PALOMA

Also by Brooks Harrington

No Mercy, No Justice: The Dominant Narrative of America versus the Counter-Narrative of Jesus (Eugene, OR: Cascade, 2018)

PALOMA

—Happy Are Those—

Brooks Harrington

WIPF *&* STOCK · Eugene, Oregon

PALOMA
Happy Are Those

Copyright © 2022 Brooks Harrington. All rights reserved. Except for brief quotations in critical publications or reviews, no part of this book may be reproduced in any manner without prior written permission from the publisher. Write: Permissions, Wipf and Stock Publishers, 199 W. 8th Ave., Suite 3, Eugene, OR 97401.

Wipf & Stock
An Imprint of Wipf and Stock Publishers
199 W. 8th Ave., Suite 3
Eugene, OR 97401

www.wipfandstock.com

PAPERBACK ISBN: 978-1-6667-4102-5
HARDCOVER ISBN: 978-1-6667-4103-2
EBOOK ISBN: 978-1-6667-4104-9

VERSION NUMBER 052322

This is a work of fiction. The characters, institutions, and events described herein are fictional. Any resemblance between these and actual persons, institutions, and events is coincidental.

Unless otherwise noted, Scripture quotations are from New Revised Standard Version Bible, copyright © 1989 National Council of the Churches of Christ in the United States of America. Used by permission. All rights reserved worldwide.

For Maxine,

my love, wife, friend, conscience, and partner
for more than forty-four years

"Happy are those who are poor in spirit, for theirs is the
kingdom of heaven.

Happy are those who mourn, for they will be comforted.

Happy are those who are meek, for they will inherit the
earth.

Happy are those who hunger and thirst for justice, for they
will be satisfied.

Happy are those who are merciful, for they will receive
mercy.

Happy are those who are pure in heart, for they will see
God.

Happy are those who are peacemakers, for they will be
called children of God.

Happy are those who are persecuted for justice's sake, for
theirs is the kingdom of heaven."

Matthew 5:3–10 (author's translation)

"Do not resist evil with evil."

Matthew 5:39 (author's translation)

"God is love, and those who abide in love abide in God, and
God abides in them."

1 John 4:16b (NRSV)

Contents

Part Two Resumed: Happy Are Those Who Hunger and Thirst for Justice

Part Three Resumed: Happy Are Those Who Are Meek

Happy Are Those Who Are Meek

"What's worse?
That nightmare or my life?"

— Monday, September 9, 2019, 1:00 a.m. —

The backyard was dark, murky, and in a fog lit by a bright moon behind broken cloud cover, without the streetlight that normally stood at the side. The yard seemed familiar but strange, disorienting and foreboding. In her mind, it was her father's backyard to his house on Hale Street in Fort Worth. The cannibalized truck was up on blocks as usual, just as it had been for years. The usual trash and junk were strewn around—loose papers and garbage and rusty box springs and cannibalized air conditioners, and the washer-dryer and the old refrigerator with their doors removed. The piles of empty paint cans and the dead tires and the broken truck wheels were there in the weeds as usual. But the light was wrong, even in the middle of the night. And there were no train tracks to the east, and no grain elevators. There was nothing to the east but deep darkness. And there was no sound at all—no noise from the highway that was just on the other side of the train tracks, no noise from Samuel Avenue up the hill to the west, no music playing, no breeze moving, no dogs barking, no cats yowling. She thought she wanted to get out of there. But as she was pulled deeper into the yard, through the dark and the murk, she saw a tall pile of dirt that didn't belong there.

She approached the pile of dirt slowly and dreadfully. The dirt was dark and shiny, much different than the red clay of the yard. The top of the pile was even with her eyes as she stood beside it. Protruding from the top of the pile was a rounded hump of earth, like a freshly covered grave. She picked up an empty coffee can. She crawled on top of the pile next to the hump, and began to scrape and dig with the can, scooping the earth to the side. She uncovered a body within the dark hump. Frantically, she began to dig and brush the earth from the face with her hands, trying to clear an air passage. She discovered it was her mother. The skull was protruding through the skin and hair at the top of her head, but she recognized the face. Her mother sat up suddenly and grabbed Paloma by the arm. She screamed and pleaded for her mother to let her go and yanked back with all her strength, trying to run. But she did not have the strength to get away. Her mother said nothing but held her there. Then her mother uncovered her own stomach, exposing a hole oozing blood and pus. Her mother thrust Paloma's hand into the hole. Paloma's brother and sister and her daughter Cynthia were beside them. Paloma tried to get free again, screaming at her daughter to run. But her sister and brother held both of them there as her mother took out a pipe, filled it with the ooze from her stomach, and lit the pipe. Her brother, sister, and mother passed the pipe among them. Methamphetamine smoke curled around their heads obscuring their faces. Her mother handed the lit pipe to her daughter. Paloma screamed, lunging toward the pipe, trying to snatch it from her daughter's hands. Her mother and brother held her back. Paloma pleaded for her daughter to stop, weeping and crying for help from anyone. John Levi appeared and tried to take the pipe away from Cynthia. But a group of strange men led by Luther and Angel were suddenly there, pulling John Levi away. As her brother and sister held Paloma back, her daughter took long pulls on the pipe, the glow from the bowl illuminating her face, making her look like a demon. The smell of the meth burned Paloma's nostrils. Then her daughter, her face contorted, began screaming at her, "You did this to me! You did this to me!" Paloma took the pipe and took a long draw on it, chasing the meth high—the energy and the power and the focus, the new identity, the escape. The burning smoke filled her nose and lungs but provided no escape. Her mind slowed. She took another draw and another. She felt herself dying. Even meth had turned on her. Weeping, she sunk onto her knees in the dirt, and threw the pipe at the group of strange men who stood with their penises out of their jeans. A bonfire flared where the pipe hit. The men, Luther, and Angel began dancing around it, laughing at her. She looked for John Levi, but he was gone. Luther, Angel, and the men chanted, "You ain't never going to get away, Paloma. You ain't never going to get away from us."

Paloma awoke suddenly. *"It was a dream again. This time it seemed so real."*

"What's worse? That nightmare or my life?" she said aloud.

She could hear blood pulsing in her ears. Her body ached and it was hard to move. Her bad leg hurt from lying on the hard cot. She felt dead. She had crashed after days of meth high before. "Hello again," she said. "Are you finally going to kill me?"

She felt hungry and thirsty, nauseous but still craved food.

The sour, sweet odor of meth hung in the air and the taste of it coated her mouth. The meth that Luther and Angel manufactured in their house always smelled to Paloma like a mix of burnt plastic and cat urine. Her nostrils burned. She sneezed, causing pain to shoot through her eyes into her forehead. She struggled to open her eyes, which were caked with sleep. When she got them open, they burned and watered.

Paloma lay still a long time, trying to muster energy and resolve. She was wrapped in a dirty blanket. She could not find her clothes. Angel had hidden her clothes before, to keep her from leaving. The bedroom was stifling hot. No air was moving. Luther had sealed the house windows so meth couldn't be smelled outside. Paloma's blanket was soaked in sweat. She examined her body for bruises and welts. She found no bites or sores. But the area between her legs was swollen and very tender. She tried to remember the men who must have used her but could not. Meth always wiped out her memory, which was one of the things she craved about it.

She didn't know what day it was. She couldn't remember what had happened to bring her to Luther's house, how many days she had been high, or what day she had given in to smoking meth and being used by Luther's customers. She felt sure she had burned her bridges to the job that John Levi had gotten for her. She even felt relieved about that. She didn't want to go back to that place now that the people there knew about her. She knew from past experience she probably had been unable to sleep for days while high. She had probably focused for hours at a time on some activity like washing the tables in the club bar Luther owned on North Main, or counting the bottles behind the bar or the number of freckles on a man's arm. She had probably chain-smoked and binged on tequila to maintain her high. She had probably never stopped talking because she felt so much smarter than anyone she encountered. She probably had belittled everyone who opened her mouth. She probably had eaten nothing. She was sure she had preached that anyone who didn't use meth was a fool and a coward. And probably, if the meth was good enough, she had hallucinated. She couldn't recall when or where she had last seen or talked to her daughter, but she really hoped that she had not called her if she was hallucinating.

And she knew to a certainly that she had engaged in self-destructive, degrading sex with strangers to pay Luther and Angel for the meth.

But now meth death was here again. She knew she had found the escape from her life and herself and her past that she felt she needed at the time. But now she and her life and her past were back, and they were worse than ever. She was paying the price she knew she would pay when she used again. Her child had been paying the price for years, just as she had paid the price when she was a child.

"Please, don't let me be pregnant." She had been on the pill, but she was sure she had missed days and days.

Her skin was starting to itch all over. She stopped herself from scratching, knowing this was going to plague her for a while and that no lotion or salve she could use would lessen it.

The craving for meth was returning. But she had to get home. Who had been feeding Cynthia? *I've got to get home.*

Paloma heard a groan. Her head and hip and her back ached as she turned her neck. She saw another form in the bed. It was Angel.

Then she heard John Levi's voice.

Chapter Two

"I have made this hell deeper."

— Monday, September 10, 2019, 2:00 a.m. —

"Paloma!"

"Paloma! I know you are in there! It's John Levi!" Pause. More silence. "Come on, Paloma! Don't give up! You've come so far! You know you cannot trust these men!" Pause. Weaker. "Cynthia is worried sick about you! Let me take you home!"

The only light came from the headlights on his pickup, which cast shadows of his body onto the front of the house. John Levi pulled and pushed and pushed and pulled at the seven-foot-tall double gate made of vertical iron bars in front of Luther Bodine's house on Lulu Street. The two doors of the gate would have swung inward and apart from the center had they not been held closed by a chain and padlock. The gate was set in an ancient fence made of stones and iron poles set in concrete, with jagged, broken glass set into the top. The gate and fence and the window bars were the only parts of the property that seemed durable. Inside the fence was a clapboard house, with rotting boards and peeling paint and iron bars on all of the windows. The only money put into the exterior of the property was to keep people out. John Levi had tried to walk around the perimeter of the property, searching for a way through or over the fence. But the house was set so close to the houses on either side that he couldn't get between them. When he walked around the street corner harshly illuminated by a bright, buzzing street light and then down the alley to the back of the house, he saw the forms of three huge dogs in the back yard in the dark, barking at him. So he went back to banging the front gate hard, trying to break it open. He could see only one light on toward the rear of the house. He wasn't certain

Paloma was in the house, but this is where she always came when she was trying to escape her life and herself. And he had been told by Seth that he had heard Luther and Angel say she was inside.

"Paloma! Just yell out. I know you are in there!"

Silence. The early morning was heavy with humidity. John Levi didn't see lights coming on inside the neighboring houses. *"Has this old man got everyone in this neighborhood so scared of him that they won't even check out this commotion?"*

"Luther! Open the door and talk to me! I know you are in there."

"Get away from my house, Preacher, or I'll let my dogs out on you. And I'll let Angel out on you. He's spoiling to kick your ass."

"Open this gate, Luther. Just let me talk to her."

"Goddammit, she ain't here! Get away from this fence or I'll call the police!"

"The last call you are going to make is to the police. Just let me look around your house. If she isn't in there, I'll leave peacefully."

"I thought preachers always had to be peaceful. You are waaaay in over your head. We ain't in landlord-tenant court now. There's no deputy here to protect your ass. How about if I let you in, and then let Angel shoot you for trespassing."

"I'm not leaving here without her, Luther."

"You here to save her soul, Preacher? Or do you want her body for yourself?" Luther mocked John Levi as he always had. "How's that been working for her? Or do you care about her at all? She's just your little Christian project, ain't she? Your Christian trophy, the woman you saved from sin. It's all about *you*, not her." Pause. John Levi could hear muffled voices from inside the house. "I'm telling you, she ain't in here. And if she is, she don't want anything to do with you."

"I'm not trying to save her soul. I'm trying to save her body from you and your drugs. I was told that Angel drugged her to get her in there. I'm trying to get her back to her child so she can find some happiness."

"Man, do you talk a lot of shit. Maybe she's already as happy as she can be. Ever think of that? Maybe she don't want to be saved from me? Maybe she knows that I'm the only one she can trust to give her what she needs to make her happy just the way she is, not the way you want her to be. I'm the one who loves her, not you."

"You don't love her, Luther. You don't love anyone or anything, not even yourself. You just want to use her."

"I'm warnin' you now. Get away from here, Preacher. If you don't want to save souls, you best go back to lawyerin' full-time. But lawyerin' or preachin', you ain't gettin' in here tonight."

Paloma had told him that the room where Luther and Angel got young women high and used them was in the back of the house. He had to get into that room. So he had to get through this gate.

He considered calling the police to ask for a welfare check on Paloma. But if the police came, Luther would deny that Paloma was in there and would refuse to let the police in without a warrant. And if the police did go in and found Paloma and drugs there, they'd arrest Paloma too.

"Paloma! Just let me know for sure that you are in there! Just give me a word! Then I'll get the police to get you out."

Paloma's shrill voice cried from deep inside the house. Her words seemed slurred and unusually raspy. "John Levi, leave me the hell alone. Go away!" She coughed out, "I don't want to be saved. I don't want you. I want you to leave me alone!" Her voice rose higher. "Go away before you get me and you both hurt."

Angel's voice boomed out, "I told you to keep quiet, bitch. Say another word and see what happens to you."

"Hell, she's really in there . . . Hurt?" He jumped into his 1953 Chevrolet pickup, painted his alma mater University of Texas burnt orange, an old, heavy truck with a rounded, solid grill. He backed it into the middle of the street perpendicular to the curb and pointed it at the gate. *"Am I really going to do this? . . . I've got to get her out of there. If I call the police and they search the house, Paloma will be arrested. If I just leave her in there, she and Cynthia lose all the progress they have made. And I lose her to these predators."* He gunned the engine, tires screaming, and rammed the gate. The truck shuddered and bucked but the chain broke and the gate slammed open. He scrambled out of the cab and into the front yard. *"What are you doing? You are about to get yourself killed!"* He paused and reconsidered. He couldn't undo what he had done.

The front door of the house flew open. Luther stood in the door with a baseball bat. A Rottweiler boiled out of the door and charged John Levi. John Levi grabbed a rusted lawn chair lying on its side in the yard and held it between himself and the dog. The dog charged the chair, knocking John Levi to the ground. He scrambled to his feet and ran to Luther and the open door, the dog right behind him. The dog bit him hard on his calf. He wrestled the bat from the surprised old man and hit the dog repeatedly in the head and ribs. The dog yelped but kept boring in, biting harder and growling louder, forcing John Levi deeper into the living room.

Angel came out of the back of the house, nude and holding a handgun, yelling incoherently. In the chaos, the dog charged Angel. "Caesar, Caesar, stop!" Angel screamed at the dog. The dog bit Angel on the thigh, grinding his teeth into the leg and shaking him. Angel hit the dog on the head with the hand gun, but the dog would not loosen his grip. Luther ran to the dog, grabbed his collar, and tried to pull him away. John Levi wanted to run into the back of the house to look for Paloma, but Angel, Luther, and the Rottweiler barred his way in the narrow door. Angel put the muzzle of the handgun tight against the dog's back and fired. The dog yelped and slunk to the floor. The sound of the shot was deafening. "Goddamn you. You made me kill my dog!" Angel yelled. He pointed the gun at John Levi and fired it just as John Levi hit Angel's arm with the bat. The flash of the muzzle exploded sharp light into the darkness of the room. The bullet hit Luther in the chest, knocking him back against the wall. "Goddamn you. Now you made me shoot my daddy." Angel pointed the handgun at John Levi. John Levi dodged to the left and hit Angel full in his face with the bat just as he fired again. Angel went down screaming, losing his grip on the handgun. John Levi looked down at the cruel young man who had enslaved Paloma for so many years to drugs and prostitution. The vision of Paloma when he first saw her came to him . . . emaciated, strung out on meth, trembling, sick . . . suffering and vulnerability peering out of her eyes. All that Paloma had told him about the ways that Luther and Angel had used her and other young women came to him. He stood over Angel and saw evil incarnate. Now was his chance to act in the way he had wanted God to act, to rid this evil from Paloma's and Cynthia's lives. John Levi raised the bat over his head and brought it down on Angel's head as if he were driving a stake. The sound of the metal bat hitting Angel's head was like a hammer hitting concrete. Angel's skull depressed where he was hit, and blood spurted from the fissure. Luther was groaning, his breathing shallowing, a mix of air and blood spewing from the sucking bullet hole in his chest. John Levi stood over Luther with the bat upraised, but Luther went still. John Levi looked back at Angel. Angel and Luther were both as still as death.

A neighbor came to the door, peered in through the darkness, and ran away.

John Levi collapsed on the floor, his legs unable to hold him, his heart pounding, his hands shaking so much he couldn't hold the bat, unable to catch his breath, his ears ringing from the sound of the gunshots and the crack of the metal bat on Angel's head. John Levi rolled over and vomited. He rolled back over. *What have I done? I was almost killed. Who was that person who hit Angel with the bat when he was down?*

"John Levi! What did you do?" Paloma stood in the dark of the doorway from the back of the house, wrapped in a blanket. "What did you do!?"

"Paloma, are you all right?" He could barely hear his own voice.

"I'm wasted but I'm more all right than you are."

"Let me get you out of here."

Paloma started screaming at him. "Didn't I tell you to leave? Didn't I tell you? Why wouldn't you leave me alone!? Why wouldn't you let me be who I am? Are you so arrogant that you think you can fix anything or anyone you decide to? You think *you* are God?" She stood over him, slapping him in the head. "I told you before to stop trying to fix me! Now we are both screwed!"

Angel lay dead still, blood still flowing onto the wood floor from his head. Luther wasn't moving. The dog was whimpering. John Levi could feel blood sticking his trouser to his leg where the Rottweiler had bitten him. The bite burned like fire. *What did I do? I almost died in this hell. I have made this hell deeper. I have put myself in it and I haven't gotten Paloma out.*

Paloma ran into the kitchen and came out with car keys. Before John Levi could get his legs to work to stop her, Paloma ran out the front door of the house, through the broken gate, jumped into Angel's Camaro, and roared away, still clad only in a blanket.

John Levi felt unable to move. *"I murdered him. I didn't even try to knock the gun away from him. I just beat him to death. Where did that come from?"*

. . . Then, *"I didn't help Paloma and I ruined by own life. There is no way I can spin this."*

. . . Then, *"All I can do is to own up to it, tell the truth of it. I can't run from what I did. I'll wait here for the police."*

Time passed until he became aware that a neighbor of Luther's was pulling and the jerking him to his feet, pushing him out the door and gate, into his pickup. "Get the hell out of here *now*!" said the man. The front grill of the pickup was smashed in but he could still drive it.

"Why are you helping me?"

"You did this neighborhood a good deed, Preacher."

"You think they are dead?" John Levi asked dumbly. He heard approaching sirens.

"Get out of here *now*!"

"I need to stay here and tell the police the truth. I have to own up to the truth."

"Man, you don't get this, do you? You weren't even here. This was a drug deal gone wrong. Those people got what they had coming. Get out of here *now*!"

PART TWO

Happy Are Those Who Hunger and Thirst for Justice

"Momma says the church lies to people."

— Sunday, September 16, 2018, 7:00 p.m. —

The Reverend John Levi Jones, thirty-eight years of age, licensed to practice law in the State of Texas since 2005 and ordained minister of the United Methodist Church since 2016, sat in his office on the first floor of the fellowship building of Peace United Methodist Church in the impoverished North Hills neighborhood of Fort Worth. He was alone in the building, which was the way he felt about this ministry. Few people had attended his evening worship service and only three children from the neighborhood had appeared for free pizza.

He pondered the improbability and imprudence of being pastor of this church. His parents, friends, old girlfriends, colleagues, and competitors in his prior practice of law warned him against leaving law and entering ministry. The step was truly quixotic. Heedless of the warnings, he had left his civil litigation practice five years before, entered seminary, received ordination, and asked for this small inner-city church in one of the poorest, most violent neighborhoods in Fort Worth. He had made all the money he would ever need at the law as a personal injury plaintiffs' attorney. But he had not remained happy in that calling. Due to tort reform legislation, the actual jury trials had all but dried up. Now every case was just tedious discovery, motions hearings, and then settlement. He missed the drama and the rush of trial. He missed closing argument, when he was the center of everyone's attention, all eyes and ears riveted to him and his words, the futures of his client and his opponent at stake. And he yearned for another profession that would plunge him deeper into the daily lives of the poor he had represented at law. So he harkened to an older ambition.

John Levi had been raised in Faith United Methodist Church, located south of downtown Fort Worth. He was the only child of wealthy parents. His father was a partner in an oil well services company. His mother was a stay-at-home mom whose leisure was spent playing bridge and serving on Republican Party committees. Their happiness came from accumulation of things and pleasures, and their inclusion into the circles and clubs of rich Anglo people like them. They were grooming their son John Levi to the same happiness. His success at academics and his friendship with sons and daughters of the equally rich was the button on the cap of their status.

John Levi attended every worship service at Faith Church, including Wednesday and Sunday evenings. The church youth group had a very active, creative drama ministry, and John Levi was its star. He had the memory and presence of an actor. The youth director of the church held a seminary degree in sacred drama and its theatre program was prodigious. But the greatest attraction of that church to John Levi was its senior pastor, Dr. Graham Forster, a silver-haired, spell-binding preacher who packed them in for every worship service. As a teenager John Levi sat as close to the pulpit as he could, fantasizing about becoming a Dr. Forster.

At the University of Texas John Levi majored in drama. But when confronted with the reality of an actor's life, scraping by waiting tables between auditions and poorly paying productions, he knew that such a life would not be enough for him. He decided to utilize his dramatic talents as a trial lawyer, and entered UT law school. His father wanted him to enter the business field, preferably his oil business. The law was a way to mediate his father's demands and John Levi's own sense of what would make him happy. Law was close enough to an establishment profession for his father to pay for John Levi's law school so long as he concentrated on business, and oil and gas law.

But on graduation John Levi didn't go into a law practice representing businesses. During law school he gave increasing amounts of his time to legal clinics helping the poor. He experienced great satisfaction in that work. After passing the bar, John Levi joined a firm that sued businesses on behalf of working men and women. He was very successful. The struggles of the working poor awakened his capacity for empathy. He still lived among the very comfortable and enjoyed the benefits of privilege. But when the practice of law was no longer a source of happiness to him, as law quit satisfying his desire to move people with his words and presence, he took the unconventional step of applying for seminary and ministry. He was unmarried and childless, so had no family responsibilities to hold him back. His initial goal in ministry was as self-centered as his goal had been in law. He wanted to make a booming success of an inner-city ministry and use it as a stepping-stone to appointment to the pulpit of his home church when its senior pastor retired. Then hundreds of people every Sunday would hang on his every word. He thought this would bring him true happiness.

Seminary broadened his goals. His studies absorbed him more than he expected they would. Before he went to seminary the only scripture he knew was from Matthew 25: "In so much as you do it to the least of these, you do it unto me . . ." He was taken over by the life and teachings of Jesus, particularly by the Sermon on the Mount and the Beatitudes. Self-promotion took something of a back seat, though it would always be a force.

After a year in this ministry at Peace, he was sure he was failing in his goal. He had never allowed himself to fail at anything. Not enough people were responding to his preaching. Ministry was turning out to be harder than trial law. How do you know when you are winning? How do others know you are winning? How do you keep score? Ministers kept score by the numbers of worshippers attending their services and the amounts of their salaries. But people were not flocking to hear his sermons and John Levi was not accepting any pay. There were just too many cultural barriers between him and the people of the impoverished church neighborhood. And people from comfortable neighborhoods did not want to hear and live the teachings of Jesus about wealth and poverty.

That left the numbers of poor people he was helping outside of worship as his only potential measure of success. The number was not nearly high enough to satisfy him. Not enough people in the church neighborhood trusted him enough to come to him for help. He seemed to have so little in common with them. He didn't speak their language in so many ways. *"There are hundreds of families in real need in this neighborhood. Why won't they trust me?"*

He was in his office when he heard a voice calling timidly from the main meeting hall. He found a teenaged girl standing shyly inside the outside door.

"Yes, yes. Please come in," said John Levi. "Welcome. Did you come for the pizza? We have plenty left."

"No," said the young lady. "I came to ask for help."

"God is good! Someone from the neighborhood asking me for help!" he thought.

"Can I get you some pizza?"

"I don't need any pizza. I already ate," said the girl.

"A piece of pizza or two wouldn't hurt you. It's good. You could take some home. You like pepperoni?"

"Well . . . maybe one piece."

"Then sit down while I warm some up. We have plenty. You can tell me about the help you need while you eat."

The girl looked doubtful. "I got no money and Momma won't let me accept charity."

"This wouldn't be charity," said John Levi. "This would just be neighbors being neighbors. You'll be doing me a favor. If you don't eat this pizza, I'll just have to throw it out."

"She doesn't want me accepting any help from any church. If she found out I was here, I'd be in trouble."

"What does she have against the church?"

"Momma says the church lies to people."

"What lies?"

"That God answers prayers. That God cares."

"Really? What would cause your Momma to say such things about God?"

"She says to just look around. Her momma died of stomach cancer when she was little, and she had to go work when she was my age to make a living to support her sister and brother. She says she prayed to God to save her momma, but her momma died. She says that she prayed to God to keep her daddy from drinking, but he is still drinking. Now he is sick. She says cheating people always get what they want and honest people get nothing."

"I look forward to meeting your momma. Where is she?"

"At home asleep, about to go to work."

"Sunday night at 7? Where does she work?"

"At a bar."

"I thought bars can't be open on Sundays."

"This one is."

"What does your momma do at that bar?"

"She's a waitress. She's an entertainer."

"Who does your momma entertain?"

"Men at the bar . . . Can I have that pizza now?"

John Levi went into the kitchen and lit the gas range. He pulled three pieces of peperoni pizza out of the freezer. While he waited for the oven to warm, he looked into the meeting hall. The girl was extremely thin. She smelled of musty clothes and body odor. She had black hair and green eyes and light brown skin. Her hair looked like it had not been washed for a very long time. She wore no makeup. Her clothes were too small for her and there were holes in her blouse. The bottoms of the legs of her jeans were tattered. Her tennis shoes had holes in the sides and her little toe protruded out of one. She looked as if she were about to cry.

John Levi put the pizza pieces on a cookie sheet and slid it into the oven. He walked out into the hall and sat down opposite the child.

"Let's start with names. Mine is John Levi." He reached out and shook her hand. The girl's hand was sweaty.

"I heard the preacher here is a lawyer. Where can I find him?"

"That's me. Tell me your name please."

"I'm Cynthia."

"It's very nice to meet you," said John Levi. "You are welcome here anytime. Maybe you will even come to Sunday service with your momma sometime."

"You will never see my momma in your church," said Cynthia.

"Because of the way she feels about God?"

"And she says the church just takes from people without giving them anything but false hope."

"How does your father feel about this?"

"Don't know."

The oven timer dinged. "Pizza time," said John Levi.

Cynthia wolfed down two pieces of pizza.

"So why do you need a lawyer-minister?"

"We don't need a minister," said Cynthia. "We need a lawyer. A free one."

"Free lawyers are hard to come by in this city," said John Levi. "Particularly free lawyers who are any good. Why do you need a lawyer? Is your momma in trouble with the police?"

"Why would you say that?" asked Cynthia. "You think that she must be a criminal because she works in a bar?" Cynthia got up to leave.

"No, Cynthia. I apologize. Please don't go. She must be in some kind of trouble with the law or you wouldn't be looking for a free lawyer. Tell me what help you need."

"We are about to be evicted. And the only other place we could live is my granddaddy's. If we go back there, CPS will put me in foster care."

"Why foster care?"

"Because my granddaddy's house has holes in the walls and sometimes doesn't have running water or toilets, and because he drinks and uses drugs, and because men live there who drink and use drugs with him."

"Do you know why the landlord wants to evict you?"

"The papers say it is because Momma didn't pay the rent," said Cynthia.

"If she didn't, there may not be a defense."

"She says she paid it," said Cynthia.

"Then why would the landlord want to evict you?"

"I don't know. I never know with Momma. Maybe because she didn't pay it. Maybe she spent the rent money on drugs. She won't tell me her business."

"Do you want me to drive you home after you finish your pizza? Maybe I can talk to her there."

"She's probably already gone to work."

"What if I stop by your home tomorrow to talk to her?"

Cynthia thought for a moment. "Let me try to get her to come here to talk to you. I'll tell her you might represent her if CPS tries to take me from her. She cares about that more than the house. "

"The eviction may be a lost cause if she hasn't paid the rent."

"When will you be here tomorrow?"

"All afternoon. I'll give you my cell phone number in case tomorrow afternoon won't work for her."

"We don't have a phone."

"I'll be here all afternoon. Finish your pizza and I'll take you home."

"In that orange pickup?"

"That's the one."

"All right."

"Do you have enough food in the house? Can I give you some more pizza?"

"Momma will be mad," said Cynthia.

"Then we'll take it a step at a time. I can feed you whenever you come here. Your momma doesn't have to know for now. What is your momma's name?"

"Paloma Ibarra," said Cynthia.

"Paloma. It's a beautiful name. I haven't heard that name before."

"It's Spanish for 'dove.'"

"And your last name?"

"Ibarra."

Well, Cynthia Ibarra, if you are done with your pizza, let's get you home. Tomorrow is a school day."

Chapter Two

"That's the difference between me and other addicts. Addicts lie."

John Levi drove by Cynthia's house the next morning after she had gone to school. He had purchased some groceries—milk, eggs, butter, bread, hamburger, taco shells, cheese, tomatoes, salsa, lettuce, apples, and oranges—hoping her mother was not too proud to accept the food. But the house was dead still. He left the non-perishable food in bags on the front porch. He took the dairy products to another family in need in the neighborhood and went to the church. *"We definitely need to find funding and space for a free food bank in the church. That's our next step. So many hungry children in this neighborhood."*

He was sitting in his office researching Texas landlord-tenant law on the internet when he heard a voice call impatiently from the next room, "Well, I'm here."

John Levi walked into the main meeting room. She was standing just inside the outside door. John Levi caught his breath. She was not the person he was expecting. He didn't know who he was expecting but it wasn't this woman.

Paloma Ibarra stood with her arms folded over her chest, staring back at him as he gawked at her. She was a shade over five feet tall. Her skin was olive colored. She was very thin. Her face was diamond shaped, gaunt and lined. Her forehead had deep worry lines. Her eyes were huge and dark brown with the slightest amount of eye liner and more deep worry lines at the corners. The gauntness of her face made her eyes look even bigger. She had a dimple on her left cheek. Her lips were full with very little lipstick. There was a deep scar in the shape of a flattened C from the right corner of her mouth to the point of her chin. She had dark brown hair that was parted in the middle and hung to both collar bones. Her hair was wet from a recent shower. She was dressed in an oversized, grey sweatshirt with the Dallas Cowboy star on the front. She wore baggy, light blue jeans and clean, cheap, dark blue tennis shoes. She wore no ring, bracelet, or necklace. The paint was chipped on her fingernails. Not so much by her face but by her hands and neck, she looked to be in her late twenties to early thirties. So she must have given birth to Cynthia when she was only a few years older than Cynthia is now. She trembled. She was sweating. She looked in pain.

Paloma looked at John Levi with an expression of cynicism, resignation, resentment, strength, and arrogance all at once, as if life was throwing everything at her and she was throwing everything right back.

John Levi was thirty-eight. He was thoroughly Anglo, five feet ten inches tall, and carried one hundred seventy pounds, lean without much in the way of muscle, a swimmer's body although he never swam. His hair was combed back and jet black, streaked with some premature grey. His eyes were hazel. He had a high forehead, a long, narrow nose, and a square jaw. He had never been married or in a lasting relationship. But he was not inexperienced with women. Before ministry, he had dated a series of "fill-in-the-blank women," as he called them, each one largely indistinguishable from the others, mostly law students or lawyers who were so well dressed and groomed that they didn't look real and who were all identically intent upon their career ambitions and pursuit of a conventional family life with great material comfort. In contrast, this woman looked real. Really real. Her face had the most history and . . . pathos he had ever seen etched in a face.

"Are you going to say something?" she asked. "Or are you just going to stare? Should I leave? Do you not help Latinas?"

"Oh, no, no, no. No—I mean, yes, yes, yes. I will help anybody I can help. Within reason," he added hastily. "If I didn't help Hispanic people in this neighborhood, well, I'd have no business being here. Won't you sit down?"

"Who told you that you could bring food by my house?" There was anger in her voice.

"I meant no disrespect. Only trying to help your daughter. I am sorry if I overstepped."

"You think I can't take care of my daughter?"

"I apologize. I should have asked you first. Won't you sit down? Can I get you something to drink?"

"How about some tequila?"

"No . . . um, no . . . we don't have any alcohol," he stammered. Then it occurred to him that she was defending herself from a vulnerable position to make him more uncomfortable than she was. "But then you know we don't have liquor here, don't you. Please sit down."

Paloma walked to a chair against an exterior wall of the room. She sat down, her arms still folded. John Levi sat in another chair about ten feet away from her.

"Let me introduce myself. I am Reverend John Levi Jones. I have been a licensed lawyer in the state of Texas since 2005. How can I help you and your daughter?"

"If you are a lawyer, what are you doing in this church?"

"I left full-time law and became an ordained minister. But I am still licensed to practice law."

"Why the hell did you go into ministry?"

"That's a long answer. I'll just say that I was called to it."

"By who?"

"By God, I hope."

"Must have been a collect call."

"Come again?"

"A collect call. God made the call but you have to pay for it."

"That's a good one. I'll have to remember that. Why don't you tell me your name?"

"Paloma Maria Ibarra Serrano."

"So, Paloma Serrano."

"No. Paloma Ibarra. You haven't had much contact with Latinos, have you?"

"Why do you say that?"

"The first last name is the father's. The second is the mother's. We go by the father's. So I'm Paloma Maria Ibarra Serrano, and I go by Paloma Ibarra."

"Got it. Thanks. I'm John Levi Jones. *Mucho gusto.* Er . . . nice to meet you. May I call you Paloma?"

"Or Lomie, if you like."

"I think I'd prefer Paloma. It's a beautiful name."

"Up to you."

"Call me John Levi. I'm sorry I don't speak Spanish."

"I don't speak much either. My family has been here for generations."

"You are trembling. Are you cold?"

"I'm fine."

"Your daughter told me you are facing eviction."

"What did you do wrong to get yourself stuck in this piddly-ass church in this shitty neighborhood? You must have really pissed somebody off. I mean, can I trust you?"

"Yes, you can trust me. Let's stick to the law for now. Texas landlord-tenant law is stacked in favor of the landlords. There may not be much that any lawyer can do for you. But unless you have access to another free lawyer, why don't you trust me enough to tell me about your situation?"

Paloma looked at him, and sighed. "I am not going to let myself be talked down to and I am not going to be pitied or judged. Understand?"

"Understood. Have you have been through an eviction before."

"Look around this neighborhood. Most people here have been evicted one time or another. They just haven't fought it like I have."

"Have you ever won an eviction suit?"

"You mean have I ever succeeded in getting the justice of the peace to prevent the eviction?"

"Yes."

"No. But I have been able to strike a deal with the landlord to let me stay."

"You are obviously a woman with her feet on the ground."

"Where else can feet be?"

"Paloma, you are clearly a very intelligent woman. How far did you go in school?

"I started the ninth grade. But I got my GED later. And I've read everything I could get my hands on. I am not dumb. You looking down your nose at me already?"

"Just the opposite. Let me ask some questions. When is the eviction hearing?"

"Tomorrow morning at 9:30."

"Tomorrow morning." He whistled. "That doesn't give us much time. Has the hearing been continued . . . delayed before?"

"I know what 'continued' means. Yes, twice."

"At your request?"

"Once at my request and once at Luther's."

"Then it is unlikely I can get it delayed again. Is Luther the landlord?"

"Yes."

"What can you tell me about him?"

"He's a miserable piece of manure who sells drugs and pimps teenaged girls."

"I want to hear a lot more about him. Is there a written lease?"

"No."

"Was there ever a written lease?

"No."

"Then you are what the law calls a 'tenant at will.' He can evict you with thirty days' notice even if you are current in your lease payments. When did you receive notice?"

"When a constable served eviction suit papers on me about two weeks ago."

"You didn't receive a written notice to vacate before that? A piece of paper posted on your door or given to you?"

"No."

"You are sure?"

"I am damned sure."

"Then we actually may be able to get this particular suit dismissed and delay the eviction."

"I don't want to just delay the eviction. I want to stay in that house at least until the end of this school year. I don't want those bastards to get their way. The house is close enough to Cynthia's school that she can walk. I don't have a car. She has a few friends in the school for a change, so I'd like to stay where we are. Besides, I could never find another place. I can't pass the criminal background check for a new place and I can't pay the security deposit or the moving expenses or the rent."

"Paloma, the law doesn't work that way."

"We made an agreement."

"Who?"

"Luther Bodine and his son Angel and me."

"When did you enter into this verbal agreement?"

"A year ago this month."

"But not in writing?"

"No."

"How do we prove it?"

"I'll tell the judge about it."

"And they'll say there was no such agreement. Do you have anything at all? Like a text or an email or a note that refers to the agreement or even to the existence of an agreement?"

"No."

"What about receipts for the rent you paid? Check stubs or money orders?"

"Nothing like that."

"How much in monthly rent have you paid them in the last year?"

"Nothing in cash. I paid them in services."

"You've never paid them any money at all?"

"None."

"What services?"

"I worked in their club as a hostess."

"Where is the club?"

"North Main."

"Name of the club?"

"The Hacienda."

"And in exchange for your working there as a hostess, you get to live in your house rent free?"

"Not rent free. I told you. My rent was my work as a hostess."

"Paloma, rent is money. If you don't pay money, you don't pay rent. What were your work hours?"

"Basically, whenever they wanted me at night. I was on-call. I was their on-call girl."

John Levi frowned at her. "Do you mean that?"

"Are you shocked, Mr. Preacher Lawyer?"

"No, I am not shocked. I am just thinking you would be better off finding another place to live to get away from them."

"Is that what you think? Then tell me. How would I pay the money rent for the new place? Where would I get the moving expenses and the security deposit? Are you going to pay it? Your church? Are *your* feet on the ground now?"

"So, to be clear, the agreement you had was that in exchange for prostitution you didn't have to pay money rent but you could live in the house."

"It wasn't prostitution when I wasn't being paid, was it?" She paused. "This has to be confidential, right? Attorney-client secrets, right? You can't tell anyone without my permission, right?"

"Right."

"It wasn't always sex. Most of the time, they used me as a lure to get men to their house where they manufacture meth. When the men got high, I could try to sneak away."

"But sometimes it did require sex acts?"

"Yes."

"How often?"

"When I couldn't sneak away before they got too high to use me. Sneaking away after they got high was easy."

"How often has that been?"

She shrugged. "Too often."

"Did you use meth too? Was that part of the deal?"

He waited but she didn't answer.

"Why would you use meth?"

"You've never used it, have you? I don't know why I am telling you this. For all I know, you are an undercover cop. You sure as shit will never get it." She looked down at her hands for a long time. Her hands were shaking. "How can you possibly get this? I use it to escape my train wreck of a life. I use it because it's the only time that my feet aren't on this miserable ground. I use it because there are times when I can't not use it. I feel guilty as hell about it because of Cynthia. But I just can't stop for good."

"In exchange for these services, you received meth and a house?"

"Yes."

"But never any money?"

"No."

"Paloma, how old were you when you started . . . working for Bodine at the bar?

"I didn't work at the bar. I worked at the club."

"How old?"

"Fourteen."

"How old are you now?"

"Thirty-one."

"So you were sixteen when you gave birth to Cynthia?"

"Seventeen."

"Okay . . . I need to research this, but my initial reaction is that this is an illegal contract. If you testify to this and the justice of the peace believes you, and I am sure this Mr. Bodine will deny it, the court can't enforce an illegal contract. But that means you can't stay in the house. And if you testify to the terms of this agreement, you will be incriminating yourself. You have an absolute right against self-incrimination."

"The Fifth, right?"

"Yes, the Fifth Amendment to the U.S. Constitution."

"I know about that."

"You've been in criminal court before?"

"Duh, yeah."

"What have you been convicted of? In adult court?"

She shrugged.

"Paloma, I need to find this out before I go to court with you."

"Just look it up."

"You're too embarrassed to tell me? Please don't be. I am not going to judge you."

"Mostly bad checks. Some prostitution. One assault."

"No drug convictions?"

"None."

"Why not?"

"Because I have never been stupid or high enough to carry drugs on my person. So can we beat this eviction?"

"Sorry to say it, but based upon what I know now, and I just drove up so to speak, probably not."

"So this old man and his scum-sucking son can cheat me, use me, and throw me away, and the law won't do anything about it!"

"Is that what they did? Then why do they want to end the arrangement?"

"They don't. I do."

"Good. Very good. What caused you to decide that?"

"They started giving me doses of stronger meth to put their hooks into me deeper. At first I would smoke some weak stuff just to get the johns to use and then leave. But Angel started giving me some really powerful shit, and I got really wasted. I got so wasted I was hallucinating. They told me that I cut my own chin and sliced off this earlobe." She pointed to the wounds. "Then Cynthia started cutting herself because I was leaving her alone at night so much, and I promised her I would stop using and working for these bastards. I tried to stop. But I couldn't make it financially, and I couldn't make it without the meth. So I started with them again. I got into meth more than ever. Angel started using me again. Once he had sex with me when I was high while the customers watched. He used me in a way I would never have agreed. He really hurt me. One of the johns was *filming* it on his cell phone. The men were laughing while he was doing it to me. Angel would show the film to men in the club to get them to come to the house. The first I knew what he had done to me that night was when I saw the film playing in the back room of the club. I was so humiliated and angry that I broke all the glasses and bottles I could get my hands on until Angel threw me to the floor. So I called it quits and told them that if they didn't let me have the house free until the end of this school year, I would go to the police and show them the film."

"You have the film?"

"A person Angel sent it to then sent it to me."

"Paloma, has Angel treated other young women this way?"

"Yes."

"Have you seen it?"

"Yes. And I have heard it going on from the other side of the door."

"Where has all this happened?"

"In the club and Luther's home on Lulu Street."

"Any of it in your house?"

"No! My child is there."

"Would any of these other victims testify to this?"

"Doubt it. Too afraid."

"Aren't you afraid?"

"No."

"Why not?"

"What can anybody do to me that hasn't been done?"

"Does Luther know his son is doing this?"

"Sure. He's been there when it has happened. Lots of times."

"What did they say when you told them you would go to the police?"

"All kinds of shit. That I would never go to the police. That if I did I would be in more trouble than they would. That they have the police in their back pockets because they supply them drugs and women. That I could never stay away from their meth. That I could never get or keep a straight job that would pay my bills. When I quit like I said I would, I got these eviction suit papers."

"Do you think they told you the truth about the police?"

"Who knows?"

"Paloma, why did you continue with Luther and Angel?"

"I needed the house. I needed the meth. What else could I do?"

"You could get a job as a waitress."

"Not in a nice place where I could make enough money, not with my record. And where would I get meth when I needed it?"

"Where did you get money to live on after you quit the Bodines?"

"Food stamps. And I cleaned houses for a little cash."

"When did you last use?

"Two days ago."

"Where did you get it?"

"I had some put away."

"Are you addicted to meth?"

"Yes."

"Do you always tell the truth?"

"Yes. That's the difference between me and other addicts. Addicts lie, mostly to themselves. I won't. I may not tell the whole truth. But I won't lie."

"I have some coffee brewing. Can I get you some?"

"Yes, please."

John Levi read through the suit papers. "The only ground for eviction in these papers is for non-payment of rent. You aren't referred to as a 'tenant at will.' That tells me there is no lawyer on the other side. May I keep these until tomorrow?"

"Sure."

"Your daughter told me that you were working last night. Where?"

"At another bar farther north up North Main toward the airport."

"Named?"

"The Landing Strip."

"What do you do there?"

"Hostess, tend bar, clean up."

"How much are you paid?"

"Tips."

"Only tips? How can you survive on tips?"

"Surviving is the best I am hoping for. I am doing okay for now. A lot of the men that came to The Hacienda are now coming to The Landing Strip."

"Because of you?"

"Because of me."

"Are you performing the same services for them that you did in the other bar?"

"No."

"Are you still using?"

"Two days ago. Aren't you listening?"

"Do you want to quit for good?"

Long pause. Paloma's eyes went dead. "I don't think I can."

"But do you want to?"

"I don't know."

"Is this an example of your refusal to lie?"

"Yes."

"So men will soon quit coming to your new employment if you don't do for them what you did at Luther's."

"Some will."

"And your tips will decrease. Is your new boss pressuring you?"

"Not yet. He hates the Bodines."

"So when the Bodines found out you were working for a competitor and their customers were going there, they filed the eviction suit?"

"And put out the word that I am mentally ill and dangerous. And that I have VD."

"Do you?"

"Don't think so."

"Are you?"

"I'm not mentally ill. But don't screw with me."

"Will you show me your house?"

"I'll give you the address."

"Will you drive with me over there?"

"Not a good idea."

"Why not?"

"Because a preacher doesn't need to be seen with me. People know who I am and what I do. Some people around here won't let their kids be around my kid."

"Paloma, I am not like that. I want to help you if I can. But I need to see your house."

As John Levi and Paloma walked together to his truck, he noticed that she walked with a pronounced limp.

"Why are you limping?"

"My leg got broke when I was a kid. We couldn't afford a doctor and it healed wrong on its own."

Paloma saw the look on John Levi's face. "My mom was high all the time and my dad was drunk. Our house was a dump. They were afraid to take me to the ER. They thought I would be placed in foster care if the hospital people found out how we lived."

"So you've had this limp most of your life?"

"One good deal after another," she said.

"Does your leg hurt?"

"Sometimes. Mostly when I dance." She saw the look on John Levi's face. "I'm just messing with you. What do I have to dance about?"

Paloma and John Levi climbed into his old burnt-orange pickup. Paloma scrunched down low in the seat so she couldn't be seen. As he backed the truck up, she said, "It looks like the paint job on your truck is new. You choose this color?"

"Sure did."

"What the hell for? You get a deal on it?"

"I went to University of Texas. Burnt orange is Longhorn color."

"Never saw a burnt-orange cow."

"Once again, Paloma, you see through me."

They drove south on Oscar Street from the church, across Northeast 28th Street, made some turns and arrived at her house on Irion Avenue.

"You want to look at the house? Go on in. You don't want to be seen going into that house with me. I'll stay here." said Paloma.

"How will I get in?"

"There's no lock."

"No lock? Texas landlord-tenant law requires the landlord has to provide security locks."

"Didn't know that."

"Did you ask him to replace the locks?"

"I just said I didn't know that."

John Levi walked to the front of the tiny house. There were two front doors, side by side. It was originally a duplex. There was a narrow front porch with space underneath for raccoons, possums, and rats. A sagging roof extended over the porch. There were circular holes in both doors where the doorknobs should have been. As Paloma had said, there was no way to lock those doors.

Inside each front door was a tiny living room. An unframed doorway had been cut in the interior wall between these two rooms, making the house into one residence. In one room were a huge TV, an old VCR, and two beanbag chairs. The other living room held only a card table and three old chairs. The only light in each living room was a bare bulb hanging from a wire from the ceiling. One light did not work. The floors were bare concrete. The paint was peeling from the walls. Water-damaged sheetrock was hanging from one ceiling. When John Levi looked up through the sagging ceiling, he saw sunlight coming through the shingles of the roof above. There were exposed electrical wires in both rooms. There was one window air conditioner unit in the front room with the TV. It did not work.

There were two kitchens, one for each of the original units. One of the kitchens had an ancient gas range with four burners and an oven, and an equally ancient refrigerator holding only milk, butter, bread, Dr. Peppers, and TV dinners. The cabinets between the range and the refrigerator contained dry cereal, pancake mix, canned vegetables, soup, chili, and macaroni-and-cheese mix. There were three plates, three glasses, and three cups. There were assorted utensils in a drawer. Another cupboard held one frying pan, one sauce pan, and a casserole dish. The other kitchen had a gap where a range and oven had once stood, and another gap where a refrigerator had been. The linoleum of each kitchen was cracked and uneven. Cocked rat traps were on the floor of each kitchen. There was a dead rat mashed in one.

Each original unit contained one bathroom, one bedroom, and a small room for a washer and dryer off a hallway. The washers and dryers had been removed from both units. One of the bathrooms had a working bathtub and shower combination. In the other, there was a gap where the bathtub had been. One of the bathrooms had a working sink and a working toilet without a seat. The other bathroom did not. There was cold but no hot water. There was mold on the wall and ceiling of the non-working bathroom. In the working bathroom, some makeup and over-the-counter medicines were in a cabinet with a cracked mirror.

There was a bedroom in each unit. In each bedroom, there was one sleeping bag on the floor. There was no other furniture in the bedrooms. Clothes were in cardboard boxes. In Cynthia's bedroom were some of her school books. In Paloma's were stacks of old paperbacks—lots of contemporary American history and John Grisham novels.

John Levi had not known that people could or would live in a place like this. He stood quietly in the working kitchen considering how to speak to Paloma about this place without embarrassing her further. When he was ready, he walked out to the truck.

"Why is there no hot water?"

"Angel removed the hot water heater and never brought it back."

"How long ago?"

"Last Christmas."

"Where do you wash clothes?"

"Laundromat up on Northeast 28th."

"Where did you wash your hair this morning?"

"In the shower."

"Without hot water?"

"Yes."

"Cynthia doesn't like cold showers?"

"Hates them. She showers at school when she can. Look, I know it's a dump. It's the best I can do right now."

"Actually, what struck me the most about the house, other than it being in such sad shape, was how clean you keep it and the number of books. Are you the reader?"

"I have always been embarrassed at my lack of schooling. When people hear I only finished eight grade and have nothing but a GED, they think I am dumb. So I don't want to talk dumb. I wanted to get away from Luther eventually, but I knew couldn't if I had bad grammar. When I was a teenager and lived at Luther's house or in an apartment with two other girls and worked at his club at night, I kept myself from going crazy by reading. There was a used book store down Main from the club. I pestered him to buy me books. And I worked on my grammar."

"What an admirable woman," thought John Levi. *"She deserves so much more than what she's received."*

"The ceiling in the living room, the missing security locks, the mold in one of the bathrooms, the exposed wires, and the lack of hot water and working air conditioner and washer-dryer—was the house like this when you moved in last year?"

"Yes. And I know what you are thinking. Why would I let my daughter live in this hole? You should have seen my dad's house where we were living."

"I wasn't thinking that, Paloma." He was thinking how unfair life had been to this woman and how limited her choices had been. He was wondering what she and her daughter could hope for now.

Chapter Three

"Are you calling me a liar, Preacher?"

— Tuesday, September 18, 2018, 9:30 a.m. —

John Levi spent the night reviewing the landlord-tenant provisions of the Texas Property Code. He searched the internet for the ownership and taxation records of the property Paloma and Cynthia lived in on Irion Avenue, the criminal conviction records of Paloma and of Luther and Angel Bodine, and Luther Bodine's marital and family court history.

At 8:00 a.m. the next morning, Paloma came out of the house without letting Jon Levi come to the door. She was wearing a tight, black jersey top with a high neck and a full, long, tan skirt. Her hair was in a ponytail. She wore very little makeup and no lipstick. A large hoop hung from one ear. The other ear lacked a lobe. *Not only does she have this injury, but she wears a hoop on the other ear as if to call attention to it.* He saw for the first time that a small cross was tattooed on the back of her hand.

Paloma was not trembling as much as she was the day before but was still fidgeting as if in pain.

They drove in his pickup to the JP Court.

"Paloma, have you ever heard of an Edith Yancey?"

"There was an Edith Yancey who was Luther's wife."

"Why do you think they were married?"

"I guess I just assumed it. They lived together. "

"In your house or in the house where Luther and Angel are now?"

"In the house where Luther and Angel live on Lulu. The house where all the shit happens."

"What happened to Edith?"

"Don't know. She just disappeared about two years ago."

"Is she Angel's mother?"

"No. Angel's mother is a woman that Luther used like he has used me. Luther got her pregnant when Luther was much younger. She left with Angel when he was about fifteen to God knows where. Angel just showed back up maybe three years ago."

"So Edith Yancey was gone when you reached your arrangement with Luther and Angel and started living in the house on Irion?"

"Yes."

"Who was living in the house just before you moved in?"

"No one. Luther told me it had been sitting empty for years."

"Ever since Edith left?"

"Maybe."

"Does Edith Yancey have any relatives who live around here?"

"Not that I know of."

"Let me change the subject. Are you 110-percent certain that you never paid any money rent for this house? "

"I already told you that."

"Sometimes people remember things after they think about them for a while."

"No, I never paid them a cent for anything. Not even for a beer?"

"Another subject. Is Angel's middle name Luther?"

"Yes."

"And is he about thirty-six?"

"I would guess so. He is about five years older than me."

"And you are thirty-one?"

"Yes. Now I get to ask you some questions. Did you check out Luther's and Angel's criminal record? And mine?"

"Luther Roy Bodine is fifty years old. He has six old criminal charges for family violence, meaning that he was charged with assaulting members of his family or household. But every one of those was dismissed."

"What does that mean?"

"Probably that the victims got cold feet and would not testify."

"Who were the victims?"

"Three times the victim was Edith Yancey."

"Does Luther have any drug charges?"

"No. But he has an old conviction for arson, for which he did five years in prison in his early twenties. And he has a burglary conviction from his late thirties for which he served three years."

"What about Angel?"

"Here is where it gets interesting. Some family violence charges against Angel were dismissed. But he has a conviction from Houston for sexual assault of a child. He served five years in prison on that charge and is on parole. He must register as a sex offender wherever he lives for the rest of his life. And I don't think he has registered here in Fort Worth. A failure to register is a criminal offense in itself and surely a violation of his parole. So there may be an arrest warrant out for him. I am guessing on that."

Paloma looked hard at him. "Thank you for helping me. I would never have been able to find all that out. How do we use it?"

"Luther will have to testify to make his eviction case. But under the law I am not supposed to tell the judge about charges that did not result in convictions, and or about the arson and burglary convictions because they are so old."

"Why the hell not?"

"The law prevents it."

"The law sucks."

"Sometimes it does indeed."

"What if Angel testifies?"

"Then I can use his child sex abuse conviction. But I doubt he will testify."

"If there is a warrant out for him, won't they arrest him if he walks into the courtroom?"

"I doubt that he will come if he suspects there is a warrant. Even if he does appear, I doubt that constables have the power to check for the warrant or to arrest him on it."

"What did you find about my criminal record?

"Two prostitution convictions. All of those when you were in your twenties. You have four bad check convictions, one a year for the last four years, and an assault conviction from six years ago on your adult record. Who did you assault?"

"No one."

"Then why did you plead guilty?"

"Because the judge wasn't going to believe my side. If I pled I got probation. If I went to trial I went to jail. Have I got a chance today?"

"We—we have a chance. But I am going to ask you not to testify. I just do not want you to testify under oath to the sex and drug use you described to me."

"But I want to expose them."

"You don't know me yet, but I am asking you to trust me on this. They have to put on their evidence first. Let's wait to see what I can do to their case before you decide whether to testify. Okay? I have something to work with without exposing you on the stand."

John Levi continued. "But I do need to tell you this. A justice of the peace in Texas does not have to be a lawyer. The JP in our case is about your age. His name is Joseph Newell. He was a cop on the Fort Worth PD. He left the police force after only seven years of service. He ran for JP and the big pay raise that comes with the office. He was probably elected because his mother is a Republican Party Committee woman for Tarrant County and because he had financial backing from the landlords' association."

"So I am fucked again."

"Let's say we have our work cut out for us. But, again, I have found some things to work with. And even if we lose in this JP Court we can get a new trial on everything in the County Court at Law. Just stay with me and do not lose your cool, no matter what lies Luther or Angel tell. Paloma, do not lose your cool. Have you ever played poker?"

"No. But I have seen it played in the club."

"Keep a poker face. Do not speak, no matter what lies you hear, unless I call on you. Okay? Understand? I predict that Angel and Luther are going to try to talk to you before the hearing, to tell you that you have no chance to win and that you, Cynthia, and your belongings will be out on the curb by nightfall. Then they will offer to drop the eviction if you will come back to work for them. I am asking that you refuse to talk to either of them. Let me do the talking."

"Okay."

"There will probably be a bunch of cases before us in this court, so we'll just have to sit and watch until our case gets called."

John Levi and Paloma arrived at the court. He made sure to keep Paloma by his side when he went to file his appearance as attorney for Paloma in the clerk's office. Then they went into the courtroom.

On the front row of the public pews to the far right were six middle-aged women. The uniformed bailiff was speaking to them by their first names. Scattered throughout the rest of the courtroom were tenants. The only thing in common they had with one another was that they all looked scared and poor and they were all without counsel.

John Levi looked for Luther and Angel Bodine. He wanted to give them a copy of his entry of appearance and to repeat Paloma's threat of going to the police with the video of Angel's sexual assault of her. He wanted them to know that they had some skin in the game now that Paloma wasn't as alone and vulnerable as before. His main goal was not to win the eviction suit, which he doubted he could do in this court, but to back the Bodines away from Paloma. But he did not see them.

Justice of the Peace Newell took the bench. He was dressed in a red plaid sport jacket and black slacks. The jacket was tight and skimpy, emphasizing his muscular physique. His biceps stretched smooth the fabric. He looked like a cop going to church rather than a judge. His hair was blond and cut close.

Newell nodded good morning to the group of middle-aged women. He offered no such greeting to the tenants. He called one of the women by her first name, and invited her to come forward and identify her cases on his docket.

This first lady stepped inside the well of the court and identified her list of cases. The bailiff then called the tenants in each of these cases to come forward in turn. These uniformly scared and fumbling people sat at the table opposite the lady, who was sworn to the truth. In each case she identified herself as an employee of a property services company, not of the landlord, identified the apartment complex, provided Justice Newell the first page only of a multipage written lease agreement, and read from a list of rent delinquencies provided by the landlord. Newell then turned to the tenants in each case to ask if they had in fact failed to make any of the monthly rent payments identified by the lady. If they admitted this, or even if they didn't, he ordered them evicted and gave them a limited amount of time to get themselves and their personal property out. If they did not do this in the time given, constables would move their belongings to the curb. The reasons that tenants tried to give the court for their inability to pay their rent—unemployment or illness or the need to spend scarce money on other necessities—went unheeded by Newell. "'You don't pay, you don't stay' is the law," said the justice, "and no excuses." So Paloma and John Levi watched a sad parade of crestfallen tenants leave the court. Paloma sat next to John Levi, muttering, "It's not fair. It's not fucking fair," while John Levi shushed her.

For over an hour each of these ladies was allowed to testify without objection to matters of which they obviously had no personal knowledge. Each of them worked for a different property services company hired by the respective landlord to handle these hearings. They were mere talking heads reading documents provided them. It took more time to call the case and get the tenants into their seats than for Justice Newell to hear the so-called evidence and order eviction.

Ten thirty came and still no Bodines. *Maybe he won't appear and I can get the case dismissed,* John Levi thought. Paloma sat nervously looking back at the courtroom doors for Bodine to enter.

Newell took a break. One of the remaining tenants whose case had not yet been called asked to talk to John Levi. John Levi went with him to a tiny conference room off the outside hall. He brought Paloma with him so she wouldn't be able to talk to the Bodines alone if either of them appeared.

"Sir, are you a lawyer?" asked the youthful man, with the mother and their baby in the mother's arms next to him.

"Yes, I am."

"Can you help us?"

"I'm sorry. Tell me your names please."

"My name is Elisha Rogers. This is my wife, Mimi, and our daughter, Kaesha."

"My name is John Levi Jones This is Ms. Paloma Ibarra. Mr. and Mrs. Rogers, I am sorry, but I am only here to help one person. I am really not practicing law actively any longer."

Elisha pleaded. Mimi was crying. "Please sir. We have no one else. We weren't able to stay up on our rent because my hours got cut at work and we had a bunch of medical bills for the baby. I almost paid all my back rent but the apartment management doesn't care. They want to bust my lease so they can charge the next tenant more. I was hoping the judge would tell my landlord to give me more time. I tried to talk to the lady here on my case, but she said she has no authority to negotiate with me. I called my landlord, but he said it is too late."

"I just can't help you, sir. I am sorry."

The family started to leave.

"Wait," said Paloma. She stepped in front of John Levi. She had tears in her eyes, which startled him because she had seemed so hard until now. "Can't you do anything for them?"

"Paloma, if I stand up for these people it might irritate this judge and he might take it out on us in our case. Besides, I don't think I can be of any real help to them."

"You can keep them from feeling so alone. I don't care if it hurts me. How can you sit there and watch this shit going on without trying to stop it? I don't expect to win here anyway. But I want us to ty to throw a wrench into the wheels of this machine. Please do what you can for them. If you don't, I don't want you to be my lawyer."

"Do you know this family?"

"No. But I know their situation. I have lived it my entire life."

John Levi looked at Paloma in wonder. *Where did this empathy come from?*

"Elisha, Mimi, please come back a minute. Let me ask you a few more questions. How many rent payments did you miss altogether?"

"Eight."

"How long ago did your apartment company first give you notice threatening eviction?"

"Four months ago."

"Did they give you time to catch up?"

"Yes."

"And when you couldn't meet their deadline to pay up in full, they filed for this eviction?"

"Yes."

"Then I won't be able to do much for you. But because of Ms. Ibarra's request I will do what I can."

The mother with the baby turned to Paloma and hugged her. "Thank you, thank you, thank you."

Paloma said to Mimi, "Don't get your hopes up. The law won't let him do much."

Justice Newell resumed the bench, this time in shirt sleeves, and called the Rogers family's case. John Levi walked into the well of the court with the family and directed them where to sit. The woman who was representing the residential services company looked startled. John Levi was the only lawyer to walk into the court well that morning.

"Your Honor, my name is John Levi Jones. I am a member in good standing of the State Bar of Texas," and gave his State Bar number. "I am here representing the Rogers family, respondents in this case."

"When were you retained, Mr. Jones?" asked Newell.

"Just now, Your Honor."

"Then you will need a brief continuance to prepare and to work out your fee arrangements?"

"Thank you, but no thank you, Your Honor. I am taking this on *pro bono*. We are ready for this trial."

"Did your new client pay his rent in timely fashion? Is the apartment owner's petition for eviction wrong?"

"Excuse me, Your Honor. But the first issue is whether the landlord can present competent evidence to prove its case. The landlord has that burden of proof. My client does not have the burden to disprove it."

"No kidding," said the Justice. "Call this case." The clerk did so. Newell then called on the lady for the property services company to testify. She stated her name, took out the rent summary from the landlord, and began to read.

John Levi stood immediately to object. "Your Honor, I object to any and all testimony by this nice lady. Texas Rule of Evidence 602 forbids any witness to testify who does not have personal knowledge of the matters about which she seeks to testify. This witness has not laid this necessary foundation of personal knowledge."

"Yes, of course," said Newell. "But this is a JP Court. The rules of evidence are relaxed here because so many lay people come here for quick justice."

"Yes, Your Honor. But the fundamental requirements of due process are not relaxed in any court in the United States. And there is no more fundamental requirement than that a witness may only testify to matters within her personal knowledge."

"Mr. Jones, you have sat here all morning and heard property service agent after agent testify in the same way this lady proposes. If I sustained your objection now, wouldn't I be admitting that I should not have allowed the testimony in all these previous cases? I have been accused in the past of being biased in favor of landlords. In fact, I am just trying to follow the law and move things along efficiently and fairly. Why should I treat this case any differently than the other cases this morning?"

"In those other cases no objection was made to the testimony. I am objecting in this one case. I am addressing only this case and surely not the entire system of evictions. At least not at this time, I am not. I ask permission to question this witness to determine if the necessary foundation of personal knowledge is present."

"Any objection to this?" asked the Justice of the witness.

"No, sir," said the witness, who looked like she wanted to flee the court.

John Levi asked the witness's employer.

"So you do not work for the landlord and owner of the apartment where this family leased their home?"

"No, sir."

"Have you ever even been to that apartment complex?"

"No, sir."

"Have you ever talked to any employee of the landlord? Or the landlord?"

"No."

Can you name any employee of the landlord?"

"No, sir."

"Who is the landlord?"

The lady refers to her sheet. "Two Brothers LLC."

"You only know that because it is on that sheet you have?"

"That's all I know about anything in this case."

"Who are the two brothers?"

"No idea."

"The only matters about which you are prepared to testify are those set forth on that sheet before you about my clients' rent payments?"

"Yes, sir."

"You have no personal knowledge that anything on that sheet is true or false, correct?"

Hesitation. "I guess not."

You don't know what rent he has or has not paid?"

"Correct."

"You don't know how the information on that sheet was compiled by the landlord, correct?"

"Correct."

"You don't know who typed that sheet or whether they know the truth of what is on it or how they know this truth, correct?"

"Right."

"And what you and the court and I do know is that the landlord chose to pursue the eviction of the Rogers family from their home without sending a witness with actual knowledge of the facts stated on their petition for eviction."

"I guess that is right."

"You Honor, on that basis, I object to any testimony from this honest lady."

The justice addressed the witness. "Ma'am, you have testified to these kinds of matters in my court many, many times. Have you ever had personal knowledge of what you testified in any of those cases?

"I can't think of any such case, Your Honor."

The justice looked at John Levi. He looked back at the witness. "Do you have any other testimony to offer . . . other than what is set forth on that piece of paper in your file?"

"No, sir."

"Mr. Jones, do you have any witnesses?"

"No, sir."

"I didn't think so. Everyone stay where you are."

The justice went into his office. Time passed. John Levi noticed a middle-aged man enter the courtroom. John Levi leaned to Paloma, who sat on the first row of pews. "Is that Luther Bodine?" he whispered. Paloma nodded. *"Good,"* thought John Levi. *"I get to cross-examine him. I am enjoying being in court again."*

The justice re-entered the courtroom and sat down at his desk. John Levi guessed he had made a call to a real judge and had made notes. Newell read, "On the particular record before me in this particular case, the particular objection under Texas Rule of Evidence 602 having been made by the respondent in this case, I sustain the objection and deny the eviction and judgment for back rent requested by the landlord. The petition is dismissed."

Elisha stood up and shook John Levi's hand vigorously. Mimi stepped into the well of the court and hugged him. John Levi asked them to wait for him in the conference room.

"Why didn't you tell the other people in those other lawsuits to object?" John Levi heard Paloma ask from behind him. He turned and saw she was standing in the first row of pews. As John Levi was about to rescue Paloma from herself, the justice asked, "Are you speaking to me, young lady?"

"Yes. I am speaking to you. You could have told every person in your court today to say, 'I object.' You could have asked all these people who testified for the landlords if they knew what they are talking about. You could have stopped every one of those evictions this morning!"

John Levi stepped between Paloma and Newell, blocking their view of one another. "Paloma, be quiet!"

Paloma stepped out from behind John Levi. "But you let these evictions go on. This isn't a game. This is about people's homes. People in hard times."

"Paloma, shut up!" John Levi started pulling her out of the courtroom.

"Mr. Jones. Is this also your client?"

"Yes, sir. I apologize. This is all my fault for not instructing her about proper court decorum. She is under a great deal of stress and is highly emotional."

"Bring her into the well of the court," said the justice. "Ma'am, you will be quiet now or I will hold you in contempt and put you in jail for the night." He looked at his docket and at the only other person remaining in the courtroom. "Are you Luther Bodine?" the justice asked.

"Yes, Judge," said the man.

"Mr. Jones, is this Paloma Ibarra?"

"She is, Your Honor, and again I apologize. This was my fault."

"No, it wasn't your fault, Mr. Jones. Mr. Bodine, come forward. The court calls the case of Luther Bodine versus Paloma Ibarra. The parties and Mr. Jones will be seated at table. I am going to see that justice is done swiftly in this case. And teach this woman some respect for the law."

"Your Honor, I request a recess of a few minutes so that everyone can calm down and so I can instruct my client once again about proper courtroom behavior." Paloma sat glaring at the justice.

"No, Mr. Jones. We are going to get this done. I am sure that you will appeal any decision I make that does not go your way. So we are getting on with this."

Luther Bodine was about five feet eight inches tall, with long white hair in a ponytail. He wore wire-rim glasses with lenses tinted blue. He wore a western-style, long-sleeve, white shirt with faux pearl snap buttons,

Wrangler jeans heavily starched and creased, and ostrich skin cowboy boots. He smelled of nicotine and caffeine. He had a thin build but a gut that made him look pregnant. He sat down at the petitioner's courtroom table, smirking at Paloma, who icily avoided his gaze.

The justice addressed Bodine. "Your petition for eviction states that Ms. Ibarra has failed to make her agreed rent payments. First, let me ask you if you have personal knowledge of this."

"Yes, Judge. I surely, surely do. No one knows as much about this as me, Judge. Except that woman there," gesturing at Paloma with his thumb.

"How do you have this knowledge?"

"I own the property and manage it myself. I am the person she was supposed to pay and didn't."

Newell looked down at John Levi and smiled as if to say, "*So much for that.*"

"Do you have the lease agreement with you?"

"There was no written lease. We just gave our word. My word is strong as stone, Judge. Hers is strong as a wet tortilla." Bodine grinned at John Levi.

Newell turned to John Levi. "During the recess in the last case, I called downtown about you, Reverend John Levi Jones. You have quite the reputation as a trial lawyer. So I am assuming that you know that residential lease agreements don't have to be written to be enforceable under the law."

"Of course, Your Honor."

"Well, we took care of that too, didn't we? Mr. Bodine, when did the lease term begin for the property listed on your petition?"

"September 1 last year."

"Did Ms. Ibarra move into the property in September of last year?"

"Yes, she did. She surely, surely did."

"And has she lived there continuously from then until today?"

"Yes, she surely, surely has."

Newell was proving Luther Bodine's case for him.

"Have you given her at least thirty days' notice to vacate?"

"Yes, I have."

"But she has not?"

"No, she is still there."

"How much rent has she paid you since last September?"

"Zero."

"Zero? Then why have you taken so long to evict her?"

"Just trying to help her out. Hoping she would see the light."

"Are you also asking for a judgement in your favor for her unpaid rent, Mr. Bodine?"

John Levi jumped from his counsel chair. "*Excuse* me, Your Honor. But there is no request for unpaid rent in Mr. Bodine's petition."

Newell looked through the petition for eviction again. "Yes, Mr. Jones. You are correct again. But I will approve a trial amendment to allow Mr. Bodine to request back rent."

"For the record, I object to this amendment."

"There is no record being made, Mr. Jones. As you can see, there is no court reporter. We are not even making an audio recording of this proceeding. Because you did not request it."

"That explains a great deal, Your Honor."

"What do you mean by that, Mr. Jones?"

"That you were quite serious when you said earlier this morning that most court rules don't apply in JP Court."

Bodine interrupted. "I am not asking for back rent, Your Honor," he said grandly.

"Very generous, indeed. I might it call it very Christian of you. Reverend Jones, I can't imagine what you could ask Mr. Bodine to prevent the court from granting this eviction. But go ahead."

"Hopefully, I can bring some things to light that are now in darkness, Justice." John Levi smiled innocently at Newell.

"Mr. Bodine, you say you are the owner and landlord of this property on Irion?" asked John Levi.

Bodine had not taken the witness stand for the court's questioning, so Luther and John Levi were sitting no more than four feet apart, with Paloma sitting to John Levi's opposite side. Bodine sat facing John Levi, with his left leg crossed over his right knee, wagging his foot so his boot was inches away from kicking John Levi with each wag.

"Yes."

"Are you 'surely, surely' the landlord and owner of the property on Irion?"

Bodine quit grinning and squinted at John Levi. "You heard me say so."

"Your authority to lease this house to Ms. Ibarra is 'surely, surely' because you are the landlord and owner?

"Yes."

"It's not because the owner made you the agent to lease it? You are claiming to be the sole owner?"

"Yep."

"So if the house violates the Fort Worth property code because it lacks any security locks, you as owner had absolute authority to have locks installed."

"I don't see what you are getting at," said Bodine.

"I am asking if you 'surely, surely' acted as if you were in fact the owner of the house on Irion. You didn't replace the missing locks. But an owner would have."

"Yes. But she wasn't paying me rent."

"We'll come on to that in a moment. The house has a hole in the roof? And sheetrock falling off the ceiling in the living room under that hole? And water leaking in? And mold? And exposed electrical wires? And no hot water heater, so no hot water? Right, Mr. Owner of the house on Irion?"

"I don't know about any of that. She never told me," pointing at Paloma.

"You know I did," responded Paloma.

"Ms. Ibarra, you will be quiet until Mr. Bodine or your lawyer questions you. One more outburst and I will have you removed from the court," said the justice.

"Mr. Jones," Newell addressed John Levi, "If you had any experience in Texas landlord-tenant law, you would know that defects in rental property do not excuse non-payment of rent."

"Thank you for your kindness in pointing that out to me, Your Honor." John Levi smiled sweetly at Newell. "But what I am showing is that he has not acted as if he is the owner of the property, particularly for such a fine Christian man. And that is because he is not in fact the owner."

"His ownership is in dispute?"

"Oh, very much so, Your Honor. May I proceed?" The justice nodded, more interested.

"Are you calling me a liar, Preacher?" asked Luther Bodine, leaning even closer to John Levi.

John Levi leaned in farther so that their two noses were almost touching. "Yes, Mr. Bodine. I surely, surely am."

Newell said, "Okay, I don't want to hear the phrase 'surely, surely' again during this hearing. And I am instructing you, Mr. Bodine, and you, Mr. Jones, to slide your chairs farther apart from one another . . . That's it. A bit farther . . . Now, Mr. Jones, if you have something to prove, I suggest you get to it."

"Mr. Bodine, who is Edith Yancey?"

Glare. "She is my wife."

"When did you marry?"

"2014."

"Was there a marriage ceremony?"

"We are common-law."

"Did you file a common-law certificate with the county?"

"Didn't know there is such a thing."

"Where is she now?"

"Hell if I know."

"When did you last see or have any communication with her?"

"Christmas 2016."

"Let me refresh your recollection about that, if I may. You were charged with assaulting Edith Yancey three times, and the last time was on Christmas Eve 2016."

"What does that have to do with anything? I was never convicted."

"Is that when you last saw her, Christmas Eve of 2016? Did she leave town and end any contact with you just after Christmas Eve of 2016?"

"So what?"

"Here's 'so what.' I am handing you now a certified copy I obtained from the Tarrant County website last night of the latest deed to the house on Irion. It shows that Edith Yancey is the sole owner of the property. Correct?"

"That's what this says."

"Your Honor, I offer this deed into evidence as Respondent's Exhibit 1."

"It's admitted," said Newell.

"This shows that Edith Yancey came into sole ownership of this house in 2012, two years before you say you and she entered into a common-law marriage."

"I may have got wrong the date we became married."

"A few seconds ago you said 2014."

No answer. Bodine glared harder at John Levi.

"This property belongs solely to Edith Yancey. And it came into her sole ownership before you claim, without documentation, that you and Ms. Yancey became married at common law. And you testified earlier that your only authority to rent this house to Ms. Ibarra is that you are the owner. But isn't it true that you are not an owner of this property. You just took control over it when Ms. Yancey fled town?"

"I am her husband. So what she owns, I own too. So I own that house."

"I'll put aside for now the principle that property owned before marriage is the separate property of the owning spouse, not both spouses." John Levi looked at Newell, who nodded at him. "Let me explore your marriage claim a bit more. Who is Elmira Bodine?"

"She was my first wife."

"Isn't she your present wife?"

"No, Edith is. I told you. How many times do I have to tell you?"

"Until you tell us the truth, Mr. Bodine. What year did you marry Elmira Bodine?"

"1990."

"Did you two always live together in Tarrant County, Texas during your marriage?"

"So what?"

"Does she still live in Tarrant County, Texas?"

"Yes."

"Mr. Bodine, I ask you to assume that no divorce suit has ever been filed in Tarrant County to end the marriage between you and Elmira Bodine. Do you claim to know of any such divorce suit?"

"No," sullenly.

"Have you ever filed such a suit?"

"No."

"Have you ever been served with such a divorce suit?"

"No."

"So as far as you know, you are still married to Elmira Bodine?"

No answer.

"Mr. Bodine?"

No answer.

"So, since in the great state of Texas a man can only have one wife at a time, you can't ever have been married to Edith Yancey?"

"I suppose so."

"And so you could never have any ownership interest in or authority over Edith Yancey's house on Irion by virtue of marriage to her?"

No answer.

"And so you don't have the legal standing to file this eviction suit."

"Whatever you say, shyster."

"Mr. Bodine, just as Ms. Ibarra must exercise proper courtroom decorum, so must you," admonished the justice. "Do you have any other basis for claiming an ownership interest or legal authority over that property?

"I paid the property taxes on the house last year and this year," said Bodine.

"Why would you do that," asked the justice, "when you didn't own it? To keep it from being condemned and seized by the city?"

"Yes, Your Honor. So that Ms. Ibarra and her children would have a place to live."

"That house was abandoned for years before you claimed to rent it to Ms. Ibarra, correct?" asked John Levi.

"If you say so."

"Do you say so?"

"Yes, I say so," he snarled.

"And when you claimed to be able to lease it to Ms. Ibarra, you told her you owned it when you did not. And since you have had no contact with Ms. Yancey for so long, she certainly didn't tell you could do so. "

"Whatever you say."

"Answer the question, Mr. Bodine," said the justice.

"Yes, what he says is correct," he growled.

"One more area of questioning and I will be done . . . Mr. Bodine, you testified that Ms. Ibarra has paid you 'zero,' I believe you said, in rent during the entire term of the so-called lease."

"Yes. Not a peso."

"Ms. Ibarra worked in your club on North Main in Fort Worth called The Hacienda when you claimed to lease the house to her, right?"

"Yes."

"She was a waitress and a hostess there for you?"

"Yes."

"And she provided other services to your customers, at your direction?"

"Like what?"

"You tell us, Mr. Bodine."

Newell seemed really interested now.

"She did some things on her own I didn't ask her to do."

"Like what?"

"Prostitution."

Newell looked at Paloma, who looked down at her hands folded on the table, biting her lip.

"Where did she provide these prostitution services, Mr. Bodine?" asked John Levi. "At your club? Or at your home on Lulu?"

Bodine stared at John Levi and Paloma. "You are getting in over your head, Mr. Jones."

"Either object or answer the question, Mr. Bodine," said the justice.

"I object," said Bodine.

"On what grounds?"

Bodine fumed. "You tell me, Judge."

"Answer the question, sir," said Newell.

"Let me repeat. Did Ms. Ibarra provide any of these prostitution services you claim you did not ask her to provide at your home on Lulu Avenue?"

"I don't remember."

"You don't remember? Would it refresh your memory if I showed you a video taken at your house on Lulu of your son Angel having sex with her when she was high?"

Bodine stared daggers at Paloma.

"You know of such a video, don't you Mr. Bodine?"

No answer.

"You have seen the video, haven't you?"

No answer.

"You have played the video in your club as entertainment for your customers, haven't you? Haven't you and your son Angel both played it?"

No answer.

"Mr. Bodine, to your knowledge, have the police been shown this video?"

"How would I know that?"

"You would know because they would have arrested your son Angel for rape and parole violation. But that hasn't happened yet, has it, Mr. Bodine?"

"No, that hasn't happened."

"Isn't it true that Ms. Ibarra never paid you any rent because the agreement you and Angel made with her was for her to provide services to you and your clients in exchange for her being able to live in the house on Irion rent free?"

"No, that is not true."

"Then tell the court how much you have paid her for her work in your club and her services in your home since September of last year when she moved into the Irion house."

"I haven't paid her anything, because she wasn't worth anything."

"So your claim is that she worked in your club for . . . nothing?"

"Yes, which was what she was worth."

"But you let her live in the house without her paying you any rent for more a year out of the goodness of your Christian heart? No connection between her work and that house at all?"

No answer.

"In fact, you provided something else in pay to Ms. Ibarra, to get her to perform these services for you and your customers. You provided her methamphetamine manufactured in your home on Lulu and sold to your customers there."

The justice intervened. "Mr. Bodine, I am required to advise you that you have the right to refuse to answer any of Mr. Jones' questions about drug use or any other potentially criminal activity, on grounds that your testimony might incriminate you."

"Your Honor, I withdraw that question. But I have another."

Luther sat simmering.

"Mr. Bodine, what you thought would happen today is that you would testify to lies, that Ms. Ibarra would be all alone and unrepresented in court, that you would get your order of eviction, but that you would then not have the order executed and would not actually have Ms. Ibarra and her child evicted."

"Why would he have intended that, Mr. Jones?" asked the justice.

"Because he could then hold that order of eviction over Ms. Ibarra's head to make her come back to work for him. He wanted to use a house he doesn't own to continue to own Ms. Ibarra."

"Mr. Bodine?" asked the judge.

"All of that is a lie."

"Do you have any other questions of this witness, Mr. Jones?"

"No, I am finished with him."

"Good idea. Mr. Bodine, do you have any additional evidence?"

"No, Judge," Bodine said glumly. "I just want to get out of here." Bodine rose from his chair and stormed out of the courtroom.

"This hearing is still going to proceed with or without you, Mr. Bodine," the justice called after him. Bodine kept walking.

"Mr. Jones, do you still have a motion?" asked Newell.

"Yes, Your Honor. I move that this eviction suit be dismissed with prejudice. Do you want me to present an argument?"

"That's enough Mr. Jones," said the justice. "You've done more than enough. The court grants the motion."

"Ms. Ibarra, there is no excuse for the way you spoke to me earlier. But I understand your emotion. You were deceived by this man Bodine. You need to get away and stay away from him and his son. But you are a squatter in that house. You have no legal authority to live there because this man had no authority to let you stay there. You need to find another place to live as soon as possible. That is not a matter before this court now, but that is my advice to you. I suspect Mr. Jones would agree with that advice. The court is in recess. Mr. Jones, approach the bench."

John Levi did so. Newell waved him to the side, where he joined him.

"I am told you are in ministry now. What church?"

"Peace United Methodist on Oscar Avenue."

"Then what are you doing here?"

"This poor woman and her child were being cheated and used by these men. I had the opportunity to help her. I couldn't say no."

"You know I was a cop?"

"I read that, Judge."

"I know from experience that there is so much need in that neighborhood. Once people find out that you can help, there will be no rest for you."

"That is what I am hoping for."

Newell smiled at him. "One more word for you, Reverend. Watch your ass with the Bodines. They don't respect God or the law and they damn sure have no respect for your being a minister or a lawyer. "

Justice Joseph Newell and Reverend John Levi Jones shook hands and parted.

"How did you help me and my daughter?"

— Tuesday, September 18, 2018, just before noon —

John Levi and Paloma walked out of the courtroom. But Paloma grabbed John Levi by his arm, jerked him to a stop, and stepped in front of him.

"Why were you making nice with that man? You saw what he was letting happen to those poor people in his court."

"Paloma, we have to pick the hills we are willing to die on. The law was letting it happen, not him."

"But he had the power to stop it, and he didn't. He is just hiding behind the law to keep his cushy job. And you were letting him."

"I let him? *I* just won your case. And I won the Rogers' case. You are mad at me because I didn't win every case? How about a simple 'thank you'? You think it is going to help in the future, if I ever come back to his court to try to help you or someone else, to get in his face now? There are speeds between full stop and one thousand miles an hour, Paloma. Pick your races. And you need to appreciate who is on your side."

"So who is on my side?" she yelled.

"I just proved that *I* am," he yelled back.

"On my side?! How did you help me and my daughter? We still have to move! Where will we move? You say you want to help but you just put on a show. You could have helped all those people but you just sat there."

John Levi jerked open the door to the conference room and stepped inside. Paloma followed, still steaming.

Elisha and Mimi Rogers jumped up from their seats and rushed toward John Levi. Elisha grabbed his right hand and began pumping it again. Mimi hugged him, her face buried in his shoulder, sobbing "Thank you." Their baby lay in a car seat, sleeping. John Levi looked at Paloma and raised his eyebrows. *"See? Like that."*

"What will you do now?" John Levi asked them.

"I am going to finish paying off my back rent," replied Elisha. Mimi nodded.

"Are you crazy?" blurted Paloma. "Why on earth?"

Elisha was startled. "We are honest people. We owe the money. It's only fair. When they see how honest we are, they will treat us right."

"Paloma, let me talk please." Paloma snorted and bit her lip. "Mr. Rogers, please hear me. This landlord is not a human being with a conscience. It's a business. It's inhuman. Its only goal is to make a profit. These property managers marked you for eviction. We have now made them angry. They will be looking for any reason to file for eviction again. And they will probably make life difficult for you while you stay. Are you hearing me?"

Elisha nodded yes. Mimi was still in tears.

"Because of this hearing we just went through, you no longer owe any back rent. They sued you not only for eviction but for the back rent and they lost the case. So the court said you don't owe."

"But I do owe morally, and I want to pay."

"My advice to you is to keep the money you were going to pay them for back rent to use to move into another place."

"But we can't afford another place now. Where will we go?"

"Mr. Rogers, here is my card. Call me at my church tomorrow and we will get together about where you can live. I am new at this but maybe I know some people who will help."

"I'll call you tomorrow as soon as I get off work at 3:30," said Elisha.

John Levi then remembered the words of Justice Newell to him when they parted at court moments before. *"I know from experience that there is so much need in that neighborhood. Once people find out that you can help, there will be no rest for you."*

And he remembered his own words in response. *"That is what I am hoping for."*

John Levi and Paloma left the Rogers and walked outside the municipal building to the parking lot.

"Paloma, I also would like to talk to you about where we can move you and your daughter. Did you have breakfast this morning? May I take you to lunch?"

"I told you that you don't want to be seen with me."

"We can go to another part of town if it would make you less uncomfortable."

"You motherfuckers!" Paloma suddenly screamed and began running toward the parking lot.

John Levi saw Luther Bodine and a younger man standing next to his pickup. The younger man was holding a car key and there were scratches in the paint.

"Hey!" yelled John Levi. "Hey! Stop that!" running after Paloma. *That other man must be Angel.* Angel was as short as Luther, maybe five feet six, but lean and muscular. He was dressed in a black dress shirt with the collar open to mid chest, multiple chains around his neck, tight black dress pants and black leather cowboy boots with pointed toes. His black hair was slicked back with pomade. He had a black goatee.

Paloma did not stop. She ran full speed straight into Luther. She knocked him against the truck and bounced him onto his ass, so he was sitting on the parking lot, his back against the driver's-side door. Paloma slapped him repeatedly, open hand and then back hand in the face. She yelled, "You rented me a house you didn't even own!" over and over. Luther covered his head with his arms and tried to roll away. As he did so, Paloma kicked him. Angel—and it was Angel—leaped behind Paloma, wrapped his left arm around her face, and jerked her away from his father. Paloma stomped her foot down on the top of Angel's foot with all her might. He howled and cursed. He dropped his arms to around her waist, picked her up, and slung her into the bed of John Levi's truck. "You bitch! You bitch! You got no sense at all!" he yelled.

Paloma sprang up and was poised to leap out of the bed onto Angel when the constable who had been on duty in JP Court ran hollering for everyone to stop.

John Levi was frozen scared. He had never been in a real fight in his life. He was undone by Paloma's courage and violence. He felt the urge to stop Angel when he picked up Paloma but was unable to move. *How do I grab him? What do I do when he turns on me?*

Luther Bodine pulled himself slowly to his feet. Paloma stood poised in the bed of the truck, one foot on the side wall. Angel was smoothing his hair back into place.

The constable turned to John Levi. "Reverend Jones, did you see what happened?"

John Levi found it hard to catch enough breath to speak. But he managed to wheeze, "As Ms. Ibarra and I were leaving the court, we saw these two men standing next to my pickup. This man," indicating Angel, "was using his keys to scratch my paint job."

Luther said, "That's a lie. We didn't even know this was his truck. We were admiring it. The scratches were already there when we walked up. This bitch attacked me without any reason. Look, my nose is bleeding."

The constable separated the Bodines and Paloma and ordered them to stay where they were. "Who are you?" the constable asked Angel. Angel refused to answer.

John Levi worked up the courage to speak. "Constable, he is Angel Luther Bodine. I suggest that you detain this man until you run a warrant check on him."

"Paloma, is this Angel Bodine?" John Levi asked Paloma.

"Goddamn right it is."

"Constable, if you run a warrant check, I believe you will find a parole warrant out for him. He didn't go inside the court because he feared he would be arrested. He is on parole after conviction for sexual abuse of a child out of Harris County. He is a lifetime registered sexual offender. I believe he has moved back here to Tarrant County and has failed to register. "

The constable turned to Angel. "Is this true? Are you Angel Luther Bodine?"

"I don't have to answer you."

The constable had no handcuffs and no radio or phone to call for help. And there was no other law enforcement person in the parking lot.

John Levi handed the constable his cell phone. "Why don't you call 911? It will carry more weight if you make the call instead of me."

The constable dialed. He turned his back and cupped his hand over the phone to hear and be heard. As he was turned, Angel ran. The overweight constable ran after him, but it was no contest. Angel arrived at his Camaro well ahead and roared off. The constable fumbled with a notepad in his breast pocket but could not get it out in time to record the license plate number and could not remember it seconds later. He stumbled back out of breath.

"What is your son's license number?"

"What son? Don't know," replied Luther. "I still can't think straight because of the way this woman assaulted me. I think I have a concussion. Aren't you going to arrest her?"

The constable kept everyone in their place until a Fort Worth police officer arrived. The officer separated them to question them individually. The officer wanted to talk most with John Levi about Paloma's assault of Luther. John Levi called the constable over while he told the officer of what had occurred in the courtroom. The constable confirmed John Levi's account.

"So you are saying that this man Luther Bodine had the assault coming?"

"I am saying that he invited it. And that Ms. Ibarra was preventing more property destruction."

"Did you actually see either man scratching your paint job?"

"I saw the scratches and the key in Angel Bodines hand as he stood next to my truck."

"So not this man Luther Bodine?

"No."

"I am going to give this woman a Class C citation for simple assault. She can tell her story to the justice of the peace."

"Officer," Luther Bodine called out, "I don't want to press charges."

"Good decision. That takes care of that," said the officer.

"What about an outstanding warrant for Angel Bodine? Can you confirm that?"

"I have. There is an outstanding parole violation warrant for him. You have any idea where he is staying?"

Paloma called out. "I can give you the address."

Luther said, "I changed my mind. I want to press charges."

The officer replied. "Too late. I already wrote that you declined."

Before John Levi and Paloma left the municipal building parking lot, after the police and the constable had left, Luther Bodine drove his pickup next to John Levi's and said, "You made yourself some enemies today, Mr. Jones. Enemies who always settle their scores."

John Levi walked to Bodine's truck and stood with his face in Bodine's.

"Help me with something, Mr. Bodine. How do you live with the way you treat young women like Paloma? How do you sleep at night?"

"Save the sermon, Preacher. You got no idea what my life's been like. No fuckin' idea."

"Mr. Bodine, if you or Angel bother Paloma or my church, I will go to the police with the video Paloma has of Angel raping her."

"Rape?" he snorted. "That girl can't give it away fast enough. She ain't never been raped by anyone. She likes it too much. The two things she craves in this world are cock and meth."

"You better hear me, Bodine."

"And you better hear me, Preacher. We Bodines don't go to the police to take care of our problems. We handle 'em ourselves. You're wastin' your time tryin' to stick up for that woman. She ain't gonna' change 'til the day she dies." He laughed and roared off in his pickup.

"I'm not going to the police for help," said Paloma to John Levi. "Appreciate you trying to back him off me, but I'm not talking to the police."

"Paloma, these men are criminals. They are exploiting young girls. They need to be stopped. If you tell the police what they have done to you and what you have seen them doing in their house, the police can get a warrant, search the place, and put a stop to them."

"Your problem is that you believe in fairy tales. You think the police would trust *me*? I had a part in every crime that I could tell the police that Luther and Angel committed. They'd charge me too. You've seen my record. I'd have to do time. Who'd take care of Cynthia while I was in jail? You? My drunk dad? I got mad once and threatened to go to the police. Luther told me that he would kidnap Cynthia and sell her out of state if I did. No, sir, I am never going to the police. And you aren't for me. To hell with that."

"How can there be a God when the world is filled with men like Luther and Angel Bodine? And women like me?"

— Tuesday, September 18, 2018, just before 1:30 p.m. —

John Levi was able to talk Paloma into going to lunch with him. He went online the night before to research typical symptoms during withdrawal from meth. He learned that Paloma was likely feeling famished, exhausted, jittery, and hopeless. He learned that she was feeling an extreme yearning for more meth. She might experience hallucinations or delusions. He was particularly concerned that she was a threat to hurt herself, another common symptom of withdrawal. She had certainly been self-destructive in court and in the parking lot. What he didn't find listed as a common symptom of withdrawal was anger, which poured out of her.

As they drove to a barbecue place on the other side of Fort Worth, Paloma took her hair down and let it fall around her face. Her head nodded forward so her chin rested on her chest and she fell asleep, snoring lightly, little bubbles forming on her lips. When they arrived, he had to gently poke her awake. They entered the restaurant and stood in line cafeteria style. She was having trouble staying awake as they moved through the line. She shuffled just behind him and leaned forward with her forehead resting against his back. John Levi was moved by her leaning against him. For all the loud objections she had made, perhaps she was beginning to trust him. He ordered barbecue brisket, pork ribs and chicken, potato salad, pinto beans, and Texas toast, divided between two plates. She was silent when he was ordering. He ordered so much to make sure he got something she liked.

They got to a booth in the back, with John Levi carrying the loaded tray. As they sat on opposite sides of the table, he opened a Dr. Pepper, put a straw in it, and put the top of the straw in her mouth. She slowly revived as she sucked it down. She loaded her plate with ribs and began to eat in silence.

He interrupted her eating. "I'd like to say grace." He bowed his head and said, "Lord, bless this food to our nourishment and forgive us our sins. Thank you for placing Paloma and Cynthia in my path. Help me to help them. Help them to trust me. In Jesus' name we pray. Amen."

He looked up and saw that she was sneering at him as she chewed.

"What?" he asked.

"What is the point of asking God to bless food to our nourishment? Do you think this food won't nourish us without God's blessing? You think it will be more nourishing with a blessing?"

John Levi drew a blank.

"And if God put me and Cynthia in your path to help us, why did God take so damn long to do it . . . And just how have you helped us? We still don't have a place to stay."

"Paloma, I don't claim to know why God does what God does or doesn't do. But I do know about myself. And I know that I'm not done trying to help you. I've never experienced anyone get angry over a blessing before eating."

"What's in this for you? You help us so you can brag about it to your church people? Because it will make you feel better?"

"Why are you so angry about this?"

"Because I have had church people claim to want to help me before. But they do just enough to feel good about themselves but not enough to really help. And when things get hard, they disappear."

"Paloma, I promise you, I am not going to disappear."

"Yes, you will. And quit bullshitting me in your prayers. God doesn't nourish us. Food nourishes us. That prayer wasn't to God. It was to me." She went back to eating.

He stared at her. Her face was devoid of any fat. Her head was a skull with skin stretched taunt. But he could see a beauty in her eyes. He pictured Paloma's daughter Cynthia's face, and vowed that Cynthia's would never look like the one before him.

He looked at her hands and saw a tattoo of a cross on the inside of her right wrist. *Interesting. At some point in her life she believed in God.*

Paloma perked up more as she ate. She pushed the plate away and wiped the barbeque sauce off her mouth and fingers with a toilette. She looked John Levi full in the face. "Why *are* you doing this? What are you after?"

"I am just trying to help you and your child."

"Why? What's in it for you?"

"Just knowing I am helping you."

Paloma leaned back against the padded booth back, drawing on her soft drink straw.

"Can I ask you a question?" he asked her.

"You can ask."

"Why did you get a cross tattoo?"

"Young, dumb, and foolish, I guess."

"Did you believe in God when you got it?"

"Every child believes in God."

"You don't now?"

"How could I?"

"What do you mean?"

"How can there be a God when the world is filled with men like Luther and Angel Bodine? And women like me?"

"Women like you?"

"Okay. So maybe . . . maybe God is punishing me for the way I have been. But why do Luther and Angel Bodine always get away with everything?"

"I don't have an answer. Or I don't have one that won't sound weak." John Levi looked at Paloma intently, drawn into the pain in her face and through the barriers that her past placed between them.

"Have any others?"

"Others what?"

"Other tattoos?"

"Is that a pick-up line? I get that line at the club. 'Kin I see your tattoos, Babeee? You wanna' see mine, Sweet Thang?' You want to see my tattoos, Mr. Preacher? Is that what you are after?"

"Paloma, I am learning how badly you have been treated by men. I am not one of those men."

"Then why did you ask about my other tattoos?"

"Just making conversation. I shouldn't have. I apologize."

"That is the second time you have apologized to me in two days. You *are* a different kind of man."

John Levi furrowed his brow. "Second time?"

"The first time was when you apologized for bringing food to my house."

"Here's another one. I apologize for the way life has treated you. And particularly how the Bodines have used you and gotten away with it so far. And for how God has not protected you. So far."

"So far? You are putting a lot of pressure on yourself. Or on God." She sucked on the straw. "Sometimes I think I need to apologize. But not to God. To myself."

"Can you forgive yourself?"

Paloma closed her eyes. "You want to know how badly those scumbags have treated me? I have two other tattoos . . . which you will never see. One is about two inches below my belly button. It says, 'Luther's.'"

"'Luther's'? Like, L–U–T–H–E–R–apostrophe–S? Like 'this belongs to Luther'?"

"Yep. The other one is in the small of my back just above my butt crack. It says 'Angel's.'"

"Tell me why you agreed to have those done."

Paloma laughed derisively. "Who says I agreed? A friend of theirs did it to me when I was passed out in their house."

"They think they own you."

"They have owned me . . . I can't help wondering why you left the law. You sure seemed to be good at it in court this morning."

"I want to find another way to help people than I did in the law. A fuller way."

"Fuller? By trying to change them?"

"By trying to help them change their lives for the better."

"What kind of law did you do?"

"I represented people who had been injured by someone else's wrongdoing."

"Did you make a lot of money at that?"

"Pots full. In a very short time."

"So you were helping them and yourself."

"I hope I was helping them . . . Yes, I was helping them. And myself. But money will only help people so much."

"What other way is there?"

"To help people make better choices. To help people know they are not alone . . . Now please don't get angry again. To help people know that is a greater power on their side. Just because people have money doesn't mean people will make the right choices. I have helped clients get rich who blew the money within a year and went back to being just as poor and miserable as before. Money isn't always the answer to misery."

"I'd like to try that answer . . . So how do you propose to help me? What if I can't be helped? And why me of all the people who could use your help?"

"Because I can. Because I want to. Helping you will make me happy."

"*How* do you propose to help me?"

"By helping you help yourself and your daughter. To get you out of the clutches of meth and the Bodines. To get you out of that disaster of a house. To help you find a job that isn't dangerous and degrading."

"The answer to most of that sounds like money to me."

"Partly. But a part of the answer is for you to start believing in yourself. You wouldn't have chosen the life you have been living if you truly believed in yourself and your own dignity as a child of God."

Paloma blew up as suddenly as if John Levi had lit a match near a gas leak. "What the hell do you know about my life? You think I wouldn't be stuck in that house, stuck screwing a piece of shit like Angel, screwing strangers for meth, if I only *believed* in myself? Well, hallelujah! Let's just sing 'Kumbaya' while you show me the yellow brick road to my brand new life!"

Other diners were turning toward the sound of Paloma's voice. John Levi tried to quiet her down.

"God damn you. God *damn* you! Don't you shush me!" she hissed. "You think the spirit of Jeeeeesus is going to give me the power to turn my pig's ear of a life into a silk purse? You think I haven't tried church? You think I haven't asked Jeeesus for help? I grew up in the Bible-banging Baptist church, for God's sake, my sins washed away in a dunking when I was twelve, my soul saved by Jeeesus' blood. Church ladies have been taking me to Sunday school since I was a little kid. But the other kids in the class wouldn't come near me because I was dirty and I stunk and I had head lice. And their parents complained to the preacher that I was even there. Jeeesus wasn't anywhere to be found when I was thirteen and my mother started bleeding from stomach cancer more than Jeeesus ever did on the cross, and my worthless papa got more worthless, and I was the only one who could raise any money to keep my brother and sister fed. And you know how I raised that money, Preacher? You know how? Any fucking way I could, Jeeesus' disapproval be damned. And the only way I knew how was with this body and this face."

"I know I look like hell now. But when I was young a man couldn't walk by me without stopping and drooling. Particularly the way the Bodines dressed me. You should have *seen* me then. I don't care whether you were a preacher or lawyer or the pope; you couldn't have resisted me back then. An oilman took me to the Kentucky Derby when I was sixteen years old. I've been taken to Vegas by high rollers more times than I can remember.

For a while I thought that one of those rich pedophiles would set me up in an apartment and get me away from the Bodines. But when I had Cynthia when I was seventeen, and then when I turned thirty, those kinds of men were done with me. That left me with Angel and Luther and their kind of scum in the backroom of that club and their hell hole of a house. "

Paloma's fury had exhausted itself and her. She lay back against the padded booth seat, her eyes closed. Then she started to retch. She ran to the ladies restroom while John Levi sat impotent for the second time since the fight in the parking lot. John Levi sat for twenty minutes that seemed like an hour. She emerged, and though he expected her to walk out the restaurant door, she returned to the table and began to eat potato salad without looking at him.

"Paloma. I am so sorry. I am so sorry."

"That's four times. Save it. You got nothing to be sorry about." She kept eating.

"Let's talk about your daughter. Let's just find a way to help her. Tell me about her."

"What do you want to know?"

"Who's Cynthia's father? Can he help her? Could we get child support from him?"

Paloma stared at him. "Don't know who her father is. I went through this when I applied for food stamps and Medicaid. Her father is legally unknown."

"What's Cynthia like?"

"Scared. Sad. Too meek and gentle for this world."

"She's fourteen?"

"Yes."

"Boyfriends?"

"I sure hope not. Don't think so."

"Has she reached puberty yet?"

Paloma stared at him again, frowning.

"Is she sexually active?"

"Doubt it. But you never know. I leave her alone at night so much. But I am not taking any chances. I have her on the birth control patch."

"What are her grades like?"

"Bs and Cs."

"Does she have a favorite subject?

"Music. She plays the flute. Or she did when I could afford the rental."

"Does she take part in any school activities?"

"No. She is too shy and scared, and I can't afford the fees. She and her clothes have been too dirty."

"What does she have to be shy and scared about?"

"What doesn't she have to be shy and scared about? You've seen the house we live in. You know my work hours. You know . . . I have a favor to ask."

"Anything."

"Can I have a beer?"

"Sure."

John Levi bought her a Negra Modelo and joined her so she wouldn't feel so self-conscious.

"A preacher who drinks beer. You damn sure ain't no Baptist. Maybe you are different," she said.

After they had drunk half their beers, he asked her, "What is life like for you when you aren't angry? What is it that makes you feel happy?"

She scrunched her eyebrows together. "I don't remember. Okay. Now it's my turn. I got angry and told you a lot of my story. I never do that with anybody. What's yours?"

"What's my what?"

"You're stalling, Bubba. What's your story? Woman-wise? Children-wise? It feels like you are looking for a cheap thrill. Maybe a little stranger from the wrong side of town?"

"No wife. No child. No live-in girlfriend."

"Never?"

"Nope. Never."

"You gay?"

"No. What makes you ask that?"

"You are a good-sized, good-looking guy. You say you have pots full of money. Being gay is one explanation for why a man like you doesn't have a wife or a child or a steady screw."

"It's not that simple. There have been plenty of women in my life. But none of them for long. And I have been careful about getting a woman pregnant. And so have they."

"So, why not marriage and family?"

"Never fell in love. Never felt any one of them couldn't do without me. Never felt that way about any of them. Plus my work takes all my passion."

"You hate boredom then. You hate routine. You want . . . variety. A crusade. Am I your crusade?"

"No, you are not, Paloma. But you astonish me. You have just nailed me."

"I watch a lot of PBS."

They both laughed and finished their beers.

"At the risk of another blowup, I want to return to the subject of what you will let me do to help—help your daughter anyway."

"I'll keep it under control. Just don't talk about God."

"Then you can't ask about why I am doing this. Or doubt my sincerity."

"Okay."

"Okay. In no particular order, but maybe all at once. We need to get you healthier, meaning off meth and eating better. What is the longest you have been able to stay off meth since you started using?"

"About seven months once."

"Ever been to in-patient rehab?"

"Once. Left before the program was done."

"Why did you leave early?"

"Nothing they were saying inside was going to change my life outside."

"How were you able to stop for seven months?"

"I found out I was pregnant with Cynthia."

"Then you *can* stop using meth when you need to protect somebody else from it."

"Never thought of it that way, but you are right."

"Does it occur to you that Cynthia and you both need you to be off meth now as much as when you were pregnant with her?"

"You have a point."

"We need a new place for you and Cynthia to live—maybe a temporary place before a more settled one. Eventually we need to find you a safe, decent-paying job. And we need to get you some reliable transportation. The job will require some new clothes for you. So why not for your daughter, too? . . . Paloma, you look so depressed."

"How can I possibly get all that done? You think I haven't tried before. The hole I am in is just too deep."

"May I say—and don't get angry please—that it will also require you to want this so much that you will accept the help I can get you. And, to repeat, you have to believe you can do it."

"Lots easier to say those words than to do them."

"Yep, kind of like prayer."

"What?"

"Easier to say the words of a prayer than to believe them."

Paloma actually smiled at him.

"To start with, I would like your permission to check you and Cynthia into a Residence Inn for a while."

"I don't want charity."

"Paloma, you are going to have to put that dislike of charity away for a while, for the sake of your child. You must get out of that house on Irion now. You heard Justice Newell say so. And you need to be where the Bodines can't find you, particularly Angel. You have any other place you can move tonight, beside a motel?"

"No."

"Then the choice is between being on the street or accepting my help."

"You have to promise to let me pay you back some day."

"I promise. But that is on you. It is not a requirement of mine."

"Another question."

"Okay."

"It seems like you are going to be spending your own cash on us. The neighborhood is filled with people in need. Where will you draw the line? Who will you turn down?"

"You let me worry about that."

"John Levi"—this was the first time she called him by name—"I'm asking again. Why me and my kid? You can't help everyone. Elisha and Mimi Rogers at the courthouse? Once word gets out that you are really willing to help people, with money, there will be no end to the asks. You just won't be able to help everyone. It will wear you out. So, again, why me?"

"Because you have suffered so much. Because you have been so alone for so long. Because those men have so misused you. It would make me happy to be able to protect you from them, if you will let me. Please just trust that I won't disappear."

"One thing I hope you won't ask me to do."

"What's that, Paloma?"

"Come to your church service. I am a lot of things. But I'm not a hypocrite."

John Levi drove Paloma back to the house and helped her to pack up what clothes and household items they owned. They put some of those things in an unused closet at the church. John Levi called a nearby Residence Inn and reserved a suite with a small kitchen. Paloma and John Levi shopped for groceries and then checked in to the inn. They picked up Cynthia from her school and drove to their new, temporary home. Cynthia was thrilled to see the indoor swimming pool, and immediately took a hot shower and washed her clothes in the in-house laundromat.

As John Levi left for his own home, Paloma gave in to gratitude. She stepped outside their new front door as he was leaving, closed the door behind them so Cynthia couldn't see, and hugged him for a long moment. Then she stepped back inside to make supper.

Tears came to John Levi's eyes. He thought to himself, *"Best hug I've ever had."*

PART ONE

Happy Are Those Who Mourn

Chapter One

"Santa only brings presents to good little girls, Lomie."

— Wednesday, December 25, 1992, 7:00 a.m. —

Paloma is five years old. She had awoken to first light in her upstairs bedroom in her mother and father's house on Hale Street in Fort Worth. She was hungry, but she had eaten the last of the food for supper the night before—dry cereal without milk. She had gone to bed alone in the cold house. Unless her mother or father had been to the store and come home with groceries after Paloma went to bed, she would be going hungry today. Paloma usually dealt with this hunger by staying in her sleeping bag as long as she could.

But it was Christmas Day! At five years of age, she had learned all about Santa Claus and his reindeer and his sleigh full of presents. Of course the presents! The mother of her girlfriend Xochi from preschool had taken both little girls to a shopping mall. Paloma had waited her turn to sit on Santa's lap and asked him for Barbie's Ice Cream Parlor, thinking she would not only have a doll to love and keep her company but also ice cream to eat. Even if her parents hadn't bought her any presents, she was hopeful that Santa had. So Paloma shrugged out of her sleeping bag, pulled on some jeans, tennis shoes, and her oversized men's sweater, and walked downstairs.

She was still all alone. The house was silent and cold. There was no food. There were no presents. Merry Christmas.

Paloma looked out of the front window. In Xochi's house across the street Paloma could see through their window a Christmas tree with lights burning. And she could see Xochi's mother taking presents from under the

69

tree and handing them out. And she could hear Christmas music coming from the house.

Paloma walked upstairs and crawled into her sleeping bag.

She was roused by a knocking at her front door. She went downstairs and found Xochi's mother on the front porch with a plate of Christmas treats.

"Merry Christmas, Lomie. Here's a plate of Christmas goodies for you and your parents. May I speak to your mom?"

"She just went out for groceries."

"Are you sure, sweetie? I didn't see a car."

"She just went out for groceries. She'll be right back."

"Would you like to take these cookies and *pan dulce*?"

"Yes, ma'am."

"Xochi wants you to come over later to play with the Barbie's Ice Cream Parlor she got for Christmas."

"I'll have to ask my mom when she gets back. We are going to have a big meal later."

"Well, you are welcome to come over anytime. Merry Christmas. Remember, the baby Jesus was born today. And he loves you." The lady smiled and handed Paloma the plate of green and red cookies and the *pan dulce* and returned to her house.

Paloma took the plate, walked back into the kitchen and sat at the breakfast table. She devoured the two pieces of *pan dulce* and half of the cookies. She wrapped the plate with the rest of the cookies in an old newspaper to keep the roaches from getting at them and put the plate in the refrigerator for her parents.

Paloma brought her sleeping bag down into the front room. She sat in the bag looking out her front window, far enough back not to be seen from the outside. She saw children on the block playing with their new toys—footballs and skates and Frisbees and even a bicycle. She fell asleep in the bag.

She felt her mother kissing the top of her head. Her mother stumbled and sat down hard next to Paloma. She reeked of smoke and beer. Her eyes were red. Her hair was a bird's nest. She was eating one the Christmas cookies.

"Merry Christmas, Lomie," she smiled. "Where did we get these cookies?"

"Xochi's mom brought them."

"You didn't let her in the house, did you?"

"No, Momma. Did you bring any food home?"

"Have you eaten up all of our food again?"

"I'm hungry, Momma."

Paloma's mother's words were slurred and she was having a difficult time sitting upright. "I need to sleep. I'll go out and get us some food later."

"I'm hungry now, Momma. I have a tummy ache I'm so hungry."

"That's probably from all the cookies you ate."

"Can I go to Xochi's house? I was invited."

"No, you can't. You stay away from them. That woman is just trying to get you away from me so she can get more food stamps."

Tears welled up in Lomie's eyes.

"Why are you crying now?"

"Santa didn't bring me any presents, Momma."

"Santa only brings presents to good little girls, Lomie." She picked up Paloma's sleeping bag, wrapped herself in it, and lay down on the couch.

After her mother was fast asleep, Paloma whispered to her sleeping form, "Did Santa bring you anything, Momma?"

Chapter Two

Can't be too careful
with a precious only son."

— Wednesday, December 25, 1985, 6:00 a.m. —

John Levi is five years old. He had been awake most of the night. He was too excited to sleep. He lay in bed, his eyes wide opened, staring at the ceiling, waiting for the streaks of dawn to appear. First light was the signal to crawl as quietly as he could out of his bed, put on his robe and slippers, and sneak down the stairs to the living room and the Christmas tree.

There, he saw the same presents stacked around the base of the tree that had been there for weeks. But he also saw a wealth of unwrapped presents that had come overnight from Santa—a shiny new red Schwinn bicycle with training wheels, a football, football helmet, and shoulder pads, a baseball glove and a bat, a video game system, and some WWF action figures.

And on the brick base of the fireplace, he saw the glass of milk and the plate of cookies he had left there for Santa Claus. The milk was three-fourths gone and only cookie crumbs were left on the plate.

He lay down next to the presents and chose the WWF figures to play with during the interminable time before his parents came downstairs. He looked at the figures of Hulk Hogan, George the Animal Steele, Junkyard Dog, Jimmy Hart, Terry Funk, Hillbilly Jim, Classy Freddie Blassie, Hercules Hernandez, the Iron Sheik, and of course Randy Savage. John Levi loved to watch WWF. Now he staged a tag team match in the middle of the living room rug, carefully dividing the rubber figures into two teams of five each.

He heard the family's cook and housecleaner, Eugenia, walk up behind him. "Merry Christmas, John Levi," she sang. "I brought you some goodies to tide you over. You won't be eating brunch until 10:00 or so. Some company is coming over."

Eugenia placed before him a plate with two cinnamon rolls, two sticky buns, an orange, and an apple. John Levi ignored the fruit and tore into the pastry.

"Eugenia, do you think I could take my bicycle outside for a ride?"

"You best wait until your parents get up. Do you already know how to ride?"

"I already learned on my friend's bike."

"But this one has training wheels," said Eugenia. "I guess they are just being careful. Can't be too careful with a precious only son."

Chapter Three

"I've got to find a way to get some money."

— Friday, March 8, 2001, 11:00 a.m. —

Paloma is fourteen years old.

"What are you doing this weekend, Lomie?"

"Oh, I thought I'd rent a limousine, drop by Billy Bob's honky-tonk with my entourage, and dance the two-step all weekend. What do you think I'm doing? Taking care of my brother and sister while my dad gets drunk somewhere. Trying to find some way to feed us besides shoplifting from the Fiesta."

Paloma and her best friend Alicia sat in the back of the library of North Hill High School, where they were both freshman. They had known each other since kindergarten. Alicia was one of Paloma's few friends. Paloma was the butt of jokes and bullying by other girls. Her clothes were tattered. Her hygiene was lacking. She was small and thin. She was easily offended, rarely smiled, and did not share the interests of other girls in music and movies and boys. And she was secretive. She shared none of her life with a drug-addicted mother who had just died of stomach cancer and a failed father who was disabled by alcohol. A life lived in a hovel with holes in its walls on an unpaved dirt road south of 28th Street, a house too embarrassing to invite even a dear friend like Alicia to visit.

"I've got to find a way to get some money. To keep the electricity and water on and to buy food and shoes and to clean our clothes. My dumb brother gets suspended from school every week for fighting kids who make fun of his clothes. My little sister keeps getting sent home for head lice. The shampoo to treat the lice is expensive. Any ideas how I can make some money?"

"My mom would be happy to cook for you. You can use our washer and dryer."

"She's already had to do that too often. I'll never be able to pay her back."

"Is your dad drinking more than he did before your mom died?"

"Not really. He's always been worthless."

"You could help my aunt clean houses. But she doesn't work on weekends."

"If I drop out of school to clean houses, the school will report me and CPS will be called. We are *not* going into foster care again. But I have to keep the lights and water on."

"What would you do if you had some money?"

"I'd pay the light and water bills in advance so I wouldn't have to worry for a while. I'd get the refrigerator fixed. I'd get a lock box to keep the food stamps from my father so he couldn't trade them for beer. I'd buy my sister and brother some new clothes and shoes."

"And for you, Lomie?"

"Maybe some clothes from the secondhand shop. Comforters for the sofa and cots where we sleep. A portable radio. Maybe a little makeup . . . What's the point in thinking about this?"

"My mom says you are the oldest fourteen-year-old in the world."

"That's mean."

"No. She says it because she feels bad for you. She says your childhood has been stolen from you . . . Lomie, have you cried over your mom?"

"No."

"Why not?"

"I'm afraid my sister and brother will hear me. I'm afraid I'll never stop."

"When did you last laugh . . . out loud?"

"Don't remember."

Alicia saw the darkness come over Paloma again. Paloma's face became hard and her eyes cold like a cheap doll's. In Paloma's mind she was seeing her mother's body in the ER, lying on the gurney just after she had died, her belly swollen, the rest of her body emaciated, her face drawn and thin, and vomit caked on her lips. Paloma was there with her father, Humberto, who was wailing in drunken grief. Paloma had to keep her emotions in check to hold him and herself and everything else in her world together. Then she was remembering a night not long before, when her sister and brother were lying together under a thin quilt on a pad on the floor of the house.

Her sister was crying from hunger. Her brother was in a dead sleep from lack of food. Her father was gone God-knows-where drinking God-knows-what. That night Paloma walked up the hill alone in the chilly air, clad only in sandals, jeans, and a thin jacket, to an all-night convenience store with only a dime and two pennies in her pocket. She begged the man behind the counter for just two little cans of Vienna sausage, one for each sibling. But he refused unless she would go into the back room with him to do what she would not do. So she stood outside to beg loose change from customers, but then ducked into the shadows when a police cruiser approached, afraid to enlist the officer's help for fear he would investigate her home and call CPS. She stumbled back to the house empty-handed, angry and hungry, cursing God or whatever force runs or refuses to run the world. As she walked back in the dark, she remembered how she could not shame Humberto to reapply for Medicaid for his children so her brother could get the Ritalin he needed to calm the hell down and give him a chance to stay in school.

"I've got to make some money this weekend. Or I've got to call CPS myself to get Lilly and Rickey into a home where they will be fed."

Angela Martinez came around the corner of a book stack to the table where Paloma and Alicia sat. They had just seen Angela making out with a boy two years older. Angela was dressed in a sequined top that fell short of the top of her tight jeans. She was in the same freshman class as Paloma and Alicia but always dressed in a revealing way. She had often been sent home by the school vice-president to change clothes. Still, Angela was always flashily dressed and always with a different boy. Yet her parents had no more money than any other girl in the class.

"I heard what you said, Lomie. I know how you can make some good money this weekend."

Paloma flared at her. "How do you know I need money, Angela? Were you listening to our conversation?"

"If you didn't want me to hear, you should have talked quieter. And anybody can see you need money just by the smell of you and your clothes."

Paloma stood up and stepped toward the much larger Angela.

"How can she make good money?" interrupted Alicia.

"Same way I make my money. You think my family can afford these clothes? I make the money myself. And my boss buys the clothes for me."

"Like I said. Doing what?"

"It's easy. There is a bar on North Main. Bunch of drunk, high old men there who like young girls. The man who owns the place keeps me safe. I only do what I want to do. No one can force me."

"So what do you do?"

"Bring them their drinks. Sometimes I sit with them when business is slow. Laugh at their jokes. Dance with them. Get them to buy me wine at seven dollars a glass. Only it isn't wine at all; it's grape juice. And I get two dollars for every glass they buy me . . . They'd love you, Lomie. You are young and would be really pretty if you cleaned up and wore some makeup. Just the way these guys like us."

"The only money you make is from the wine?"

"No, you get tips. The drunker they get, the more they tip you. I make at least fifty dollars a night. You can make more money than that if you want. I once made a hundred twenty-five dollars on one Friday night."

"*Fifty dollars a night!*" thought Paloma. She started thinking what she could buy for her siblings with one hundred dollars for two nights work.

"Don't you get in trouble with the police?" asked Alicia.

"All this happens in a private club in back of the bar. So the police would have to have a warrant to get in there. They never have and never will. That's what Luther says."

"Who's Luther?"

"The owner of the club and bar. The one who takes care of me while I am there."

"Angela, why are you telling me about this?" asked Paloma.

"Because I get what Luther calls a recruiting fee for every girl our age who starts working there."

"How much?" asked Paloma.

"Two hundred dollars. If you start working there, you can make a recruiting fee too."

Angela said, "Paloma, don't even think about this. We'll figure something else out."

Paloma asked, "How many girls work there a night?"

"There's a bar in the front and a club in the back. One or two girls in front and two or three in the back . . . Look, Lomie, you can try it out. If you don't like it, you make some quick money and never come back. You'd be surprised which of the girls in our class have tried it."

"Let me think about it. How do I get in touch with you?

"Here's Luther's phone number. I'll call him about you now. But if you are going to try this, you need to be in contact with Luther by 8:oo tonight so he can arrange some clothes for you. You can't wear what you wear to school . . . And Lomie, if you try it and stay with it, I'll even give you fifty dollars of my recruiting fee."

"I'll think about it."

Angela left.

"Lomie, you can't do this. It's too risky. Why would you want to be around those old men? You know what they'll actually want from you. You've never even had a boyfriend. And what if you get arrested for being underage in a bar? If you go to juvie court, who will take care of Lilly and Rickey?"

"Angela, I'm desperate. If I do this—I said 'if'—it will be for one weekend only. I've got to pay the light and water bills and buy some food. But I need you to promise me one thing. You can't tell your mother or anybody about this. You can't. You promise?"

"Okay."

"Say, 'I promise.'"

"I promise. But you have to call me in advance if you are going to do this, to tell me where the bar is. And you have to call me as soon as you get home. Now you have to promise."

"I promise."

"How strange to have someone worried about me," Paloma thought.

"I understand that you and your family can use some extra cash."

— March 8, 2001, 6:30 p.m. —

A silver Ford Crown Victoria with a black vinyl rear roof pulled up to the house on Hale Street. Paloma was poised at the door to run out to the car before the driver came to the door and saw the condition of the house. But the driver, an Anglo man looking to be in his mid-thirties, dressed in blue slacks, a gold shirt with fancy stitching on the chest and shoulders, and cowboy hat and boots, bounded out of the car and met Paloma before she could get out the front door.

"Paloma? Good. Just as cute as Angela said you were. I'm Luther, as if you hadn't guessed."

Bodine took Paloma's right hand in both of his and shook it warmly. Paloma saw the multiple gold rings on both of his hands. She saw the three gold chains around his neck. *"Who is he trying to impress?"* she thought.

"I understand that you and your family can use some extra cash. I am so glad that you will let me help out. Mind if I look around?"

Bodine pushed through the front door and took an uninvited tour of the house. He saw a living room with sheetrock peeling off the walls and showing bare studs. He saw a couch that looked inhabited by rodents, an end table with one leg missing, and a table lamp with a torn shade and no bulb. He saw a kitchen with a refrigerator that was not running and that emitted a foul order. Through the kitchen window he saw a backyard with junked cars and rusty propane tanks and broken metal mattress frames, with Lilly and Rickey playing in the wreakage. He saw stairs missing step boards leading up and a second floor he could look into from the first floor because of gaps in the flooring. He saw a first-floor bathroom with a toilet with a broken seat and a dripping sink faucet.

While Bodine took his tour, Paloma stayed with her head down at the front door.

Bodine returned to her. "Your father around?"

"No."

"Know when he will be back?"

"Any moment," she lied.

"Any other grown-ups live here?"

"*I'm the only grown-up who lives here*," she thought. But she said no.

"You embarrassed by this house? Don't be. It's not your fault. I understand that your mother died recently and your father is . . . having a hard time dealing with her passing. I hope you'll let me help. You need a better refrigerator. I have a friend in the used appliance business and I'll see if he will let you have the use of a trade-in."

"I can't accept charity," said Paloma.

"Very admirable. But 'pride goeth before the fall,' to quote Proverbs, and pride is not going to get you a working refrigerator. Maybe just a loaner? Think about it. Have your sister and brother eaten yet?"

"No."

"Have you?"

"No."

"Is that why you need the money?"

"Partly."

"There's a *taqueria* up the road. Let's get you and your kids some tacos. My treat. I'm hungry too. Can we leave them here alone for a moment?"

She didn't have any choice about leaving them alone if she was going to make some money. Her father had been gone for two days, and there was no one she could ask to babysit who wouldn't call the police or CPS about their living conditions and abandonment.

"Yes, sir. Like I said, my dad will be back any moment."

"What's your dad's name?"

"Humberto Ibarra."

"I think I know him."

"If you run a bar, I am sure you know him," replied Paloma, and immediately regretted being so revealing.

Bodine drove to a stand-alone *taqueria* hut called "Emilio's." They returned to the house with twelve beef, cheese, onion, salsa and tabasco tacos. Paloma ran inside the house and put seven of the tacos in their individual wrappers on the drain board next to the leaky sink. Then she called Lilly and

Rickey into the kitchen. Their eyes opened wide when they saw the tacos. Paloma doled out four to Enrique and three to Lilly. They sat down at the white plastic kitchen table and chairs, and devoured the tacos like dogs that hadn't been fed for a week. Watching them eat made Paloma even hungrier. She began to feel clammy and light-headed.

"Lilly and Rickey . . . Lilly and Rickey!" she repeated louder to get their attention. "I need you to stay here alone for a while I go to a new job."

"Why?" asked Lilly.

"Because we need money for food, silly." Paloma kissed Lilly on her dirty hair.

"Can we come with you?" Rickey asked.

"No."

"Why not?"

"Because my boss won't allow it."

"When will Papa be home?" asked Lilly.

"I don't know. Hopefully soon. But I need you to do more than stay here alone. I need you to stay in the house and keep quiet. Rickey, I need you to look after your sister and not let the neighbors know you are alone."

Rickey and Lilly nodded solemnly. Their dead mom and their semi-alive father had told them and told them of the evils of a foster care system that would separate them into different foster homes.

Lilly began to tear up. "Lomie, can't you stay here with us. It's scary here in this dark house."

"I wish I could, Sweet Pea. But I have to make us some money. So I need you both to be brave and quiet. Just 'til Papa gets home."

The children turned back to their tacos.

Paloma returned to the Ford. Luther was waiting, still in the driver's seat. "So . . . let's eat," he said. He tuned in some country music on his radio and the two of them ate the tacos in silence.

"So, can I show you my club so you can decide about working there?"

"Is it a bar or a club?"

"Bar in the front. Private club in the back. Anybody can get in the bar. Only patrons we screen for high character can get into the club. We are very choosy. You'd be working only in the club."

"How much will I make this weekend?"

"I'll start you off with a sweetener of two hundred dollars, just for coming. To prove to you that my heart is in the right place and that I can be trusted. You'll make maybe fifty dollars a night on top of that, maybe more. Will you come take a look? No commitment. You say 'no' and we'll bring you right back here."

"Okay."

"Who will look after the kids?"

"No one."

"Before I take you to the club, I want to take you to a clothing store that specializes in ladies your age."

"Mr. Bodine, I can't afford new clothes."

"I'll pay for them to get you started. Employers provide uniforms for their employees. It'll be like that."

"So will the cost come out of the two hundred?"

"No. In fact . . ." and he took a wad of cash out of the glove compartment, counted out four fifty-dollar bills, and handed them to her. "As promised. You will learn that I am a man of my word."

Paloma had never before seen a fifty-dollar bill, much less four of them. She kept looking at the money and the handgun in the open glove compartment. Bodine had left the compartment open so that Paloma could see the gun. "Paloma, I know how to protect my own. You are safe with me. I promise that nothing bad will happen to you while you are with me."

"Why are you doing this for us, Mr. Bodine?"

"Luther. Call me Luther. Because I want to help. No other reason. It's selfish, really. It makes my heart feel good to help a beautiful young lady in a string of bad luck get off to a better start in life."

"Luther," she hesitated, "I am afraid to keep this money on me. Can you keep it until the end of the night?"

"Like money in the bank, Paloma dear. Like money in *your* bank," said Bodine. He stuck the bills back in the glove box and closed it.

"If I decide not to work for you, do I still get this money?"

"Paloma, would that seem fair to you? Would I be teaching you about fairness if I gave you this money without your giving me anything in exchange?"

"No, sir."

"All right then."

CHAPTER FIVE

"Ah, another unspoiled beauty."

— March 8, 2001, 7:30 p.m. —

Bodine drove to a former church renamed Bonitas Chiquitas. Luther used his own key to enter what was once a small chapel. The pews had been removed. Against the outer walls were racks of gaudy clothing on hangars. To the right were tops and blouses arranged by size. To the left were jeans, slacks, and skirts also by size. And in the center, back against the wall where the pulpit and altar had been, were shelves of footwear.

"Elvira," called out Bodine. "Elvira! Are you closed?"

An overweight woman entered the room from the back. She wore a multicolored dress the size of a small tent. Her fleshy arms extended from the puffy short sleeves, her upper arms tattooed, one arm with a cobra and the other with the Virgin of Guadalupe. A glass ring was on every finger of her hand, each ring a different color. Her hair was a dull black without highlights, clearly a home dye job. White eye shadow was caked on her eyelids with heavy black eye liner rimming both eyes and false eyelashes protruding half an inch. She had a small mouth, small ears, and an upturned nose. Her round cheeks were heavily rouged. Reaching out from under the hem of her dress as she walked forward were almost square feet balanced on entirely too narrow high-heeled sandals.

"Always open for you, Luther. You know that." She apprised Paloma. "Ah, another unspoiled beauty," said the woman. "How many outfits for this one?"

"Let's start with one top and one pair of jeans. Then some shoes and a makeover."

"Shampoo and a shower? Is she working tonight?"

"I hope so," said Luther. "The works."

Paloma started to protest, but Elvira took her in hand to the rack of tops on the right.

"I'm guessing a size two or a small for you, right sweetie?"

"Probably. I've lost some weight."

The tops were of various bright colors, sheer, usually sequined, and always low-cut. Most were short-sleeved or sleeveless. Elvira picked three tops for Paloma to try on. Paloma chose the most modest of the three—sky blue, no sequins, and short sleeves.

For the jeans, Elvira chose a tight, blue designer pair with waist below the navel and thread designs on the rear pockets. Paloma got to choose her own footwear and picked open-toed sandals.

Elvira took Paloma in the back through the curtained doorway to an apartment with a living area, a bedroom with a large bed with a mirror on the ceiling above, a bath with a toilet and a shower, and a kitchenette. A dressing table in the bedroom was covered in lipsticks, mascara, eye shadow and liner, rouge, and powder. The closets were empty. No one seemed to be living in the apartment at the time.

"Honey," said Elvira, "let's get you cleaned up a bit." Paloma was mistrustful but certainly needed a shower. "You can lock the bathroom door. Shampoo, conditioner, soap, and a new Bic razor are in the shower. Use all of them. Shave your legs and under your arms and tidy up your bikini line. You'll find a clean towel under the sink. Deodorant, new toothbrush and toothpaste, and an unused comb are in the medicine cabinet over the sink. After the shower, use all of them. Then wrap yourself in a towel and come out. I'll be the only person out here. "

Paloma hurried through the shower and shampoo. She had not enjoyed a hot shower in forever but she did not linger. She did what she was told to do after the shower and then stepped into the bedroom area.

"Here is a bra and panties. Go back into the bathroom and put these on. Then come back out and we will see if they fit."

Paloma was getting accustomed to doing as she was told. *"This is starting to be fun,"* she thought. Elvira had guessed right on her sizes. *"This woman must have done this before plenty."* The bra and bikini panties were shiny, sheer, lacy, and black. Paloma had never worn black underwear before. She put them on and adjusted the bra straps. They felt sweet against her skin. She looked at herself in the bathroom mirror. For the first time ever, she liked the way she looked and thought that a boy might like it too. She wondered what it was like to have a boy find her attractive. Then guilty thoughts intruded. *"I wonder if Lilly and Rickey are okay. I wonder if Papa came home?"* But then she stopped herself. *"I deserve some time off. I'm their sister, not their momma. I deserve to feel pretty for a change."*

When she stepped out, Elvira unwrapped Paloma's towel from around her. Paloma drew back and grabbed at the top of the towel to try to keep it in place. But Elvira reassured her. "Just to see if the bra and panties fit you . . . Oh yes, very nice. You are developing into a beautiful young lady . . . You have started your period? I mean, generally?"

"Y . . . y . . . yes." Paloma stammered. "A year ago." Elvira wrapped her back up in her towel.

"My goodness," said Elvira, "girls develop so much faster now than in my day. Let's sit you down in front of the mirror."

"Where's Mr. Bodine? Don't I have to hurry?"

"Oh, he'll be back when I call him. No rush."

"What do we have to do?"

"We are going to complete the picture, darling. We are going to do your hair. Then a manicure. Then a pedicure. Your hair will be easy. You have naturally thick, gorgeous hair. But your nails—oh my goodness."

Chapter Six

"I want you to call that number."

— March 8, 2001, 8:00 p.m. —

Elvira answered her ringing cell phone.

"Elvira, this is Luther."

"Yes, sir."

"Is the young lady still in the shower?"

Yes."

"I want you to do something."

"Something else?"

"Yes. Get a pencil and some paper. I need you to write this down."

Pause.

"Got 'em."

"Ready?"

"Yes, sir."

"1–800–252–5400."

"Okay. What number is that?

"CPS statewide hotline. I want you to call that number and report that two children younger than ten, a little girl name of Lilly and a little boy name of Rickey, have been left alone in a house in the 2600 block of Hale Street in Fort Worth. Their father is a drunk and has left them there alone for days. The mother is dead. Tell the hotline operator there is no food in the house and that it's unsafe and unfit for the children. That'll do it. Read that back to me."

Elvira read back her notes.

"Call that in. And then call 911 and tell the police the same thing."

"They'll ask my name and how I know this."

"Do not give a name. Tell them you live nearby and have seen the children there alone many times, but that you are afraid to give your name because the father is violent."

"Does this have anything to do with the young lady in my shower?"

"None of your business. But do not tell her anything about this conversation or the calls you make. Never. Got it?"

"Yes, sir."

"Make the calls right now. And then tear up the notes you just made."

CHAPTER SEVEN

"Don't you worry. You are as safe as you can be with me."

— March 8, 2001, 9:00 p.m. —

Luther picked Paloma up at Bonitas Chiquitas. Paloma tried so say a final thank you and goodbye to Elvira, but Elvira insisted they would be seeing each other again.

Paloma was amazed at how good she looked. Her hair was black, full, and silky, parted just off to the side of the top of her head, hanging down to both collar bones, a golden bow in place just over her left ear. She wore gold hoop earrings. She had just a hint of eye shadow and liner, "to look young and fresh," counseled Elvira. Her clothes were tight, revealing her developing figure. Her midriff was bare. Her nails looked the best they ever had. And she had chosen for herself a wonderful perfume from the array on Elvira's dresser, a French perfume called Quelque Fleurs, which just had to be very expensive. She was nervous about the reaction to her of the customers at the bar and club and whether she would be worth the money Luther was going to be paying her. And she kept thinking about Lilly and Rickey, particularly about Rickey's habit of getting himself into trouble. She asked Luther if they could swing by the house to check on the children, but Luther insisted that it was too late. Then his gushing compliments diverted her.

Luther parked behind The Hacienda. It was a rectangular-shaped building of painted gray concrete blocks with a flat roof, no windows, and a non-descript door. The only identifying sign was painted on the outside of the door. That door stood open so the sign was facing the wall. A single bulb light was over the door. A narrow side of the building fronted North Main.

The building was set to the side of the lot. A wide gravel parking lot took up the center and other side of the property. The parking lot was already filled.

Luther put his arm around Paloma's shoulders as they walked to the entrance. "Don't you worry. You are as safe as you can be with me."

A shallow vestibule and then another door were just inside the open front door. Bodine pushed open the inner door to reveal a bar with seven booths on the left wall, maybe eight tables with four chairs each down the center, and a wooden bar with bar stools the length of the room on the right. On the wall behind the bar were shelves of liquor bottles. At the center of the bar were beer taps. The bar was well lit. There were two televisions mounted high on the wall, one at either end of the bar. A jukebox in a corner was blaring a Willie Nelson song. This was the very first bar Paloma had seen in person, but it looked like every single bar she had ever seen on television or in the movies. Surprising to her was that there were many fewer people in that bar than vehicles parked outside.

Luther stooped to introduce her to the bartender, a middle-aged man named Lupe. "Nice to meet you," said Paloma. "*Mucho gusto*," said Lupe, and turned immediately back to watching a Dallas Maverick–Golden State Warrior game. Luther ignored the patrons in the bar and stepped to a door in the back wall. He took out his cell phone and dialed it. "It's Bodine. Open up." The door swung inward. A huge man was standing sentry duty inside the door.

Paloma and Luther stepped through the door into another world. This was the private club Luther had told her about. On the ceiling was an old disco ball, spinning and casting what looked like fireflies around the room. She saw men around a roulette wheel, three poker tables, two blackjack tables, and a bunch of slot machines. The club was crowded and soon to be packed. She smelled marijuana, which she recognized because men had smoked it with her papa at the house. There was only one other female in the room, a teen dressed much like her. None of the customers had females with them.

Luther signaled one of the bartenders to cut the power to the jukebox. Luther stood on a chair. "We have a new hostess with us tonight. This is Lomie. Her very first time here, and, I'll bet, in any bar. So I want each of you to be on your very best behavior with her. Watch your language and keep your eyes and hands to yourselves. Treat her as if she was your own daughter. If you step over the line, Seth," motioning toward the door sentry, "will be escorting you out. *Comprende?*"

Customers turned or stood to get a good look at Paloma. She felt the flush of embarrassment rising in her face.

"Let's all give her a big Hacienda welcome. And let's make it well worth her while in tips tonight. Her family has fallen on hard times and they could use the money."

With that, customers clapped and whistled, more rising out of their seats.

Paloma felt dazed. She had expected to be as anonymous as a waitress working at any restaurant, going about her work inauspiciously as order taker and food bringer. She would have preferred that to being made a center of attention to all these men. She followed Luther to the bar, walking between tables as men called welcome to her. She was painfully self-conscious about her tight clothing and her bare midriff. Despite Luther's warning to them, she could sense the eyes of these men following her. It felt the same as when her papa brought men to their house. "*I'll get through the night and that will be the end of this,*" she thought.

Luther introduced her to the two bartenders and the young female she had noticed when she came in. The girl's name was Maria. "Maria, show her the ropes. Let her shadow you for about an hour. She'll get the hang of it quickly. And tell me if anyone gets out of hand with her," said Bodine.

Sitting behind the bar was a young man who looked to be about nineteen or twenty, playing a video game. "This is my son, Angel. Angel, this is Lomie. Leave her alone."

"What about with me?" asked Maria. "What if someone gets out of hand with me?"

"You can take care of yourself," said Luther.

"If she shadows me, am I going to owe her some of my tips?" asked Maria.

"Just do as I say. It won't be long until she is on her own," replied Luther.

Maria was not friendly. She coolly gave Paloma a drink order pad. The bartenders showed Paloma the different types of alcohol in stock.

"Most of these guys will order some kind of beer or whiskey. But some will order a mixed drink with a fancy name. Just follow me and write down what I tell you," said Maria.

This arrangement went on for about an hour and a half. The hardest part was hearing the orders over the loud music and drunken talking. The bartenders were as friendly as Maria was not, and they seemed familiar with what different customers wanted even if Paloma couldn't hear the order.

When Paloma started working alone, Luther had Angel shadow her. Angel was small and wiry and sullen. He did not speak a word to her except to point out a table that needed more drinks or to help her spell a drink order.

The bar became more crowded. The new arrivals kept asking her name and to know more about her. Most of the new ones headed toward the gambling area. She was hustling drinks so hard that she ignored them.

Then Luther told Paloma and Maria that he wanted them to divide the club into areas, with each of them assigned to their own part of the room. He separated the room into the half farther away and the half closer to the bar, which included the gambling area where the big tippers were gaming. He assigned Paloma to the area farther away. That part included a closed corner room.

Paloma knocked repeatedly on the door of that room and heard nothing in response. She looked back to Angel. He gestured to her with his hand, signaling to go in. She pushed open the door.

She was bowled over by the fumes in the air. "Close the door," was the unison cry. She saw men and a few women sitting in booths around the walls. They were smoking, some with cigarettes that looked like they had rolled themselves and some with small glass pipes. The air was heavy with sweet-smelling, pungent smoke, though there was an air conditioning vent that was sucking the fumes out. "Anyone want a drink?" she cried. Two people ordered beer on tap. Paloma left the room, closing the door tightly behind her. She went to the bar, delivered the order, and returned with the beer.

Even though the customers in this back room were not ordering much in the way of drinks, Luther told her to enter every twenty minutes to check. He wanted her to go around to every booth and ask. And he ordered her to take glasses of beer into the room, on the house, even though the customers were more intent upon smoking than drinking.

After an hour and a half of this, after entering that room at least six times, Paloma began to feel differently than she had ever felt before. She quit worrying about Lilly and Rickey. She quit worrying about anything. She lost track of the time. She was filled with energy. She felt tremendously alert. She felt peaceful and happy. And she felt strong. She began to smile at the customers and laugh at their jokes. She started having a hard time making change. And she was aware that Luther and Angel were studying her intently.

One of the women in the back room invited her to take a puff on the glass pipe she held. "Just once. See if you like it. What's the harm?" But Paloma said no.

Hours passed. The club began to thin out. Soon it was last call. Paloma looked at the clock and saw that it was 2:30 a.m. She had been hustling from table to table and room to room for more than five hours, but she was still brimming with energy.

Maria and Paloma presented their tips to the bartenders. These were added to the tips from credit cards and from the tip jars at the bar. The two bartenders and Seth, the door sentry, and bouncer divided 75 percent of the tips equally between the three of them. That left 25 percent of the total to be divided between Maria and Paloma. Paloma's share of the tips alone was more than seventy-five dollars! Paloma felt ecstatic. If Luther paid her the two hundred dollars he had promised, then she'd be able to . . . but she couldn't remember why she had wanted to make that money.

"Time to close up," said Luther. "Let me drive you home."

"Luther, do I still get my two hundred dollars?"

"Of course you do, Lomie. But I had to pay that money in my glove box to a distributor tonight. So I have to run by my house to get more funds. It won't take a minute."

Chapter Eight

"Lomie, if it's CPS, they will be looking to take you in too."

— March 9, 2001, 3:00 a.m. —

As they walked to Luther's truck, Paloma felt her energy leaking away. A heavy fatigue and a liquid sleep rolled over her. She was getting a headache behind both eyes. She hoped she could stay awake until she got home. But she dozed as Luther was driving. She awakened as he was getting back into his car, which was parked in front of a house on Lulu Avenue. Luther handed her a roll of twenty-dollar bills. "As promised," he smiled. "Interested in working tomorrow night? Can you use the money?"

"Yes," said Paloma, yawning. "But before I tell you for sure, let me see how Lilly and Rickey did tonight."

Bodine drove the Ford to Paloma's house on Hale. As they turned the corner onto the block Bodine and Paloma saw a police cruiser and two uniformed officers in the front yard of the house talking to Paloma's father, Humberto, who was having a difficult time standing. One of the officers was shining a flash light in Humberto's face. Another car was parked in front of the house. They saw periodic flashes of light coming from inside the house.

Paloma tried to jump out of the car but Luther held her by the arm. "Lomie. Lomie! Let's see what's going on before you get in the middle of this. Sit back! Sit back so they can't see you, I said!" Luther drove by the house, turned the Ford around down the block in the dark and parked. As they drove by the house, Paloma saw that her father was crying and holding a sheath of papers in his hand.

"Something has happened to Lilly and Rickey. I just know it. Why did I leave them alone there?" cried Paloma.

"Just sit here for a moment. Let's see if the cops leave soon. Then we can find out what happened. Maybe they are looking for you."

"Why looking for me?"

"You just said you were the one to leave the children alone there. Look, I don't know. Let's just wait here awhile."

"Luther, just drop me. This isn't your problem."

"Lomie, when Luther Bodine takes someone on to help, Luther Bodine doesn't abandon them in their hour of need. Just sit still for a while."

A woman came out of the house carrying a camera.

"That's what the flashes were. She was taking photos of the house with a flash camera." said Bodine.

"Why photos of the house?"

"Maybe they think the house isn't fit for you kids to live in. Maybe they are looking for evidence to show a judge. I have seen this kind of thing before."

"Oh, hell. It must be CPS. Now we have to go into foster care," said Paloma.

"Let's wait and see, Lomie. We don't know yet."

"I bet one of the fucking neighbors made a complaint. Like their houses are so much better."

"Lomie, if it's CPS, they will be looking to take you in too."

"I know it." Pause while she was thinking. "Maybe I need to go with my sister and brother. They can't lose mom and then me too."

"That's not the way it works. Chances are that you all will be separated, because of your ages. So don't be a hero."

"How do you know that?"

"You learn a lot of things in a bar. Lots of sad stories come to a bar."

The woman and the police drove off. Paloma jumped out of Bodine's truck before he could stop her and ran to her father.

"What happened, Papa?"

"I dunno. They were here when I came home. They said they were PCS." His words were badly slurred. But Paloma spoke drunk from years of practice with her father.

"You mean CPS?"

"Dunno. A woman and man were putting little Lilly in their car when I was walking up. I was crying for her not to leave me but they were giving her a burger. The police were chasing Rickey around the back yard. They finally caught him but he bit one of them, so he may be in trouble again. Then they drove away with my children." He began to cry.

"What are the papers?"

"Dunno."

Luther stepped forward. "May I see those?"

Humberto recognized him. "Mr. Bodine. How come you here?" He gave Luther the papers.

"I was trying to help Paloma make a little money for your family."

"Lomie?" Her father turned toward her. "Why did you leave the kids alone?"

Paloma erupted. "Why did I leave them? Why did *I* leave them? Why did *you* leave them? Why do *you* stay away for days at a time? Why do *you* drink up all our food stamps? Why are *you* a fucking drunk? I left them to make some money so they could eat and so the lights and water could stay on. I left them because they lost their mother and never had a father. Who was going to feed and take care of them? Not you! Only me! *Only me!*"

Paloma was so loud that lights were coming on in houses down the block.

Humberto lashed out at Paloma, trying to slap her in the face. But he was too drunk and Paloma was too fast. When Humberto lunged at her, he fell flat on his face in the dirt of the yard and lay there crying and moaning.

"Lomie, we have to get you out of here," said Bodine. "You can't stay here tonight. The neighbors are probably calling the police right now. If the police come back, they will take you with them. Your father is going to blame you. You could end up in juvie for abandoning your sister and brother."

Paloma was too ignorant of the law to know that a fourteen-year-old couldn't be charged and incarcerated for leaving her siblings alone. She was afraid of being arrested. She was afraid of being put into foster care. She couldn't stand the thought of staying at the Hale Street house with her father.

"Where can I go?"

"To my house. You'll be safe there. You can think it through there after you get a good night's sleep."

Chapter Nine

"She is better off going to church with her own kind!"

— Friday, March 8, 1994 —

John Levi is fourteen years of age.

"John Levi. John Levi. Are you home?" John Levi's mother, Amanda, called as she came in the door of the kitchen.

"Eugenia?" she asked the maid. "Is John Levi home from school?"

"Yes, ma'am," answered Eugenia, interrupting her scrubbing of the oven. "I believe he is upstairs in his room. Or maybe he is taking a swim."

"Thank you, Eugenia. Would you be a dear and get the wine out of the trunk of my Mercedes? Put the white wine and champagne in the cooler in the TV room and the red wine in the rack in the dining room, please. Thank you."

Mrs. Jones put her purse down and punched the buttons of the home telephone to listen to her messages. Then she looked out the picture windows to the heated pool. Not seeing her son, she climbed the stairs and knocked on his bedroom door. John Levi was sitting on his bed, watching a DVD of Shakespeare's *Midsummer's Night Dream.*

"Hi, Mom."

"John Levi, I need to talk to you."

"Uh-oh. What have I done now?"

"Jenny Leeves tells me that you haven't asked Krissy to the freshman dance tonight. Isn't it late to ask her?"

"I'm not taking Krissy to the dance."

"Are you going?"

"Planning to."

"I don't understand. I thought this was all decided. Eugenia is to drive you to pick up Krissy at her house and then drive you to the school for the dance. Krissy's parents and your dad and I are going to the country club for dinner and dancing. Why haven't you asked Krissy?"

"First I have heard of it is right now."

"First you have heard of what?"

"Me taking Krissy to this dance."

"John Levi, you and Krissy have been a couple since you were in grade school. We just assumed. She did too, I am sure. You know that Krissy's father and your father are business partners. So this involves more than you and her. What's happened? Did you and Krissy have an argument?"

"No argument. I asked somebody else."

"Somebody else? Who?"

"Her name is Zaira Trejo."

"That's an odd name. Do we know her family? Are they members of the country club?"

"No."

"Who is she?"

"I met Zaira through Faith Church. She lives in the church neighborhood and she comes to the youth group. She and I are the leads in the church play next month. She's beautiful, Mom. And smart. And a great actress. We have so much in common. I really like her."

"Is she Mexican?"

"No, Mom. She's American."

"You know what I mean . . . Does she go to Country Valley School?"

"No, Mom. I told you, she lives the church neighborhood south of downtown. She goes to Paschal High School."

"What do her parents do?"

"I don't know, Mom. Does it matter?"

"Well, honey, have you thought this through? How will she fit in with students at a private school like ours?"

"She'll be with me. So she'll fit in fine. She'll be with me. And all the boys will wish she were with them."

"Honey," Mrs. Jones sat down on the bed, "this is very bad timing. Your father's business is going through a hard time with . . . oh, I don't know why. But times are hard for your dad and Mr. Leeves. They are both really stressed. And with all the political ugliness over all this racial stuff, I am afraid that people at the school and our friends will see your bringing this Mexican girl as some kind of political protest."

"Mom, she's not Mexican. She was born here. She is her own person. It's nothing like what you say. I really like her, Mom. She's a beautiful person. We talk about plays and drama. All Krissy wants to talk about is shopping and trips and parties. Just meet Zaira, Mom. You'll love her. More than that, you'll admire her. Give her a chance."

"It just seems like a really bad time for this, John Levi."

"When would it be a good time, Mom?"

"Don't take that tone with me, young man."

"What tone?"

John Levi and his mother could hear Mr. Jones climbing the stairs, having come home from work.

"Let me handle this. You know your father's temper. And don't argue with him. There is no point."

Mrs. Jones left John Levi's bedroom. John Levi rose from his bed and put his ear against the door. But his parents had gone into their room down the hall. All he could make out was some muffled words, mostly his father's.

After about twenty minutes, John Levi's father entered his room.

"What I want to know is how long Faith Church has allowed kids from the church neighborhood to be in our youth group?"

"Zaira has been going to our group all school year."

"Are there others?"

"A few."

"John Levi, we have you in the most exclusive and expensive private school in Fort Worth for three reasons."

John Levi could always rely upon his father to have three reasons—not two, not four—to support all his positions.

"First, so you could get the best possible preparation for your college career. Second, so you could get to know young men you will be doing business with during your entire life in Fort Worth. Third, and just as important, to protect you from exposure to people like those in the church neighborhood. I am extremely disappointed in our senior pastor and our youth minister for letting this . . . what's her name . . . Zachariah Treejoe? . . . participate in our youth group. I have a call in to Dr. Forster right now."

"Father! Please do not do that! You want the church to kick Zaira out of the group? A church group? A *Christian* church group? Dr. Forster preaches every Sunday that the kingdom of God is for everyone, that the church should welcome everyone. He preaches from that Gospel teaching—I don't know which Gospel—'Insofar as you do not help the least of these, you do not help me.'"

"So you are admitting that she is the least," said Mr. Jones.

No, I am saying that you think she is the least. But you haven't even met her. She has done nothing wrong. She does everything right. She is great. Why would you want her excluded? Because of where she lives?"

"Do not argue with me, young man! You are going to call this . . . what's her name?"

"Zaira Trejo."

"And give her some excuse. Tell her you are ill or something."

"You want me to lie to her?"

"You are being melodramatic again. I never should have let you be involved in this drama stuff. It will lead nowhere. You need to be concentrating on economics and mathematics. People in drama are just strange . . . Do you want to spare her feelings? Then give her some excuse. I don't care what. Except do *not* tell her that your parents have forbidden you to take her."

"She predicted that I would have to back out. She predicted that my parents would forbid me to go when they found out. I said no, that she was wrong about my parents. Because my parents are Christian."

"What does being Christian have to do with it? This is about your future. She is better off going to church with her own kind!"

"Her own kind!? What kind is that? Beautiful? Smart? Talented? Hardworking? Father, she has two part-time jobs to help her mother take care of her brothers and sisters on top of being an honor student and being a great actress. Or do you mean poor and Hispanic? Do you think it won't hurt her to find out she was right about you?"

"Don't you talk back to me! You will call her now and back out. It's on you to make an excuse that won't hurt her. I don't really care. This is on you for even thinking of taking her to Country Valley. Then you will never see her again."

"So you will have her kicked out of the church?"

"No. I will not allow you to go back to that church."

"I love that church. I am the lead in the next play. Do I have any say in this?"

"Not until you are paying your own way, you don't."

"So I can't go to church at all?"

"Don't be daft. There are plenty of churches in this part of town who would never let our children interact with . . . those people."

"So forget the teachings of Jesus?"

"John Levi, you will stop this disrespect right now! You will call Krissy now and ask her to the freshman dance. Tell her that you forgot that you had not asked her and you are sorry. We'll go on as if this never happened. One day you will thank me. And we will speak nothing about this to anyone."

"No, sir."

"'No, sir,' what?"

"No, sir, I'm not taking Krissy to the dance. You said it yourself. I am ill. And no, sir, I am not going to be responsible for the church excluding Zaira."

"Tell me this. How were you going to get this Treejoe girl from her home near downtown to the dance at Country Valley?"

"Since I'm fourteen and don't drive yet, I was expecting to get there in the usual way. Eugenia was going to drive us just as she has driven Krissy and me so many times."

"You were going to ask Eugenia to drive at night into a part of town as dangerous as just south of downtown? In our new Mercedes?"

"She could drive the Chrysler, like she always does. Father, if you ever talked to Eugenia, she would have told you what part of Fort Worth she lives in. And you would know that she lives in a part of town—Stop 6—where you would also not want her to be driving your new Mercedes. And the church is close to downtown. I go there at night a lot."

"John Levi, I do not have the time or the patience to deal any more with this foolishness. As I say, someday you will thank me. Either ask Krissy or don't go. But you aren't going with this Treejoe girl. If you defy us about this, you will not be receiving the BMW we promised you when you get your driver's license. That's final. And we will have to reconsider whether you can continue to use drama as your extracurricular activity."

"Drama is not just an extracurricular activity for me, Father. It is a passion."

"Passion doesn't get a house like this. Or a BMW. Or a girlfriend from a good family like Krissy's. Business does."

"Father, at least meet Zaira."

"We will not."

John Levi called Zaira and told her he was ill. She didn't believe him. John Levi's father did not persist in forbidding him to attend Faith Methodist. And he received his BMW. But Zaira Trejo never again set foot in that church. After John Levi obtained his driver's license and his car and could go places his parents couldn't monitor, he telephoned Zaira repeatedly and went by her apartment when she wouldn't call him back. Zaira's mother told him he was not welcome there. Zaira was too disappointed in him to ever speak to him again.

CHAPTER TEN

"What did you do to me, Angel?"

— May 8, 2001, 8:00 p.m. —

Paloma is fourteen years old.

"Luther. Luther. It's Paloma. Can you pick me up?" Paloma was calling Luther Bodine's home phone.

"Well, listen at the chicken who wants to come home to roost. Why would I do that, given the way you ran out on us?"

"You know why I left. You wouldn't protect me from your son and that hairy pile of fat."

"The way Angel tells it, he needs protection from you."

"Luther, please. I have no one else to call and nowhere else to go. Please pick me up."

"Where are you?"

"In a motel in west Fort Worth off Las Vegas Trail."

"I heard you were being put in foster care."

"I am. But they don't have enough foster families for teenage girls so they are keeping me in this motel for now."

"Alone?"

"No. I have a female guard sleeping in the room with me. She won't let me be alone. She keeps me from calling anyone."

"How are you calling me now?"

"From a phone in the laundry room of the motel. I snuck out when my Nazi was taking a shower."

Much had happened since the early morning of March 9, when Paloma's siblings had been placed in the foster care system. CPS and law enforcement looked for Paloma to take her into custody just as they had

Lilly and Rickey. Luther lied that he had a friend in the court system and was monitoring the progression of the CPS case about Lilly and Rickey. They had been placed in two separate foster homes. Paloma's father had been appointed a free attorney to argue that the children should continue to live with him. But Humberto was too drunk to show up for the court hearings. He was also refusing to work the services—alcohol addiction treatment, job referral, counseling—that would give him any chance to obtain the return of his children. CPS had so far been unable to find another relative who would take the children, so Lilly and Rickey were in placements with strangers in the foster system.

When Luther told Paloma that Humberto hadn't even shown up at court for the emergency hearing, she was furious. "I never want to see his sorry ass again!" she yelled.

Paloma had nowhere to stay except Luther's house, unless she wanted to go into a foster home. Her only incentive to do so would have been if she and her two siblings could be together. Since Lilly and Rickey weren't living together, there was no good reason for Paloma to turn herself in. She hid at Luther's house on Lulu Street. She couldn't return to school because she would have been turned in to CPS investigators.

At first it was tolerable. She slept and ate and slept and read every book she could get her hands on and made herself pretty during the days. Then she worked at The Hacienda from 8:00 p.m. to about 3:00 a.m. every night. Luther would not allow her to use a phone. "We can't trust anyone to know you are here," warned Luther. She was cut off from her old world and her few friends. Luther arranged for her to obtain three more sets of clothes from Elvira at Bonitas Chiquitas. Luther fed her very well, with takeout of whatever she wanted whenever she wanted. She had been blossoming into young womanhood when she met the Bodines. With the attention to her grooming and her weight gain and her wardrobe and her regular sleep, she had become adorable.

Even when there were other teenage girls working in the club, Paloma was assigned by Luther to wait on the customers in the back room, where the air she breathed was thick with marijuana and methamphetamine smoke. So she was high when she returned to the Bodines' house every morning. Angel sat on the couch in the television room, urging Paloma to join him as he smoked marijuana blunts or a pipe of meth. At first she refused, partly because she was repulsed by everything about Angel. But she was tempted when the meth she breathed at work began to wear off and withdrawal came. The times she was high from the back room were the only times she wasn't depressed about every aspect of her life—about Lilly and Rickey, about her dead mother and her drunk father, about her own captivity and the threat of foster care, about her dead-end future. So one morning when she had started to withdraw and had a terrible headache, she gave in to Angel. She took a pull from the marijuana blunt and felt relief. In mornings to come she took more than one pull, and then many more than one.

Then she took a single, deep pull from Angel's methamphetamine pipe, a single act which ushered her into an alternate existence of boundless self-confidence, energy, and well-being. Meth freed her of her past, present, and future, of her despondency, of her loneliness, of the injustice of the world, of the cruelty or indifference of whatever god was responsible for the world being the way the world is. Paloma looked forward to escape into this bright, illusory world. She knew it was illusory when she wasn't high and was suffering the torture of withdrawal. But she hungered for this world when she was not in it. It was as if she had married meth, so thoroughly had she given herself to it. After she started using meth she had to be encouraged to eat, to shower, and to brush her teeth. She began to lose track of the days of the week. She dreaded the crash dive when the drug was wearing off, so she began to smoke before she went to work and even during work when she took hits off the customers' pipes. She invited the groping of her body by the men in exchange for their meth. It was her husband Methamphetamine who was touching her. After weeks of daily, frequent use, Paloma had become a naturalized, true, and committed citizen of the sovereign nation of Methamphetamine, a nation that would tolerate no traitor to any other allegiance.

Luther and Angel then recruited Paloma into the underground of sexual exploitation. At the time Paloma still had enough of her wits and soul to recognize that this had been the Bodines' destination for her all along. Paloma's descent into this underground was the price she had to pay for her continued citizenship in the nation of Meth.

It happened early one Saturday morning after the club closed. Angel and Luther brought home one of the high rollers from the back room whose name Paloma had never learned. This nameless man, hulking and hairy, probably in his forties, had been the leader in encouraging Paloma to take pulls from his meth pipe in exchange for his liberties in pawing her. Paloma planted herself as usual in a corner of the couch, impatiently waiting for Angel to share his pipe. This time the fat, hairy man entered the TV room with Angel and Luther. Luther sat in his big easy chair and Angel sat in the far end of the couch from Paloma. This man sat between Angel and Paloma. He took a glass pipe and meth crystals out of a pouch he pulled from his jacket, lit the pipe, and handed it to Paloma for the honor of the first puff.

It was the strongest by far Paloma had ever used. It wasn't just meth. It was meth laced with something else. Three puffs and Paloma was lost in still another reality in which her senses were dulled, not heightened, in which everything and everyone moved slower, in which sound was muffled, sight darkened, thought slowed, and strength sapped.

She began to awaken. She had no sense of the time. She was in her bedroom at Luther's. The shades of the windows in her bedroom were closed. The room was only dimly lit. She was lying under covers without any clothing. She was nauseated. She felt the worst pain she had ever experienced across the entire front of her head. The front of both her hips and the muscles in the inside of her legs ached. She felt a burning wetness between her legs. She reluctantly moved her hand there. She was swollen and exquisitely tender to touch. She withdrew her hand and raised it before her eyes. She was able in the darkness to bring her eyes to focus on her hand. Her hand was red with blood. She panicked. What had happened to her? She could remember nothing after the few puffs she had taken on the hairy man's pipe.

She became aware of a body lying behind hers, its back to her back. She moved her hand behind her as she lay on her side and felt . . . hairy skin. She slowly turned her head to look. It was the man from the back room of the club who had brought his own meth pipe to Luther's house. He was hairy, fat, bald, ugly . . . and nude. He was breathing in snorts.

Paloma rolled out of bed, struggling to free herself from the covers. She stood down from the bed, took a step, and accidentally kicked Angel in the head. Angel was lying on the floor on a blanket next to her side of the bed. He grunted and punched at her foot. "What the hell!" he grunted. "Get off of me, bitch."

"What did you do to me, Angel?" She kicked him in the neck. "What did you do to me?" The pain in her head and between her legs was strong but her anger and disgust were stronger. "Why am I swollen and bleeding?" She reached her hand between her legs again, wiped some blood on her hand and smeared it on Angel's face. "*What did you do to me?!*"

"Bitch!" Angel jumped off his blanket. He was nude. He grabbed Paloma by the neck with both of his hands and lifted her off the ground, cutting off her air. "You want some more? *You want some more?!*"

Paloma kneed Angel in his groin. A guttural sound escaped from his throat and he bent forward. He kept his hold on Paloma's neck and slapped her hard in the face twice. He threw her on her back and came down on top of her. He reached his hand between her legs.

"*Stop it!*" Paloma felt Angel's weight being jerked off of her. From the floor, she saw Luther with his arms wrapped around his son, dragging Angel out of the bedroom. She heard Luther yelling, "You are about to screw this whole thing up! You had no business joining in on that girl! She is for customers only, not you!"

"Joining in? Joining in on me?" She felt dirty and degraded and spoiled. *"This is the bottom,"* she thought. *"I can't sink any lower—at fourteen."* She had to get out of there. The instrument of her degradation still lay unconscious, a hirsute lump in the bed as heavy as a black hole, the entire mattress curving down to him. She found stuffed in a chest of drawers the old clothes she had been wearing when she first met Luther. She put on the panties and stuffed a handful of tissues into the crotch. She put on the rest of the clothing, slipped into the bathroom, experienced burning during urination, was shocked at her reflection in the mirror, and tiptoed back through the bedroom and into the hallway. She peered into the TV room and saw the glass pipe, a bag of meth crystals, the remains of two smoked marijuana blunts, and a half-empty bottle of Jack Daniels sitting on the coffee table. She slipped farther down the hallway and heard Luther's muffled talking to Angel in their back bedroom. She walked through the living room and opened the front door. She saw that the front gate was chained and padlocked shut. The stone fence and iron gates were too high for her to climb. She walked back into the kitchen. She could make out Luther yelling at Angel: "Use your damn head. Her mother is dead. Her father is a drunk. Her sister and brother are in foster care. She lives in a rat trap. Anywhere is better than where she lives. We are all she's got. She's worth a fortune to us, if you leave her alone. We do not eat the produce, Angel, We sell the produce. Leave her to the customers to eat. She'll help us sell the dope too. But we have to keep her fresh." She looked out the back door into the back yard. The dogs were sleeping in their pen without their usual run of the yard. She was startled to see that the gate to the backyard was partially open. She snuck out the back door, and tore across the yard and out the gate.

She ran as fast as she could for as long as she could, which was not far or long. She was undernourished from her obsession with meth and had not had any exercise for weeks. She was coming down from meth and whatever else she had been given. But she was terrified that Luther or Angel would come after her.

She had been a virgin until last night. She had no experience with sex. *"I'm not a virgin any longer,"* she thought. *"What if they didn't use a rubber? What if I am pregnant . . . at fourteen? What if that man has VD? Then so do I! Why else would I feel burning when I pee? Where can I get help? I have to stay away from the police. If they catch me, they'll put me in juvenile detention for abandoning Lilly and Rickey."*

She was already feeling hungry for another hit of meth. This real world was too much, too sad, too hopeless.

Paloma scuttled sideways like a crab, looking furtively over her shoulder for the Bodines as she ran.

The only haven she could think of was Alicia's home. She was afraid to go to her father's house on Hale, suspecting that the neighbors who had called CPS had been instructed to call the police if they saw her. There was nothing and no one there for her anyway. Maybe Alicia's mother would hide and help her. She scuttled south on Lulu to 33rd Street, turned east on 33rd, then south on Schwartz, crossed the railroad tracks, and hid in some bushes to see if they were coming after her. When she saw no one after her, she walked all the way down Schwartz to Northeast Loraine, where Alicia and her mother lived.

By then it was about 8:00 a.m. It must have been a school day. Paloma knocked softly and then harder on the front door. No response. She walked into the backyard and crawled into an empty playhouse. She had played in there with Alicia since they were in elementary school. She sat and waited. She fell asleep.

She was awakened by the crunch of the tires on the gravel driveway. She crawled out of the playhouse and stood up. Alicia's mom was reaching into the backseat of her car for a grocery bag when she saw Paloma.

"Oh, Lomie! Oh, thank God! Oh thank you, Lord Jesus! Oh, Lomie, sweetie! Where have you been? We have been worried sick about you!" Mrs. Garcia dropped her bag on the driveway and ran to Paloma, taking her in her arms. Engulfed in the warmth and safety, Paloma began to cry, sobbing into Mrs. Garcia's coat. "Come inside with me, sweetie. You are okay now. You are safe now."

Mrs. Garcia sat Paloma at her kitchen table. "Can I warm you up a breakfast burrito? Made them myself just yesterday. You look as if you haven't had anything to eat in days."

"That would be wonderful."

Mrs. Garcia busied herself at her stove. She put the plate with the burritos and salsa before Paloma on the table.

"Where have you been, *hija*?"

Paloma chewed and thought. She was afraid to tell Mrs. Garcia the truth. She needed to ask about pregnancy and disease, but she was afraid that Mrs. Garcia would kick her out if she knew where Paloma had been and what she had been doing. "I left town. I was staying with an old friend of my momma's."

"Where are you going to stay now?"

"I don't know."

"Paloma, you know that Lilly and Rickey are in foster care?"

"I know."

"You know that CPS is looking for you?"

"Yes, ma'am."

"Have you been hiding from them?"

"Yes."

"Why? They could find you a better place to stay than at your father's house."

"I don't want to go to foster care. I want to get Lilly and Rickey back." Paloma had been taught by her mother and father from her earliest age that losing a child to the foster care system was the greatest failure and *the* evil to be avoided. It wasn't just the loss of food stamps. It was the shame of it. So every truthful story of a bad foster home setting, of foster parents who were only in it for the monthly payment, was exaggerated and spread by families under threat of losing children to the system.

"But you can't take care of them, honey. You can't take care of yourself."

"Who says I can't?"

"Sweetie, you are only fourteen."

Paloma thought, *"I can take care of them and myself. Through Luther. I could make enough money to get us an apartment. I wouldn't have to stay at Luther's overnight every night. I could make a lot more money there than anywhere else."* But of course she did not say this aloud.

"Could I stay here for a little while? I wouldn't be much trouble. I promise. I'd clean and cook and get a job and pay you rent."

Mrs. Garcia took Paloma's plate and went to the sink, buying time before responding. She came back and sat beside Paloma.

"Honey, you have to go to school. It's the law. My husband won't let you stay here. His work hours have been cut and we are barely getting by. He just won't agree."

Paloma looked at her blankly. *"Can I trust her to ask about pregnancy? And VD? But if I do, I will have to tell her what happened and what I have been doing."*

Paloma's craving for meth, for escape, was growing.

Mrs. Garcia asked, "Paloma, how did you get those bruises around your throat? Let me look at you." Paloma ducked her chin against her chest and tried to pull her sweatshirt up around her neck to block Mrs. Garcia's inspection, but Mrs. Garcia would not be denied. Mrs. Garcia looked and then pulled a kitchen chair beside Paloma's. "Who choked you, Lomie? Was it your father?"

"No!" Then more quietly, "No, it wasn't my father."

"Was it one of the men who hang out at his house?

"No."

"Who was it, then?"

No answer. Paloma shut down.

"Lomie, tell me where you have been."

Paloma began to tremble and sweat. She felt exhausted. She wanted to give up.

"Lomie, do you want to lie down in Alicia's bed?"

"Yes. Just for a minute."

Paloma slept soundly until Mr. Garcia came home for lunch. Mrs. Garcia stopped him just inside the kitchen door to tell him Paloma was in the bedroom asleep and to ask him not to get angry.

"Not get angry! I told you I don't want her here! That family is bad news! Her father is nothing but trouble! Her little brother is studying for prison!" Mrs. Garcia tried to quiet him. "You know the police are looking for her! Do you want to get us arrested?"

Mr. Garcia used the house phone.

"The police are on their way. Don't go in there."

"Francisco, she will think I betrayed her."

"You didn't betray her. I did. I did what I had to. She is used to being betrayed by her father."

One police officer arrived within ten minutes. He had already called CPS. Paloma was still dead asleep when the officer and the CPS investigator entered her room and gently shook her awake. Paloma started up. It was the second time that day she had awakened to discover she had been betrayed.

Paloma felt the urge to run, but lacked the energy and strength. The young female CPS investigator knelt beside her bed with the office standing just behind. "You are Paloma Maria Ibarra Serrano?" asked the investigator.

Paloma shook her head no.

Both the officer and the investigator turned to Mr. and Mrs. Garcia.

"Yes," said Mr. Garcia. "She is Paloma Ibarra."

"How did you get those bruises around your throat?" asked the investigator.

"Don't remember."

"Paloma, we can protect you if you will just help us," said the investigator.

"I *said* I don't remember."

Paloma glared at Mrs. Garcia as she was taken out of the house and put in the backseat of the police cruiser. Mrs. Garcia was in tears and mouthed, "*Lo siento mucho*" as Paloma was taken out, not wanting her husband to hear her apology. Paloma was driven to Humberto's house on Hale. The investigator wanted to get his signed permission to take Paloma to the county hospital for examination and treatment of her throat. But Humberto was out drinking. So Paloma was taken to a CPS office. The investigator prepared an affidavit and court petition for CPS to take emergency custody of Paloma. This would give CPS the power to obtain medical care and shelter her until the next court hearing. Paloma had to stay in that office until the next day. There was no shower or bath in the offices, so she had to take a sponge bath in the sink in the ladies' restroom. She lay on a cot under lockdown with a distant supervisor. She could not sleep. She was in withdrawal from meth and worried about her brother and sister, about what Angel and the hairy man had done to her, about pregnancy and VD, and about when and where she would get her next hit of methamphetamine.

The next morning a judge signed an emergency order giving CPS temporary custody of Paloma. She was taken to the county hospital, where a care team tried to take her history and examine her. Paloma denied that she remembered what had happened to her throat. She did not reveal her sexual assault. She did not want to inform on Luther and Angel because she feared that working for them was the only way she could make enough money to get herself and her siblings out of foster care. If she could make enough money, she could hire a lawyer for her father and free Lilly and Rickey from the state, even though she was going to be the one to take care of them. And she was anxious about where else besides Luther's she could get her next puff of meth. The meth was doing her thinking.

Paloma CPS case was combined with Lilly's and Rickey's. The case could result in their father's paternal rights being terminated, so they could each be in foster care until turning eighteen. An attorney was appointed by the judge to represent Paloma's interests. Paloma didn't trust the attorney or the judge with the truth, so she told them nothing. Paloma also refused to speak to the CPS caseworker.

Because of Paloma's refusal to cooperate with CPS and the court, she was labeled a flight risk. She was kept in a secured motel under close supervision with other teenage girls of similar disposition. Tutors held desultory classes for the girls. There were a lot of fights. Horror stories about the foster care system were shared among them. Paloma was unable to see her siblings because of CPS staff shortages and her refusal to talk. Her father was not interested in seeing her or talking to her on the phone. Her court-appointed attorney told Paloma that she feared Humberto wanted his paternal rights and duties terminated. Paloma could not obtain any solid information about how long the court case would last. She felt utterly abandoned.

So she telephoned Luther as soon as she could.

"Paloma, why are you calling *me*?"

"Because I can't stay here and I have no one else to turn to."

"I was wondering when you would finally figure that out. What do you want from me? Just to pick you up and take you somewhere? You think I'm a fuckin' taxi service?"

"No. I want to come back to work for you. I can't talk long. I don't have time to talk this out now. Can you just pick me up at Las Vegas Trail and I-30?"

"No. We need to have an understanding now before I come. What do you want?"

"I come back to work for you, doing what you say, if I can. In exchange, you pay me enough to hire a lawyer to get my brother and sister out of foster care, and to rent a place where the three of us can live."

"Doing whatever I say?"

"Please, Luther. Yes, whatever you say. If I can."

"And you pay me for the meth you smoke?"

"I am not going to smoke any more meth."

"Bullshit. I never seen anyone take to meth like you have . . . I'll tell you what. We'll work out the meth part. You just promise to come back to work for me and do what I ask, and I will see to it that you get paid enough to hire this lawyer and to get your own place. But you have to promise to stay nights at my place when I ask you to. And to provide . . . services to our customers. But, Lomie, I'll take care of you. I'll protect you. Things will never go too far again. You will only do what you want to do. I apologize for what happened."

"Just get me out of here and help me get my children back."

"*Your* children?"

"My sister and brother."

"I am sending Angel for you in the Crown Vic. He'll be there in forty-five minutes. He won't wait for you for more than an hour."

"Please, not Angel."

"Yes, Angel. Start doing what I say. You ride with Angel." He hung up.

"Daddy." Angel had been standing at his father's elbow listening during the conversation. "That bitch will not do what you tell her to do. Look how she ran away after the first time."

"That's how the meth comes in. That little girl is a natural-born whore and meth addict. She'll stay with us for the meth, not the money or the children. Go get her. But get the hell out of there if you see anything suspicious."

Paloma locked her supervisor in the bathroom, slipped out of her room, took back stairs into the basement where the motel washing machines were located, and crawled out a window.

When Paloma arrived back at Luther's house on Lulu, Luther's tattoo artist friend was waiting for her. At first, Paloma balked at having "Luther's" and "Angel's" tattooed on her lower belly and back. But she submitted after Angel gave her a hit from his meth pipe.

Chapter Eleven

"I want this baby. I need this baby. She's my lifeline."

— February 2004 —

Paloma is seventeen years old.

"I knew it. Goddammit, I told him."

Paloma looked at the cross on the pregnancy stick. She felt faint, and not only because it had been so long since she had eaten. She pulled the ragged birth control patch from her shoulder and threw it in the toilet.

Esmeralda, one of Paloma's apartment mates, ran into the bathroom. "What's wrong? You told him what?"

Paloma showed Esmeralda the positive pregnancy stick.

Esmeralda was only fifteen. "What does that mean?"

"See that cross? It means I'm pregnant, you ignorant dope," she yelled.

"But you are on the patch." Esmeralda pulled up her sleeve. "Just like me. You can't be pregnant."

"Obviously, Ms. Rocket Scientist, these things aren't foolproof. And I have been the fool. I told Mr. Luther Bodine that these patches have to be replaced every week. I told him and told him. But 'Noooo,' he says. 'My supplier says you can go longer than two weeks per patch.'"

"Who's his supplier?

"All he tells me is that it's a customer of his who owns some pharmacies. Who knows if that is true. Who knows if anything Luther Bodine says is true."

"What are you going to do now?"

"I don't know. Have a baby, I guess. I can't even see my sister and brother, but I am having a baby. My life is totally screwed."

"Will you have to quit using?"

"I need to use right now," she thought. *"How in the world will I be able to quit?"* But then, *"Maybe this is a good thing. Maybe this will give me something to live for, a reason to get away from Luther. But how?"* She couldn't envision all she had to do, much less how and in what order.

When Paloma escaped from CPS in the motel, she went right back to captivity to Bodine and meth. She was not pregnant and she did not have a disease from that first sexual assault. Within a few months, Luther enticed two more teenaged girls from miserable situations to work for him. Luther's house was too small for the three girls, Angel, and Luther to live. Angel couldn't be trusted around them. So Luther moved the girls into a cheap two-bedroom apartment off North Main Street, and convinced Elvira, the proprietor of Bonitas Chiquitas, to supervise them day to day and keep the apartment stocked with groceries and supplies. All three of these young ladies were hiding from their families, CPS, or the law, and were restricted to The Hacienda, Luther's house, their apartment, and the tinted interior of the Crown Vic. Elvira locked the door to their apartment from the outside when any of them were there. They weren't allowed to use a phone.

Luther claimed that he paid an attorney to defend Humberto in the termination case about Lilly and Rickey. He did not tell her that Humberto already had a free, court-appointed attorney. But Humberto did not want to be a father to his children, would not mount a defense to the termination suit, and insisted to the skeptical judge and CPS workers that he had no idea where Paloma was. Paloma was unable to see her siblings or to know what was going on with them.

"What do you mean, 'What am I going to do with the baby?' demanded Angel. "You are going to get rid of it. That's what you are going to do!"

Angel had been told by Esmeralda that Paloma was pregnant, and he had driven directly to the apartment where Paloma was lying in her bed.

"Get rid of it?" she asked. "'It'? *'It'?!* Is that all a baby is to you?"

"You are going to have an abortion. That's final."

Paloma hated Angel. He was always intimidating, degrading, and belittling. He thought he could touch wherever, whatever, and whenever he liked on any of the Bodine captives. He treated all the young female employees that way. Luther was an ambassador of gentility compared to his son. And she was sure that Angel had been the one who had anally assaulted her the night she ran away in 2001. She hadn't decided how she wanted to respond to her pregnancy, but she automatically defied Angel.

"I am not. I've decided to put this baby up for adoption."

"Stupid *puta*! Where are you going to live for the next seven months while you are pregnant? And after your mutt is born? Who's going to feed you?" He leaned his face down into her face. She could smell the cigarette smoke and whiskey on his breath. "Where are you going to get your meth?" He sneered. "Not from us. We aren't running a charity here."

Paloma jumped out of bed and shoved her face into his, standing on tiptoes. "Oh yeah, *bastardo*? Where can I get an abortion where they won't find out that I'm underage? And how I got pregnant? And what you and your father have been doing to me?"

"How about if I just abort it right now by kicking you in your skinny belly." He grabbed her by her hair and twisted her down on her knees.

Luther burst into the bedroom. "Angel! *Stop!* What's wrong with you?"

Angel jerked Paloma up by her hair, lifting her off her knees, and then threw her down. "She says she wants to keep the baby! Can you believe it?" He pushed by his father and left the apartment.

Luther put his hands gently under Paloma's arms, lifted her up, and sat her on her bed. Then he sat in a chair across from her.

"Are you sure you are pregnant?"

"The stick was positive. This was the second one. I have been feeling sick to my stomach in the mornings. I haven't had my period in almost three months. I have to pee every two hours. My breasts are getting tender. I am even more tired than usual. I can't seem to get enough sleep. I am as hungry as I can be, and I haven't been hungry in two years. I cry at the drop of a hat. I'd say that the only stronger clue would be if a baby fell out of me . . . This is your fault, Luther. I told you and told you that I needed the patches replaced more often." She lay down and buried her face in her pillow. "Now what I am going to do?"

"I need you to trust me, Lomie."

"I couldn't trust you about the patches. I can't trust you to protect me from that asshole son of yours. Why should I trust you about this?"

"Any idea who the father might be?

"What do you think? It could be any of two dozen guys, none of whose names I know. And none I would want as a father to my kid. And none who would *be* a father to my kid."

"How long have you suspected you were pregnant?"

"Too long . . . But I kept using, Luther. I kept smoking meth. What if I have injured my baby?" Paloma rolled away from Bodine on her side in bed and began to cry. She cried for a long time. She fell asleep. She woke up thinking Luther was still there. "Do you have any crystal on you?" she asked. But she discovered that now it was Elvira who was sitting on the bed next to her, stroking her hair.

"Poor thing. You must be in shock. But you need to get moving on this, if you are going to . . . take care of the pregnancy."

"How can I do that? How can I pay for it? Who can consent for me? What do I tell them about how I got pregnant?"

"Lomie, there is a clinic here in Fort Worth where they see dozens of young girls in this predicament every month. They don't ask a lot of questions. They don't ask for money. They don't care about your age."

"What if I want to keep this baby?"

"Have you been using meth while you've been pregnant?"

"You know I have," she said, tears welling up in her eyes.

"Then wouldn't it be best for this child to . . . terminate?"

"Maybe it would be best for everyone if I terminated me."

"Please don't say that, Lomie. Please don't say that. I know things seem too much for you now. But we can put this behind you in a few days. Things will be back where they were, and you will have learned a great lesson about taking care of yourself."

"I don't want things to go back to the way they were. My life stinks. I am all alone. I am already used up."

"No you aren't, Lomie. You have Luther and me. Luther saved you from CPS and your daddy. He has given you a place to stay and all the pleasures and excitements of meth. You know what life is like for almost everyone, Lomie? It's boring. It's routine. No ups and downs. No thrills. You have all this excitement. You are more attractive every day. There is not a man in the world you couldn't have. Someday some handsome, rich man is going to come along and take you out of all this. Then you can have all the kids you want. But not now. You can have your fun now."

"Fun? You call this fun? What man would want a meth addict who has been used by so many men?"

"Life is long, Lomie. Life is long. Things can change. Love is blind. Some men are attracted to a woman with . . . this kind of experience. Maybe an older man will come along and want to save you from all this."

"It just seems so wrong to kill this child."

"It's not a child yet. It's a tiny knot in your tummy. Maybe a damaged knot because of your drug use . . . How would you take care of it? By leaving The Hacienda and Luther? Getting a job doing what? Waitressing at night and on weekends? Working at a dry cleaner or a warehouse? Or on an assembly line? You have an eighth-grade education and a worthless GED. So the best you could do would be minimum wage or a little above. You know how much rent is? Child care? Car payment? You have to be able to get to work. Medical care for your child? Ever heard of a copay?

"You sound as if you have helped someone through this before."

"I'll tell you a secret if you promise not to tell anyone. I've been through all this myself."

"Working for Luther?"

"Working for Luther," she said.

"You worked for Luther? Like I do?"

"Yes."

"And got pregnant?"

"Yes. I haven't always looked like this. I was young once too, and not as long ago as you think."

"Did a man ever take *you* away from all this?"

"There have been special men in my life. Still waiting for that special, special one. But I'll tell you this. My life would have been a lot different and a lot worse if I hadn't ended my pregnancy."

Paloma sat up in bed, gathered her knees to her chest, and wrapped her arms around her legs. "But have you ever really been loved? Or loved anybody? A child will love you."

"I have loved and been loved. And I have been free to leave when things got boring or hard. I just ended things a few weeks ago with a man who was a lot of fun. But I was free to end it so I did. You can't do that with a child. Unless you are someone like your father."

Paloma winced.

"Lomie, let's live in the real world. You can't take care of a baby. You can't give up meth and weed, and you have probably already damaged the child by using meth. Next pregnancy can be planned. That's not this one . . . Are you afraid abortion will hurt? "

"Yes."

"It won't. The procedure will take maybe thirty minutes and you will be recovered and back at it in forty-eight hours. And this clinic I am thinking of will help you with birth control. More dependable than a patch. Maybe an IUD or an implant."

"What do I do next?

Luther drove Paloma to the clinic in east Fort Worth. As Paloma was getting out of the car, she asked him, "Aren't you coming in?"

"No, Lomie. Think about it. I am not family. Now remember what we talked about. You have lost your ID. You never had a driver's license. Give them your actual month and day of birth but change the year so you are eighteen, not seventeen. Your mother is dead, and your father is a drunk whose whereabouts are unknown. If you could find him, you would still be afraid to tell him for fear he would hurt you. He has hurt you before. Use your father's house on Hale as your address. Say you are living there with a friend's parents. You have dropped out of school. You got pregnant when you got drunk at a party and had consensual sex with a strange boy. You don't know his name. You hadn't seen him before and haven't seen him since. Do not say anything that will cause them to call the cops. And above all, do not mention me or The Hacienda or weed or methamphetamine. Got it?"

"Got it." Paloma paused.

"Chances are today will just be an interview, an exam, and signing some consent forms. We'll have to bring you back for the actual procedure."

"Why the delay? Why can't I get this done today?"

"They want you to have time to think about it."

"You sound like you have been through this before with someone."

Luther did not respond.

"Did you help Elvira get an abortion?"

"What? Elvira? Bonitas Chiquitas Elvira? Fat Elvira?"

"Yes, Elvira."

"No, definitely not Elvira."

"Did she ever work for you doing what I do?"

"Hell no. Just look at her. Why do you ask such shit?"

"She told me that she once worked for you doing what I do and that she got pregnant and had an abortion and it was the right decision."

"Oh, she did, did she? Well, I just asked her to help you make the right decision. I guess she tried to make it easier on you by telling you a story."

Paloma sat inside the clinic across the desk from a nurse practitioner. The walls were covered with drawings of the female reproductive system and babies in different stages of development in the uterus. And there were posters listing dos and don'ts.

"My name is Cynthia Cerrillos. I am a nurse practitioner here at the clinic. I have read your application for a termination." Cynthia looked closely at the young woman across the desk sitting with her arms crossed over her chest and her legs crossed tight. She certainly looked older than the age of eighteen written on her application and history. "Do you have any questions?"

"What is a nurse practitioner? Why am I not seeing a doctor?"

"You will see a doctor, of course. You are seeing me in addition to seeing the doctor. A nurse practitioner is somewhere between a nurse and a doctor. I have a lot of experience as a labor and delivery nurse, and have gone through additional training and licensing, and am supervised by a physician. I can do things some things that a nurse cannot, like prescribe medication. But I cannot do things that a doctor can, like perform surgery or termination. The clinic has doctors and nurse practitioners on staff, which enables us to see more patients sooner. Any more questions about that?"

"No."

"First we want to make sure you know what your options are. What other questions do you have? We want to answer all of your questions."

"Is everything I tell you confidential?"

"Particularly since you are eighteen, yes, it is confidential. The only exception might be if you were to tell me about child abuse when you were under eighteen. Those things I would have to report to CPS or law enforcement. Everything else is confidential. Other questions?"

"Will God punish me if I have an abortion?"

"We can't answer religious questions."

"Why not?"

"If you are worried about that, you should talk to a priest or minister. We are not qualified to answer that question."

"Will an abortion hurt?"

"No, it won't hurt you physically."

"What about otherwise?"

"You mean emotionally? Psychologically?"

"Yes."

"We can refer you to licensed professional counselors whom you can speak to about that . . . Paloma, do you have anyone who can help you make this decision?"

"No, ma'am. I am all alone." Paloma's voice cracked as she said this.

Cerrillos came out from behind her desk, sat in the chair next to Paloma, and took her hand. "You aren't all alone anymore. We are here for you, whatever you decide. If you want to talk about God or your worries or anything else, I am here to listen as long as you need. But this is your decision. No one can make it for you . . . We can help you decide but we can't decide for you. Are you looking for someone else to take the responsibility to decide for you?"

"No, ma'am. I'm not. But I *am* sick of being alone . . . Will an abortion cause my baby pain?"

"To give you the truest answer I can, I need to do a sonogram to see how far along you are in the pregnancy. We will do that and a vaginal exam in just a moment."

"Does this place offer any other help besides abortion?"

"Yes. Abortion is just one option. Another is prenatal care for you and your baby during pregnancy and postnatal care for you after delivery or termination. And we can refer you to an adoption agency if you are not sure you want to terminate but you don't feel you can raise the child. We also have caseworkers here to help you access services."

"Will I be in trouble with the law if I decide to get the abortion?"

"No, dear. You will not be in trouble with the law."

"Will anyone know I had an abortion?"

"Only those you tell. In the future you may be asked about your medical history. Certain job applications involve a potential penalty for not telling the complete truth. But generally, it's nobody's business but yours and whoever you decide to tell."

Cynthia smiled at Paloma. "Take your time. We do not want to make you feel rushed. Although if we are going to perform the termination, the clock is ticking a bit depending upon how long you have been pregnant."

"What's next today?"

"The sonogram and the vaginal exam. I'll do those. And we'll need you to pee in a cup and to draw a little blood from you."

"You mean a needle for the blood?"

"Yes. There will be a little stick. I won't be bad."

"Will the sonogram hurt?

"No. We spread a little jelly on your belly and then use a sonogram machine to look at your fetus in your womb. From that we can estimate how many weeks you are since conception and how the fetus is doing."

Cynthia noticed that Paloma seemed uncertain.

"I can tell you have another question, or a worry. What is it? How can I help?"

"If a mother has used meth during the pregnancy . . . If I have used meth . . . will you be able to tell from the sonogram if my fetus was injured?"

"No, Ms. Ibarra. That is beyond the capability of this sonogram. It would be years after birth of the child before anyone could have an opinion that meth use damaged the fetus. It is medically more complicated than that. But, no, this sonogram will not tell us that."

"What are the chances that my baby has been damaged by my meth use?"

"I can't tell you that. I doubt that the doctor can tell you that. But we can ask her when you meet her."

"Any more questions? Ready for the exam?"

Paloma Ibarra, Nurse Practitioner Cynthia Cerrillos, and Dr. Ashwini Bashkar gathered in Dr. Bashkar's office after the sonogram and exam. Cerrillos had conducted the sonogram. But after she had started the vaginal exam, she had asked Dr. Bashkar to join her.

"Ms. Ibarra, your written application and history state that you have engaged in only one act of sexual intercourse. Are you sure about that?"

Paloma looked from face to face. "Yes," she replied. "Why do you ask?" She could hear the blood pounding in her ears.

"Because there are signs of repetitive trauma in your vagina. And there are signs of trauma to your anus. The exam is not consistent with one or even a few acts of intercourse."

"Do I have VD?"

"No, you do not. The blood test was negative, and there are no signs of disease in the exam."

Cynthia interjected. "We are not blaming you, Paloma, or trying to make you feel ashamed. We are just concerned for your safety. Based upon your application, you have no family support group. Even if you have a termination, we are concerned that you will return to the setting where you were treated like this."

"I don't know what you are talking about."

"Ms. Ibarra, I have another concern. According to your application, you are barely eighteen. But you have no driver's license, and no ID or documentation of any kind. This is very unusual for a young lady your age. Plus, if you are using meth, you are endangering yourself and your baby. If you are seventeen or younger," Dr. Bashkar paused, "you may be a victim of child abuse and we are required by law to report our concerns to CPS and the police."

"I *am* eighteen! I thought what I tell you is confidential."

"It is. Unless the confidentiality is overridden by the law requiring us to report child abuse."

"I tell you that I am eighteen. My mother died of cancer and my father is a drunk. I just never had the chance to get a driver's license. We couldn't afford drivers education and I didn't have a car to practice driving in or anyone to teach me. It's not my fault I don't have an ID."

Cynthia tried to calm her. "We believe you. We know this is a really scary time for you."

"I want to leave," said Paloma.

"Paloma, just give us a few more moments. Let me talk alone to Dr. Bashkar for a moment."

"Are you going out to call CPS?"

"No," said Dr. Bashkar, "just to talk. Word of honor."

The two women stepped out. Paloma tested the door to see if they had locked her in like she had been locked in at the apartment. The door was not locked. She walked out and down the hallway, into the reception area, and out the front door. Luther's Crown Vic was nowhere to be seen. Paloma felt abandoned again.

She had just experienced an awakening. Seeing the images and shadows of her baby on the sonogram and having Cerrillos point out the beginnings of her baby's anatomy awakened another set of yearnings.

Cynthia stood beside her. "What did you decide to do? We have a place for you to stay here overnight to sort out your options."

"Are you trying to keep me here until the police come?"

"No, Paloma. We don't have a good enough basis to report you. So we will observe confidentiality. Your secrets are safe with us, at least through tonight. I promise you we will not report you if you stay with us overnight. Most of all, we want you to be safe until you decide."

"I don't have anywhere to go anyway. And I am starving. Do you have anything I can eat?"

"Of course."

Paloma went back inside out of faith in Cynthia Cerrillos. She had just met Cerrillos but she was desperate for someone she could trust. And Cerrillos was so gentle and reassuring. *"I wonder if I will be that way with my child?"* Paloma thought. *"I would like to be."*

The next morning, Paloma and Cynthia met again in her office.

"What arc you thinking?"

"I want to keep this baby."

"Really?" Cynthia had been trained not to push back on the decisions made by the young women who come into the center. But she had been trained to explore with them the realities of those decisions. "Are you thinking about adoption or raising the baby yourself?"

"Raising her myself."

"Her?"

"I just know she's a girl. I don't know how I know it. I just know it."

"That's sweet. Sometime an expectant mother just knows." Cynthia smiled. "How will you be able to provide for the baby?"

"I don't know. I just know I want to raise her."

"So I take it that termination is off the table."

"I want it to be off the table."

"Is this because you are tired of being all alone?"

"Yes. Partly, I guess."

"Then let's talk about people who might help you while you are pregnant. Then we can talk about people who might help you to raise your baby after you deliver. You must have some relatives."

"None that would help me. Like I said, I am all alone."

"Let's put who might actually help aside for now. Let's just make a list of relatives. Sisters, brothers, aunts, uncles, cousins, grandparents, great grandparents, great aunts, great uncles?"

"My sister and brother are in foster care, and are too young anyway. There was no relative who would take them in. So I don't know who would take in me and my baby."

"Any aunts or uncles?"

"My father has a brother but he lives in Mexico. My mother had two sisters, but I don't know where they are."

"Grandparents?"

"All dead."

"Great grandparents?"

"Dead. There is a great aunt on my mother's side who lives in Oklahoma."

"That would be your maternal grandmother's sister?"

"That's right."

"When did you last have any contact with her?"

"She came to my mother's funeral. She wanted to take me and my sister and brother to live with her when she saw what a mess my father was making. But he refused."

"There it is! Let me slow down. That great aunt may be your answer. How long ago was it that this lady wanted to take you in?"

"I was thirteen. I'm seventeen—sorry, eighteen—now." Cynthia pretended she didn't hear the mistake. "So five years maybe."

"How old is your great aunt?"

"In her sixties, I think."

"Is she married?"

"Widowed. I doubt that she has remarried but I don't know."

"What's her name?

"Mildred Mayfield."

"Children of her own?"

"Yes. My mom's cousins. They are probably grown and gone."

"Where does she live?"

"Walters, Oklahoma."

"What does she do?"

"She's retired. She worked as a teacher for years. Big-time church woman. Deaconess or something."

"That sounds promising."

"Why do you say that?"

"Some church women walk their talk. That's all. Do you have her telephone number?"

"No, ma'am."

Cynthia called information for Walters, Oklahoma.

"Here's a telephone number for Mildred Mayfield in Walters. Do you want to try to call her or should I?"

"Do you think I really might be able to have this baby? And keep her?"

"One step at a time. I know you are anxious to get this decided but let's slow down. We don't know if Ms. Mayfield is willing or able to help. We are just exploring all the options. I also want to talk to you about adoption before you decide. There is a wonderful place here in town—Edna Gladney Center for Adoption—where you could live and go to school and get excellent prenatal care while you're pregnant. And you could be certain that your baby would go to a loving home. And termination continues to be a possibility."

Paloma's teared up and she gritted her teeth. "I want this baby. I need this baby. She's my lifeline."

"But are you her lifeline?"

Paloma darkened. "If I have an abortion, no one is my baby's lifeline."

"Of course. Anyway, one step at a time. It will be your decision. Let's just line up all your choices. Then you can decide."

"Cynthia," said Paloma, "I am going to have this baby. And I am going to keep her. And when I do, I am going to name her Cynthia. You are the first person who has ever been on my side about anything."

Cynthia hugged Paloma.

"I'll never forget you, Paloma. All of our ladies are special. But there is something extra special about you."

Chapter Twelve

"Your parents all agree that a procedure is by far the best decision."

— December 1997 —

John Levi is seventeen years old.

John Levi's parents, Gerard and Amanda Jones, were met at the door of the Leeves' home by Larry Leeves. Gerard said to Larry, "Again, Larry, we can't tell you how sorry we are about this." Amanda began to sniffle again.

They walked into the Leeves' living room, with its beige carpet and beige sofa and beige upholstered chairs and its earth-tone landscapes. Amanda walked to a family portrait in the dining room of Larry, Jenny, and Krissy when Krissy was eight. "Oh, you put this back up. Wonderful. I have always *loved* this," she gushed to Jenny. Jenny replied, "It reminds us of better times."

Jenny Leeves sat in an armchair across the coffee table from the couch. John Levi and Krissy were holding hands and seated on one end of the couch. Larry Leeves and Gerard and Amanda Jones took their places in the vacant spaces in the couch and chairs. The housekeeper brought a tray of coffee and soft drinks and set it on the coffee table. The Leeves were Church of Christ and no alcohol was ever allowed in their home.

John Levi had arrived at the Leeves' home before his parents to talk to Krissy about their plans for their baby. Krissy was in turmoil but thought she wanted to have the baby and then put the child up for adoption. John

Levi had pledged to support her, although he would be relieved if she had an abortion.

Of course, Gerard Jones tried to take charge. "Krissy, I want you to know that Mrs. Jones and I will stand with you and your parents in helping you reach the best decision for everyone. And we will help financially with whatever the implications are of your choice. And," and he paused and looked at everyone in the room in turn, "we will be completely and totally discrete about this. This is no one's business but the people who are here in this room. Do you both agree?" Gerard asked, looking to Krissy and John Levi.

"Agree to what, sir?" asked John Levi.

"Agree that this entire situation should be kept confidential within the people in this room?"

"How long will we be able to keep this secret? Krissy will start to show soon." John Levi spoke again for himself and Krissy.

"All right then," interjected Mr. Leeves. "Do we agree that we keep this a secret as long as we can?"

"If you want," replied John Levi. "I just don't know how long that can be."

Mr. Jones asked Krissy and John Levi, "Have either of you told any of your friends? Tell the truth now. Krissy, you must have felt tempted to confide in your girlfriends."

"No, sir, I haven't. I don't want anyone to know yet . . . I feel so stupid," said Krissy.

"John Levi?"

"No, sir." John Levi looked at Krissy. Krissy looked back at him and nodded silently at him, as if to say, *"Go ahead. You say it."*

"Won't how long this can be kept secret depend upon what she and I decide about this baby?"

"You mean what she and her parents decide," insisted Mr. Leeves. "But it would be better if we all were on the same page. And I am confident we will be."

Krissy gripped John Levi's hand harder and snuggled closer against him. Krissy was seventeen, like John Levi. She was blond, trim, and always immaculately dressed and coiffed. She wore a cashmere sweater and a plaid skirt. A gold cross hung by a gold chain from her slim neck. Tiny diamond studs were in her tiny ears. Her complexion was flawless. She had a monthly, standing appointment with her dermatologist. She had small features, small round lips, and small, bright blue eyes. She also had a small personality that always sought affirmation from her parents and friends. It was that need for affirmation that led her to have sex with John Levi. He only tepidly wanted it with her. He thought of her as a friend and steady date but not as a sexual partner. He was not as attracted to her sexually as he was to some other girls. But Krissy's closest girlfriends claimed they were no longer virgins and pressured her to share their experience. Seeking the girlfriends' affirmation, she had sex one time with John Levi. When he did not have a condom, she was too embarrassed to tell him she was not on birth control. She just wanted to get it over with and relied upon the odds against her getting pregnant from only one act. She was more timid than stupid about it, while John Levi was just stupid. Neither of them enjoyed the sex, which was physically painful and scary for Krissy. She felt too vulnerable and exposed during their lovemaking. Even before she discovered she was pregnant, she vowed not to have sex again until she and John Levi were married. For all of her life Krissy Leeves had been sheltered by her parents' wealth from any unpleasantness. This one foolish act dismantled her shelter.

Larry Leeves began his previously agreed presentation. He, Jenny, Gerard, and Amanda had held their own private meeting in advance of this gathering, just as John Levi and Krissy had held theirs.

"We parents had a meeting about what is in everyone's best interest," said Larry Leeves. "Your parents all agree that a procedure is by far the best decision."

John Levi spoke up. "A procedure? You mean an abortion, don't you? Or do you mean an adoption procedure?"

"Let's not be crude. It's an abortion. But let's just call it a procedure," said Mrs. Leeves.

"But Krissy and I are not sure we want an abortion. We may want to give this child up for adoption."

"But Krissy, dear," Mrs. Leeves blurted, "have you thought about what that will require of you? And of us?"

Mrs. Leeves looked for the husbands to take over. When they did not, she kept talking. "Where will you go while you are pregnant? You can't stay here. You can't stay at Country Valley School. They don't allow pregnant students to attend."

"Yes, they do, Mother," responded Krissy quietly. She named a student who continued in school while she was pregnant.

"But Krissy, that girl is very different than you. And her parents are very different from us. She was a scholarship student. An affirmative action student. She had nothing to lose from it being known that she was pregnant. If you stay in school and don't have the procedure, you will forever be known as that girl who had a baby in high school out of wedlock. The girl who couldn't control her animal urges. Girls from good families don't do this. You could never show your face again at our church."

"Even if I did the right thing for the baby by putting it up for adoption?" asked Krissy.

"That would not change the fact that you conceived this child in a sinful act," said Mrs. Leeves.

"But what will God say if I have an abortion?"

"A procedure, darling. A procedure," said Krissy's mother. "Don't you worry about God. You just let us make this decision and God will consider that this is all on us."

Mrs. Jones inserted herself. "Krissy . . . Precious, we just want what is best for *you*. Think of what you would have to give up just in the short term. This is your senior year in high school. This should be one of the best years of your life. You wouldn't be able to go to your senior prom. You wouldn't be able to go on the senor trip to Cancun in the spring. You will miss all the senior parties. And next year, do you think you could still go to TCU and pledge a sorority? This baby will be due in the summer. Do you think a sorority will pledge you if you just delivered a baby? You will never be able to keep that a secret."

"But I want to do what is right for the baby too. John Levi," she asked, almost whispering, "do you really want me to have this baby and put it up for adoption?"

"I know that you will make the right decision, and I will support you whatever it is."

"That's very admirable," said Mrs. Leeves. "But I am asking you both to listen to the voices of reason and experience in this room. All of us are agreed that the right decision here is to have the procedure. We have already been in contact with a doctor. By this time next week, this will all be a bad dream. No one else has to know or will ever know."

Mr. Jones stated, "We will of course share in any expense," as if it was decided.

"Krissy," asked John Levi, "do you want to think about this overnight? So you know it is your decision and not someone else's? Then you and I can get together tomorrow morning to talk privately."

"I am really tired. Can't you stay with me tonight?" she asked John Levi.

"Out of the question," said Mr. Leeves. "If it is to be Krissy's decision alone, which I do not agree is the case, then Krissy needs to be alone to decide alone."

The Joneses said goodnight. Krissy and John Levi were granted a moment alone before he left.

"Will you still be my guy, no matter what I decide?" she asked him.

"I'll always be your guy." He hugged her close.

"If it were your decision to make alone, what would you do? What would you tell me to do?"

"Krissy, I do not want you to violate your conscience."

"John Levi, answer my question. I need to know what you would do."

"I am not going to tell you what to do. But if I were the one who is pregnant? Just between you and me? I'd have the abortion."

"Why? What about the baby?"

"I didn't say it would be right. I said that is what I would do. And I am not saying that is what you should do."

"Why would you do that?"

"Because it would change my life too much right now to be pregnant and have a baby. This is our senior year, like your mom said. We have too many ambitions and plans. If the baby were born, how would it stay secret that we had a child but failed to raise it? What would people say?"

The next morning, John Levi called and called Krissy's private phone. He drove by the Leeves' home and knocked on the door. The house was dark. Krissy did not answer his calls that morning or that day or the next day. The day after that his mother told him that Krissy had the abortion and had gone out of town for the holidays with her parents. She asked that he give her time alone to recover. What his mother insisted on most was that he tell no one, ever—not even his closest friends—about the pregnancy or the abortion.

After the "procedure," John Levi offered to take Krissy to their senior prom and to accompany her to the senior parties. But her parents and his parents forbade it. Mr. and Mrs. Leeves found Krissy a date to all these functions—a young, well-mannered man from a good family who was already a freshman at TCU majoring in accounting. Mrs. Leeves saw to it that Krissy received an IUD, even though Krissy swore tearfully that it was not needed. John Levi decided not to attend any of these senior festivities. When Krissy and John Levi encountered one another around Country Valley School, Krissy avoided his eyes. After they started college, they had no more contact with one another.

Chapter Thirteen

"Never have. Never will."

— July, 2011 —

Paloma is twenty-four years old and Cynthia is seven.

Paloma had been summoned to an 8:00 a.m. meeting with the human relations director of the nursing home where she had worked as a nurse's aide for two years. She was at the end of an all-night shift and was fighting sleep. She was directed via intercom to enter Ms. Patterson's office. She sat in a chair opposite the director's desk.

With no pleasantries, Ms. Patterson said, "Ms. Ibarra, we are going to have to let you go."

"Let me go? You mean fire me?"

"Or you can resign, which will make it easier for you to get another job."

"Why are you firing me?"

"You tested positive for marijuana in your last urine sample." Ms. Patterson showed her the test result on a single piece of paper.

Paloma briefly considered feigning surprise and indignation, but quickly decided to avoid the hoax. "So what? Are there any complaints about my work?"

"Just the opposite. Our patients love you. Especially the men. And our staff loves you too."

"Then why are you firing me? I have never been high at work."

"It's the law. We cannot employ a nurse's aide who tests positive for any illegal drug."

"Can't you just throw that piece of paper away? Just this once?"

"The drug testing agency sends these results into the state board."

"Then can't you give me a warning? Or put me on probation? Or cut my pay? Ms. Patterson, I really need this job. I just got my daughter back a few months ago."

"I can't make an exception. The state licensing authorities are always looking for us to violate their rules."

"Ms. Patterson, please. I didn't smoke it myself. I was at a party where it was in the air and I must have breathed it in enough to test positive. Was the test number really low?"

"Ms. Ibarra, it doesn't matter to the state if it was low so long as it was positive. We have to let you go. We have absolutely no choice."

Paloma thought, *"Screwed again . . . by myself."* Alicia, her apartment roommate, had paid for a babysitter for her children and Cynthia, and had taken Paloma to the first party she had attended in months. When Paloma walked in, she smelled weed in the air and thought that she should leave. But the music was so inviting and she was in so much in need of a break from her life that she stayed. One minor mistake and she was out of an ideal job. The nursing home was a thirty-minute walk from her apartment. Paloma had no car, so she had to find employment nearby. Because of its location and her hours, the job at the nursing home had been a godsend, despite the low pay. Now she had lost it.

"How much time do I have?"

"You are terminated today."

"Today?" She soaked that in. "How much severance pay?"

"None."

"How about if I resign?"

"Still none."

"Can I get unemployment? Do you know?"

"I am not allowed to advise you on that."

"Ms. Patterson, be a human being, please. Do you know if I can get unemployment if I resign instead of being canned?"

Ms. Patterson sighed. She left her desk, made certain that her office door was shut tight, and returned to her desk. "You didn't hear this from me, okay?"

"Okay."

"If you are fired for cause, particularly for drug use, you probably won't be able to get unemployment. If you resign, you definitely won't receive it. But if you resign, you will have a better chance of getting another job. When we receive an inquiry from a prospective employer, we will simply confirm the beginning and ending dates of your employment and that you resigned."

"What about if I am fired?"

"We will only give your beginning and ending dates and refuse to give any other information. Which will let the prospective employer know that you were fired."

"So I am cooked."

"Yes . . . Anything else."

"No."

"Do you resign?"

"Yes."

"Sign here." Ms. Patterson had already prepared Paloma's resignation document, exonerating the nursing home from any wrongdoing and from any responsibility for unemployment for her.

When Paloma was pregnant with Cynthia seven years before, Cynthia Cerrillos of the pregnancy center had explained Paloma's predicament by telephone call to Paloma's great aunt Mildred Mayfield. Paloma and Mildred spoke at length, and they agreed that Paloma could live with Mildred during pregnancy. Paloma took a bus to Walters, Oklahoma. She delivered her daughter Cynthia at the hospital in Lawton, which was about twenty miles from Walters.

Mildred was a generous hostess whose household was rigid with rules. Paloma was a loving and attentive mother to newborn Cynthia, who seemed not to suffer any ill effects from Paloma's meth use. But Paloma lived with Mildred for only a year after Cynthia was born. When Paloma turned eighteen, she was no longer in danger of being placed in foster care back home. She left Cynthia with Mildred and returned to Fort Worth with the goal of getting Lilly and Rickey out of foster care. To accomplish this she needed a stable, healthy residence, a steady job, reliable transportation, and affordable child care. Paloma did not think she could accomplish her goal if she had Cynthia with her. Her plan was to set up in Fort Worth with a home, job, car, and child care, and then to reunite all three children with her. A side benefit of her plan was to get out of Walters, its crushing boredom, and Mildred's exhausting rules.

Mildred Mayfield lectured Paloma that she had no business leaving her baby behind. Mildred didn't know how long she could care for Cynthia alone. Paloma had no support in Fort Worth, Humberto continuing to be a worthless drunk. Just as he had chosen not to be a father to Lilly and Rickey, Humberto did not want to act as a father to Paloma or a grandfather to Cynthia. When Paloma arrived back in Fort Worth on the bus from Walters, she thought she had arranged for a place to stay with Alicia, her ninth-grade friend. But upon arrival she was informed by Alicia that Alicia's newest boyfriend had just moved in. There was no longer room for Paloma. Paloma then had the options of slinking back to Walters, crashing at her father's dump of a house on Hale Street, or going to the women's homeless shelter off Lancaster in Fort Worth. She chose the shelter.

The only employment that Paloma could find was with a company that cleaned one of Fort Worth's pricier downtown hotels, only a short bus ride from the shelter. The hours were steady and decent, but the job paid only fifty cents more an hour than minimum wage. She couldn't earn enough at that rate of pay to afford her own apartment or car. She applied for Section 8 housing, but the waiting period was months long. She spoke by phone to Cynthia every week, but Cynthia was too young to carry on a conversation. Mildred pressed Paloma about when she was coming back to Walters or taking Cynthia to Fort Worth with her. Paloma kept making promises to Mildred she couldn't keep.

Mildred finally gave Paloma an ultimatum. "I am too old and sick to take care of this child by myself. Come back to my house to take care of Cynthia or take her with you. Whichever it is, you have one month. After that, I am going to call CPS here and say Cynthia has been abandoned by her mother." Paloma pleaded with Mildred to give her more than a month, but Mildred was unrelenting. Paloma hoped that Mildred was bluffing, but she knew she had to make more money soon.

So Paloma started acting as the middle person in the sale of drugs on East Lancaster. She had vowed when she left Luther Bodine that she would never be around drugs again. But she needed the money to avoid Walters and to bring her daughter to Fort Worth. Paloma introduced herself to the suppliers of the marijuana, cocaine, and meth to the unsheltered homeless on Lancaster. Paloma set a goal of accumulating five thousand dollars for a security deposit for an apartment and a down payment on a car from one of the "we tote the note" car lots on East Belknap. Then she would drive to Walters in triumph to pick up her daughter.

Paloma would sit in a supplier's car until a homeless person lingered on a particular street corner signaling that he or she wanted drugs. Paloma was then dispatched from the car to find out what drugs were wanted and to tell the buyer the price. She would receive the money and place the order for the drugs through a cell phone. She told the buyer to wait on the corner until another person delivered the drugs. Paloma would take the money to the supplier in the car and receive a cash percentage of the sale. Paloma never touched the drugs and so could not be arrested with them on her person. But there was the risk of arrest by an undercover cop posing as a buyer and working with a team of police to identify the various players in the scheme.

One night Paloma was arrested. A police car with its lights flashing and sirens screaming pulled beside her as she was walking back to the supplier's car. Two police officers jumped out and put her against the car.

They searched her, expecting to find drugs but were disappointed when they nothing but a wad of money in her hand. So they charged her with prostitution just because she was a young female walking alone at night in that neighborhood. She was taken back to the downtown precinct in cuffs, shackled to a desk, and questioned by a detective. The detective wanted her to make a sworn statement about the details of the drug sale operation in exchange for dropping all charges against her. Paloma claimed ignorance and denied prostitution. She was taken before a magistrate, who ordered her bond at one thousand dollars. She could not find a bondsman to post the bond because she had no fixed address. So she sat in jail for five days on the false charge until a court-appointed defense attorney negotiated a sentence of time she had already served in jail in exchange for her plea of *nolo contendere* to prostitution. This attorney advised her that this plea would not be treated in the future as a guilty plea. And if she didn't take this plea deal now, she would sit in jail for another month before the chance to exonerate herself at trial. This attorney was wrong about the future effect of a *nolo contendere* plea and he knew he was wrong. But his caseload was backbreaking, he was only paid a limited amount by the county for a misdemeanor like a first-time prostitution charge, and he had to move some cases to final disposition to receive his pay from the system. She followed his bad advice, was brought to court, pleaded *nolo*, and was free to go.

Paloma's drug-selling side job on East Lancaster was over. She had not accumulated her full goal of five thousand dollars as Mildred's deadline approached. But she was able get a waitressing job at an IHOP during the days and at a downtown steak house during the evenings. She was eventually able to make enough at both jobs to pay the monthly rent on a one-bedroom apartment, to buy an old car, and to send a one-thousand-dollar money order to Mildred. By then, Mildred had grown to love Cynthia so much that she would not have given her to Paloma if Paloma had come for her.

Weeks turned into months, which turned into years. Paloma entered her twenties and Cynthia grew from a toddler to a little girl. Paloma still telephoned Cynthia every week. Cynthia was always eager to speak to her mother. Paloma visited Cynthia at Mildred's at least four times a year. Paloma could tell that Cynthia was better off staying at Mildred's in Walters than with her in Fort Worth. Mildred was retired on a decent pension. Paloma was a single working mother with low-paying day and night jobs and no child care.

A regular customer at the IHOP had been a regular at Luther Bodine's Hacienda when Paloma was working there in her teens. This customer recognized her and offered Paloma meth in exchange for sex. When Paloma refused and dumped the remaining syrup on his pancake plate in his lap, the customer informed the owner of the IHOP of Paloma's past. The owner fired her and banned the customer from the restaurant for a single month. The owner and the customer attended the same church.

Paloma's application for Section 8 housing was denied because of her plea of *nolo contendere* to the prostitution charge. She was informed by the public defender service that it was too late for her to withdraw her plea and dispute the charge.

Then Mildred was diagnosed with ovarian cancer. The cancer was virulent and poor Mildred died within two months of her diagnosis. Cynthia had only her mother to take care of her.

Because she had no driver's license or credit card, Paloma was unable to rent a van or pickup to transport Cynthia and her things to Fort Worth. She nursed her clunker of a car to Walters and back, loading it with clothes and toys until it squatted dangerously low on its already shot suspension. Cynthia had lived more than six years with Mildred and was scared when Paloma had to throw away so many of Cynthia's possessions to make the move. Cynthia was grieving Mildred. Cynthia was quiet and withdrawn. Paloma was direct about her own thoughts and feelings, and was unfamiliar with Cynthia's moods. It was an awkward trip to Fort Worth and a difficult adjustment after they arrived. Paloma had lost her day job at IHOP and had to keep her evening job at the downtown steak house. She was forced to leave Cynthia alone at night in the small apartment in the middle of city of almost a million in population, quite a change from Walters, Oklahoma.

Paloma worried twenty-four hours a day. How would she gain Cynthia's confidence? How would she help Cynthia understand that her only choice had been to leave her at Mildred's for so many years and that she had to go to work at night? How could she make Cynthia feel safe while she was alone during the night? How would Paloma obtain health care for Cynthia? How would she answer Cynthia's inevitable questions about her father? How would she help Cynthia make friends? How could she make ends meet without taking another job and spending even more time way from Cynthia?

The same day that Paloma's old car gave up its ghost, Alicia, Paloma's old friend from school, asked her to share a two-bedroom apartment. Alicia had a child of her own. Her boyfriend had just moved out on her. She needed a roommate to share the monthly rent. Paloma's share would be less than half of what she was paying for her own apartment. And Alicia's place was in a much safer neighborhood than Paloma's.

Alicia worked at a nursing home as a nurse's aide. The home was hiring and conducted its own in-house training program for its new hires. The home was within walking distance of Alicia's apartment. The job paid much less than Paloma made as a waitress. But Paloma's expenses would be cut radically with much reduced rent and no car expenses, and she was now eligible for food stamps for Cynthia and some food through the WIC program. Alicia and Paloma could essentially share a position, with one of them working twelve-hour day shifts four days a week and the other working twelve-hour night shifts on the same dates. Paloma watched Alicia's child and Cynthia during Alicia's shifts and turnabout during Paloma's.

Paloma dedicated every possible hour off work when Cynthia was not in school to be with her. She learned that Cynthia loved silence, so Paloma did not push her to talk. Cynthia delighted in doing chores with Paloma. They cooked together, cleaned together, washed dishes and did laundry together. It was a silent, busy time very well spent. Cynthia loved the Candyland and Chutes and Ladders board games she brought with her from Walters. Paloma was willing to play these games with her whenever Cynthia wanted, no matter how tired Paloma was from her shifts. Cynthia also loved to read. Paloma had only finished eighth grade but she had dealt with her depression and isolation over the years by reading every book she could. Every night Paloma was home they took turns reading aloud to one another. On Saturdays when Paloma was not working, Cynthia and Paloma rode together on the bus to a Half Price Books to buy one paperback for Cynthia, usually a travel book, and one for Paloma, usually a John Grisham or James Patterson novel.

Then Paloma was fired by Mrs. Patterson for the marijuana test.

Paloma was concerned that Alicia would be fired too. While Paloma had merely breathed in some marijuana smoke in the air at the party, Alicia had actually smoked a blunt.

As Paloma was walking away from Ms. Patterson's office, she ran into Alicia. Paloma had just ended her shift when she was told to report to HR. Alicia was beginning hers when she received the same instruction. Paloma told Alicia she had been fired and what was probably about to happen to Alicia.

"I'm not going in," said Alicia. "I'm not going to give them the satisfaction. Just for marijuana? To hell with them. Let's go back to the apartment and get wasted."

"The kids are back there. We can't do that. We need to figure out where we are going to work . . . I feel so stupid. This was such a good deal we had going. Not the first time I have let drugs mess up my life."

"What do you mean?"

"Never mind."

Paloma and Alicia started making phone calls to nursing homes located on bus lines. They discovered that they couldn't duplicate employment sharing a twenty-four-hour-a-day job. They started applying alone for wait-ressing jobs, warehouse jobs, cleaning crew jobs, any job on a bus line. None of them led to employment. Alicia's family members loaned her money to pay her part of the rent and the utilities, but Paloma had no one to help her.

"Don't you have any family to make you a loan?" asked Alicia.

"Never have. Never will," replied Paloma.

Alicia found herself a day job as a cashier at a convenience store in the neighborhood of the apartment. But the income was far less than was needed for the total rent and the utilities. Paloma would have to find a night job so that she and Alicia could continue to stay in that apartment, Cynthia could remain in her school, and Paloma and Alicia could between them provide child care for their children.

Alicia pressured Paloma to contribute her share. Alicia's family members were tapped out. Tension was thick between the two of them. Paloma and Cynthia couldn't sleep from worry.

Then Paloma was arrested and charged with passing bad checks at the local Fiesta food store. She had sweet-talked the assistant manager to accept three checks made out to "cash" for a total of almost five hundred dollars. When it came to light that her bank account was closed for overdrafts, this manager called the police and Paloma was arrested. She could not make bond and sat in jail for nine days. Alicia visited Paloma in jail to tell her they were about to lose their apartment. Alicia and her child were going to live with Alicia's mother. But Cynthia couldn't come with them.

"Don't you know anyone who will take Cynthia in until you can get out of this bad check fix?" Alicia asked her.

Paloma replied again: "Never have. Never will."

"Should I call CPS?" asked Alicia.

For a long time, Paloma sat silently in her cubicle of the jail's visiting room, a thick glass separating her from Alicia, both communicating through telephone receivers. Alicia knew this was a momentous decision for Paloma, so she gave her time to think in silence.

Eventually Paloma said to Alicia, "Here is a number I want you to call. The number belongs to Luther Bodine, if the piece of crap is still alive. Or maybe Angel Bodine. Whichever one of them answers, tell them I am in jail on a bad check charge. Tell them I have a seven-year-old daughter who only I can take care of. Tell them I need to work nights and have my days free. Tell them I want to come back to work nights at The Hacienda. Tell them I need them to make my bail, only 10 percent of the two-thousand-dollar cash bond, and that I will pay them back out of my tips. Ask them to come see me here in jail."

"Why didn't you think of this before you passed the bad checks?"

"Just make the call. I will use my one daily phone call to call you tomorrow at 5:00 p.m. If I haven't heard from them, don't leave me hanging."

It was Angel Bodine who showed up at the jail the next day in the late afternoon.

"Where's Luther?" asked Paloma, controlling her revulsion to Angel.

"I'm running things now. Luther's old and sick. Waddaya want? "

"I need my job back at The Hacienda."

"*Your* job?" Angel sneered.

"I need the same job I was doing before. Only at The Hacienda, not at your house."

"We have too many hostesses now."

"You know how men like me. I haven't lost it. I can see you leering at me right now. You know I'll make you a lot of money."

"You are more damn trouble than you are worth."

"Angel, be a human being for once. I've changed. I have a daughter I have to provide for. I have to work nights. I am not going to run away this time. You can depend upon me this time around."

Angel chewed on his toothpick. "Just how desperate are you for this job?"

"What do you mean? Desperate is desperate."

"What are you prepared to do to *prove* how desperate you are?"

"*What a miserable excuse for a man! Someday someone is going to take him out. Maybe it will be me.*" "What do you want, Angel?"

"I am asking how desperate you are. Desperate enough to spend one night with me in my bed at the house, smoking crystal just one more time? Just one night? A night I will videotape so I know you will never go to the cops?"

"Fuck you, Angel. *Fuck you!*"

"Actually, that's right. Fuck me." he sneered. "Desperate enough to come back to work when I say and where I say? At The Hacienda and at our house? Desperate enough to attract men to our house to buy drugs? And to use with them when they want? Just how desperate are you?" Angel smiled his sweetest, phony smile. "See, you don't know everything that's going on here, Lomie. Your friend . . . what's her name? . . . Alicia . . . that's it. Alicia reached me on the phone, not Luther. And you know what she did? She told me the address of your apartment. And she let me visit there if I would bring her some weed. I met your daughter Cynthia. What a good, pretty girl. Looks like a young you. And what a shame if she were to be picked up by CPS and put in foster care because her mom is a jail bird, a whore with a habit."

"What are you threatening, Angel?"

"Either we make your bond and you spend your first night with me at my house doing whatever I want, or I leave you here and I call the CPS hotline . . . Oh, and if we bond you out and you don't honor the deal I just made you, I call the CPS hotline then, too. In fact, I call CPS whenever you piss me off. So you better keep me happy."

"Does Luther know about this?"

"I told you I am running the show now."

"Why did I trust Alicia? When have I ever been able to trust anyone?" thought Paloma.

"If Jesus' teachings are true, why does God allow so much injustice to continue?"

— October 2004 —

John Levi is twenty-four years old.

"So what brings you in to see me this afternoon?" asked Father Gutierrez.

"Couple things. How much time do you have for me?"

"Maria, please hold my calls," the father called out to his secretary. "All the time you need."

"First thing, I want to talk about your sermon last Sunday."

Father Sergio Gutierrez was the only priest at Saint Jude Catholic Church in the Montopolis neighborhood of Austin, one of the economically poorest areas of the otherwise thriving city. Montopolis was more than 60 percent Hispanic. Maybe half of those were undocumented. Almost every citizen of Montopolis lived below the federal poverty line. Father Sergio was in his late thirties, the son of undocumented immigrants from Mexico. His parents had moved to the Montopolis when Gutierrez was appointed pastor there. The father had started his undergraduate studies at the University of Texas intending to become a lawyer. At the end of his sophomore year he had answered his call to enter the Roman Catholic priesthood and had gone to seminary at Assumption Seminary in San Antonio before continuing his preparations in Boston and Rome. He had been appointed to Saint Jude only two years before. He immediately organized ministries to help his impoverished parishioners with their earthy burdens—a food bank, a clothing bank, and a ministry of microloans. John Levi had been referred to Saint Jude and Father Gutierrez by the senior pastor of the large United Methodist close to the University of Texas campus because of John Levi's desire to combine his training in the law with faithfulness to the teachings of Jesus about the poor. John Levi helped organize a law school–approved *pro bono* legal clinic at Saint Jude and recruited other UT law students to help.

"I have a bunch of questions. Your sermon on Matthew 5, verses 5 and 6. How 'happy are those who are meek, for they shall inherit the earth,' and how 'happy are those who hunger and thirst for justice for they will be satis-fied'? *How* is it that we happy ones who hunger and thirst for justice will be satisfied? Who will satisfy us? God? Or ourselves by achieving justice? And how in the world can we achieve justice by being meek?"

Father Gutierrez usually enjoyed John Levi's questions. They always poured out of John Levi and they kept Gutierrez sharp. On some occasions, he was impatient with the questions. *"Can't he take anything at all on faith? Or on the authority of the Church? This is what I get for encouraging a Prot-estant law student to be a part of the congregation."* But for the most part he enjoyed the conversations with this young man who was using the ana-lytical approach of a lawyer to find a way to walk the Christian walk within his chosen profession. That this young man came from such a privileged, insulated home made the conversations all the more interesting.

"As I preached last Sunday, Jesus is not saying that *achieving* justice is what makes us happy. It is our hungering and thirsting for it that makes us happy, fulfilled people. Jesus' audience really couldn't control whether or when they achieved justice for themselves. And any justice achieved even today is likely to be subjective. One person's justice is likely to be another's injustice. So Jesus' teaching is that the yearning for justice, the hungering and thirsting for the world to be put right by God, makes us happy, satisfied people. I know that is a hard thing for a law student to accept. The practice of law is all about results. So what is the justice for which you have a hunger and thirst?"

"Since I have been providing legal help to the people of Montopolis parish, I have been exposed to so much undeniable injustice. Nothing about this injustice is merely subjective. Landlords who don't care why their ten-ants have fallen behind in their rent or if the tenants have another home to go to when they are evicted. Cheating used car dealers. Payday and title loan companies that exploit the ignorance and need of the poor. Employers who are so intent upon maximizing their profits that they treat their employees like nothing more than costs of doing business. It seems like a rule that the wealthy exploit the poor and powerless. I never knew there was so much of this. And I never cared before."

"And your personal exposure to all this has made you hunger and thirst for an end to these injustices?"

John Levi hesitated. "If Jesus' teachings are true, why does God allow so much injustice to continue and for so many poor people to be exploited? If the teachings aren't true, why am I devoting so much time to a legal clinic in a church? And why am I so unhappy at all this injustice? When can I expect to start feeling happy?"

"A true hunger and thirst for justice comes from the center of our beings. Not just a passing preference or a wish. But a constant *hunger*. An abiding *thirst*. Like the hunger and thirst for God. A need for what you cannot do without. That is much of what Jesus is describing here. Not so much an order to his disciples to hunger and thirst. How could anyone obey such an order if that hunger is not there in the center of his or her character? You either have that hunger and thirst or you do not. This is Jesus' description of the way members of the kingdom feel. Do you think the Jesus could be right about this?"

"I never thought about it that way. I don't know."

"So where else besides this parish did this hunger and thirst come from for you? Did you grow up with it?"

"No such hunger and thirst for justice in my home. Or my school. Or among my friends. There was a preacher—a great preacher really—I grew up listening to, Dr. Graham Forster. He proclaimed a passion for social justice from the pulpit."

"Did he live out that passion?"

"He preached it."

"That's not enough. Did he live for the poor? Was their struggle his struggle?"

"No. It was something he advocated."

"Then was this a true passion? A true hunger and a thirst for something this Dr. Forster could not live without? Or was his an ideal only?"

"I see your point."

"This hunger and thirst growing in you comes through your encounters with the endless injustices that the poor suffer. But realize that not everyone who is exposed to these injustices comes away with such a hunger and thirst. I think that God is the reason that these encounters are causing your hunger and thirst. God is the difference for you. In the Parable of the Good Samaritan, two very religious men walked by the man lying beaten in the road. Only the Samaritan stopped. He stopped because God had put it in his heart to stop and to hunger and thirst for justice for this poor man who had been treated so unjustly by the robbers. Are you becoming like that?"

"You mean that I cannot *not* hunger and thirst? That I cannot walk by?"

"Yes."

"That's a little scary."

"It should be scary. Being possessed by the hunger and thirst for justice is frightening. But then again, what would you prefer to possess you?"

"I don't know."

"In my experience, some *personal* experience of injustice is needed to get the dissatisfaction out of the front of someone's mind as an idea and under their skin as a hunger. For me, it was the personal experience of poverty and injustice toward me and my parents and family when I was growing up. My parents came to this country without documents when I was three years old. They stayed despite all the indignities to give a better life to their children. They are hard-working, community-minded people, an asset to any neighborhood. They have been *neighbors* to people around them. But they have been taken advantage and demonized and belittled by some at every turn of their lives here. My hunger and thirst for justice started at my mother's breast. But you . . ."

"My life has been just the opposite. I never wanted for anything. No, that's not true. I wanted for meaning in my life—and passion. How can anyone be passionate about accumulating even more money and stuff? I think I went into drama because of the roles I could play of men who were passionate about something. That's what originally attracted me to Jesus. His passion."q —] I don't mean the passion of Holy Week. I mean his passion for the kingdom. His passion to rescue the poor from their plights."

"Was there some story you encountered, some specific story of injustice that got under your skin?"

"There was this family I represented through the legal clinic near UT law school. I really got close to them. I had enrolled in the UT law clinic because I wanted a few pass-fail academic credits. But the stories of the people who needed legal help and had nowhere else to turn changed my view of the world."

"Tell me the story of this family."

"A married couple with four children. One of the children is severely autistic, and another has microcephaly and will never develop beyond a three-year-old's mental capacity. Can't swallow well, so always at risk for pneumonia. The mother can't work outside the home because she needs to care for these two children 24-7. So the other two children don't get the attention from the parents that they hunger and thirst for. The father is a truck driver. Owned his own rig and contracted for a percentage of his load. Had to be gone on trips for long periods. The longer he was gone, the more money he brought home. But he was really needed at home when the child with microcephaly developed severe pneumonia. He had to take a break from hauling loads for the trucking company. The company gave his slot to another driver. He had no income for an extended period. So he got a loan from a title loan company. He had to put up his rig for collateral. Outrageous interest rates. The title loan company could only get away with charging this exorbitant rate because of the need of this family and the statute passed by our legislature. The minute he was late on a payment, this company seized his rig, even though the rig was worth thousands of dollars more than the principal on the loan."

"Were you able to help?"

"Kinda. I obtained an injunction against the seizure, and they had to return the rig. But he still had to pay off the loan, including the accumulated interest charges."

"So he still owed?"

"No. Look, I was stupid. I was so taken over by this family. They invited me to their house for supper twice. They were doing everything right, everything they could, and were still at the mercy of this heartless company and this terrible loan contract. Their need and their love for one another melted my heart."

"Okay. But how were you stupid?"

"I couldn't let them stay under that debt. I just couldn't. So I sold my BMW and paid their debt off."

"You didn't."

"Yeah, I did."

"Wow. I am impressed, John Levi. God is good."

"Well, my parents weren't impressed."

"I'll bet."

"They bought me that BMW when I started law school. It was the second one they had bought me. It had every possible accessory. It was a sweet car. I avoided telling them I sold it for as long as I could. But a friend of mine at law school told her parents and they told mine. I should have told my parents about it at the start. I bought an old Jeep for basic transportation from part of the proceeds of the sale of the Beamer. I was going to have to go home in that Jeep someday."

"Were you honest with your parents about why you sold the BMW?"

"Eventually. But that isn't to my credit. The details had already gotten back to them."

"How did they take it?"

"Like I was ungrateful. Like I was trying to make a political statement. Like I was turning their back on them and their ways. They said it was embarrassing for them with their friends. My mom cried and my dad got angry, as usual. My dad said what I had done was like spitting in his face."

"How did you respond?"

"I asked him if the car was *my* private property or not. He is such a believer that owners of private property have the right to do with their property whatever they will. I really got him where he lives with that question. Father Gutierrez, I am not trying to defend my parents. But they are so insulated from the poor. They don't know the stories of any poor people. The poor are just caricatures to them. They are afraid of the poor. The ideology of wealth has them totally in its power."

"How did your classmates react?"

"I got a whole new set of friends. My old friends thought I was a fool and made fun of me, but my new friends thought that what I had done was admirable."

"What did you think?"

"I go with fool. But it sure made me feel good to help that family. Maybe the most selfish thing I have ever done."

"As in, 'Happy are those who hunger and thirst for justice, for they will be satisfied'?"

"Oh my God! Father, it was right there in front of me! How amazing. That Jesus . . ."

Father Gutierrez gave John Levi a moment. "Do you want to stop?"

"Not if you have more time for me."

"Plenty of time for you, John Levi. I am getting as much out of this conversation as you."

"You preached an entire series on the Psalms. It was great, Father. Opened my eyes. What yearning for God's justice in so many Psalms. But the Psalms raise a lot of questions for me. A major premise of them is that there is a third party involved in every encounter between the unjust powerful person and the impotent victim. And that third party is God. The oppressor wants to deny that. But the psalmist says God *is* there. So one day, and one day soon, the oppressor is going to get his. Justice is going to be done in favor of the powerless. Like in Psalm 37."

Father Gutierrez took out his Bible, opened it to Psalm 37, and slid it across the desk to John Levi. "Show me what you are talking about."

"Here it is. Verses 7 through 10. 'Be still before the LORD, and wait patiently for him; do not fret over those who prosper in their way, over those who carry out evil devices. Refrain from anger and forsake wrath. Do not fret—it leads only to evil. For the wicked shall be cut off, but those who wait for the LORD shall inherit the land. Yet a little while and the wicked shall be no more; though you look diligently for their place, they will not be there.'"

"And?" asked Father Gutierrez.

"And the oppressors are still here. They do *not* get justice. A lot of people get rich screwing the poor. And they die fat and happy in bed. The premise of the Psalms seems untrue to me, especially in this parish."

"The Church teaches that God will mete out justice at the Last Judgment."

"So is that when those who hunger and thirst for justice will be satisfied? At the final judgment but not before? Is the Last Judgment coming in 'a little while' as this Psalm says?"

"Are you familiar with Dr. King's paraphrase of Theodore Parker, the nineteenth-century abolitionist? 'The arc of the moral universe is long, but it bends toward justice'?"

"So all of life is random and unjust in the interim? I mean, do we hunger and thirst for justice more than God does? Being born into a rich home meant that I never encountered a problem that my parents' wealth could not fix. Except the problem of a meaningless life. But I see children in this parish who, through no fault of theirs or their parents, must learn only to endure their problems, because there is no fix."

"And you hunger and thirst for that not to be so?"

"Yes. But does God? If God does, then why doesn't God fix it?"

"I don't know. When you get an answer to that question, let me know. Do you doubt that you are happier now that you have experienced the suffering of the poor' and hunger and thirst for it not to be so, than you were when you were growing up in a home insulated from the injustice of the world?"

"I am happier now—and sadder."

"And that hunger and thirst for justice, the happiness and sadness that comes with it, can result in your ending a lot of injustice in the world as a lawyer. Another beatitude of Jesus is, 'Happy are those who mourn, for they will be comforted.' I believe that the mourning Jesus is talking about in that saying is the mourning for the brokenness and injustice in the world. You are mourning this injustice. Do not give up hope that you and the victims of the random injustice will one day be comforted."

"Whatever that means," replied John Levi.

"The promise of Jesus is that one day we will know what that means. In the meantime, the human community seems to be divided between those who hunger and thirst for a justice that is not yet present and those who are happy with the way things are now in their favor, between those who mourn the way the world is for the poor and those who don't give the poor a thought. What I think Jesus is saying in these teachings is, 'Truly happy are those who care about people who are suffering, and truly unhappy are those who do not care.'"

"That brings me to the second point I need to talk to you about. Have time?"

"What's that?"

"My career path in the law was all set. I didn't suffer the *angst* of most law students about their futures. Until now."

"Why's that?"

"My dad is an owner of an oil well service company based in Fort Worth. My future was all decided for me . . . by him. I was going to college, major in business, or if his wildest dream came true, petroleum engineering. Then his plan was for me to come back to Fort Worth and eventually take over the company while he rode into the sunset on his golf cart."

"Doesn't sound like the John Levi I know."

"He and my mom hated that I was into theatre. 'Childish,' he said. 'Irresponsible.' So when I decided I wanted to go to law school, he modified his plan for me. He would pay for law school and I would concentrate on business law and oil-and-gas law. Upon graduation I would join the big establishment law firm in Fort Worth that has handled my father's legal affairs for decades. I would start with my own major client—my father's company. Eventually, I would take over his company and he would . . ."

"Ride into the sunset on his golf cart?"

"Exactly. He had threatened to refuse to pay for my undergraduate education when I majored in theatre, but my mom turned that around. Then he threatened that he wouldn't pay for my law school until he came up with this second plan. If he had known that I was spending so much of my time in our legal clinic here, he'd probably already have threatened to withhold the money again."

"And now your hunger and thirst for justice is preventing you from following the plan."

"I have decided to accept a job at graduation from a plaintiff's personal injury firm in Fort Worth, representing plaintiffs in workers' compensation, industrial injury, and product liability suits. So I have decided to drop the corporate and oil-and-gas law courses and concentrate on civil litigation courses. I have already arranged for loans to get me through this last year of law school without his money."

"So what are you asking me?

"Do you feel I am doing the right thing?"

"John Levi, that is not for me to say. That is for you to say. Let me ask you this. How did you *feel* when you were on track to follow your father's plan?"

"Bored. Resigned. Trapped. Angry . . . In that order."

"How do you feel now?"

"Excited. Energized. At peace."

"There is your answer. One more question. Have you prayed about this?"

"Prayed what?"

"O Lord, show me the path you want me to take."

"That's scary too. What if it were to come to me that God wants me leave the law altogether and volunteer full-time at Saint Jude?"

"My point is that you need to develop a prayer relationship with God. But it sounds to me that God has already answered the prayer you didn't pray."

"How's that?"

"You said you feel 'excited, energized, and at peace.' That's how I felt when I decided to leave law school and prepare for the priesthood. Is 'excited, energized, and at peace' the same as being 'happy'?"

"Yes, Father. I think you are on to something there."

"Your mommy is not going to let your father cut you off. Not her little boy. That's one of those injustices of life in your favor. Accept it and use it for the good of others."

CHAPTER FIFTEEN

"If I am used up, who used me up, you bastard?"

— Saturday, September 19, 2017, 9:00 p.m. —

Paloma is thirty years old.

"What do you mean I can't come in?" Paloma demanded. When Paloma had tried to enter The Hacienda club from the bar, the bouncer had stopped her. "Seth, let me in."

"Angel says you can't come in tonight."

"Why not?"

"He didn't tell me why. You just can't."

"Is he here?"

"He told me not to tell you."

"Get him, Seth. Tell him to come here now, or I am going to call a cop."

"Don't think you want me to tell him you said that."

"Just get him."

"Can't. I am afraid to lose my job. You know how mean Angel can be."

"Seth, do you remember when you and your family all had the flu last winter? And I cooked and brought food to your house for a week?"

Seth nodded.

"And Angel threatened to fire you if you didn't come to work, even when you were throwing up out your eyeballs? He didn't care about you and he didn't care about the customers who would get sick because you were catching? Remember all that?"

"Yes."

"So are you going to do what I ask?"

Seth closed the door to the club while he went to plead with Angel.

When Angel bonded Paloma out of jail six years before, Paloma was indeed desperate to keep Cynthia with her. So she worked when and where Angel said. There were times when she begged Luther to protect her, but Angel was running the operation. She had to work more nights than she wanted, and she had to work at both The Hacienda and the house. She threatened to quit when she was worn out from the sex and the meth. There were periods when she refused to work for Angel at all. But then her money would run out and she had to return because the work made her much more money than she could make elsewhere.

Despite the sexual abuse and her meth addiction, Paloma had become a very attractive woman and *the* attraction at the club and the house, much in demand by the Bodines' high-rolling patrons. She was taken by some of these high rollers to Vegas, New Orleans, and the Bahamas for weekends of gambling, gluttony, drunkenness, drugs, and lust. These men paid the Bodines a fee for the money they lost because of Paloma's absences. These rollers paid Paloma generously. She made enough money to afford her own modest apartment, her own car, and child care, private flute lessons, and counseling for Cynthia. She was able to get meth without having to pay money at the Bodine club and house. And she was able to keep her sexual favors to the men at the Bodine house from being automatically required. When her meth use became so frequent that her resistance to Angel's most degrading demands weakened, she would disappear from work. Then Angel and even Luther would threaten to end the relationship with her for good. But Paloma made them too much money for them to follow through on their threats. And she had always came back to work for them for the money and the drug.

But as Paloma aged into her late twenties, she became less in demand. Her competitors for the attention of the customers were newly recruited teenage girls. So Paloma made much less money. When Paloma turned thirty years of age, Angel began reducing Paloma's shifts at The Hacienda. She had once worked at least six nights weekly in her teens and twenties, but the number of her shifts precipitously decreased. There were long periods when she could only work as a sexual magnet at the house and lost the easier tip income from the club.

Cynthia reached her teens and began to battle serious depression and an eating disorder. When Cynthia began to cut herself, Paloma would sometimes refuse Angel's demand to work so she could be home with Cynthia. But Cynthia's cutting increased Paloma's depression, causing her hunger for meth to increase. So when she needed to be home with Cynthia she needed meth even more. When Paloma told Angel and Luther that she needed to miss work because of her daughter's depression, Angel suggested that Paloma start Cynthia on weed and meth. Paloma would never again make the mistake of appealing to Angel's or Luther's humanity.

Paloma's shifts were reduced so much and she had to miss her assigned shifts so often that she faced eviction from her apartment and repossession of her car. She picked up a bad check charge and was placed on probation again after she made restitution. She had to clean houses during the day to supplement her income. She applied for work on the assembly line of a company that refurbished cell phones. She worked a few shifts as a waitress at a Tex-Mex restaurant. She still fell into a deeper financial hole.

As spotty as her work had become with the Bodines, she had always been able to rely on a shift at The Hacienda club on Saturday nights. So she was shocked and angry when she showed up for work that Saturday only to be told by Seth that Angel had forbidden her entry into the club. She had made the Bodines too much money to be treated like trash and discarded now that she was thirty and used up.

Seth came back from looking for Angel. "Angel said to go into the office behind the bar and wait for him."

"Why can't I go talk to him in the club? Why do I have to wait out here?"

"Paloma, I don't know. I am just bringing you the message. I can't let you in the club. Luis will unlock the office door for you."

Paloma walked behind the bar and into the tiny office after the bartender unlocked it for her. She sat in the dark office, lit only by a fish aquarium, for more than thirty minutes until Angel walked in.

"You tryna' get Seth fired?" Angel sneered.

"I'm trying to work my shift here. You know how much I need the money, Angel."

"*Your* shift? *I* decide who works shifts here and you ain't working tonight."

"Why not? I always work Saturday nights."

"Yeah, unless you decide you don't want to work. You need to learn that I decide when you work, not you."

"How much money have I made you and your father over the years?"

"'Made' is right. You are over the hill, Lomie. Nothing worse than a used-up, over-the-hill, junkie whore."

"If I am used up, who used me up, you bastard?"

"Me and about a thousand other guys."

"Angel, just let me work this shift. I *need* the shift. My daughter and I are about to be evicted. I've got nowhere else to put her."

"Well, boo-freaking-hoo. Not my problem."

"You know I can make you money tonight. Who is working instead of me?"

"We have two new, sweet little teenage girls working their first shifts tonight. Just came from Bonitas Chiquitas. Remember when you started here at—what was it?—thirteen?"

"Fourteen."

"Whatever. When you started here at fourteen, you yourself took some used-up, over-the-hill junkie's shifts. You remember that. The wheel spins."

It occurred to Paloma that maybe she *was* all used up and over the hill. And it occurred as well that the real reason she wanted to work tonight was to get into the back room of the club and get a lung full of meth. She had child care for Cynthia all taken care of until tomorrow morning. She hungered for a night's escape.

"What about at your house when the club closes? Can you use me there?"

"You dyin' for meth, Lomie? Is that what this is about?"

"Angel, don't make me beg."

"Have I come to this?" She thought. *"I am begging the biggest asshole God ever suffered to live to let me be used by strangers for meth."*

Angel began to laugh. "Look how you are shaking and sweating, Lomie. There's not a man alive who would pay to screw a junkie like you tonight."

Luther walked in the door of the office. He had been listening over an intercom to the conversation.

"I have a deal for you, Lomie," said Luther. "For old time's sake. We will let you work at the club tonight and every Saturday night for tips only. But you also have to work at the house whenever we call you."

Angel growled, "I thought that I am running things now."

"You are running things as long as I let you," replied Luther.

"For tips and meth only? Nothing for the sex?" asked Paloma.

"I will throw in something else. Since you won't be able to stay in your apartment, I have a house I can let you live in so long as you hostess at the club on Saturdays and perform your usual services at our house whenever we call you. So house, tips, meth, and weed for your services."

"Where is the house?"

"On Irion. Not far at all from your daddy's old house."

"Can I see it first?"

"Take it or leave it now, *puta*," said Angel.

"A neighbor like what?
Like in the Bible?"

— 2008 —

John Levi is twenty-eight years old.

"Why in God's name do you propose that we waive our legal fee? I've never done that in my entire forty-eight-year career."

"We have to waive our fee to be able to get this kid the minimum of what he needs to live."

"This is that oil field explosion case?"

"Yes."

"Take me through it again."

John Levi was a junior partner to James Hennigan, one of the best-known plaintiff's personal injury lawyers in Texas. John Levi had been with Hennigan since he passed the Texas bar in 2005. Hennigan led an obsessively extravagant lifestyle. He once told John Levi that his hobby was to sample the cuisine on first-class flights to Europe and back. His favorite cuisine was the curry on Air India. But his profligate ways meant that he never had any money saved, was always in the IRS bull's-eye, and had to keep taking in money endlessly. He was in his late sixties, obese, and in poor health from drinking and eating to excess. Because of his history and reputation, he was still able to attract high-dollar plaintiff suits. But he then turned them over to John Levi to do all the work. This was a valuable arrangement for John Levi because he was able to work early in his career on big, challenging lawsuits against excellent defense attorneys. John Levi received 25 percent of every legal fee he brought in by settlement or trial verdict.

"His name is Dub Taliaferro. He is a good ole boy from Olney, Texas. Never finished high school. Went to work to help feed his widowed mother at age fourteen."

Hennigan smirked. "Is this a lawsuit or a Dickens novel?"

"What are you smiling at? This kid is terribly hurt," asked John Levi.

"Mind your mouth, young man. I'll smile when I want to. Go on."

"Dub worked for a fly-by-night oil pipe recovery company. They contract to recover old production pipe out of wells that are no longer producing."

"How?"

"To pull the pipe out of the hole, it has to be separated from the bottom of the pipe string cemented to the bottom of the hole. They use what they call a 'gun,' which is actually a kind of bomb. The gun is lowered by electrical wire into the bottom of the pipe hundreds of feet below the surface and exploded by an electrical current. This breaks apart the string at the bottom. Then they pull up the pipe string and unscrew the forty-foot lengths one at a time for reuse in another well."

"So did Dub work on the rig floor?"

"No. All he did was to drive the truck that delivered the gun to the site. He got to the location before anyone else, took the bomb out of the back of his truck, and put it on the tailgate. His employer had already hooked it up by a long length of electrical wire to a generator in his truck. Dub lay down in the seat of his truck to wait for the salvage crew to arrive. When they drove up, Dub got out of his truck and walked around to the rear to where the bomb was. Then . . . it just blew up."

"Oh my God. How close was he?"

"Maybe four feet."

"How did he even survive?"

"I'd call it a miracle except for how badly he was hurt. Both eyeballs were blown out of his skull. Four fingers of his right hand and most of his right chest muscle were blown away. He suffered second-degree burns over his entire right side."

"Did his employer have workers' compensation coverage?"

"Of course."

"So his medical bills have all been paid for."

"Yes."

"How much so far?"

"Over six hundred thousand dollars and counting."

"And he gets a piddling amount of monthly benefits from the insurance, just because he was injured on the job?"

"Yes."

"And to get any other damages, we have to prove that someone else besides the employer was at fault."

"Yes. Since Dub's employer had workers' compensation insurance and Dub didn't die, we can't sue the employer. But even if we are able to prove that the manufacturer of the gun is liable, the workers' compensation insurance carrier gets reimbursed for the medical bills off the top of our recovery. And if we stick to the contract we have with Dub, we also get 40 percent of the total recovery. So, let's say that we can prove that the manufacturer of the gun is liable because of some defect. If we recover two million in damages, and we take 40 percent of that total for our fees after subtracting our litigation expenses, his recovery is down to close to one million because of our expenses. Then if the workers comp insurance carrier takes its six hundred thousand for reimbursement of the medical bills it paid, Dub is down to four hundred thousand dollars. And then the insurance carrier doesn't have to pay a penny more in medical bills until he has paid four hundred thousand in new bills himself.

"So we just have to get him a lot more than two million dollars. Shouldn't be that hard with his lost income, future expenses for his daily care, pain and suffering."

John Levi ignored Mr. Hennigan's use of "we."

"Mr. Hennigan," John Levi took a deep breath, "the evidence of liability is not enough to get us before a jury. The judge will likely dismiss the case before we get that far."

"Why?"

"The Occupational Safety and Health Administration investigators determined that the gun was detonated by a radio signal from an Air Force jet flying out of Dyess Air Force Base in Abilene. OSHA investigators also determined that this signal was capable of causing the detonation because some of the control components of the bomb had corroded."

"So the potential for corrosion is a design defect in the manufacturing process. And the lack of warning to the employer of the potential for corrosion is a marketing defect. We just need to get a testifying expert to swear to the defects, so we can avoid a motion for summary judgment. When we get to a jury, jury sympathy will get us a big verdict."

"Who is the manufacturer?" asked John Levi.

"How should I know? That's your job."

"Then maybe you could give me some advice about this. The bomb was blown to smithereens. OSHA couldn't gather enough fragments to identify the manufacturer. We do know from Dub's employer that the bomb was really old. It had sat in their shed for more than a decade, exposed to water dripping through the roof. This employer has no records of where it got the bomb or who manufactured it. Who do we sue?"

"Then why are you asking me to agree to waive our fee? Doesn't sound like there will be a fee."

"I was able to find an engineer in Cleveland who was so moved by Dub's injuries that he gave me a report that the bomb 'had to have been' manufactured by a company out of Houston that used a chemical component that was susceptible to degradation. So I sued that manufacturer and it is now the defendant in our suit."

"Well there you go. Good work."

"Not a 'go.' This expert gave me the report to try to help Dub get a settlement, with the understanding that the expert would never testify at deposition or trial."

"Again, why are you talking about our waiving our fee?"

"I've worked out a tentative arrangement with the lawyer for the manufacturer and with the lawyer for the workers' compensation carrier. I took them to see Dub and they were really moved by his condition and situation."

"Defense lawyers moved by pity for a plaintiff? Never heard of such a thing."

"Really?" asked John Levi. "Never? You've never been moved by pity for a client?"

"Not enough to waive my fee."

John Levi frowned.

"Who do you think you are frowning at?" said Hennigan. "Clients are not our friends. They are just parties with us in a contract. Under the contract, we obtain them money and we get a percentage. Contracts are legally binding under the law, and the law, young man, is sacred. We are warriors of the law, not warriors of pity. It would be an injustice to waive a fee for any reason, including out of pity. If word got around that I had waived a fee, other parties to my contracts would ask me to do the same thing. There would be no end to it. I earned a fee in this case because of the work done by me over the years that caused Dub's case to come to me. John Levi, listen to me. You can't let yourself get so personally involved with someone who is merely a party to a contract with us."

John Levi stared at Mr. Hennigan coldly. "The two reasons the manufacturer may be willing to pay us something is, first, pity for Dub, and, second, because I said I would ask you to waive any fee. If you insist on a fee, they won't pay anything."

"You had no right to do that."

"I didn't have the right to say I would ask you?"

"Now you make me out to be the bad guy."

"Unless you do the right thing."

"I am going to ignore you said that . . . for now," he said ominously. "What will keep the workers' compensation carrier from exercising its right to take the money paid by this manufacturer as reimbursement for the medical bills they have already paid?"

"If we waive our fee—I say 'if'—the manufacturer will pay enough money to buy an annuity that pays Dub six thousand dollars a month tax free for the rest of his life, and the workers' comp insurance company will waive its right to claim any of that money for past medical expenses or to stop paying Dub's future medical bills."

Hennigan's mouth dropped open onto his double chin. "Why would they do such a damned fool thing?"

"Because it's the right thing to do, Mr. Hennigan."

"Bullshit. They are willing to pay something because of what kind of lawyer I have been." He blinked. "What kind of lawyer I *am*. And because of the cost to their clients to defend our suit. Wait a minute. You aren't telling me something. Have you made a side deal to get the fee all to yourself?"

John Levi had become increasingly resentful of his absent senior partner's ways. He wanted to tell him where he could put this partnership. But then what would happen to Dub and to his own goal of becoming a famous trial lawyer? He took a deep breath. "Mr. Hennigan. I am a young man in life and in the law. I respect your experience and all that you have accomplished. I am grateful for the opportunity you have given me. I am not a man who would even consider such ingratitude and dishonesty. And I think that if you agree to this most generous arrangement, your reputation among lawyers will be even more legendary. This will lead to even more cases being referred to you."

Color rose in James Hennigan's face. Who was this youngster to be speaking to him like this? But this youngster had already proven to be a naturally talented trial lawyer. Hennigan counted on making a lot of money off John Levi without having to do any work himself. He no longer had the energy or interest to try lawsuits. He had been a real warhorse of a trial lawyer. But his wars were over.

"Maybe there is something to what you say. But you should have consulted me before you got so deep into this discussion. A little humility is a good thing in a young lawyer," lectured Hennigan. "Let's both simmer down and think about this. Do the other lawyers have to have an answer today?"

"No. We have the weekend."

"Then let's both take the weekend. I'll see you back here on Monday for lunch." Mr. Hennigan never came to the office earlier than lunchtime. At lunch at his club he drank a martini or two and then went home.

John Levi decided that he wanted to attend Father Gutierrez's worship service in Austin. After a sleepless night with the image of Dub's wounds in his mind, his eyeless face and fingerless hand and burn scars, John Levi was on the road by 5:15 a.m. But he ran into traffic north of Austin and was only able to walk into the sanctuary as the Father was beginning his homily. By pure coincidence Gutierrez preached on the Parable of the Good Samaritan from the tenth chapter of Luke's Gospel.

The Father began with the background of the question the Jewish Torah expert asked Jesus about the verse in Leviticus, "You shall love your neighbor as yourself."

"'Just who *is* the neighbor we are required to love?' asked this lawyer of Jesus. The question is urgent to those of us who aspire to live by Jesus' teachings because 'love' in the Bile is never just a feeling. Love is always found in actions of generous mercy. So like the lawyer, we ask Jesus the identities of these neighbors who are to receive our acts of merciful love," Gutierrez said.

Gutierrez continued, "In our secular culture we think of love as a personal option, not a legal obligation. Who and how we act mercifully is up to us. Failure to act mercifully could never be the cause of legal punishment unless we have some special relationship with the person needing our love and mercy, such as our child. The victim in need of loving mercy in Jesus' parable was a stranger to the Samaritan. In our legal system, our only obligation to a stranger is not to harm him or her wrongfully. We have no positive duty to help such a stranger. Not so, says Jesus in this parable, for those who would be members of the kingdom of heaven."

Gutierrez preached, "Jesus tells us nothing in the parable about whether the victim deserves the Samaritan's mercy. All Jesus tells us is that the victim is in need and lying on the road which the Samaritan walks. So the lesson to us is that we are not only to love people whom we decide are blameless, people whom we decide are not responsible for their own plight, or people whose conduct we approve of. The neighbor, says Jesus, is anyone in need whom we find in our path. Anyone."

He continued, "Remember the first question of the lawyer—'What must I do to inherit eternal life?' The central lesson of Jesus' parable is that mercy to persons in need is *the* requirement to obtain eternal life—not belief in proper dogma, not membership in the church, not faithful receipt of the sacraments, not contribution to the budget of the church. Mercy to whomever is in need and in our path, regardless of whether they are in our family or group or whether we approve of their conduct, is our first calling. As our Lord said on another occasion, recorded in Matthew's Gospel, 'Happy are those who are merciful, for they will receive mercy.'"

"You may ask, 'How can I show this loving mercy to *every* person in need who is in my path? I have limited resources. I have family and others who depend upon me.' This is a valid question. In the parable this Samaritan had the resources to bandage the victim's wounds, a donkey at hand to carry the victim, and the money to pay for his room and board. We do not know what other persons depended upon the Samaritan. What we do know is that the Samaritan used his resources at hand for the victim without excuse. He did not see the victim's plight and say merely, 'My thoughts and prayers are with you' and walk on by. Instead he stopped and loved this stranger in need with the resources he had available."

Father Gutierrez paused and smiled again at his congregation. "I can hear our Lord saying to us now, 'Go and do likewise. Use generously the resources at hand to help those in need in your path.'"

John Levi was unsettled that he had happened upon this sermon on the Parable of the Good Samaritan much in the way the Samaritan had happened upon the man in need. John Levi had driven to Austin to Father Gutierrez's service on a whim and because he had been unable to sleep Saturday night. He had no foreknowledge that the sermon would have this parable as its scripture. And the Father could not have known the situation that John Levi was in about Dub and Hennigan. "*So what resources do Hennigan and I have at our disposal to act with loving mercy toward Dub?*" thought John Levi. "*Unlike the Samaritan and the injured man on the road, Hennigan and I do have a relationship with Dub. What excuse could we have not to help him with the resources we have at hand?*"

John Levi approached Father Gutierrez as he stood in the exit door greeting his parishioners as they left the service. When the father saw John Levi, he cried out and hugged him. "So good to see you! What brings you here? I wish you had given me warning." Gutierrez looked into John Levi's face and saw that something was wrong. "I have a few minutes before the next service. Please come into my study."

Gutierrez sat John Levi in one easy chair as the father sat in another one. "Tell me," he said.

John Levi told the father about Dub Taliaferro, the lawsuit, what he wanted to do for Dub with the settlement, the proposed waiver of the legal fee, and Hennigan's reaction. John Levi applied Gutierrez's morning sermon and Jesus' parable to John Levi's and James Hennigan's obligations to Dub.

"I take it that Mr. Hennigan has no interest in following the teachings of Jesus."

"I am sure he would say that the teachings have no application to law practice. I also doubt that he has any interest in those teachings in his private life."

"Do you have the power to make him do what you want?" asked Gutierrez

"It's complicated."

"I thought you'd say 'no.' How do you mean 'complicated'?"

"I don't have the power to force him directly to agree to the arrangement I discussed. Indirectly, I can threaten to quit if he doesn't agree. He is too obese, drunk, and lazy to try the lawsuit himself. He would have to find some other young lawyer to replace me fast. If we don't go through with this arrangement, the manufacturer will file a motion to dismiss right away, and we won't even get the case to a jury."

"So I am hearing that you have no chance to win this suit. And if you lose, you and your boss receive no fee. But the agreement you made will get Dub some money without winning it. And you receive no fee from that."

"That's right."

"Then why in the world won't Hennigan agree?"

"He might. Or he might think that if he pushes me to keep working the case, we can get more money. But to do that I have to find a whore of an expert to make up a liability theory that will survive a motion to dismiss. I don't even think we can prove which company manufactured the bomb. I have looked for such a whore. It turned my stomach but I have looked all over the country."

"It sounds as of you and this Hennigan are not a good match. Have you thought about working for someone else?"

"You bet I have. But that won't help Dub. He signed the contract with Hennigan, not with me. If I quit Hennigan, Dub probably must stay with Hennigan. There goes the chance to help Dub with the settlement I worked out. So I need to persuade Hennigan to accept this settlement arrangement."

"I know you to be very persuasive. Surely, he will come around."

"I hope so."

"Then why are you so troubled?"

"Okay, this is what is really bothering me, Father. For all his present . . . shortcomings, James Hennigan has this once-earned but now-undeserved reputation as a plaintiff's trial lawyer. That means he gets a lot of what we call 'looks' at a lot of potential lawsuits referred by other lawyers. The lawyers sign up the client and then refer the case to Hennigan to try. Hennigan still gets his choice of big suits. When he accepts a case, he gives it to me to try. I am still new in the law. On my own I could never, ever get the chance to handle such important cases so early in my career. I couldn't sleep last night worrying about Dub *and* worrying that I have burned my bridges with Hennigan by the way I talked to him. I was self-righteous and condescending. Even if Hennigan accepts my recommendation on this case, I am afraid I am on my way out the door. There goes my chance to make a name for myself so early in my career. I need to learn to keep my mouth shut more often."

"So you put Dub's welfare over your ambition. Are you regretting that now?"

"Father, there is one more thing. I admitted to myself last night that one of the reasons that I worked out this settlement was that I didn't want to be the one to lose the lawsuit if I couldn't get it settled."

"John Levi, Give yourself a break. That's what plaintiff's lawyers do, isn't it? They work up their case and then settle it for what they can get if the proof isn't there. The difference here is you are offering to waive your legal fee."

"But it isn't just because of Dub's need that I want to help Dub. It is partly because of my fear of losing. I couldn't have gotten the insurance carrier and the manufacturer to consider settlement if I hadn't broken the ice by offering to give up the fee. This is no way to develop a reputation as a kick-ass trial lawyer."

"You are critical of yourself because you had mixed motives, some out of concern for yourself and some out of concern for Dub."

"I guess so. Actually, I'm afraid it is all out of concern for myself. "

"That's not what I am hearing, John Levi . . . I have to go lead the 11:00 a.m. service. If you want to stay, I can take you to lunch, and we can talk this out some more."

"I need to get back, Father. I am so grateful for your time."

"I want to leave you with this for your drive back to Fort Worth. You have always been so taken with our Lord's Beatitudes. In one he says, 'Happy are those who are pure in heart, for they shall see God.' You remember that one?"

"Of course."

"Of course you do. I am hearing that it bothers you because you have mixed motives in wanting to do the right thing for Dub."

"Yes."

"So you are not 'happy' because you are not 'pure' in heart. You are mixed in heart. And that bothers you."

"Yes, I am bothered."

"Think about this, John Levi. We humans are only very rarely without mixed motives in doing the right thing. We are rarely 'pure in heart.' But our Lord didn't say that we are *only* happy when we are pure in heart. That would mean that we are almost never happy. So my advice to you is to be happy that you are trying to do the right thing to help this poor young man regardless of your mixed motives. Almost all of the good that we humans do in this world is with a mixed heart. So be happy on your drive home. And let me know how this turns out."

John Levi worked the next morning in his office on the watch for James Hennigan to come in to the office. When he saw Hennigan walk by at 11:30, John Levi followed him to his office. "Mr. Hennigan, sir, I wonder if we can talk about this oil field explosion case now rather than at lunch. I have an oral deposition in Dallas at 1:00 p.m. and I have to leave soon.

Hennigan walked to the chair behind his desk, sat down, and pulled out a pack of French-manufactured cigarettes. "Come on in."

John Levi sat in one of the stuffed leather chairs in front of Hennigan's ornate, carved mahogany desk. "I want to apologize for going so far in these discussions with the other side without getting your approval first. It will never happen again."

Henniga, swiveled his chair so he was looking out his window and away from John Levi, said, "I am relieved to hear you say so."

"Second, if you are still having any misgivings about waiving our fee under the arrangement I have explored with the other side, would you consider coming with me tomorrow to meet Dub and see his condition?"

Hennigan swiveled back to face John Levi. He took a long draw on his cigarette and blew the smoke toward John Levi. "No, I would not."

John Levi wanted to believe that if Hennigan just witnessed for himself Dub's injuries and the condition of the double-wide trailer Dub and his mother lived in outside Olney, his heart would be moved to agree to waive the fee.

"Young man, you are trying to manipulate me."

"No, sir, I am just trying to show you why waiving the fee is the right thing to do."

"Right by whom? "asked Hennigan. "Right by me?"

"Right by Dub Taliaferro, sir. Right by us too."

"How about this? How about if you waive your part of the legal fee . . . ?"

John Levi interrupted Hennigan before he finished his question. ". . . I'd be happy to, sir."

". . . and I keep mine?"

"Then we would be back to square one with no winnable case and no fee at all."

"Tell me again why I should do this."

"Because of Dub's pitiful condition."

"Son, every client I sign up is in pitiful condition. That's why their cases are worth so much money. If you start waiving a fee every time your client is in pitiful shape, you might as well start representing people in traffic court. You won't be able to keep a law office open."

Hennigan rose from his chair, grunting as he did so, walked around his desk, and half-leaned and half-sat on the desk in front of John Levi.

"I admire your passion, John Levi. I do. But I do not admire your judgment. Or your self-righteousness. You give off this air, at your young age, of being such a moral authority, such a holier-than-thou Joe. You are actually trying to guilt me into giving in to you. You even had the manufacturer's lawyer, Joe Freed, call me over the weekend to congratulate me for being such a humanitarian."

"Sir! I never suggested that anyone call you about this or any other case! I never even thought about that. When did Mr. Freed call you?"

"Yesterday. He and I have opposed one another in many a case over the years. I knocked his jock in the dirt in every case we have had together . . . before this one. He actually said that he had never before suspected that I had a human bone in my entire body. You have made me look bad, young man. You have made me look like I am over the hill. "

"That was not my intent, sir. My intent was just to help a neighbor in need."

"A 'neighbor'? Is this what this is about? You live next door to this man in Olney? I thought you have a condo in Fort Worth?"

"Not a 'neighbor' like that, sir."

"A 'neighbor' like what, then?"

"Like nothing. Let's forget I called him a 'neighbor.'"

"No. Answer me. A 'neighbor' like what?" Hennigan started laughing. "Like in the Bible?"

"Yes, sir."

"You see, holier-than-thou-Joe, we aren't in vacation Bible school here, young man. This is the real world of high-dollar litigation. Get your feet on the ground. This ain't a game of bean bag."

Hennigan drew himself up to his full height, standing over John Levi as John Levi remained sitting. "Here is what you are going to do. You are going to get out of Sunday school and back into the practice of law. Today you are going to write and email a letter to Joe Freed and the lawyer for the workers' comp carrier. I want to see a draft of the letter on my desk before you leave for your deposition today. You are going to withdraw the nonsense you discussed with them. You will be certain to refer to it only as a discussion, not as a settlement offer. You will write that Mr. Hennigan is becoming even more involved in this suit, that he is about to identify multiple experts who will place indefensible liability on the manufacturer. You will remind them of the horrific injuries of my client and make a settlement demand of eight million dollars to expire one month from today."

"Sir, what experts are those? You have a line on these experts? I should have come to you before."

"No, I don't have any experts. You are going to find these experts. Turn over some more rocks. This the way the game is played. We are going to get a larger settlement offer just on the threat of my being involved."

"But sir, a larger settlement offer won't help Dub unless the workers' comp insurance carrier agrees to waive its reimbursement right to past and future medical bills. They only agreed to make that waiver because we were giving up our fee."

"You do what I say. I want that letter on my desk in fifteen minutes. Before I go to lunch. Hurry up."

John Levi went into his office and typed up a letter. When he returned, Hennigan was on a phone call with a travel agent, standing with his back to his desk and looking out his office window. John Levi left the letter on Hennigan's desk and left the firm offices. The letter read:

Mr. Hennigan:

I resign effective as soon as I finish this afternoon's deposition in Dallas.
Below is the schedule of future oral depositions in Dub's case if you persist in your decision not to waive your fee to settle the case. Even if you do settle it on that basis, I do not want to handle your lawsuits anymore.

Respectfully,
John Levi Jones

P.S.: If you don't want to take back Dub's case from me, I will take the case with me and I will make the settlement by waiving my fee. Then your reputation will not be damaged. The expenses that your firm has incurred to prepare Dub's case amount to about twenty thousand dollars so far. If you let me take Dub's case with me, you may subtract that expense money from what you owe me for the fees I earned that will be coming in after I leave for other cases I worked on for you.

CHAPTER SEVENTEEN

"I am the one who is unwanted."

— Tuesday, February, 13, 2018, 1:30 a.m. —

Paloma is thirty-one years old and Cynthia is thirteen.

Light had vanished from the house so abruptly that it scared Cynthia. The darkness was like a beast that broke in and scared the light away. She held her breath, waiting for the return of the light and heat. She was wrapped in a sleeping bag in her bedroom finishing in longhand her essay on *Oliver Twist* for her eighth-grade honors English class. The floor lamp next to her had gone suddenly dark, and the light and heat from the coils of the space heater had buzzed off. Cynthia sat in the dark and cold, hoping for only a temporary outage. She was alone in the house on Irion. She could hear the sparse late-night traffic and a railroad whistle in the distance, but no other sound beside her beating heart. The dark persisted, so Cynthia rose from the floor, her sleeping bag draped over her shoulders and trailing her like a cape, and crept to the front room, walking barefoot on the rough cement floor. She looked out and saw that lights were burning in the other houses on the block. *"Angel didn't pay the light bill. Mom must have pissed him off again. Or he is just screwing with her again."*

Cynthia returned to her room. She squatted in her sleeping bag. She checked the power reserve on her cell phone and saw that it had only 28 percent remaining. She turned on the flashlight feature so she could see to finish her essay. She did all that she could do until the phone power was exhausted. She rose again from her sleeping bag, walked into the bathroom, pulled down her jeans and panties, squatted over the toilet that had no seat, urinated, redressed, and washed her hands in the frigid sink tap water. She took a steak knife, a book of matches, and a candle out of the drawer next to the sink and returned to the bedroom.

She lay down in the sleeping bag, still wearing all her clothes for warmth, listening for the sound of her mother coming into the house. It was only 1:30 in the morning, so she didn't expect her mother to come home by then from The Hacienda, assuming she would return home that night at all. But she listened anyway.

Hearing nothing, she tried to fall asleep, but she felt dread crawling into her. Monday had been a bad day. Her momma had been missing since Saturday night starting when Angel swung by the house to pick Paloma up. Her momma left Cynthia only a few dollars for food, which Cynthia purchased from a convenience store. Monday morning she arose early enough to walk in the dark to her middle school nine blocks away to eat a free breakfast in the cafeteria and avoid being seen by her classmates. She had hoped to shower and shampoo in the girl's gym dressing room before school, but found it was closed for repair of pipes burst by the cold weather. So she had to endure Monday's classes with dirty hair in her usual dirty clothes. She passed up a free hot lunch rather than sit dirty in the lunch room. When she was leaving school to walk home, she passed by the gymnasium, where the band was rehearsing for Thursday night's basketball game. Cynthia had been a member of the band until her mother could no longer afford the rent on her flute.

When Cynthia was around people, she only succeeded in keeping herself together by being withdrawn. But when she was alone in her house, loneliness, hopelessness, and anxiety took control of her. The only way she could defend herself from the feelings was by focusing all her pain into self-inflicted cuts.

As she lay on her back she lit the candle, pulled down her jeans, and used the knife to finish cutting "unwanted" in the skin of her upper right thigh. She daubed at her cut with toilet paper and fell asleep.

At 7:00 a.m. she was awakened by her mother.

"What's this, Sweetheart?" Paloma asked her. Paloma was holding the knife with the bloody tip that Cynthia had left beside her sleeping bag when she went to sleep. "What's this?"

Cynthia crawled out of her sleeping bag and wiped her hair out of her face. She saw her mother, gaunt, red-eyed, and disheveled, standing over her holding the knife. Cynthia panicked. She stood stammering before her mother. Paloma looked down, and her eyes widened. She saw the waist of Cynthia's jeans down around her knees, the cuts on Cynthia's upper thigh just below her panties on the right leg, and the bloody bathroom tissue clinging to the cuts.

"Oh Sweetheart, what have you been doing to yourself?" Paloma took Cynthia in her arms and tried to hug her. Cynthia pushed her away. Paloma jerked Cynthia roughly to her. She bent down, pulled the tissue from the cuts, and peered at them. *"Unwanted."* she thought. *"I have given her my disease."* "Cyn," she said, "this is my fault. This is all my fault. I am the one who is unwanted. You are a beautiful young lady, a beautiful daughter." Cynthia began crying and Paloma embraced her, rocking back and forth with her.

Paloma tucked Cynthia back into her sleeping bag and went into the kitchen. She could still hear Cynthia crying softly from the bedroom. Paloma's head was aching, her hands were shaking, her entire body was jittery, her vision was blurry, and she felt exhausted. The usual post-methamphetamine self-loathing was on her. She had used meth at Luther and Angel's house for three straight nights and crashed there during the days. She was making so much money being used by men, and was getting so high on meth to be able to do it, that she had not dared leaving Bodine's house to check on Cynthia. She was afraid what Cynthia would say to her if she called. And she forgot about her and the rest of this world when she was high. Now she had to own up to the consequences of leaving her daughter so alone for so long, and rally to take care of her.

The electricity was still out and there was no natural gas flowing to the range. But there was a camping stove that ran on butane on the back porch. Paloma took a pot from the countertop, filled it with water from the tap, dragged the stove into the kitchen, lit the butane burner, and began heating the water. When the water boiled, she lowered the flame under the pot, retrieved a cake of hand soap and towels from the bathroom, soaked the towels with hot water, lathered them with soap, returned to the bedroom, and cleaned the dried blood off Cynthia's cuts. She then washed the soap off her leg with a clean, wet towel. She looked in the bathroom for an antibiotic ointment, though she could not recall ever buying any. Then she washed and dried Cynthia's face and neck.

"Why don't you stay home from school today? Let me catch up on my sleep and then we can spend some time together. I made enough money this weekend for us to have a nice steak dinner at a restaurant in the Stockyards."

"Momma, I have to go to school. I have an essay that is due in honors English that I hope to have published in the school literary magazine. The teacher told me that my writing is getting good enough. I have to get dressed and leave now."

Paloma's head was throbbing, and she felt nauseous. "You can't give up a day of school so I can show you that you aren't unwanted?"

"Momma, I need to go."

"Can you run to the store to get me something to eat first? I haven't eaten since Sunday morning, and I feel sick."

"Momma, please let me go now."

"What about your leg?"

Cynthia suddenly started screaming. "What about my leg? What about my hair? What about my clothes? What about a shower? What about lights and heat? What about head lice and rats? What about food for me, your only child? Did you even think about me this weekend? You didn't even answer my calls! I didn't know if you were dead or alive and you didn't care of I was! Do you know any other mothers who leave their daughters all alone without food for days without checking on them?"

Paloma was in shock over Cynthia's fury. But she thought, "*Yes. I know of a mother who left her children alone without any of that. She was my mother. And now I have become her.*"

Cynthia grabbed up the clothes she had been wearing the Friday before and ran with them into the bathroom, slamming and locking the door behind her.

Paloma stood stark still. Cynthia had never raised her voice to her before. Suddenly Paloma was infected by her daughter's fury and she ran to the closed bathroom door and began pounding on it, yelling, "Don't you talk to your mother like that? Why do you think I was gone this weekend? To make enough money to take care of you; that's why! You think I wanted to be gone doing what I was doing?" But Cynthia made no response, and Paloma felt herself getting weaker and sleepier from the effort and sicker from the meth wearing off. Paloma took out her cell phone and started to telephone Angel to come back to pick her up. But her guilt stopped her. She put her lips to the door and said, "I am sorry, Cyn. I didn't mean it. Go to school and we will talk when you get home. We will go to the laundromat tonight to clean your clothes and check into a motel where you can shower." Then Paloma walked into her bedroom and collapsed into her sleeping bag. She fell asleep almost immediately.

Paloma awoke with Cynthia standing over her. It was late afternoon. The inside of Paloma's sleeping bag was soaked with sweat. She had thrown up on the concrete floor next to her bag. She had her recurring dream of digging up her mother from a grave in her daddy's backyard and of Cynthia smoking meth. Paloma had a terrible headache behind her eyes. Her heart was racing. Her entire body was shaking as if she were freezing.

She looked up at Cynthia. "I promise I am going to quit this time, Cyn. Never again."

Cynthia closed her eyes and shook her head slowly. "Go back to sleep, Momma. We'll walk to the laundromat and the motel in a few hours."

Paloma fell back asleep into her nightmare. Cynthia walked back into her bedroom and into her own nightmare.

Humberto walked into Cynthia's bedroom. Cynthia jumped, startled.

"I am sorry, Cynthia. There was no lock on the door so I just let myself in. Where is your mother?" Humberto's speech was thick.

"In her bedroom. Don't go in there. Let her sleep."

Humberto stood swaying, licking his lips and blinking.

"What do you want, *Abuelo*?"

"Could you spare me any money?"

"I am leaving law and going into Methodist ministry."

— March 26, 2014, 3:00 p.m. —

John Levi is thirty-four years old.

"My Goodness, John Levi. What brings you here?" Amanda Jones looked up in surprise from her magazine to see her son standing in front of her. Mrs. Jones was seated on the leather couch in the den of her home, a glass of white wine in her hand.

John Levi bent down and kissed his mother on the cheek.

"It's been a while since I have seen you. No reason for me not to see my mother just because my father has . . . disowned me. Unless you have disowned me too."

"Such melodrama. Your father hasn't disowned you. You are the one who can't be around him without picking an argument. And it embarrasses him, with all the newspaper coverage you have been getting for your lawsuits against corporations. It hurts your father that you are so judgmental." She paused. "I would never disown you."

"Mother, my being judgmental isn't what bothers my father. He is my model for being judgmental. What bothers my father is that my judgments are different than his. He doesn't want to be around anyone who disagrees with him or Fox News. That's why he doesn't allow you to express any of your own opinions."

"Oh John Levi, listen to you. I don't have any of my own opinions." She smiled from making a joke. "I run this house. Your father runs our opinions."

"He told me he didn't want to see me again until I decided to quit persecuting businesses. Is that your opinion too?"

"Oh, he did not."

"His words exactly, Mother. He once told me that corporations are people just like my clients. He claimed that the Supreme Court says so. 'You shouldn't demonize them,' he said. 'Business is hanging by a thread in this country.' He is more concerned about businesses than about me or my clients."

"Let's not quarrel. You are here now. Sit next to your mother." Mrs. Jones patted the couch next to her. She glanced at her watch. It was only 3:00 p.m. on a Wednesday, and Gerard Jones wasn't due home until 5:30 at the earliest. He had a standing tee time at their country club at this time on Wednesdays, which was why John Levi had chosen to drop in to see his mother during this afternoon.

John Levi had left his relationship with James Hennigan six years before and had started a law partnership with two other young lawyers. He made a quick fortune in plaintiff's personal injury litigation and had achieved something of the reputation he craved. Ironically, it was his settlement of Dub Taliaferro's case, which Hennigan had let John Levi take with him, which had brought referrals of high-dollar suits from other lawyers. John Levi had indeed waived his fee to settle the Taliaferro case, which gained him a unique reputation among his peers. To those of the James Hennigan school of law practice, he was guilty of shameless grandstanding. To others it was evidence of how much John Levi actually cared about his clients. When Dub took his own life with a shotgun months later because the monthly income which John Levi secured for him was not enough compensation for his blindness, deafness, disability, and pain, Texas newspapers publicized the tragedy. John Levi was celebrated as the hero who had done his young, innocent, selfless best to provide for Dub. Cases also poured into the new firm through direct calls from clients wanting that kind of compassion in a lawyer.

In 2011, three years before this conversation with his mother, John Levi had tried a wrongful death case before a jury in Houston for a mother and children whose undocumented husband and father had been killed on the job by dangerous manufacturing machinery which had already killed three other employees. The jury found the employer guilty of gross negligence and awarded forty million dollars in punitive damages. The case was settled confidentially for thirty million dollars within a month of the verdict and the money came in a month later. John Levi's new firm received twelve million dollars to be divided among the three partners. So at the age of thirty-one, after only six years of law practice, John Levi took home a four-million-dollar fee from this one lawsuit. His firm had other cases and won other large fees. But legislative caps on damage amounts and the desire of defendants to settle cases confidentially to avoid the risk of huge and public damage awards radically reduced John Levi's opportunities to do what he loved most—try jury cases representing the working poor who had been done an injustice by inhumane corporate practices.

John Levi suspected, ungenerously but realistically, that some of his father's disapproval of his law practice was stoked by resentment that John Levi had made so much money so quickly and without the risk and work of running a business. John Levi's financial worth already far exceeded his father's, who had been slogging at his business in the volatile Texas, Oklahoma, and New Mexico oil patch for decades. His father's friends hated lawyers and considered them to be leeches and threats. His father was embarrassed at his son's success in the law, even though money was how his father kept score of life's success. John Levi's money was not respectable money. John Levi made things worse through what Gerard Jones considered to be an ostentatiously modest lifestyle despite his fortune, buying only a two-bedroom condo close to downtown Fort Worth, driving an old, noisy, burnt-orange clunker of a pickup, and wearing unpressed suits in a false display of solidarity with his clients. Gerard Jones thought his son made a show of phony humility.

John Levi's mother did not approve of his bachelor, work-obsessed life. She wanted a granddaughter to mould into her own image. She wanted the affirmation of seeing John Levi playing golf and poker with his father at their club, attending club dances, eating dinner in the club dining room with his parents, and marrying a young woman from one of the club's "good families."

After John Levi had seated himself on the far end of the couch from his mother, she asked, "So what really brings you here? You didn't drop by just to say hello."

As emotionally distant as his mother and John Levi had been while he was growing up, as distant as she had seemed to be from her husband and from herself, she knew John Levi.

"I have news, Mother. I am making a career change. "

"Oh, wonderful! Your father will be so glad to hear it!"

"Doubt it."

"Then dare I ask what the change is?"

"Mother, I am leaving law and going into Methodist ministry."

"What? What do you mean? Say that again."

"I mean that I have enrolled in seminary at SMU, am giving up my law partnership, and am going to become an ordained Methodist minister."

"What on earth for?"

"Mother, you wouldn't understand."

Amanda Jones rose from the couch, went to the bar, and poured herself another white wine. "Get you anything, dear?" John Levi said no, watching her for any emotional response to his announcement.

She sat down in a chair across the coffee table from him. "Please don't condescend to your mother, John Levi. Your father isn't here. I want you to tell me why you think you are doing this."

"I don't want to argue about it with you. I am not seeking your approval. I am just letting you know before you hear it from someone else."

"So you refuse to explain why you are doing this. What am I supposed to tell our friends about why?"

John Levi didn't care what she told their friends. But his parents, for all their attempts to channel his career decisions, had made it easier for him to accomplish what he had in the law by paying for his education. So he owed them some explanation.

"The shorthand version is that I have come to believe deeply in the gospel."

"Goodness. How grand you sound . . . Doesn't everybody?"

"No, Mother. No, they don't. I have come to believe in Jesus' good news to the poor. I want to try giving myself to it."

"To the poor? That sounds more like politics than religion. What brought this on?"

"If you really want to know, it started with the free legal clinic in southeast Austin during law school. And the preaching of a Roman Catholic priest and the ministries of his church. He really opened my eyes to what Jesus actually did and taught. I saw firsthand the constant difficulties of the poor. The unfairness of their lives. The indifference of comfortable so-called Christians, who are really just churchians. It all really got under my skin. The only hopeful voice I heard in that poor neighborhood was coming out of Father Gutierrez's church."

"You aren't going to convert to Catholicism! You know that all those priests are pedophiles."

"I told you, Mother, I am entering the *Methodist* ministry. And your comment about priests—my God. Father Gutierrez is a fine man who has given up a great deal for his calling. This is why I didn't want to talk about this with you."

"You sound so self-righteous."

"And you sound so bigoted."

"Are you *trying* to hurt my feelings?"

"No, but you can't expect me to remain silent when you say something stupid like that."

"Maybe I should just stay silent while you preach to me."

John Levi looked at his mother. The emotional distance between them was even increasing. She seemed smaller and smaller to him. He wondered if she was seeing the same thing about him.

"Do you want me to be happy?" he asked her.

"What a question. Of course I do. I'm your mother. I brought you into this world. We have given you everything, every advantage, to make you happy."

"Which do you want more? For me to make you and Dad happy? Or for me to make me happy?" And he thought to himself, *"And to make God happy?"*

"John Levi, your father and I know what will make you happy. You are just doing this to be different. Why do you feel this hunger to be so rebellious? We have done everything we could for you. We would do more if you let us. If your father said the sun rises in the east, you'd make some involved argument that it actually rises in the west."

"Do you want to hear what makes me happy or not? If you don't, I'll just go."

"Of course I do, dear."

"Let's see if you do. What makes me happy is using my abilities to help poor families survive and defeat their poverty. To fight their injustices with them. To help them understand they are not alone. Being able to use my abilities and resources to fight the injustices being suffered by these families has already made me happy. And now I want to do that in the name of Jesus. I believe that Jesus put this hunger in my heart."

"Whatever does ending injustice have to do with Jesus?"

"That church in southeast Austin had ministries that helped people in that neighborhood in the name of Jesus. A food and a clothing bank. English classes for Spanish speakers. Job referrals. Boys and girls clubs to keep them away from gangs. A microloan program. A real community of people helping one another."

"Loans? The church making loans?"

"Small loans through a non-profit owned by the church, to help people get out of poverty."

"Why are you telling me about this Catholic church?"

"That is the kind of church I want to build here in Fort Worth. That would make me truly happy."

"You don't want to be at Faith United Methodist?"

"I want to lead a church in a poor area of Fort Worth." *"At least to start,"* he thought to himself.

"Doesn't your law practice getting money for your clients make you happy?"

"I've done that, Mother. I want to get deeper into the daily lives of the people I have represented in court. And I don't want a lawsuit to be the center of my involvement. That isn't making me happy anymore. I don't love it anymore."

"John Levi, we have asked you to settle down and have a family. Surely that would make you happy. Surely love would."

"There will be a time for that kind of love, Mother. But never a time for a family focused on private school and private club and gated community. I am looking for something to be passionate about."

"John Levi, who are you?"

"I am trying to figure that out."

"Why do you reject us?'

"Mother! Let me ask a question. Are you happy with your life? Is it fulfilling to you? Are you passionate about it?"

"Of course I am."

"Really? It's not boring? Or empty of meaning? It would definitely not be fulfilling to me. I need more meaning in my life than accumulating stuff and insulating myself from all the injustice in the world. I couldn't be happy to benefit from all the injustice to the poor."

"That is what you think of us? Is that why you are always so angry with us?"

"That is what I think of your life choices, Mother. Living like you and Dad would not make me happy. I know that. Surely you know it by now."

"You sound ashamed of us."

"You have sounded ashamed of me for years. Do I at least have your blessing to try to find what makes *me* happy? Not what makes you and Dad happy, but what makes me happy with my own life?"

"Of course . . . Perhaps it would be better if you didn't discuss this with your father. Let me tell him."

"I don't plan on it. My father thinks there is only one good way to be happy in this world, and that is his way."

"Like father, like son . . . Speaking only for myself, you have my blessing to try to find if this will make you happy for now."

"Thank you."

"But there will be no real happiness for you until you settle down and start your own family. I predict that when you do have a wife and a child, your father's and my life will not look so unhappy to you. But don't tell your father that I gave you my blessing."

"Deal."

"Can we pay your tuition to seminary?"

"No, Mother, I can handle that."

"Really? How much does a minister make?"

"Effectively? Nothing."

"John Levi. I want you to let me have this last word. I just hope this isn't another way for you to draw attention to yourself. In addition to rebelling against us."

Later that day, John Levi's cell phone rang.

"John Levi, this is your father."

"Yes, sir?"

"Your mother told me about your conversation today. When I got home, she was in tears."

"I am sorry about that."

"Are you? She wasn't in tears about this ministry thing. You have enough money to have the freedom to do what you want with your life. She was in tears that you were so condemning of our lives."

"She asked me what I thought, so I told her."

"She asked you what you think about our lives?"

"I guess the conversation just tended that direction."

"John Levi, if you are indeed going into ministry, you will need to be more sensitive about hurting people. It sounds to me that you cross-examined your mother needlessly. She is a woman who needs approval. And love. Especially from her only child. Your mother has had a much rougher life than you know."

Pause. "Really. Rough how?"

"We never told you that she had three miscarriages before we had you. Because of that, she had long bouts with depression. All she ever wanted was to be was a mother. All three of the miscarriages were girls. She really wanted a daughter to be best friends with the rest of her life. God knows I have been too absent with my work and golf. She was anxious during her entire pregnancy with you. After all the disappointment, it was an act of courage for her to get pregnant again. We almost lost you too. She was on bed rest for the last four months of your pregnancy."

"Why didn't you tell me before this?"

"Because you are our child. It is not your job to bear our pain."

It occurred to John Levi that he didn't know his parents at all. *"So that's why I am an only child. So that's maybe why she talks about wanting a grand-daughter so much."*

"Would it help if I called to apologize?"

"Yes, if you listen and don't talk. And it would help if you decided to be our son and not our judge. Since she lost those pregnancies, she has always been waiting for something else to go wrong. So she is scared to get out of her routine . . . John Levi, sometimes truth is just cruel. It's too late for your mother and me to change our commitments and our lives. Truth can be the enemy of love. Your mother just wants your love."

John Levi had never heard his father talk this way. John Levi and his father had treated one another as adversaries for many years. "Yes, sir. I hear you. I'm sorry."

"John Levi, I know enough about ministry to know you are going to have to lose the sharp edge you have all the time. I hope you are not burning your bridges with your law firm. You built it, and they owe you the chance to come back if this move doesn't work out."

"Father, this is the first indication that you don't entirely disapprove of my courtroom career."

Pause. "We are not people who easily express our feelings, particularly to you. My father never once told me that he loved me. I guess I inherited that."

"Father, I appreciate your honesty."

"But I am worried that this latest career move will not make you happy. Successful ministers are people pleasers first, last, and middle. They are servants, not masters. That's not you, John Levi. Why does religion matter so much to you all of a sudden? Why not just make it a part of your life like everyone else?"

"Because this is the one thing that will make me happy, Father."

"No one thing makes anyone happy, John Levi. Hear me."

Happy Are Those Who Hunger and Thirst for Justice

Chapter Six

"You make it sound as if lasting a month at a job is a big deal."

— September 2018 —

Paloma is thirty-one years old and Cynthia is thirteen.

"Look, Momma, John Levi and I made supper." Cynthia walked fast to Paloma as she was opening and closing the door to their apartment, a huge, excited smile on her face. "We wanted to have it on the table by the time you got home."

"What's the occasion?" asked Paloma.

"Your one-month anniversary on the job, of course," replied Cynthia, purposefully not mentioning her mother's almost two-month emancipation from the Bodines and meth.

Paloma walked into the living area. She took off her shoes and dropped her purse and bag of groceries on the couch. She looked through the dining area and into the kitchen. She saw John Levi in the kitchen wearing an apron, pouring a pot full of spaghetti and boiling water through a colander into the sink, the steam rising into his face and causing him to blink and turn his head away. He dumped the spaghetti onto a large plate. The table in the dining area was set, ready for supper. Someone, probably Cynthia, had put a single red rose in a vase in the center of the table. Over the table was a shiny, sequined banner proclaiming, "CONGRATULATIONS!"

"We are so proud of you," said Cynthia.

John Levi looked up from his work in the kitchen, smiled, and winked at Paloma. "This was Cynthia's idea. I'm just her assistant."

Paloma felt proud of herself, but nervous about the pressure on her to stay free of Angel, Luther, and their meth. Cynthia was encouraging her hard to stay on the path that John Levi was opening for her.

Much had changed since that evening that Paloma and Cynthia had moved temporarily into a residence inn. The most impactful change had been Paloma's willingness to accept financial and material help from John Levi. Paloma was at first suspicious of John Levi's motives. And she didn't want to admit the obvious to him and herself that she had been failing her daughter and herself and needed John Levi's assistance to make their lives whole and happy. But Cynthia was desperate for a better place to live and for sobriety and a safe, stable job for her mother. Cynthia wanted to be free from anxiety and the urge to cut herself. So she begged, demanded, and manipulated her mother to accept each successive offer of help. Still, Paloma kept waiting for John Levi to make the kind of demands that she was accustomed to receiving from men. And she was waiting for John Levi to tire of her and Cynthia and to move on to another woman and child in need, breaking Cynthia's heart. Cynthia was getting attached to John Levi.

John Levi found Paloma and Cynthia a clean, modest two-bedroom apartment in Cynthia's school district. He and Cynthia persuaded Paloma to accept John Levi's offer to pay the security deposit, the moving expenses, and the monthly rent until Paloma could pay their way. John Levi furnished the apartment with used furniture donated by his friends or church members or purchased by him from a used furniture store. John Levi also found a nine-to-five job for Paloma as a file clerk for his old law firm. The job paid Paloma eighteen dollars an hour, part of which was secretly contributed by John Levi. He loaned Paloma the use of his second car, an older Lexus. John Levi presented Paloma and Cynthia with a one-thousand-dollar gift certificate from Target for clothes for both of them and for household and kitchen supplies for their apartment. And John Levi bought Cynthia her own flute.

John Levi was at first reluctant to spend his own money to help Paloma and Cynthia. Once he started this, where would he draw the line? But he was drawn to them. He was spending at least three late nights a week at their apartment, sometimes as many as five. There was so much that was thoroughly compelling about them. They had suffered so much and had such resilience born of the suffering. Cynthia expected and needed so little materially to be grateful and happy. Paloma was struggling with how readily Cynthia was forgiving her. Paloma was divided among her anger at the unfairness of what life had thrown at her, her defensiveness about the mistakes she had made, and her guilt about the impact on Cynthia of her mistakes. But Cynthia's incessant joy was infectious, so even Paloma had more moments of unguarded happiness. Paloma and Cynthia were blossoming physically from the regular food, the comfort and safety of the apartment, the regular hours, and the time they could spend together. Cynthia was developing into an attractive teenager, a butterfly emerging from her cocoon of poverty, depression, and abandonment. Paloma was always physically attractive, even when emaciated and actively addicted. Now she was regaining her health, filling out, and turning beautiful despite the scars on her face and her pronounced limp. Her looks turned men's heads wherever she went, making her afraid that they knew her from The Hacienda. John Levi felt honored to be an intimate witness and party to all of this change and possibility.

But there was always an undertone of fear that Paloma would disappear one day to return to meth. John Levi had not yet felt comfortable to talk to Paloma about entering an extended rehab program to enable her to cope with the brutality of her past and the reasons she was drawn so strongly to meth. Paloma was still emotionally brittle and always on the edge of anger. Cynthia hugged her at every opportunity, and John Levi avoided any talk about the future. But the fear was like a low bass note on an organ that played softly but constantly.

John Levi's financial help to them started slowly. The effects of his generosity were so positive and taking care of them made him so happy that his giving increased. The only limit was from Paloma's refusals. He finally overcame the worst of Paloma's resistance by confessing his great wealth. Every time she resisted his support he would say, "It's for Cynthia. Besides, it's not even a drop in my bucket. I'll never miss the money." And he didn't. But Paloma still worried how she would make do when his generosity was inevitably directed elsewhere.

Paloma tried to enter the kitchen to see what a mess John Levi had made and what she would have to do to rescue the meal. But Cynthia steered her to a chair at the table. "Sit here, Your Highness."

"Oh my God, you make it sound as if lasting a month at a job is a big deal."

"Cynthia's proud and happy, Paloma. Me too. Let us make a little fuss over you."

"What ingredients did you use to make the sauce?" she asked him.

"You mean there's supposed to be sauce?" He made a face. Then he held up a jar of store-bought spaghetti sauce. "Here, Cyn, give this to your mom so she can approve the ingredients."

John Levi and Cynthia brought to the table the heaping plate of spaghetti and meatballs, a pitcher of sauce, a container of Parmigiano, another plate of tossed salad, a jar of Ranch dressing with bacon bits, and glasses of iced tea.

John Levi said, "On this auspicious occasion, I am going to say thanks. If you won't bow your head, just stay silent for a moment, please." He held his open hands out to mother and daughter. Cynthia readily took his hand. Paloma sat stock still. John Levi reached out and captured her hand. "Dear Lord, we thank you for new life and limitless possibilities. We thank you for the love in this home and ask that you inspire us to trust it. Forgive us for our refusals to love ourselves in the past. In Jesus' holy name we pray. Amen." He knew better from his first meal with Paloma to ask God to bless the food to their nourishment.

Paloma stared at John Levi blankly. *"Did this man just say before God and my daughter that we should trust that he loves us? Why would he love me?"* Paloma watched Cynthia and John Levi laughing about the chewiness of the spaghetti. *"Why would my daughter love me?"*

John Levi tried to teach them how to twirl spaghetti on their forks. They pretended to be unteachable until they broke down laughing and showed him that they were veteran spaghetti twirlers. After dinner they cleaned up the kitchen and played Yahtzee at the table until it was time for Cynthia to do her homework. Then John Levi and Paloma sat on the couch in the living area, watched some television, and talked about Paloma's co-employees at the law firm. Cynthia came out of her bedroom to say good night and kissed both her mother and John Levi on the cheek. "Why don't you stay over?" Cynthia asked John Levi. When he and her mother looked startled, she said, "You can sleep on the couch. It's a pull-out bed."

John Levi hurriedly said goodnight and excused himself. "Maybe I will see you two tomorrow night after my church meetings. It may be late when I get done. It will be after supper for sure."

"Just let us know," replied Paloma.

"Call me if you need anything, anything at all."

John Levi left, looking forward to the next time he could be with them.

Chapter Seven

The church rocked with the children's noise and joy.

— September 2018 to August 2019 —

John Levi's ministry at Peace United Methodist experienced a sea change when he helped Elijah and Mimi Rogers at landlord-tenant court and when he started using his own money to help neighbors who came to Peace in material need. To paraphrase Mark's Gospel, from these small seeds grew fields and fields of mustard shrubs with dozens and dozens of birds nesting in their branches.

John Levi helped the Rogers find a three-bedroom rental house in the neighborhood of the church owned by a long-time, faithful church member. The Rogers family could live in the house rent free for six months in exchange for Elijah's renovation of the interior. Mimi turned out to have talent as a pianist and a choir director. She had a lovely alto voice. She recruited friends from their old church to join the choir at Peace. Their families attended worship. Soon Peace worship services were jumping to the sound of African-American spirituals and praise songs. Mimi led the worshippers in Latino and old Anglo hymns as well.

John Levi recruited some female paralegals from his old law firm to form a club to mentor the girls of the neighborhood. The women named the girls' club JFG, for "Just For Girls." Elementary and middle school girls flocked to the meetings. Many of their mothers were born in Mexico or Central America and were ill-equipped to teach their daughters the mistakes to avoid in this new culture. These young women lovingly provided that mentoring and encouragement.

John Levi found a bilingual seminary student from his seminary at SMU. Pedro Gonzales, himself a Mexican immigrant to the U.S. as a teenager, helped lead bilingual worship services and interacted with the Spanish-speaking adults and youth of the neighborhood. John Levi convinced his church board to pay his salary to Pedro and pay John Levi nothing so the budget of the church was not increased.

John Levi and Pedro started a boys club to mentor the neighborhood boys and discourage them from joining their older brothers' street gangs. With this inroad into the families of gang members, John Levi actually arranged for a meeting in a church building between the leaders of two warring street gangs and negotiated their agreement to stop shooting into the homes of rival gang members.

The local newspaper ran a feature article on the amazing happenings at Peace Church, lavishing far too much praise on the successful young trial lawyer who "gave up everything" to pastor this inner-city church and "save" the neighborhood. This publicity attracted more financial support and more people from outside the neighborhood to worship and help.

Peace Church added a free food pantry and clothing bank. The articles of clothing were donated by members of Peace and Faith United Methodist Church of Fort Worth, and by the new members who came from outside the neighborhood. John Levi and Pedro arranged for free contributions of food to the pantry from a non-profit in the county, and Faith Church funded the salaries of two neighborhood women who ran the pantry and bank two days a week. Faith Church also funded the salary of a children's Sunday school and children's choir director.

The Fort Worth ISD provided a teacher to lead English as a Second Language classes for adults in Peace Church on Wednesday evenings.

Leaders of businesses donated computers to help young neighborhood children with their English and math skills. Young men and women came from all over the city on Tuesday and Wednesday nights to lead the tutoring program.

A church that was without a single child to light the altar candles for Sunday morning worship when John Levi started as pastor now had over one hundred fifty children—Latino, African American, and Anglo—in the church buildings every week. The church rocked with the children's noise and joy.

The neighborhood adults were grateful for what the church was doing for their children. But what brought these adults into the church was the microloan program administered through a new non-profit corporation owned by Peace Church and funded by John Levi himself, and the free legal aid clinic that helped defend neighborhood families in their disputes with landlords, used car dealers, payday and title loan companies, and rent-to-buy furniture stores. The largest law firm in Fort Worth sent young lawyers to staff the clinic and be mentored in client skills by the great John Levi Jones himself. John Levi was soon spending half of his seventy-hour work week running this law clinic, supervising and teaching the young lawyers, learning the details of the injustices suffered by the neighborhood's families, getting to know these families personally, and representing families in court himself. Neighborhood adults who were helped through the loans and the law clinic were asked to help organize and interpret for the programs.

When John Levi started at the church, attendance at Sunday worship services numbered in the teens and twenties—all elderly Anglo members who used the service to remember the good old days when the neighborhood was completely comprised of Anglo working-class families. Now, worship attendance numbered between one hundred twenty and one hundred fifty people—children and adults, Anglo, Latino, and African American. John Levi and Pedro thought worship looked like the kingdom of heaven.

The success of the ministries of Peace caused representatives of the board of directors of Faith Church to attend worship at Peace regularly. John Levi brought to his preaching the dramatic skills he had used in closing argument in the courtroom. His involvement in the lives of Paloma and Cynthia and in the lives in the church neighborhood awakened in him an empathy that he communicated in his sermons. Because of his ministry's success and his dramatic preaching, it was hoped by some at Faith Church that the bishop would appoint John Levi to be its senior pastor and lead preacher when its present pastor retired in the years to come.

The new ministries of Peace Church also inspired opposition. When John Levi started at Peace there was a loyal but dwindling core of older Anglo members who never missed a worship service or a Wednesday evening potluck supper. Some of these veteran members welcomed their Hispanic and African-American neighbors into the church. But some were bitterly opposed to welcoming "them" and to John Levi's radical shift of Peace's focus to neighborhood needs. The veterans were accustomed to their pastor's time being dedicated wholly to them, including one visit to each household each week. But the neighborhood ministries demanded so much of John Levi's time that he had to give up those routine visits.

The greatest opposition was inspired by the bilingual worship services. It was a sacrifice for the veteran Anglo members to sit patiently while John Levi's English sermons were translated into Spanish by Pedro paragraph by paragraph. Despite the grumbling, the pastors believed that having two separate services—one in only English and one in only Spanish—would not unify the members into one church and would not foster neighborliness.

Some veteran Anglo members left the church and joined the Baptists over this issue.

A crisis occurred when the stained glass window behind the choir loft was vandalized. Some veterans were certain this was the product of the resentment of the local street gangs to the church's boys club. But John Levi received word through the street that Angel Bodine did the damage in retribution for the landlord-tenant case John Levi had won for Paloma against Luther. John Levi quietly paid for the repair of the window himself.

Cynthia started attending the weekday and Saturday JFG meetings and the teenage Sunday school classes led by John Levi and the young women from his old law firm. Cynthia sat with friends in Sunday morning worship. Paloma was still refusing to attend worship but helped with distribution of food for the food bank and with filling out the applications of persons seeking the services of the legal aid clinic. And she cared for infants and toddlers in the nursery while their parents attended worship on Sundays.

"What are you mad at? That your daughter worries about you?"

— Thursday, October 11, 2018 —

John Levi arrived at the football game just before halftime. It had started at 4:00 p.m., so it was just before 5:00 p.m. when he arrived. The marching band was already lining up behind an end zone for their performance. John Levi breathed a sigh that he had not missed the band's performance. He had been delayed at church by a family seeking help against an eviction. He scanned the people in the bleachers—it really couldn't be called a crowd—looking for Paloma. When he didn't see her, he took a seat next to some new members of the church. He studied the band. All of them wore the same uniform, of course, and so it was hard to identify Cynthia. Then he found the flutes and spotted her. She waved gaily at him.

The band was about two-thirds female and one-third male. The band simply walked onto the field in columns just as they had lined up. All members turned at once to face the stands. They then played three songs as they stood in their places. Most people in attendance had gone for concessions during the performance. The only ones who stayed to watch and listen were the families and friends of the musicians. When their third song was finished, the band marched off the field in the direction from which they had come, the three snare drummers clicking time for the steps with their drumsticks on the rims of their drums. The band director gathered the members around her for post-performance encouragement and then released them. John Levi was interested to see if Cynthia would pair up with friends as the band dispersed. He hoped she had friends. Instead, she hustled alone over to where he sat. She smiled, hugged him, and sat on the bleacher plank just in front of him. She looked excellent in her red-and-black uniform.

"How was it?" she asked.

"It was great. You clearly played the best."

"How in the world could you hear my flute in all that noise?"

"Because you played so well. Everybody around me said so." They both smiled.

"Where's Momma?"

"Stuck on the road here. She said she would ask to leave work at 4:30 instead of 5:00 to make the performance."

"Are you going to stay for the rest of the game?"

"It looks as if I'm your ride. But I'd be happy for you to sit with some friends."

"I could walk home."

"I'll stay at least until your mother gets here. You want me to hold your flute? "

"Thanks."

"Here's some money for a Coke and some chips."

John Levi watched Cynthia intently as she sat with a group of girls from the band. He was really interested to see if she was included. At first, she sat on the periphery of the group, looking toward them and overhearing their talk, but not included. But as other band members joined the group after getting refreshments and sat to the outside of Cynthia, she was included in their talk and giggling. Periodically, Cynthia looked back to see if her mother had arrived.

The game ended about 6:00 p.m., and Paloma was still not there. John Levi drove Cynthia back to the apartment. They went inside. Cynthia called Paloma's cell phone but heard only her voice mail recording. It got to be 6:30. "I'm really getting worried," said Cynthia.

"What are you worried about?" asked John Levi.

"Don't make me say it."

Just then the door opened. Paloma came in with two full bags of groceries. Cynthia ran to her and hugged her.

"Well, hello to you too," said Paloma.

Paloma saw tears in Cynthia's eyes. She looked over Cynthia's shoulder at John Levi with a puzzled look on her face. "Baby," she said to Cynthia, "what's wrong?"

"You could have called me. I was worried."

Paloma looked angry. "I think I left my cell phone here this morning. And I get home from work this late a lot. Do I have to get your permission to go grocery shopping?"

Cynthia went into her room and closed the door.

"What's that all about?" Paloma asked John Levi.

John Levi walked into Paloma's bedroom and found her phone on her dressing table. Five calls had been received from Cynthia's phone in the last forty minutes. John Levi showed the phone to Paloma as he knocked on Cynthia's bedroom door. "Cynthia, Cynthia, please open the door. I want to show you something."

Cynthia cracked open her door. John Levi held the phone up for Cynthia to see. "I just found this in your mother's bedroom. Just as she said, of course."

"Then why didn't she come to the game?" asked Cynthia through the cracked door.

"Wait a minute," said Paloma. "What game?"

"The game today at 4," said Cynthia.

"I thought that game was tomorrow."

"Mother, I told you it was today. John Levi knew it was today." The unexpressed question hung in the air . . . "*Then why didn't you?*"

Paloma was irritated at being called on the carpet by her daughter and at herself for missing the game. Before this new life, she had not been held accountable to anyone but the Bodines.

John Levi handed Paloma's phone to her. "You have a calendar on your phone?"

"Yes," said Paloma.

"Pull it up."

Paloma did so. There on today's calendar for 4:00 p.m. was "Cynthia's first game!" John Levi showed it to Cynthia.

"So the problem was that you didn't have your phone."

"Wait a minute. Do I have to account for every minute?" Paloma was really losing her temper, as she too often did when confronted with a mistake.

"Cynthia, let me talk to your mom a minute." Cynthia withdrew into her room.

"Don't you preach to me," said Paloma.

"Please take a breath."

Paloma took the bags of groceries into the kitchen and started slamming the cans into their cabinets.

"Stop for a moment, please. Just stop." John Levi took Paloma's hands and sat her at the table in the dining area. He sat down in a chair opposite her.

"What are you mad at? That your daughter worries about you? That she remembers all those years when you would disappear for days at time?"

"I was just getting groceries!"

"Yes. You did nothing wrong. You have been doing everything right. It was a bad set of coincidences . . . Can I tell you something without your getting angrier?"

Paloma grimaced at him. "I'll try not to."

"Getting angry at Cynthia's worry *is* wrong."

"I thought you just said I had done nothing wrong."

"Paloma, honest to goodness, do you just want to argue? You should have been a lawyer. Maybe I'll say something worth hearing if you'll will listen. That little girl loves you to death. Despite of how you've treated her. You know this. You could have lost her love. But you haven't. So you can be angry that she is telling you how much she worries about you and that she was disappointed you weren't there for her concert. Or you can be happy that she even cares so much . . . She adores you, Paloma. And you adore her. But you can't expect that she doesn't remember. It wasn't that long ago."

"Who the hell are you to be telling me this? You think because you have given us so much help that you can talk to me this way?"

"I talk to you this way because I am someone else who cares about you and Cynthia."

Paloma swore and walked into the kitchen. She stood looking out the window for what seemed a long time. Then she sighed, walked to Cynthia's bedroom, knocked softly on the door, and went quietly into the room, closing the door behind her. John Levi sat in the chair until he heard the sound of two people crying from inside Cynthia's room. Then he quietly left the apartment.

"You don't feel that life is good?" "How could I? Have you not been paying attention?"

— October 2018 to August 2019 —

John Levi spent between five and seven nights a week at Paloma's and Cynthia's apartment. Evening activities at the church took place four nights a week and generally lasted from 6:00 to 8:00 p.m. On those nights he would arrive at Paloma's and Cynthia's apartment at 5:00, talk to Cynthia about her school day and help her with her homework, maybe start dinner, and leave for the church just as Paloma was getting home from work about 5:45. Then he would return to their apartment after 8:00, eat the dinner that Paloma had finished and kept warm for him, do the dishes with Cynthia, and talk and watch television with Paloma until 11:00. Then he would drive to his own condo. On nights when there were no programs at the church, he would arrive at their apartment at 5:00 and stay until 11:00.

One night, as Paloma and he sat on the couch watching *The Bachelor*, which John Levi hated and Paloma loved, Paloma asked him about his girlfriend.

"What girlfriend?" asked John Levi.

"Guy like you. With all your money. Not the worst looking guy in the world. Women must be hanging all over you."

"Not since I went into ministry."

"Why is that?"

"It was not a move that anybody understood."

"You telling me that there isn't some good-looking honey at some church somewhere who would love to get next to you?"

"Not looking for that right now."

"Why is that? You are still young. You must have needs. If people knew how much time you spend here, they might think I am taking care of your needs."

John Levi flushed with embarrassment. Paloma saw the red come to his cheeks and laughed. "Oh, what an innocent little boy you are," she smiled. "Have I embarrassed you?" She tickled his side. She had put shadow with shiny sprinkles on her eyelids and under her eyebrows. She usually wore her hair pulled back for work. Now it was hanging down on either side of her face, and she was looking at him out of the corner of her eye through her hair with a smile on her face.

"How are you enjoying work?" he asked her.

"You are changing the subject."

"Yes, I am." He smiled. "How are you enjoying your job?"

"It's routine. It's boring—the same thing every day. I come in, drink a cup of coffee in the break room, pretend to listen to the other employees talk about their boring lives, go to the file room, pick up my stack of filing, pull the case files, put the docs in the right folder, rinse, repeat. If things get really exciting, I get to scan docs into the right folder on the hard drive of the computer. At first, I tried to read some of the papers I was filing. But that put me too far behind. Now I just file."

"How are you being treated? Making any friends?"

"One of the partners is an ass. Thinks because he is a lawyer he can yell at anyone beneath him. To answer your questions, I haven't made friends. Nothing in common with anyone there. Don't trust anybody there enough to share anything about my life."

"Your old life wasn't boring. How are you dealing with that?"

"It wasn't boring. But it was a twisted kind of routine. Nothing but highs and lows. Highs from meth. Lows from coming down from meth and from shame about needing and using it and what I had to do while I was high. I hated myself every time I came down. I hated Angel and Luther. I hated hating. Sometimes the highs were high enough to make up for the lows. Most of the time they weren't. But then the lows would get so low I had to escape into the highs. The worst were the bad dreams when I took a break from using. Haven't had one of those in a while."

"Are you ever tempted to use again?"

"You want the truth?"

"Yes, Paloma, I always want the truth, and you can always trust me with it."

"The truth is I am tempted almost every day. When I am at work and don't have to think much about what I am doing, my mind wanders, and I get this itch for the rush from meth."

"What keeps you from using again?"

"How happy Cynthia is."

"She is happy, isn't she? Great to see. Bad dreams about what?"

"Same one every time. I dream I am at my father's house. It's dark. Deep, silent, thick dark, heavy on my skin. I am in the backyard. There is a pile of dirt. I dig it up and find my mother's body . . . I don't want to talk about that anymore."

"Then we won't."

Paloma closed her eyes. John Levi tuned off the sound on the television.

"That's the most you have told me about using. Thank you. Let's change the subject. What makes *you* happy?"

"'Happy'? Did you say 'happy'?"

"Yes, 'happy.'"

"Haven't thought about my own happiness in a while. What do you mean . . . 'happy'? I'm happy right now sitting here with you," she said.

"Thank you. What else?"

"I'm happy not having to worry about whether Cynthia has a safe place to live, enough electricity and water, and enough food. I'm happy I don't have to get fucked for meth and a place to live. But I worry how long it will be before I have to start worrying again about the rent and the electricity."

"Why do you think you will have to start worrying about that again?"

"You got anything for me except these questions? Because you won't take care of us forever. And it wouldn't be fair to you or the other people you could help. You only have so much money and time."

"Why not?"

Paloma stuck her tongue out at him. "Come on. Quit bullshitting me. Not you."

"What do you hunger and thirst for?"

"What? Where the hell did that question come from?"

"You were talking about not having to worry about having enough to eat. So what are you really hungry for? There is a saying, 'Happy are those who hunger and thirst for justice.' What are you hungry for?"

"Like I said. Rent money. Food money. Electricity and water money. Control over my own body."

"You have all those."

"For how long?"

"For now for sure." He deflected the issue again. "What else? What would really make you happy? The kind of happiness that would make you know that life is good?"

"Life isn't good."

"You don't feel that life is good?"

"How could I? Have you not been paying attention? Most of my life has been terrible, some of it by my own making. I have been defeated by my life most of the time."

"What would make you happy now? What would make you feel good? What's your hunger?"

"My brother and sister out of prison. A life for them once they get out. A future for Cynthia. Her college paid for. There's a hunger. A great love for her—someone she can depend upon and trust."

"For yourself?"

"Those *are* for myself."

"What else?"

"For people not to know my past. For people not to *judge* me by my past. Or for them to just give me a freaking chance, you know? Do I have to say it?" Paloma looked at John Levi out of the corner of her eye through her hair again. "Love. A normal, healthy love. I've never had that kind of love from any man . . . or from anyone except Cynthia. I don't know what that would look like with a man. I've read about it. I've seen it in the movies and on television. I've never seen a man and woman in real life who had it." Paloma looked at John Levi, waiting for him to say something. He did not reply. "You know something sad?"

"What?" said John Levi. "What's sad?" *"Other than your entire life up 'til now,"* he thought.

"I've never been on a date."

"You've never been on a date? Not even before you went to work for Bodine?"

"I was only fourteen when I got sucked in by Luther. Before then I lived in a dump. Most of the time there was no running water, hot or cold. My hair and clothes were dirty, and I stunk. Boys only looked at me to make fun of me. It was cruel. Nobody cared what I was going through. I sure wasn't going to tell anyone. And there was no one around to tell me how to be a female. Then I went from being a virgin who was all alone to being a piece of ass for a bunch of sick old men. I learned the facts of life from some fat, hairy guy sweating and grunting on top of me." She saw the shocked look on John Levi's face. "My mother had died, and my father was worthless. The alternative to the Bodines was foster care for me and my sister and brother. They ended up in the system anyway. By then I was too far down the road to turn back."

"It's never too late to turn back."

"We'll see."

"So you've never experienced romance."

"What's that?"

"Back then—before Bodine, I mean—what would have made you happy then?"

"Same things as now. Rent paid. Roof that didn't leak. Hot water and electricity. Clean clothes and lots of shampoo. Plenty to eat . . . Somebody to talk to honestly . . . You know what would have made me happy then? A date to the prom. I still dream about that. Guy picks me up at my door. I am in a fancy dress. He pins a corsage on me. We dance all night. We sit at a table with friends. Somebody spikes the punch with vodka. *Don't you dare laugh!* I get elected prom queen. He drives me home, walks me to my front door, gives me a long, romantic kiss goodnight, and leaves. He doesn't try to get in my pants. Just leaves. One normal night. That would have just about done it."

She charged on. "How about you, John Levi? What makes you happy? Have you ever found it?

"The things that I thought would make me happy didn't. At least not for long enough."

"Like what?"

"Jury trials. The kick of crushing an expert witness on cross-examination. Closing argument in a big case when a lot of people come to the courtroom just to hear me. The rush of winning a big verdict. Being the best lawyer in the courthouse."

"Is that how you got rich?"

"Yes."

"Didn't that make you happy?"

"Money doesn't make you happy. Not after you have enough for what you need, that is. Money can enslave you like meth and Luther Bodine enslaved you. Again, once you have enough for necessities."

"Is that why you left that life?"

"You are not going to sit still for this. But I hope we are becoming friends."

Paloma smiled. "Risk it."

"God made me unhappy with it."

"O goodness. So we are back to God. Okay, I'll bite. How did God make you unhappy?"

"I represented clients whom the world had screwed. They were prey for predatory companies and employers. I could get them money case by case. I could get them some justice. I came to hunger and thirst for that. But those cases didn't change their world. I couldn't really bring 'justice'"—he made air quotes with his fingers—"like I wanted to. And I wanted to get *into* the lives of people like my clients. The poor and working poor. I wanted to experience their heroism with them. Their hardships and courage and endurance. I wanted their passion for just . . . surviving. Like yours. I asked you what would make you happy and you said rent money. It's real. It's true. If I asked that question of some of my old girlfriends, they would have said something like a ski trip to Aspen or to the Galleria in Dallas."

Paloma started laughing.

"Now you are laughing at me."

"Yes . . . The only reason I said rent money would make me happy is I have gone without it too long. I wish I could count on it enough to want something more. Like a trip somewhere else besides this sad neighborhood. Don't knock having enough of what you really need to dream about things you just want."

"I hear you. I am not idealizing poverty . . . making it into something good."

"I know what idealizing means."

"It's just that Jesus tells us that he, that God, is actually found in the midst of the suffering poor. God is experienced in helping the poor and sick and prisoner and stranger. Not so much in church or in prayer. Just in helping people in need. It's human nature for us to keep looking far and wide for something to make us happy, really happy, when the path to that happiness is right in front of us. And within us. Like me with the fame of being thought a great lawyer. Or you and meth. "

"And what's that ladder to happiness?"

"Augustine said it is God. He once wrote: 'We are made for you, O God, and our hearts are restless until they rest in you.'"

Paloma snorted. John Levi frowned at her.

"Who's Augustine?"

"An early church father. Why did you snort?"

"Did I snort?"

"Why did you make that noise?"

"Maybe *your* heart is restless for God. But God's heart has not been restless for mine. Or a lot of other people's. Seems like God's restless heart is pretty damn random."

"I understand why you feel that way. I think there is so much suffering and injustice that is against God's will because people who claim to be Christians do not hunger and thirst to follow the way of Jesus."

"So you are saying that it was not God's will for my mother to be a drug addict? Or for her to get stomach cancer and die with a hole in her stomach? Or my father to be a miserable drunk? Or for no one to come forward to help my family to keep me from having to go into prostitution at fourteen to feed my brother and sister?"

John Levi started to interrupt but decided to let her talk. Paloma was getting angry.

"And you are saying that it is against God's will that those fuckers Luther and Angel Bodine have used so many young women and gotten us hooked on meth? Or even for methamphetamine to exist? I mean, why doesn't God just kill Angel Bodine? We are all going to die sometime. Why not just speed it up for him?"

He waited until she was quiet. "Yes, Paloma. I am saying that all those things were and are against God's will."

"Well, that is one weak-ass God you got there. I don't hunger for God because God never has hungered for me."

"My God may be 'weak-ass,' as you put it. Another way to put that is that God is a crucified God, present in and sharing in all our suffering. That 'weak-ass God' is why I am sitting here."

"Just why *are* you sitting here? Does *this* make you happy?"

"Yes, Paloma. Maybe the happiest I have ever been in my life."

"Whaaaat? Now? But *why*?"

"Paloma, I admire and love you and Cynthia so much. I feel privileged for you to let me into your life a little. I feel God in this."

"Well, I don't," replied Paloma. "I just feel scared you are going to find something else to make you happy, like you have before."

"John Levi," Cynthia called from her bedroom, "can you help me with my algebra?"

"We will continue this conversation. If you want," said John Levi to Paloma.

"Just keep paying the rent until I can get on my feet. For whatever reason. Please."

The very next night, John Levi showed up at Paloma's and Cynthia's apartment in a sport coat, tie, white dress shirt, and slacks. He knocked on the door. Paloma answered it in a nice white blouse and dark blue skirt and black high heels. She wore a simple necklace and a long earring dangling from her one earlobe. Her hair was down like John Levi liked it. She looked wonderful. He had told Cynthia to tell her mother that it was open house at

Cynthia's school for parents to meet their child's teachers and that he would pick her up and take her. But there wasn't.

When Paloma opened the door, John Levi said, "There is no open house. We are going on your first date." He stepped inside and pinned a corsage on her blouse. Paloma turned and gave Cynthia a look. "*You* should have told me." Then she turned to John Levi. "Where are we going?"

"A steakhouse downtown."

"Give me a moment to put on a little more makeup."

"You look absolutely great right now."

"If this is my first date, I am going to look the way I want to look. So my date will ask me out again." She smiled at him.

Paloma went into her bedroom and closed the door.

Cynthia hugged John Levi. "You did good," she said to him.

Later they were seated at a table for two in a posh restaurant on South Main Street in downtown Fort Worth. Paloma was self-conscious about the corsage and left it in his car. Two lawyers John Levi knew were in the restaurant with their wives. He stopped by their table and shook hands. Paloma hung back to keep from embarrassing him, but he called her over and introduced her to them as his date. She seemed very pleased.

As they were seated, she asked, "Why are you doing this?"

"Because you deserve to be treated well. I want you to learn to expect that."

Paloma declined the offer of wine. John Levi joined her in her abstinence. As the bread and salad were brought to the table, Paloma was soaking up the surroundings.

"How much does a dinner at a restaurant like this cost? Just curious."

"About half of what it would have if we had ordered a bottle of good wine."

"How much?"

"Maybe two hundred fifty dollars."

"Oh my God. That's about half a week's work for me."

Paloma was by far the most attractive woman in the restaurant, even with her scars and her limp. He was enjoying sitting directly across the table and looking at her. Usually they sat beside one another on her couch.

"So is this really a date?"

"Of course it's a date."

"I'm surprised you are willing to be seen in public with me."

"You mean that some people in the neighborhood would talk if they saw us together like this?" He looked around the restaurant. "I think we are safe here. All those men are thinking is how lucky I am to have such an attractive date."

Now it was Paloma who blushed.

The entre was served. They both ordered filet mignon, hers the six ounce and his the ten.

As he was eating, he noticed her watching him and mimicking his table manners.

"Good?" he asked. "Cooked the way you like it?"

"I've never had anything this good," she answered. "Thanks for this."

Unlike every date he had been on ever, his date finished her steak.

When they were done and he was drinking a cup of coffee, she suddenly asked, "Tell me about your family."

"What do you want to know?"

"Anything you want to tell me."

"I am an only child. My father is an owner of an oil well service company. My mother doesn't work outside the home. She plays cards and spends money."

"Where do they live?"

"Here in Fort Worth."

"Where?"

"In a gated community for rich people close to their country club."

"They must be very proud of you."

"No. No, they are not."

"Why not?"

"Because I didn't become my father."

"Why didn't you?"

"Because his life would not have made me happy."

"Does he respect your decision?"

"I don't think so. Actually, no he doesn't. I am an embarrassment to him."

"That seems impossible."

"It's the truth."

"But you have been so successful. And now you have given up so much to help people in trouble. How can he not be proud of that?"

"He thinks I have rejected his values."

"What values?"

"He believes in money."

"What else."

"That's really it."

"Just money?"

"And all the trappings of money. Power. Comfort. Insulation from suffering. Separation from people who aren't just like him."

"He *has* to believe in more than that."

"I don't think so."

"Wasn't he always there? At home with your mother and you?"

"Yes. Except for business trips."

"Your parents—have they been together all the time you have been alive?"

"Yes."

"They made sure you were in a nice house, plenty to eat, took you to the doctor when you were sick?"

"Yes to all of that."

"Patted you on your little head and spanked you on your little butt when you needed it?"

He nodded. *"But they never spanked me once,"* he thought.

"They paid for your schooling?"

"Yeah. Except seminary."

"What's seminary?"

"Schooling to be a minister."

"John Levi, from where I sit as someone who never had any of those things, I think maybe you are taking all that for granted. My mother hadn't been a mother to me and my sister and brother for years before she died. My father was never a parent to us. They never married. They had drunken fights whenever they were together. We were always hungry, cold in the winter, and hot in the summer. Let me ask you this. Do you think you would be where you are now if not for you mother and father?"

"Where is this wisdom coming from? What would this woman be if she had had my parents?"

"No, I wouldn't be where I am. I wouldn't. You are right."

"How have you thanked them?" Paloma wasn't letting up.

"I have to think about that."

"How long since you have seen them?"

"Years."

"Years? Did you say *'years'*?"

"Yes."

"And you say they live in Fort Worth."

"Yes."

"Why no contact in so long?"

"Because we argue—about my rejection of their lives."

"You know what I think?"

"What?"

"I think that you are happy when you are helping people. So why not make yourself happy by helping them? Tell them you are grateful for what they did for you. And that you love them. It is a sin to take family for granted. Take that from one who has none."

"You have Cynthia."

"Yes, I have Cynthia." She smiled. "We need to get home to her."

As Paloma sat there across the table from him, so very attractive and wise, taking such an amazing path, John Levi had to stop himself from saying to her, "And you have me too." He stopped himself. "*What can I be feeling for this woman? What am I doing here? We have nothing in common.*"

They drove back to her apartment with the radio tuned to a country-western station. She sang the lyrics with every song.

They walked to her door. It was 10:00 p.m. She started to unlock her door but he stopped her. "You don't want to come in?" she asked him.

"No, I need to go home now. Early day tomorrow." On impulse he said, "But you want a proper date, and I want this to end like one." He put his arms around her waist and kissed her. He opened his eyes and caught her staring at him during the kiss, her eyes an inch from his. He started to pull away. She wrapped her arms around his neck, standing on her toes, closed her eyes, and kissed him like he had never been kissed before. As they parted she patted his chest with both of her hands, smiling and looking up into his eyes. She looked like a twenty-year-old. "I had a really nice time," she said. She went inside.

As he walked back to his car, she called to him. "I forgot my corsage. Can you bring it to me?"

He retrieved the orchid and brought it to her. "Why do you want this? It's already wilting?"

"As a keepsake of my first date ever, silly." And she kissed him on the cheek.

"*What have I done?*" he thought.

Cynthia greeted Paloma just inside the apartment door.

"How was it, Momma?"

"It was wonderful. He is wonderful."

"So are you, Momma."

"And now we have gotten down to the truth of it. You are trying to save God from failing them."

— Sunday, August 11, 2019 —

"You wanted to meet with me?" John Levi asked Rafer Thompson, a retired Fort Worth police detective who started attending Peace Church because of John Levi's and Pedro's efforts to keep the young boys of the neighborhood from joining the local street gangs.

"Yes, sir. Do you have the time now?"

"Yes, I have about thirty minutes."

"Can we step into your office for some privacy?"

"Of course."

It was just after noon on a Sunday and the last few people were leaving the chapel and fellowship building. Paloma and Cynthia had just said goodbye to John Levi. He usually spent his Sunday afternoons visiting the homes of church members. He planned to see Paloma and Cynthia at their apartment after evening worship and the church pizza supper for hungry neighborhood children.

Detective Thompson and John Levi went to the pastor's office. John Levi went in first and Thompson closed the door behind him. They sat facing one another in wooden chairs in front of the pastor's desk.

"What's on your mind?" John Levi asked.

"Reverend Jones, I want to start this conversation by saying that I am a 100-percent supporter of what you are doing here. I was a police detective in this district for more than a decade just before my retirement and I see a real difference in the spirit of this neighborhood because of your ministries."

"That's good to hear . . . But?"

"I am not trying to intrude. I just want to make sure you know what you are doing."

"I'm all ears."

"It's about Paloma Ibarra."

John Levi felt a catch in his chest. *Is Thompson going to tell me that she is using again?*

"What about her?"

"I hear some of your older members talking about your relationship with her."

"Members? How many?"

"Maybe a dozen. It's a hot topic at the senior citizen center."

"What are they saying?"

"That it is inappropriate for a Methodist minister to be in a relationship with a woman like her."

"A woman like what?"

"So you don't know about her past. That is what I was afraid of."

"A woman like what?"

"Reverend Jones, Paloma Ibarra is a prostitute who works for two of the most miserable men in this city. They pimp for her. She works at their club on North Main and helps them attract men to their house for drugs. She is a methamphetamine addict."

John Levi looked blankly at Thompson.

"You didn't know any of that?" Thompson asked.

"Detective, I appreciate the reason that you have told me this. But maybe I know more about Ms. Ibarra than the people who are gossiping about her. Or maybe even than you do. I am just trying to help her and her daughter. They have led tragic lives. Ms. Ibarra has changed. I am helping her. That's part of my calling as a Christian."

"Reverend, meth addicts don't change."

"Rafer—may I call you Rafer? Good. Please call me John Levi. I do not question your years of experience dealing with addiction."

"Not just addiction, but methamphetamine addiction."

"Methamphetamine addiction. But a foundation of the gospel is that people *can* repent and make new lives for themselves. That the spirit of Jesus and being a part of a loving, forgiving community can help them change. Maybe you think that is silly, but that is why I am here."

"And you think Paloma Ibarra is making a new life?"

"I do."

"She is going to break your heart."

"Perhaps, but that is part of my calling."

"To have your heart broken?"

"To take on lost causes. That brings a risk of heartbreak. One of Jesus' beatitudes is, 'Happy are those who mourn, for they shall be comforted.' I mourn what has happened to Ms. Ibarra and her daughter. I mourn that so many young women like Ms. Ibarra are used for evil, degrading purposes. I mourn that so many so-called Christians don't care about the unjust suffering in the world. Paloma and her daughter mourn what life has done to them. My hope is that we will all be comforted with their new lives. I can't save everyone, but I can help save them."

"The problem with lost causes is that they are already lost. There are so many in this neighborhood you can actually help, people who will respond to your help. You need to concentrate on causes you can win. Her life is not one of those."

"We won't know that until I try."

"Are you willing for Paloma Ibarra to take your ministries at Peace down with her?"

"What are you talking about?"

"I did some checking into things. I asked some patrol officers in this police district to check some things out for me."

"And?"

"I am told that your truck—which you know is a very easy truck to spot—is parked late at Ms. Ibarra's apartment complex damned near every night."

"Detective Thompson. Rafer. I am starting to wonder if you are a fan of the ministries we have started here. You said that older members of this church are talking about my relationship with Paloma. How would they know about it? "

"If I weren't a fan, I wouldn't be having this conversation. I would just let things unravel. The members know about it because the patrol officer I asked to check on it visited the local senior center and ran his mouth. I am sorry about that. I should not have trusted him."

"Are you assuming that I have a relationship with Paloma that is more than friendship or a pastor's with a church member?"

"Don't you?"

"No, sir, I do not."

"John Levi, people aren't blind. Despite the marks on her face and that limp, she is a very . . . a very physically attractive woman. People see the way she looks at you and the way you look at her. I am sure that she is very experienced in the ways . . . of making a man happy. You are a young, single man. It's not that you would have a relationship with a young woman. It's *that* woman. Even if there is nothing like that going on, something like that *appears* to be going on."

"Rafer, I promise you that there is nothing sexual between me and Paloma. I give you my word on that. I can't tell you everything that I know about Paloma and Cynthia because they have told me things in confidence. But I can tell you that I wanted to serve an inner-city church to help people like them. Their story is tragic. They are so admirable. It makes me happy to help them and be around them. They are so . . . real." He paused. "Look, I am just trying to help them find happiness. I have a chance to really make a difference in their lives. I *am* making a difference. I don't want to give that up. I am not going to abandon them because small-minded people talk. I am spending so much there to try to make sure Paloma doesn't go back to that old life and to protect her daughter from being abandoned again."

"But you don't have to spend so much time at night over there."

"Like I said, I am just trying to keep Paloma from returning to meth."

"All it would take for you to be kicked out of the church would be for word to get to the bishop about you and her."

"Are you going to spread that word?"

"No, Reverend, I am not. I make that promise to you. But it's going to get up the ladder to the top . . . John Levi, you aren't Jesus and Paloma Ibarra is not your Mary Magdalene."

"Agreed. Paloma Ibarra is Paloma Ibarra, not Mary Magdalene. I am definitely not Jesus."

"Listen to me, please. If you are not physically involved with this woman . . ."

"I just gave you my word that I am not."

". . . then what *are* you doing over there so many nights a week? Are you really being honest with yourself about that? A woman with that past? You are her lifeline. She probably thinks there is only one way to hold on to you."

Thompson saw the angry look in John Levi's eyes. "Okay, okay. You are just being a pastor or a brother to her. Does she understand that?"

"I am afraid that if I just drop out of their lives now, Paloma will go back to meth and her daughter Cynthia will be abandoned again."

"And you feel it is on you to stop that? That it will somehow be your fault if that happens? Reverend Jones, people who live with meth addicts twenty-four hours a day can't keep them from going back to meth. You can't stop her, not even by being there all night every night, if she wants to use again. The attraction of meth—God the Father, God the Son, and God the Holy Bigod Spirit can't stop her. She has to stop herself. There is no one on earth who wants to be more alone than a meth addict who craves the drug and decides to use again."

"You saying that people can't help meth addicts quit? That God can't help her?"

"No, I am not saying that. What I am saying that you are not long for this ministry if you think that it's on your shoulders to keep bad things from happening to the people in this neighborhood. Or to keep people in this neighborhood, or any neighborhood, from doing bad things. You ain't God."

"I don't see God doing it . . . at least not without me."

Rafer reached out and put his hand on John Levi's shoulder. "And now we have gotten down to the truth of it," said the detective. "You aren't just trying to save Paloma and her daughter. You are trying to save God from failing them."

CHAPTER ELEVEN

"Do You *See* This Woman?"

— Sunday, August 18, 2019 —

For the week after his Sunday conversation with Detective Thompson, John Levi began to reexamine why he was spending so much time at Paloma's and Cynthia's. He admitted to himself that Paloma was very attractive to him and that he had in weak moments wondered what it would be like to kiss her again and more. He was a pastor and an aspiring Christian, but still a young man. He wondered whether he would be so generous with his money if Paloma were not so attractive. But there was a wise, bright line in the Methodist church against any romantic relationship between a pastor and a church member. Crossing that line could rightly result in suspension of ordination. There was a real imbalance in the relationship between pastor and church member that calls into question whether any such a relationship could be entirely voluntary for the member. He was not sure what her feelings about him were—whether she was tolerating him for the material help he was giving, or whether she was developing true feelings for him. He could be leading her and himself on by spending so much time there, if he wasn't willing for the relationship to progress. It could even lead to his falling romantically in love with her, which would only compound the problem.

So he made excuses to Paloma to avoid being at her apartment for dinner or late at night. He still came every evening to check on them. He didn't just want to stop abruptly and he hungered to see them. But he always left before 6:30 p.m. Paloma kept asking him what was wrong. She was afraid that the time had come when John Levi had tired of them. Or that he had awakened to the fact that she would not fit in his world. Or that he could not put her past out of his mind.

Cynthia was sure that Paloma was responsible for John Levi not staying as long as he had, that her mother was not making herself as inviting to John Levi as she could, or that she was putting him off with her tactless words. Cynthia dreamed of the three of them becoming a family. But John Levi heeded the wisdom of what the detective had said to him. He didn't want to sacrifice the ministries of Peace Church to whatever his relationship was or would become with Paloma.

The next Sunday, Paloma and Cynthia sat together in morning worship. It was the first time that Paloma had ever heard John Levi preach. Before he knew that Paloma was coming, John Levi chose his sermon scripture from the seventh chapter of Luke, verses 36 through 50. He entitled his sermon, "Do you see this woman?"

In the scripture, a Pharisee invites Jesus to supper at his home. But the Pharisee does not treat Jesus as an honored guest. He does not provide Jesus with water to wash his feet, or kiss his cheek in greeting, or anoint his head with oil. But a "woman of the city who was a sinner" witnesses how Jesus is being mistreated, and bursts into the meal to wash Jesus feet with her tears and dry them with her hair, to kiss his feet and to anoint his hair with costly oil. The Pharisee's reaction is that Jesus would have known "who and what kind of woman this was" and not have allowed her to touch him if he were indeed a prophet of God. But Jesus instead asks the Pharisee, "Simon, do you see this woman?" because the Pharisee was only seeing the *sort* of woman the Pharisee judged her to be.

John Levi spoke about this unnamed woman and what might have motivated her to be so courageous in defense of Jesus. "The scripture does not tell us what Jesus had done or said that inspired this courageous, risky love from this woman. Perhaps she was not unnamed to him. Perhaps they had a history. Perhaps her past sins *had* been sexual. Perhaps she had been required to sell her body to cruel men to survive. Perhaps she had a daughter or a son and the only way for her to provide for them was with all she had—her body. Or perhaps she was the woman with the unquenchable flow of blood described in the fourth chapter of Mark's Gospel, a woman who had to skulk on the edge of community because she was considered to be unclean. Perhaps she was judged and shunned by the good religious people who knew all the purity laws of Torah but had forgotten the one great law of mercy. Perhaps one day he had seen her hiding at the edge of a crowd around him, listening to his teachings of forgiveness and hope. Perhaps he had walked through the crowd to her, and called her 'daughter,' and had taken her hand and brought her to the center with him. Perhaps he had forgiven her sins and restored her to community. Perhaps he had shared a meal with her and made her a part of his community. Perhaps he had enabled her to love herself. Surely he saw through her past into her soul. Surely, he saw *her.*"

"So she loved him. Why wouldn't she? Do we think she was the only woman to fall in love with Jesus? We would be blind if we ignored the possibility that her touching him so intimately with her hair was an erotic act for her. Clearly, Jesus inspired a depth of *every* kind of love from people. Much of the love he inspired was because he did what the Pharisee failed to do. Jesus saw people as individuals. He looked into their souls. He did not see them as the *kind* of people they were judged to be by the religious establishment. He saw them. We are called to do the same."

When John Levi finished his sermon, he saw Paloma looking at him with tears brimming up and out of her eyes.

CHAPTER TWELVE

"You have taken our church from us and given it to strangers."

— Later Sunday, August 18, 2019 —

"Mister Jones, you have taken our church from us and given it to strangers," said Jewel McKenzie.

John Levi held church council meetings on the third Sunday of every month. The members of the council were elected by the church members to act as a kind of board of directors. John Levi ensured that the council included a mix of veteran Anglo members and new Anglo, Hispanic, and African-American members from the neighborhood. He used the meetings to report on the successes of the many new ministries of the church.

The only unusual attendee at this Peace Church council meeting was a member of the board of trustees of Faith Church, who was there to observe. His name was Jim Wilson. He was a lawyer and an old friend of John Levi's. He was sent there by the Faith Church trustees to monitor and report John Levi's successes and failures. Faith Church was funding some of Peace's ministries, and John Levi was a possible successor to the senior pastor at Faith Church when he retired. Some members of Faith Church's council were concerned about how John Levi would deal with opposition to his vision of a church. Wilson had come to the right meeting to see this firsthand.

Jewel McKenzie was the most vocal opponent among the veteran Peace members to John Levi's new ministries to the neighborhood. Jewel was an eighty-three-year-old Anglo woman who had lived in the church neighborhood almost her entire adult life. She was in her twenties when she first moved to North Hill. Then the neighborhood was entirely Anglo and working class. Most of the household breadwinners worked at the meat packing plants, at the stockyards, or at what was called the "bomber plant" going back to the time when B-24s were manufactured there during the Second World War. That plant had become General Dynamics and then Lockheed, manufacturing F-16s and then F-35s. These Anglo families lived in the small, neat clapboard houses lining the streets around the church. In the 50s and 60s the neighborhood was homogenous and safe, from their perspective, unless you happened to be Hispanic or Black traveling through. Attendance at worship on Sunday and at potluck suppers on Wednesday evenings was routine and reassuring. Most of the preaching was about the atoning blood of Jesus and the need for right belief and conventional kindness to family and friends.

But the demographics of the church neighborhood had changed. The children of those Anglo parents grew up and moved out as fast as they could. Houses aged and sold when the Anglo owners left or died. The new neighbors were overwhelmingly Latino, from Mexico or Central America, many undocumented, almost all identifying as Roman Catholic but unaccustomed to attending church regularly. Some African-American families moved into the neighborhood as well. The veteran Anglo members of the church who remained in their old homes were afraid of their new neighbors and viewed Peace Church as their refuge, a return to the good past and an escape of the bad present every Sunday and Wednesday. They wanted the church to be nothing more than a place for the familiar. The only outreach to the community they approved was recruiting the rare Anglo family moving into the neighborhood to join them at Peace.

Jewel McKenzie had demanded to be included on the Peace council. It would have caused an awkward fight to prevent her inclusion. John Levi did not openly oppose her inclusion because she was generally disliked by even the veteran Anglo membership, was well known to be controlling and hypercritical of everything and everybody, and because he thought it would be better, to paraphrase Lyndon Johnson, for her to be inside the tent pissing out than outside the tent pissing in. But she had proved to always be inside the tent pissing in during her tenure. She opposed every new ministry which John Levi proposed.

"I am vehemently opposed to this new ministry. It is one more attempt to take our church from us and give it to strangers. We don't need more of these dirty, out-of-control children running around our church and damaging our property. I will not allow this to happen. And I object to how little time *Mister* Jones spends with the true members of this church. We are the ones who have built and sustained this church and we deserve and demand a pastor who will devote his time to us, not to these aliens in our neighborhood."

John Levi was spending much less time with the veteran members of Peace than his predecessor pastors had. But his predecessors had done nothing to serve the neighborhood or to bring its newer arrivals into the church. All of the recent predecessors had been rookie ministers on their way to a bigger church and a bigger salary as soon as possible or aged pastors on their last stop before formal retirement. Previous pastors had made it a point to visit once a week in every home of the thirty or so older veteran members. John Levi was too busy with the ministries to the neighborhood to continue these weekly visits. Instead he delighted driving through the neighborhood during the day with bags of groceries and clothes. He would deliver the food and clothes to the homes of families he learned were in need. He would linger to speak to the adults present, often with the teens in the households translating English into Spanish and back, about their family's problems. He spread the word about all the ministries of the church during these visits and learned about legal and financial crises the neighborhood families were facing. It was an education for him into the lives of the working poor. He began to pick up Spanish and resolved to become fluent as soon as his time permitted.

McKenzie's particular objection this Sunday was to John Levi's proposal of another new ministry to the neighborhood. He recommended formation of another non-profit corporation which would build and operate a child care center on church property to help working-class families in the neighborhood by charging minimum fees. John Levi told the council about a mother of four whose family needed her to find a job but for whom child care costs would be greater than the income she could bring home. McKenzie blamed this family for their poverty and said she would not allow this ministry to start.

Before John Levi could reply, Darla Henderson, one of the paralegals who led the ministries to the young girls in the neighborhood, spoke up angrily. "Ms. McKenzie, did you say that *you* would not allow this ministry to go forward?"

"I did."

"You are only one member of this council and one member of this church. How will you alone prevent it?"

"Young lady, I was a member and contributor to this church before you were born. All of the real members of this church are with me on this."

Darla looked around the table at the other council members present. "And I am sure that all of us here appreciate all you have done for the church over the years."

"Decades." McKenzie corrected Henderson.

"Yes, ma'am, decades. But you are still just one member now. How will you stop this from going forward by yourself?"

"Because I have a meeting with our bishop this coming Tuesday and I intend to expose Mister Jones and have him removed from this church. A group of us are going to the meeting."

The other veteran council members present looked down at their hands. The remaining five members—Darla and new Hispanic members Mr. Esquivel, Mr. Serrano, Ms. Castillo and Ms. Chacon—began yelling at McKenzie. Jewel sat back with a self-satisfied smirk on her face.

John Levi spoke up. "Let's take a breath. Jewel, I ask you to explain what you said."

"You can ask. But I won't be cross-examined."

"Please explain what you meant when you said that I had taken the church from 'us.' Who is 'us'?"

"You know very well."

"No, I don't. I thought this was the church of Jesus Christ. Who is 'us'?"

"The people who made this church."

"The members who were already here when I came?"

"Yes. And their families. And the people *we* would welcome into our flock."

"When I came here, there were less than thirty people at worship. The youngest person regularly attending was in her upper sixties. Today we had more than one hundred thirty in morning worship. You want us to go back to thirty people? If the church is limited to your 'us,' it is going to close in a matter of months."

"So? We had kept this church going for decades. It is our church. If we want it to close when we were gone, that is our right. The Methodist Church owes us a pastor who will minister to us the way we want. Instead they sent you. We don't want this. "

Murmuring in the meeting. One of the veteran members said, "'We'? You are not speaking for me or my wife, Jewel. John Levi, my wife and I will not be a part of any meeting with the bishop."

John Levi replied, "What about the needs of the neighborhood? What about the teachings of Jesus? In your mind, does a church of Jesus Christ have any responsibility to help people in need in the church's own neighborhood?"

Darla interjected, "Did you listen to John Levi's sermon this morning?"

Ms. McKenzie turned on Henderson. "This man does not preach the gospel. He says nothing, ever, about justification by faith or our being saved by the blood of Jesus or repentance. He says nothing about our sinfulness.

He does not save souls. He has turned this church into a do-gooder, bleeding-heart arm of liberal government."

She turned to the entire group. "Do you remember his sermons last month on the Beatitudes? He constantly preys upon your ignorance of the Bible in his preaching to you. Well, *this* church member knows her Bible. He said that the beatitude is 'Happy are those who hunger and thirst after *justice*.' It's not 'justice.' It's 'righteousness.' It's acting right. It's following God's law. It's believing the right things and associating with people who separate ourselves from unrighteous people. Like these unrighteous Mexicans."

"When has he ever confronted these Mexicans with their sinfulness, with their unrighteousness? Their laziness? Their noisy cars and that terrible music? With the guns they shoot off on New Year's Eve? Some things are just wrong. The way they act is unrighteous. So many people living in one house. And their children. They come into our church. No respect for us. Crawl all over it. Dirty faces and hands. Getting their handprints all over the piano that *we* saved and scrimped to buy. They contribute nothing to the church and ruin it for us." She pointed her finger at John Levi. "And you have brought that ignorant language into our worship. You make us sit there and listen to that gibber-gabber, instead of demanding that they learn our language. This is our country, not theirs."

Rather than getting nods of affirmation, people turned their faces from Jewel.

John Levi spoke to McKenzie. "Did you hear my sermon this morning about actually *seeing* people, Jewel? I am just asking us all to be led by Jesus' teachings. Jesus breaks down this barrier between the so-called us and the so-called them. He asks that we *see* everyone as part of 'us.'"

"But *you* don't see *us*," said McKenzie. You are the one who has divided this church into 'us' and 'them,' not me. You don't care about the people whose support and sacrifices have kept this church alive all these years. We are your 'them.' Someone has to be Mexican or Black for you to see them. They are your 'us.' You have no idea what we are going through, and you don't care. Our bodies are failing us. Our incomes buy less and less. We are surrounded by strangers. Abandoned by our families and our church. We are prisoners in our own homes and outcasts in our neighborhood."

"Jewel, I am sorry you feel that way. I wish there were more hours in the week. These new ministries are taking almost all of my time. I am not going to apologize for that," said John Levi, "but I am inviting all the members of this church to *see* one another as part of our new 'us'—Anglo, Black, and brown—and to join in these ministries."

"Do you *see* this man? This is Señor Esquivel. He has been married for thirty years. He is the father of five children, three sons and two daughters.

He started and runs his own tire repair shop on Long Avenue. Three of his children are now in Tarrant County College. We are honored he has joined here at Peace. He contributes financially to this church. He is not Mexican. His family has been in Texas since before your family came here, Jewel."

McKenzie tried to interrupt, but John Levi kept speaking.

"Do you *see* this man? This is Señor Serrano. He is a Marine veteran. He served in the first Iraq war. He has a son in the Marines now. He was born in Zacatecas, Mexico, immigrated to the U.S. when he was six, and became a naturalized American citizen while he was on active duty in the Corps. Now he drives a city bus. His wife of more than twenty years works as a teacher's aide at the elementary school across the street. He is active in our boys club, and she is active with Darla in our girls club. We are honored he has joined here at Peace."

McKenzie started to get up to leave.

"Jewel, I expect you to sit there and listen. You have had your say and now I want you to listen to the response. You slandered these good people. You used the most ignorant ethnic stereotypes. You did it to try to run them off from this church. Now I am asking you to sit there and learn about them." He caught himself. "But of course you are free to leave. If you do, we will take it as your resignation from this council."

"You aren't going to run me out of my church," said Jewel.

"Good. These two ladies are Señora Castillo and Señorita Chacon. Do you *see* each of them? Señora Castillo is an LVN. She works at the nursing home on Decatur Avenue. She has received award after award for the quality of her care and her kindness. He husband died of cancer years ago. She has twin teenage girls. They are cheerleaders at the high school and both work part-time to support the family. All three—Señora Castillo and her daughters—were born here in the U.S. Senora Castillo speaks Spanish and English, but her daughters only English. We are honored she has joined here at Peace.

"And this is Señorita Chacon. She has a three-year-old daughter. She is the victim of violence by the father of her child. She makes a living cleaning houses and baking. She has a wonderful singing voice. I'll bet you don't *see* her enough to recognize that she sings lovely solos with our church choir. She was born in Mexico and has her legal residency papers because she was the victim of family violence. Our *pro bono* legal aid clinic helped her get those papers. She is a lovely young lady of profound faith. We are honored she has joined us here at Peace."

"And we are honored that you are still here as part of our 'us,' Jewel."

"Señor Esquivel, Señor Serrano, Señora Castillo, Señorita Chacon." John Levi looked at each as he called the name. "I apologize for what Ms.

McKenzie has said. She has said hateful, bigoted things. In this she speaks only for herself. But it is not her fault. It is my fault for not proclaiming Jesus' teachings in a way that reached her. I would not blame you if you left the church. But I am asking you to stay with us in Jesus' work."

The other Anglo members of the council chimed in, "Yes, Yes. Please stay."

Señor Serrano, the former Marine, said, "No one is going to run me and my family out of here. I believe in what we are doing here." The others nodded in agreement.

"Jewel, since you brought one of the happiness Beatitudes up, let me quote my favorite translation of that beatitude. 'Happy are those who hunger and thirst for God to make things right.' I believe that this translation captures the real meaning of Jesus' teachings. So in our ministries to the neighborhood we are trying to help God make things just and right for our neighbors. Does your hungering and thirsting after this righteousness you describe make you happy? Does it make you happy to keep yourself separate and pure from people you judge to be sinners? Are you happy only associating with people you think are like you?"

"Of course I am."

"As long as I have known you, you have *always* seemed to be really unhappy and angry. You are cutting yourself off from your own neighbors and from knowing a lot of good people. I am sad for you."

"Can I speak now?"

"Of course, yes."

"I am happy letting God be in control. 'Be still and know that I am God.' That's Psalm 46, as you probably don't know. If God wanted these people to be fed and clothed and to get justice, then God would have done it already."

"Again, with the 'these people,' Jewel? How will God do that without us? Look around you. Does what you see in this neighborhood make you happy? Hungry children? People who work their heads off at multiple jobs and still can't support their families because they are paid so little? People who get cheated and used by landlords and payday loan companies and plasma buyers and used car dealers? Are we Christians supposed to be still about all that and wait for God alone to do something? Then why hasn't God done it? Why hasn't God changed your mind about your neighbors?"

"Because these people are unrighteous. They don't deserve justice. No, that's wrong. They are getting the justice they deserve . . . from God. How many of the people you help in your law clinic are illegal?"

"What?"

"How many of the people who you help sue our good American business people are here in this country illegally?"

"By 'American' I think you mean 'Anglo.' Most of them," replied John Levi evenly. "Although most of their children were born in the U.S. So those children are American citizens as much as you and I are."

"You don't believe that."

"Jewel, it's not a matter of belief. It is a legal fact that a child born in the U.S. *is* an American citizen. Do you want us to have a citizenship test before we donate food to a hungry family?"

"I want you to give us back our church. Go make another church for them if you'd like."

Darla Henderson spoke up. "John Levi, I think we need to say to you how very much we admire you for giving up so much to preach the teachings of Jesus and to start these ministries to help people in need. This is what the church should be. We can see the fruit of what you are doing in worship. Soon we are going to need more than one Sunday morning service because of the numbers who are coming to be a part of what we are doing. And for you to fund so many of these ministries with your own money—well, that is beyond admirable. When I think about these beautiful children and how poor so many of their families are and how badly they are treated and how much we are able to help them . . ." She teared up and couldn't continue speaking.

"They are poor because they don't belong here," said McKenzie. "And what Mister Jones is doing is not admirable. He uses his own money, so we won't be able to stop him. We've had other pastors here, snotty young men with ambitions to take this church away from us and give it to these strangers in the neighborhood, quoting Jesus for this and that. We've always been able to control them because they needed our church money to do what they wanted. But this man comes in and uses the money he got cheating people in court to shove these ministries down our throat and bring these people into our church without our permission."

Señor Esquivel stood up. "I am not going to listen to this any further. Reverend Jones, my family supports everything you are trying to do here. But I am not going to be abused. I thought this church was different."

Darla spoke up. "Mr. Esquivel, it *is* different."

"I need to get out of here now. John Levi, will you call me?"

"Of course. I am so sorry, Carlos."

Señor Esquivel walked out. Señora Castillo stood up quietly and left with him.

"See what you have done? Are you proud of yourself? Why don't *you* go to another church?" asked Darla.

"Because this is my church! This is our church! You go somewhere else! I am going to fight for our church!" yelled Jewel.

John Levi looked at Jim Wilson, the representative of the church council from Faith Church, to see how he was reacting. He was taking notes.

"I wasn't going to bring this up here. But some of you have been so disrespectful to me this afternoon, led by Mister Jones, that I am going to say it. The so-called Reverend John Levi Jones is in an immoral sexual relationship with a known prostitute and drug addict and her teenaged daughter."

John Levi noticed that Jim Wilson looked up from his note-taking.

Darla cried out, "That's a lie. He would never."

The words of Detective Thompson rang in John Levi's ears: *"Are you willing for Paloma to take your ministries at Peace down with her?"*

"They were in church this very morning. That brown-skinned Mexican woman with the limp and the scar on her chin and the missing ear. And her daughter who is just like her. This man had the nerve to invite them to our church."

"You mean Cynthia and her mother, Paloma? Is that who you mean?" Darla demanded of McKenzie. "That sweet, innocent, beautiful young teenager who is a part of our girls club? Her mother who works in the nursery on Sundays? That's who you mean?" Darla Henderson was shaking.

"I don't know or want to know their names."

"That's who she means," said John Levi. "Ms. McKenzie, you have crossed a line by slandering a woman and her innocent daughter." John Levi rubbed his eyes with his hands to regain his composure. "I am trying to understand how anything about your faith that Jesus is Lord could possibly inform what you are thinking and saying now."

"How dare you accuse me of slander! Or of being unchristian! Wait until I tell *my* bishop . . ."

"Jewel, you can stay here and listen to this, or you can leave. But I am going to speak up for these innocent people now and you cannot stop me. Now it is time for you to be quiet so I can try to undo the unjust and unrighteous—yes, 'unrighteous'—hurt you have inflicted."

McKenzie folded her arms across her chest and seethed. "You can't run me off."

"Are there any limits to what you will do to get your way, to take this church back into a past that no longer exists? It would crush this mother and daughter to hear that you have told the people here that the mother is a prostitute and a drug addict, and that this sweet teenaged girl is . . . following in her footsteps."

"I am limited by the confidential nature of my conversations with both of them. I would like to tell you the complete truth about . . . how hard . . .

their lives have been, how heroic they are, how much they are trying to put their lives back together . . . But I can't . . . And it is not my story to tell. It is theirs. I will emphatically say that they are worthy of our love and support. And even if they weren't, as followers of Jesus and as members of the church of *Jesus*—not *our* church or *her* church or *his* church or *their* church—we should help and support them."

"Was it slander to say that the woman is a prostitute and a drug addict?"

"It is slander to say that she is a prostitute. I can say that."

"So you do not deny that you have a sexual relationship with them."

"I do deny it, categorically and completely. I have just tried to help them . . . Jewel, be decent. You don't have to be a Christian just to be a decent human being. This woman has no friends. She had a terrible childhood and has been exploited by evil men. She has been cut off from community and family. Imagine what it is like to have no one to take your side. I have just been trying to be a friend to her and her daughter."

"There's a good reason why she has no friends. This woman is a prostitute and drug addict."

"You don't know that and repeating that over and over does not make it true." Silence for a moment. "I wish I could tell her whole story. But I am not allowed . . . I have to say this in fairness. She is not now a prostitute. She is not using now. Jewel, it is *unrighteous* of *you* to say what you did here about them."

"And your truck is there at their apartment every night until very late every night."

Every member of the council flinched and stared at John Levi, waiting for his answer. Jim Wilson looked at him with frown lines wrinkling his forehead.

"That is true. Or at least it has been true. That has stopped. I have just been trying to help and encourage that mother and daughter. But there has not been and will never be anything sexual or improper in the help I am providing."

"If there was nothing wrong with it, why did you stop being over there late every night?" asked Jewel.

John Levi said nothing in response.

"Are you going to keep letting this woman and her daughter come to this church?"

Darla spoke up. "I am."

"Thank you, Darla. I am too," said John Levi. "So long as I am pastor here, no one will be excluded. All will be welcomed. The greater the need, the stronger the welcome."

"So we are stuck with a pastor who thinks there is nothing improper about being at the apartment of a prostitute and drug addict late every night. Or about inviting her to our services."

"Just as I seem to be stuck with a church member who thinks we should exclude people and lies about their so-called unrighteousness, regardless of the teachings of Jesus. And who thinks she has license to say hateful things about other members of the church."

A gasp came from someone in the room. Evidently, Jewel McKenzie could say what she had about being stuck with John Levi, but he should not respond in kind about his being stuck with her.

The meeting broke up. Every church member there, except Jewel, came by to shake John Levi's hand or give him a hug. But there were quizzical looks on a few faces.

Jim Wilson waited until everyone had gone to talk to John Levi. "John Levi, let me give you some entirely friendly advice. I am on your side. What you have done here is amazing. And it is more amazing to me that a man as accomplished as you in the law would put up with having to answer to a person like that McKenzie woman."

"How happy are those who are the meek," John Levi replied.

"Never thought of you as meek. Didn't think you were particularly meek responding to her. You sounded more like a lawyer in a courtroom."

"I'm working on my meekness. I am finding it hard to be meek and to hunger and thirst for justice at the same time."

"Don't become too meek. This is too tough a neighborhood. But if you are still interested in someday becoming senior minister at Faith United Methodist Church, you can't have your truck parked outside the home of a former prostitute and drug addict until all hours every night."

"Jim, life has been terribly unjust to both the mother and the daughter. The mother was hanging by a thread. I needed to be there. And they are such amazing people. I wanted to be there. Still do. But I have stopped that for the good of the ministries."

"Have you considered what that McKenzie woman said? Maybe you need to leave some things to God alone for your own mental and emotional health?"

"And like I said to her, Jim, look around this neighborhood. What has God been doing here before?"

"This church is making a real difference in this neighborhood. Particularly for children. Are you willing to sacrifice all of that for one woman and one daughter? If you maintain that relationship, you just give people who oppose these ministries a way to bring you and the whole thing down. Better to cut it off clean with this woman and end the talk."

"I am just not able right now to jettison that mother and child. Jim, if you only knew them. If you only *saw* them for who they are and what they have been through. It would be so merciless for me to just . . . abandon them after I have put myself in their lives. "

"You don't have to abandon them. For a while, just don't go to their apartment. See them at the church with other people around."

"It will feel to them like abandonment. They already don't understand why I have stopped staying at their apartment so late."

"So what that woman said about your being at their apartment is true?"

"*Was* true. I stopped that."

"Isn't there someone else from the church who could take over for you with them? I bet that Darla would be willing to do that. She seems like a wonderful young woman."

"There's a thought. Thank you for the suggestion."

But John Levi thought to himself, "*I need Paloma and Cynthia too. And how will they understand if I flake out? How can I give in to small-minded people? This is exactly how a church abandons Jesus' teachings.*"

"John Levi, there are plenty of people in lay leadership at Faith Church who would agree with that McKenize woman about bringing Latinos and Blacks into their church. If you were to become senior pastor at Faith, would you try to do the same things there you are doing here?"

"Jim, one hill to die on at a time. This is the hill I am dying on now."

"Are you *dying* here?

"If I have to abandon that mother and daughter, something in me is going to die."

CHAPTER THIRTEEN

"You are unfit
for the Methodist ministry."

— Monday, August 19, 2019 —

John Levi walked into the dining room of a club in a downtown office building. He had received a pointed invitation that very morning to have lunch at the private club with Eugene Cockerel, the organizer and informal head of the twelve most generous financial donors to Faith Church. Although Cockerel and the others in his donor group had in the past held various positions on the finance committee and the board of trustees of Faith, now they were choosing to maximize their power outside the formal church structures. If things in the church didn't go as they wanted, if the senior pastor started staying things they didn't want to hear from the pulpit, if ministries they didn't want were organized, if wrong staff hires were made, they threatened to withhold their large donations until things went the way they wanted. Cockerel was a seventy-two-year-old former commercial real estate broker who had accumulated a private fortune by buying land outside Fort Worth city limits and selling to developers of cheaply built apartment complexes as the city expanded. The other members of the informal donor group were similarly wealthy.

John Levi was surprised to see Cockerel seated at a table with Rev. Mark Greer, the assistant to the bishop of the Central Texas Annual Conference. The Methodist Church is organized into geographical conferences like the Roman Catholic Church is organized into dioceses, with a bishop at the head of each. Ordained Methodist ministers like John Levi were members of their clergy conference, not of the churches they served. Despite the efforts of rich churches to recruit its own preachers, it was the conference bishop who had the formal power of appointment. So the financially powerful churches tried to influence the appointments by promising financial support for a bishop's pet projects and through personal relationships with the bishop and his or her first assistant. Rev. Greer was in the ear of the bishop, and Cockerel was trying to get into the ear of Greer.

Faith Church was a plum appointment for a preacher, typically coming after years of faithful service in the many smaller United Methodist churches of north central Texas. The senior pastor at Faith Church preached to a highly educated and successful congregation. The support staff was large and handpicked by the senior pastor, with the approval of the large donors. The position paid well for ministry and came with perks such as country club membership, a fancy parsonage, and invitations to the exclusive social events of the Fort Worth elite. The senior pastor typically enjoyed a long and secure tenure at Faith Church, usually interrupted only by retirement. But this security came at a price. In the parlance of the old time Methodist preachers, "no plowing too close to the corn," meaning no criticism of the economic and social system of Fort Worth that had so benefited a congregation that was insulated from the struggles of the many poor of the city. Lots of pastoral preaching was required, and no prophetic preaching was tolerated.

But all was not well at Faith Church. It was not rich in attendance at worship. Older members attended and contributed more faithfully than the younger ones. The younger members found other places to spend their time and money. So the church's future was not assured. The senior pastor was in his early seventies and in ill health. He hadn't written an original sermon in years and worship attendance was lagging. The Methodist Church as a whole was threatening to divide over the issue of homosexuality. The congregation of Faith Church was overwhelmingly in support of inclusiveness. When the inevitable schism in international Methodism came, there would be some defection of members and money to more theologically exclusive congregations. Faith Church had a huge and expensive physical plant. The attendance and contribution curve needed to start back upward and be weighted toward younger members.

That is where John Levi came in. Many in the formal lay leadership were considering urging the bishop to appoint John Levi as senior pastor of Faith Church when its senior pastor retired in a few years. Faith Church and the conference alike needed a preacher who would pack them in Sunday after Sunday. The bishop had indicated that he would not allow Faith Church to recruit a preacher from outside the conference, so its choices were limited. From within the conference, John Levi seemed to many in formal leadership to be a natural. John Levi had grown up in the church, his intellect was more than strong enough to keep the well-educated congregation engaged on that level, and he preached with the skills and a passion of, well, a successful jury trial lawyer in closing argument.

But Cockerel's elite donor group was alarmed with this potential appointment. Given his youth and short service time, John Levi's appointment to the Faith Church pulpit would be resented by the other ministers of the conference. But more significant for this group was whether John Levi's passion for the teachings of Jesus could be controlled. Jim Wilson had quickly reported to Eugene Cockerel the confrontation between John Levi and Jewel McKenzie at the Peace council meeting days before, and particularly how John Levi had squelched Jewel. Cockerel asked Jim if he thought John Levi could be tamed. Jim replied that he was unsure that John Levi would want the appointment if he would not have the freedom to preach what was in his heart. Wilson doubted that John Levi would leave unexpressed from the Faith Church pulpit any of his convictions about social injustice in Fort Worth. Jim did not say that he wondered if John Levi would accept the appointment if it meant he could not lead Faith Church into being a more ethnically and economically diverse congregation. And Jim did not mention to Cockerel Jewel McKenzie's allegation that John Levi was in a sexual relationship with a prostitute and addict. Based upon what Wilson did report, Cockerel quickly invited John Levi to lunch and included Rev. Greer in the meeting. There was considerable excitement among younger members of the Faith Church congregation about John Levi becoming senior pastor. Cockerel wanted Marshal there to take the heat if Cockerel and his donor group decided to lead the opposition to John Levi's future appointment.

John Levi only knew Mark Greer as an organization man for the conference. Greer had risen from pastor of small churches to larger churches to the conference office to the right hand of the bishop. There had never been a boat that rocked when Greer was in it. John Levi had never heard that he was passionate about anything. His reputation was as a prophet of niceness.

Cockerel and Greer rose from their chairs as John Levi approached.

"So good to see you, Reverend Jones," said Cockerel, extending his hand.

"Thank you for the invitation." Turning to Greer, John Levi said, "Hello Mark. It's good to see you. What brings you here?"

"I happened to be in the building for another meeting when I ran into Mr. Cockerel. He asked me to join you two for lunch. How are your parents?"

"Fine, fine," replied John Levi, though he had no idea. His father was not speaking to him and was forbidding his mother to return John Levi's calls.

John Levi felt sure that Jim Wilson had told Cockerel about Ms. McKenzie's claims about his relationship with Paloma. John Levi had resolved to be completely honest about his relationship with Paloma and Cynthia. *"Why should I act ashamed about trying to be merciful?"* he had reasoned. *"After all, 'Happy are those who are merciful, for they shall receive mercy.'"* He didn't think he needed to receive mercy about this relationship, but Eugene Cockerel might.

After they had seated, ordered, and started sipping their sweetened iced tea, Cockerel played the first tune of the dance.

"Tell us about all the goings-on at Peace, all the wherefores and the whatfores. I understand your worship service is busting at the seams. You may need a bigger sanctuary."

"It's a nice problem to have. We will probably go to more worship services soon. Maybe an 8:00, a 9:30, and an 11:00 on Sunday mornings." John Levi immediately shifted to his well-worn speech about Peace Church ministries to the church neighborhood and the numbers of people helped.

"Have you thought about separating your English speakers and your Spanish speakers in worship?" asked Rev. Greer.

It would have surprised John Levi if Greer was a supporter of a combined Spanish-and-English-language worship service. John Levi didn't like the idea or sound of "separating" people. But John Levi didn't want Greer or his bishop meddling in this, so he was non-committal. "We've thought about it," was all he said.

"I hear there has been some pushback to the legal clinic," said Cockerel.

"No," said John Levi, "there hasn't. It's a huge success in the neighborhood."

"I was told you received some letters from some landlords objecting to the church taking the side of delinquent renters."

"We received some letters from a landlord association. But not from church members or people in the neighborhood. Our neighbors are beyond grateful. I thought that was what you were asking me about. How did you find out about the letters?"

"One of the property owners is a member of Faith Church. He demanded that Faith Church stop subsidizing your ministries until we could get some control over you. He claimed that a legal ministry is not a legitimate function for a church."

"What did you tell him?"

"That Faith Church doesn't subsidize that particular legal ministry. And that no one can get control over you." Cockerel and Greer smiled.

John Levi didn't smile back. "The landlord association tries to elect the justices of the peace through their campaign contributions. They want the justices to evict poor families from their homes after a thirty-second court hearing with no evidence. I am happy to hear they are unhappy with the ministry."

Cockerel and Greer grimaced.

"Why am I here, Mr. Cockerel? Why is Rev. Greer really here?"

"John Levi, this is nothing sinister. Perhaps I was a bit disingenuous when I explained why I was here. I didn't want you to feel like we were ganging up on you."

"Mark, I used to try cases in which I was the only lawyer on my side of the suit with five or six lawyers on the other side. I am comfortable being ganged up on."

"We are not ganging up on you."

"Okay, 'no' to ganging up. Why are we here?"

Greer looked to Cockerel.

"It's no secret that some at Faith Church are interested in exploring your succession to our pulpit when our senior pastor retires."

"Some? Hmmm." replied John Levi.

"Are you still interested?"

John Levi paused in thought for a long time. "*Did Jim tell Cockerel about Paloma?*" he wondered.

Cockerel jumped ahead. "Seems like a man wouldn't hesitate if he were really interested in an appointment like this one."

"All right, I'm interested."

"Why the hesitation then?"

John Levi' goals had changed since he came to Peace. When he first started his training for ministry, appointment to the Faith Church pulpit was his goal and success at Peace only a means. But his time at Peace had changed him. He would be happy remaining in an inner-city church like Peace until he burned out. Once Peace's neighborhood ministries were established, he had thought about asking the bishop to be appointed to another inner-city church to found the same ministries there. If he was ever given the opportunity to fill the Faith Church pulpit, which he doubted would ever happen, he would only consider it on his terms.

"Why do I hesitate?" he replied to Cockerel. "Because I have seen and experienced things firsthand. I have seen what it's like to be poor and excluded in this city. To be cheated and used by employers and landlords and payday loan companies and plasma buyers and used car dealers. To be looked down upon. I can't unsee those things. And I won't be quiet about them. I have seen the truth of Jesus' way."

John Levi noted the look of impatience on Eugene Cockerel's face.

"You have a problem with that, Eugene," said John Levi, not as a question but as an observation. "You have a problem with a minister who takes seriously Jesus' teachings about poverty and wealth and generosity? The point that I am making is that I am not willing to be quiet about the truth I have learned in exchange for the pulpit at Faith. I am not willing to give up the happiness I feel trying to be merciful. Or my happiness in hungering and thirsting after justice for the poor in this city."

John Levi had just confirmed for Cockerel that John Levi was the opposite of the preacher they needed at Faith Church. Cockerel had already listed for his donor group John Levi's shortcomings. First, most Methodist ministers have a compulsion to be liked and an aversion to conflict. John Levi had a compulsion to be right and an attraction to conflict. Second, most Methodist ministers wanted to maximize their salaries by pleasing their church's wealthy contributors. John Levi didn't want any more money than he already had. Third, most Methodist ministers are intimidated by the worldly success of their church's leading lay members. John Levi had achieved that success himself and had turned his back on it. Fourth, most Methodist ministers are understanding and forgiving. John Levi was intolerant and judgmental, particularly of the wealthy. He took the Sermon on the Mount and Jesus' parables entirely too seriously and expected the church he led to do the same. So John Levi could not be trusted with Faith Church's pulpit. What Faith Church needed, in the thinking of the "money" in the church, was a Methodist Joel Osteen. Cockerel decided to goad John Levi into saying more in the hearing of the bishop's assistant that Cockerel could use to defeat those at Faith who wanted John Levi as future senior pastor.

"How much respect do you have for the feelings of the congregation at Faith?" Cockerel asked John Levi.

"Plenty. I am appreciative of the financial support they have provided. Faith is my home church and where I first learned about Jesus' concern about the poor. And I want them to be offered a real chance to be followers of Jesus."

"You are aware of the monetary value of the assets of Faith? And the overhead and the income needed to keep the doors open?"

"I am not."

"John Levi, the senior pastor of Faith has to be a business CEO. Faith Church is a business and needs to be run as such. Income must at least equal and should actually exceed outgo. A senior pastor can't put the assets at risk by fanaticism."

"Fanaticism? You are baiting me, Eugene. I suppose you think Jesus was a fanatic. Your point?"

"Members of our congregation are our consumers. We have to sell a product that they will be willing to consume and purchase with their offerings."

"The product being . . . ?"

"What the senior pastor preaches. What the church does in its ministries. If the senior pastor condemns the way the members of the congregation live their lives and spend their money, and if he directs the church to spend too much of its assets on ministries to people who aren't members, well, the members will just take their business elsewhere to a more reasonable church."

"Actually, the greater threat is that members will simply stay home, not that they will go to another church," replied John Levi. "And stay home is exactly what they will do if the church is only proclaiming what the secular culture is proclaiming. People have a hunger for God. If our preaching and our ministries proclaim the culture and not the teachings of Jesus, why would they get out of bed on Sundays to come to church?"

"Spoken like someone who doesn't care if Faith Church survives," Cockerel responded.

"What I care about is whether Faith Church, or any church, is a church of Jesus. What, in your opinion, is the authority for the senior pastor's preaching? The *Wall Street Journal*? Fox News? Or the life and teachings of Jesus? Who leads the church? The senior pastor or the richest donors?"

"Young man, there are plenty of good Christians who read the *Wall Street Journal* and watch Fox News."

"'No one can serve God and wealth.' That's from Jesus, not me."

"John Levi, stop!" said Greer.

John Levi did not let up. "Mr. Cockerel, what are you driving these days?"

"What does that have to do with anything?"

"What are you driving? You ashamed of it? It's a simple question. What are you driving?"

"A 2019 Mercedes S-Class sedan."

"How much did that cost you? Over one hundred thousand, right?"

"It is one sweet car. What difference does it make? I worked hard for it."

"You think you work harder than the parents in my church neighborhood who work two jobs each to feed and keep a roof over their children's head? I'll tell you what difference it makes, old man. You could have brought a Ford for thirty-five thousand, which would have gotten you down here to this lunch at this fancy club just as well as that luxury car. And then you could have contributed the difference in price to a food bank to feed poor children. You haven't heard proclaimed from the Faith Church pulpit the greater happiness that comes from helping poor children over the happiness from spending your money on luxuries you don't need."

"John Levi!" cried Greer.

"Eugene, do you have any friends who are poor, truly poor? Ever been into a poor person's house?"

Cockerel merely wiped his mouth with his napkin and made no reply.

"Of course you haven't any poor friends. So you don't know anything about their struggles. And so you are offended by my quoting Jesus' teachings about wealth because those teachings are a judgment on all of our lives. I am offended by your demanding Faith Church's senior pastor to hide Jesus from the congregation. You talk down to me, calling me 'young man' as if what I am trying to do is all about immaturity. But it is Jesus who offends you, not me. The truth is that you think that Faith Church ought to be run by you and the big money, not the senior pastor or even Jesus. And Jesus was a young man, by the way, when he taught and died for us. You have made your point. But I already knew your point. I grew up in your world of comfort and accumulation of stuff, and of separation from poor people. It is a world of unhappiness, of shallow obsession about things that have no lasting meaning and give no real joy."

"I am not unhappy," said Mr. Cockerel, gesturing around this private club and its sumptuous dining room.

"How can you be happy spending so much money on luxuries for yourself when a quarter of the children in this city are food insecure? Or when 85 percent of the children who attend the schools in the Fort Worth ISD live at or below the poverty line?"

"They are not my concern."

"Are they Jesus' concern? If you read the Gospels once in a while, you would see that they *are* Jesus' concern. So they should be Faith Church's concern."

Cockerel drank his tea and gave no answer.

"What you and I experience as happiness is different," continued John Levi. "I have decided to give Jesus' teachings about happiness a try."

"What teachings are those?"

"And now we are to the guts of the matter. The pastors who have been preaching to you haven't been passing on what Jesus says about happiness."

"So now you are criticizing our senior pastor. He will be interested in hearing that. I repeat, what teachings are those?"

"Happy are those who are poor in spirit and who are meek and merciful. Happy are those who hunger and thirst for justice. Happy are those who mourn. Happy are those who are peacemakers."

"Oh, *those* teachings. And you claim to be all those things?"

"No, sir, not even close. Especially not poor in spirit or meek, as you have heard today. But I will say that I have received more true happiness in trying to be merciful to people in Peace's neighborhood, and in mourning their plights with them, and in hungering and thirsting for justice for them, than I ever received getting and spending money on myself."

Cockerel replied, "Young man, you are one of the most arrogant and least humble men I have ever encountered. You are unfit for the Methodist ministry. If memory serves, Jesus has some things to say about arrogance and humility."

John Levi just looked at Cockerel.

"No wonder your father cannot stand to be around you."

John Levi laughed derisively at Cockerel. "You can always tell when someone realizes they are losing an argument. They turn chickenshit."

Cockerel's face turned beet red.

Greer jumped in. "You two are both over the line."

"Tell me, Jones, what does Jesus look like?" continued Cockerel.

"Now why do you ask me *that*?"

"Because you talk like you have supper with him every day."

John Levi got up to leave. "Mark, I trust you will give a full report to the bishop. Please give him my regards and my thanks for keeping me at Peace." Greer nodded and shook John Levi's hand.

"And I trust you will understand if Faith Church no longer subsidizes your ministries at Peace," said Cockerel.

"Speaking of arrogance and lack of humility, you aren't Faith Church, Eugene. Your cabal isn't either. You just think you control some of the property and some of the money."

Mark Greer walked John Levi out. "Well, you just turned over the tables of the money changers in the temple. There is another part of the Sermon on the Mount you might check out," said Greer.

"Tell me."

"The part about not retaliating. The part about turning the other cheek. He provoked you and you responded in spades. Now he may be able to cut off Faith Church's financial support for your ministries. Who will benefit from that? I hope your honesty was worth it to you. You made yourself feel good, but you didn't help anything. "

John Levi shook his head. "I don't feel good about any of that. But the truth is the truth. That man just hasn't been faced with it before."

"You know your problem? Your problem is that you are exactly right about what Jesus demands."

"How is that a problem?"

"Because being exactly right isn't enough. You need to be a bit less concerned with being right and a bit more concerned with bringing people along with you. You just can't cram Jesus' teachings down people's throats. You'll drive them the opposite direction, especially when you are right. We aren't called to love just the poor."

"Is speaking the truth the same as cramming it down people's throats?" asked John Levi. "Why is it that the rich seem to be the only ones who feel I am cramming when I am just proclaiming? That ass in there can take care of himself. He's been cramming things down his opponents' throats his entire career. I was just putting the hay down where that goat could get it."

"He's not a Methodist minister, John Levi. And don't quote me, but we both know he's not interested in following Jesus' teachings if it would cost him a buck. You are, on both counts. Just think about it . . . I'm being too hard on you. It must be difficult for you to be around that poverty all week and then come to a place like this to talk to a man like that. Hang in there. The bishop is actually a great supporter of you and what is going on at Peace. Keep doing what you are doing. And remind me never to get in an argument with you."

"He hasn't heard about Paloma yet," he thought.

"Is everything okay between you and your father?" asked Greer.

John Levi lied. "I don't know what Cockerel was talking about there."

Darla Henderson called John Levi's cell phone that same afternoon. Darla and John Levi had known one another through their work together at his old law firm. He trusted her enough that he welcomed her insights and criticisms. She left a long voice message.

"John Levi, this is Darla. I want you to know that Peace has changed my life. I am so grateful that you have given me a chance to get into the lives of the girls in the neighborhood. They are so sweet and beautiful. But I am worried about the future of the ministries. I will be happy to take some of the burden of helping Cynthia and Paloma. I know there is nothing wrong going on between you and Paloma. But what the older church members believe matters. And I wish you would be gentler with them. I know how busy you are. But maybe you could spend more time inviting them to share our vision of the church? Maybe you could have a little more dialogue with them? I could help with that. I even wonder if part of Jewel McKenzie's opposition to what we are doing is because she feels that the veteran members of the church have no say in what is happening. Granted, she is terribly prejudiced. Maybe God can change her.

Anyway, those are my thoughts. Take them for what they are worth. Let's have lunch soon. Love you."

"God? *God* might be unhappy? God is nowhere!"

— Tuesday, August 20, 2019 —

John Levi's cell phone rang at 7:30 a.m. He saw on the call registry that it was Paloma.

"Good morning, Paloma. Everything okay with you and Cynthia?"

"Yes, we're okay. I guess. But I have a favor to ask. Cynthia is on a band trip to Austin. She'll be gone overnight. So do you think you can come by the apartment tonight? I will make us some supper and we can talk. It's been awhile."

John Levi sucked in his breath. His heart rate jumped. He needed to stop being at Paloma and Cynthia's apartment at night, for the good of Peace ministries, particularly if he and Paloma would be there alone. *"Why would she want me to come when Cynthia isn't there?"* Rather than the obvious answer, he thought, *"Maybe she wants to talk about Cynthia when she's not around."* He didn't want to hurt Paloma.

"Why wait for tonight? I am going by the law firm this afternoon. I will see you there and we can talk."

Paloma was disappointed by his refusal to agree to her request. She felt rejected and angry, even though she had recently promised Cynthia not to fall into anger default so automatically. *"I guess he is just tired of us. Must not have been much of a kiss for him."*

All afternoon of the day before, Paloma had been thinking about John Levi's sermon. *"Was he thinking of me when he spoke of the woman's hair being erotic? Does he want me to do something erotic? Does he want me to*

233

take the lead?" Paloma had never believed in romance. The only "love" with a man she knew was physical and transactional. But she found herself for her first time fantasizing about a romantic relationship, wondering what it would be like for John Levi to be tender and sweet with her when he made love to her. She watched a romantic comedy on Netflix. She felt her face getting flush during a kissing scene. She caught herself pantomiming with her lips the kissing on the screen. *"What is happening to me?"* she thought. *"I know better than to believe in this happily-ever-after shit."*

Later that same night, the Sunday of the sermon, Paloma had a different dream than her usual one set in the backyard of her father's house. She was back at Luther Bodine's house. She was in a bedroom, crying and washing a man's feet with her tears and her hair. The man was one of the regulars at Bodine's. There were other men in the bedroom, naked and laughing at her. Then the man whose feet she was washing became Jesus, with long hair, a beard, and a robe. But then the man became John Levi, who took her out of the house and away from the laughing men. So she called John Levi first thing that morning to ask him to come over.

John Levi arrived at his former law firm at about 1:00 p.m. He was startled to see his name still as the first name on the sign with the title of the firm. The receptionist was new. When he walked in, she asked who he was here to see. He told her, "Paloma Ibarra." The receptionist seemed surprised and asked, "Who may I say is asking for Paloma?" John Levi walked behind the receptionist's counter to the big letters on the wall behind the receptionist's chair. He pointed to the name "Jones" in the firm title. "That's me," he said.

"Oh my gosh, are you really John Levi Jones?"

"Yes," he said, "I guess I still am."

"It's amazing to finally meet you. Wait," she said, "did you ask for Paloma?"

"Yes, I did," he said. "Paloma Ibarra."

"May I ask why you want to see her? Is this about a lawsuit?"

"Please just tell her I'm here. She should be expecting me."

The receptionist disappeared. As John Levi waited, three employees he did not know peeked through the door to get a look at him and then ducked back. John Levi went back into the outside hallway and entered a back door into the firm offices. He walked down another long, interior hallway, and turned into the open file room lined with tall file cabinets. Paloma sat at a desk, scanning legal documents and saving them to computer case files. She was dressed in tight jeans and a peasant blouse. Her hair was pulled back into a pony tail. She wore very little makeup, but her eyes and face shone.

"Hi," he said. "It's good to see you."

She looked up startled. "Hi," she said. "It's good to see you. I didn't think you would really come by."

"Here I am, as promised. Can we talk now?" he asked.

"Let's go into the supply room."

Paloma led the way to a door in the back corner. She leaned back against a set of shelves with her hands folded behind the small of her back.

"How are you?" he asked.

"I am okay. Bored silly," she laughed, "but okay."

"How is Cynthia?"

"Good . . . Wondering if we did something wrong."

John Levi hesitated. Paloma was as direct as usual. "You've done absolutely nothing wrong. You are doing everything right. Why would you wonder if you had done something wrong?"

"Because you quit staying for dinner. You drop by, say hello to Cynthia, barely speak to me, drop off some food, and then run out the door before we have a chance to talk."

"The church has kept me busy."

"Don't lie to me. Tell me what's going on. You tired of us? Gone on to your next mercy project? Found some other people to save?"

"Paloma, it's nothing like that."

"Then tell me what it *is* like."

John Levi looked hard to her. He walked to the only chair in the room and sat down. He stared at his hands. Paloma stamped her foot. "Tell me what you are afraid to. Get it over with."

"My truck has been seen parked outside your apartment late every night."

"So? What business is it of anybody's where you spend your time off work?"

"Life is different for a minister, Paloma."

"Tell me."

"A Methodist minister is not allowed to have a romantic relationship with a member of his church."

"Since when have we been having a romantic relationship? I must have missed it."

"We aren't. We haven't been."

"Then what's the problem?"

"Paloma, surely you can see this. You are a very attractive young woman. I am a relatively young, unmarried man. People know I am at your apartment until late every night. They add two plus two and think they get four."

"I haven't been enjoying any 'four.' Neither have you. Who are these people?"

"A person who hates the ministries. She wants them stopped. She wants me kicked out of the church. So she is making a stink about this. I actually was going to tell you that I need to stop coming by completely for a while. I was going to ask Darla Henderson to look in on you and Cynthia."

"Does this person know how much of your own money you are spending to support us?"

"No."

"So you are ashamed of us."

"*I am not!* I am proud of you."

"Then why are you being such a coward about us?"

"Coward? Don't you call me a coward. Not after all I have done for you."

"What you have done has been in secret. If you weren't a coward, you would be honest about us."

"Paloma, it's not like that."

"Then tell me what it is like."

"People expect Methodist ministers to be chaste."

"Chaste. You mean like a priest? Hell, not even priests are chaste. You been chaste. I been chaste. I haven't been with any man since before I met you. Tell the motherfuckers."

"I have."

"Then what's the problem? . . . I'll tell you the problem. The problem is me. The problem is that I am a Latina. The problem is my past. Do these persons think they know about me? What do they think they know? Your sermon? What did you say? Do they *see* me?"

"They don't know anything. They don't know what you have been through or how far you have come. Truth is that they wouldn't care if they knew. These particular people are blind. Paloma, it's only a few people."

"You let only a few people keep you from eating supper with us? When nothing is going on? Coward. *Cobarde.* You are ashamed of us."

"I am not. I am ashamed of myself."

"They think I am not good enough for you. *You* think I am not good enough. If you were spending this much time at Darla's place, I bet no one would say anything. Wait, why are you ashamed of yourself?"

"For putting you in this position to be hurt."

"Then don't do it." Paloma walked to him as he sat in the chair and put her hands on either side of his face. "John Levi, what *is* going on? My question isn't only why you have stopped spending so much time with us.

My question is why were you spending so much time with us? Why did you kiss me?"

"Because you and Cynthia are the most amazing people I have ever met. Because I like being around you. I feel alive when I am with you. And I kissed you because I wanted you to have a real date."

"You didn't enjoy it?"

"Of course I did."

"Then don't stop."

"Maybe I only need to stop for a while."

Paloma bent down to where her face was inches from his face, staring into his eyes. "So 'maybe' is all you can give me? Are you attracted to me?"

John Levi stood abruptly up from the chair, almost banging his head into her face. He moved two steps away from her. "Of course I am attracted to you. Any man would be. I am a minister but I am not dead. . . . But Paloma, I want you to understand that a man can be attracted to you in other ways than sexually . . . You are a completely attractive woman to me." John Levi immediately regretted that last statement.

"Why can't you be attracted to me in all ways at once?"

"Because there are lines I can't cross as a minister."

"What lines? I don't see any lines."

"Paloma, I don't want to know if you are really attracted to me." She started to speak but he stopped her. "But if you were, how could I trust that? How could we trust your feelings after all that I have done for you?" She started to speak again. "We are not in an equal position here. You could mistake gratitude for love."

He walked farther away from her.

"Look, do you *see* me? How could you?" he asked her.

"I see you enough to know that I wouldn't fit in the world where you live, the world where you come from and go back to at night." She laughed. "Can you imagine taking me to meet your parents? Or your stuck-up friends? At your country club? Where the only women who look like me are wearing uniforms and wiping up spills? You'd be ashamed of me . . . I don't know what I was thinking. What the hell was I thinking?"

Paloma felt exhausted. Like she did when she comes down from meth. She went back out to her desk and slumped down. "Did it ever occur to you that I could make you really happy? Happier than you've ever been? And that you could make me happy?"

John Levi stared at her for a long moment. "Yes, it has occurred to me."

"What makes you happy now? Why do you come around so often if you can't trust how I might feel about you?"

"Helping you and Cynthia makes me happy. Being with you makes me happy. Sharing your story."

"Why can't you just try us? Trust your feelings. Who would be unhappy if we were together?"

"God might be."

"God? *God* might be unhappy? God is nowhere! I'm right here. I'm real. These eyes are real. These lips are real. This body is real. This heart is real. My story is real. I hate my story but, man, is it real. Love these real things. God is nothing but an *idea* that you love. God is the way you wish the world would be. Well, it's not that way, John Levi. When my mother was dying, I prayed to God over and over. So many times when I was using meth at Bodine's, I prayed. Once I prayed to die. I didn't die and my world didn't change. My mother and father didn't change. Bodine didn't change. The men who used me didn't change. *I* didn't change. We are all alone here, John Levi. We'd best make the best of it. "

"How?"

"By loving."

"I do love, Paloma. I am trying to change the world in front of me by loving."

"I don't understand that love."

"Paloma, that . . . that would be a barrier between us. God is real to me. I experience God's presence when I am helping you. God is the source of that love."

"Why do you have to put the God sugarcoating on it? Why does God have to be the filling in the middle of this? You don't think you would be happy being with me and Cynthia without God? I see the way you look at me. I felt the way you kissed me. I know you want me. I see and hear how concerned you are for me and my daughter. Why isn't that enough for you?"

"Paloma, if it weren't for God, or at least my belief in God, I would never have met you. I would never have come to Peace. If not for God, I'd be bored sick at the country club. God has made me hate that life. This is the life I love. "

"What life?" Paloma walked to John Levi and put her hands on either side of his face again. "What life?"

"This life of helping people. Helping the neighborhood. Helping you and Cynthia. This life with God."

"Then have it your way. Why don't you trust that your God wants us to give us a try? You believe that God brought you here to this life and to me. Why don't you trust this life? Or you could go back to practicing law full-time and helping people that way. I hear the way the people at the firm talk about you, the stories they tell. You were a freaking rock star in the courthouse. God and all these rules wouldn't have to be part of it. You'd only answer to yourself. And to me. And to the people you were helping."

She sat down again. "What was I thinking? What was I thinking? Dumb, dumb, dumb *puta*. For a moment there, you made me forget what my life really is. You made me dream. I'll never forgive you for that."

She put her head in her hands and shook it. "You know what? You are a phony. Your fear of being seen with me isn't about God. It's about you. It's about the person you really are. All this talk about God! This 'Do you see this woman?' bullshit. You think you see *this* woman? The 'me' you think you see would embarrass you. You'd be ashamed of me. You don't have the guts to tell your church people and your friends that you might love *this* woman."

"Paloma, I love you. And Cynthia. But I can't be *in* love with you like that."

"No, you can't. And it has nothing to do with God. It's because of what isn't in you. It's because you are just like the rest. You are a phony chicken-shit. You think you are too good for me. You know what your problem really is? You couldn't be with me without thinking about all the other men who had me before you." She began to cry. "If I could do that all over, I would. I'd let my sister and brother and myself go into foster care. But I can't change that now. And if I *didn't* have that miserable past, you wouldn't be interested in me. I wouldn't be somebody for the great Reverend John Levi Jones to save. You wouldn't . . . You need to leave now. I think it would be better if you didn't come by the apartment at all. Hiding in my apartment with you is not enough anymore. You've been found out. By the church and by me."

John Levi stood frozen for a moment, afraid to respond, soaking in the truth of what Paloma had said to him. Finally he asked, "What will you tell Cynthia?"

"I don't know. I'll think of something. Probably the truth."

"Please don't tell her . . . the truth." John Levi leaned down to hug her, but she pushed him hard away.

"I want you to take back your car. I want you to stop paying our rent."

"Paloma, you are upset. Please take time before you make decisions like that. Where will you live? How will you get to work? What will happen to you and Cynthia? I want to keep helping you. I still love you two."

Paloma's face turned angry. "You think I don't have any pride? You think I don't have feelings? You've just told me that those narrow-minded, self-righteous asses in your church are more important to you than I am. These *Christians*." She spit out the word. "They don't see me and don't care to. I am too far beneath them to be seen. They think the only love that a man like you could feel for a woman like me is dirty. Given how dirty I am . . .

What's the word? 'Unclean.' Given how 'unclean' I am, a man like you could only care about me long enough to use me and then kick me to the curb."

Paloma grabbed John Levi's arm, and shoved him out the file room. "You and your God can get the hell out of my life."

John Levi was shattered by his encounter with Paloma. He couldn't eat the rest of that day or sleep that night. The next day he had the urge to call her or just show up at her door at night and beg to come in. But he knew better than to cross her when she was angry. And she would lose a lot of self-respect if she let him in.

His thoughts were a maelstrom. Was he falling in love with Paloma? Had he been lying to himself about why he was spending so much time with her at her apartment? Was his generosity to Paloma and Cynthia based more upon a longing for Paloma rather than his longing to help them? Would he have been as generous if Paloma were not so physically attractive to him? And could such a love have a future? He had zero experience being in love with any woman. He had never stuck it out in a relationship with a woman during hard times, and he knew there would be many hard times in a relationship between Paloma and him. Her wounds were part of what attracted him to Paloma. She was surprisingly bright and insightful. But what would they talk about after the first excitement of loving faded? She didn't want to talk about her past or her wounds. She couldn't appreciate his past and he had no wounds like hers.

If he loved Paloma in all the ways that a man could love a woman, what would he be required to give up for her? Given her anger about God and the church, would he have to give up ministry? And was Paloma right about God? Did God have no more reality than John Levi's wish for the way the world would be? If God exists and is present in the world, why are there so many Paloma and Cynthia Ibarras, so many Luther and Angel Bodines, so many Eugene Cockerels, so many Jewel McKenzies, so many comfortable, professing Christians to whom the teachings of Jesus mean nothing in their lives, so much indifference within American churches to the suffering and poor children in the world? Why would a loving, powerful God allow all this?

Two days after the painful conversation with Paloma at her work, John Levi gave in to his urges and repeatedly tried to call her, but there was no answer. He left her a message asking for a callback. Just as he was arriving at Peace, Paloma called him back, saying only that she didn't want him to call or come by any more. She hung up before he could reply. He called Cynthia, but her phone was out of service.

Chapter Fifteen

"You broke my mother's heart. You broke mine. You need to go."

— Wednesday, August 21 and Thursday, August 22, 2019 —

The day of John Levi's and Paloma's painful encounter at her work, Paloma developed a migraine and left work. She got home to the apartment about 2:30 p.m. She was hurting so badly that she crawled into bed in her work clothes and stayed there after calling to disconnect Cynthia's cell phone.

About 4:00 p.m., Cynthia knocked on the bedroom door and asked what was wrong. Paloma told her she was just tired and needed to sleep. "I'm okay, sweetheart. Don't worry about me. Just let me sleep a little while. Then I'll get up and fix dinner for us."

"Is John Levi coming over today?"

"No, honey. We'll talk about that when I get up."

At 8:00 p.m., Cynthia came in Paloma's bedroom again. "Momma, are you all right? I'll make us some scrambled eggs and toast. That'll be easy on your stomach."

Paloma tried to get up, but she had no energy at all. She felt a weight bearing down on her. There didn't seem to her to be any point in eating. Her migraine had gone away, replaced by the heavy fatigue. She fell back to sleep.

That night the dream in her father's old backyard returned. Paloma awoke just after midnight. Sweat drenched her sheets and pillow case again. She was gasping when Cynthia came into the room. "Momma, what's wrong?"

"I just had a bad dream. I'm okay."

"No, you're not." Cynthia sat down next to her mother and began stroking her hair. When she felt how wet she was, Cynthia retrieved a towel from the bathroom and began caressing Paloma with it, wiping off the sweat. "Are you sick?"

"I told you! I just had a bad dream! That's all."

"Momma, please calm down." Cynthia wet a facecloth with warm water from the bathroom and cleaned her mother's face. "What was your dream about?"

"Don't trouble yourself with it."

"Should I call John Levi?"

"Why call him? He's not a member of this family. I'll be all right. Just let me get some more sleep."

Cynthia took Paloma's temperature and found it was normal. "Can I sleep in your bed with you tonight?" she asked Paloma.

Paloma rolled over so Cynthia would not see her tears. "That would be very sweet." Cynthia crawled under the covers next to her mother and hugged her.

Cynthia fell asleep but Paloma could not. Her old night terrors had returned for the first time since she met John Levi. She dreaded falling asleep because the old dream would come back. It seemed she was stuck forever in her father's back yard, eternally digging up her mother's grave in the gloom and unable to escape. She couldn't put away how badly John Levi had hurt her. She felt she was lying in the pieces of her shattered future with him. She felt angry, stupid, and helpless. Cynthia would have no easier life. There was no path for the both of them out of their past and present life. How long could she pay the rent and put food on the table on the pay she received from the law firm? What if she got sick and couldn't work? How could she get a better-paying job with her criminal record and her lack of education and job experience? She was incapable of providing for herself and Cynthia without charity. Who can ever rely upon charity? Who can anyone ever rely upon? Would she ever have a loving relationship with a man who could overlook her past? In the night there seemed to be no solutions.

Paloma considered whether Cynthia would be better off if she killed herself. *"John Levi would take care of Cynthia if I die,"* she thought. *"Cynthia is the one he loves, not me. John Levi and Darla can marry and adopt Cynthia."*

Paloma craved the escape of methamphetamine. *"Maybe just one day's relief from this."* She started to say a prayer. *"There is no one to turn to except God."* Then she stopped herself. *"No, there is no one to turn to."*

The next day was a school day. Cynthia rose at the regular time, but Paloma stayed in bed. Cynthia offered to make both of them breakfast, but Paloma said she was too sleepy.

"Do I need to call your work to tell them you are still sick?"

"No, I'm getting up now."

Paloma moved slowly and deliberately like she was underwater. She tossed on a pair of jeans, an old sweatshirt, and some sandals, ran a comb through her hair, and drove Cynthia to her school. As they were driving, Cynthia asked, "Momma, why does my cell phone not work?"

"I must behind in my payment. I'll take care of it."

"Momma, are you all right?"

"Honey, I'm good. Don't worry about me."

When Paloma arrived back home, she called in sick to work and went back to bed without eating.

About 4:00 p.m., John Levi received a call from unknown number. He let it go to voicemail. Before he could check the message, two more calls came in quick succession, so he answered. It was Cynthia.

"Cynthia, I am so happy to hear from you."

"Something is really wrong with my momma."

"What?"

"She wouldn't or couldn't get out of bed. She is missing work. She couldn't get up to pick me up from school."

"Is she ill?"

"I don't know. She says she isn't. I'm afraid she is just depressed."

"Oh gosh, Cynthia. I'm afraid I am to blame for this. Did she talk to you about me?"

"No. What about you?"

"I just feel we need to take a break from my spending so much time there."

"Why?"

"We'll talk about that. I feel so guilty that she is so down."

"There's something else."

"Oh God, what?"

"Do you remember that guy Angel?"

"Angel Bodine?"

"Yes. He's outside now."

"Outside your apartment?"

"Yes."

"Doing what?"

"Sitting in his car in the parking lot, calling Momma's phone over and over."

"Cynthia, I am walking out of the church heading your way right now. Stay on the line with me. Are you using your mother's phone right now?"

"Yes."

"Do not answer his calls."

"I won't."

"Tell me what happened."

"I came home from school today and he was sitting there in his car. I don't think he recognized me at first. But when he saw me go into the apartment, he followed me and started pounding on the door."

"Did you answer it?"

"No, but he knew I was inside. He yelled that Momma had called him and asked him for some drugs. I went into her bedroom and asked her if that was so. She said she had called him but changed her mind. She told me not to answer the door."

"I asked her if I should call the police. She said no."

"Where is he now?"

"I can see him out the apartment window. He's sitting in his car and blowing up the phone."

"Describe the car for me."

"Gold Camaro."

"Hang on, I'm almost there."

"What are you going to do?

"Run him off."

"John Levi, this man is dangerous. Now that he knows where Momma lives, he'll never give up. I want to call the police."

"Do it."

"Momma said not to."

"Do it. Hang up and do it."

After Cynthia hung up, John Levi called the apartment business office. They knew him because he paid Paloma's and Cynthia's rent every month. He told them that Angel Bodine, a lifetime registered sex offender, was trespassing in their parking lot and to call the police.

When John Levi roared into the parking lot in his truck, he spotted Bodine still sitting there. John Levi parked his truck behind Bodine's Camaro, blocking him from leaving. He stood twenty feet from Bodine's car door.

Angel powered down his window. John Levi saw on Angel's face that he recognized him from their encounter outside the justice of the peace court the year before. "What's the idea blocking me in, shyster?"

"I thought you would want to stay until the police get here. Just wanted to do my part to help."

"I ain't trespassing. I was invited here by Paloma."

"Yeah, well, Paloma changed her mind . . . I'll bet the police will be able to find meth in your car."

Angel started looking back furiously over both shoulders. "Police ain't got no grounds to search my car."

"Really? Even after I tell them that you tried to sell me drugs?"

"You are fucking with the wrong *hombre*, Preacher. You better watch your back. I know where your church is. Ever fix that window?"

"I thought that was you. Now I have proof."

"What proof? You recording this?"

"I might be. You never know."

Angel started to get out of his car.

"You still unregistered here in Fort Worth?"

Angel stopped dead. "Unregistered for what?"

"You are a sex offender, Angel Luther Bodine. You are required by law to register as a sex offender wherever you live for your entire lifetime. Last I checked, you haven't registered here in Fort Worth. But if I am wrong about that, I do apologize. We can both wait here until the police arrive and they can pull the information up on their computer. Let's do that, shall we?" John Levi nodded encouragingly at Bodine. "Shall we?"

"That shows what you know, asshole. I registered. I'm good. My parole is good. I cleared everything with my parole officer. You got nothin' on me."

John Levi didn't let that surprise piece of information throw him off. "You think that's all I've got on you, Angel? I have a copy of the video your customer made when you were raping Paloma when she was unconscious. Remember that one? The one you showed in the club that pissed Paloma off so much? You know what the audience was saying while you were doing that? All the talk about her being unconscious while you were doing that to her? All the talk about meth?"

"Ain't no video. If there were, you'd have taken it to the law already."

"Maybe I haven't taken it to my police detective friends yet because Paloma told me not to. But I am telling you now, Angel. In fact, I am giving you my word. If I see you anywhere near Paloma again, I'm takin the video to the police and to your parole officer. And that will give the police all the grounds they need to search your club and your house. And your parole officer will have grounds to revoke your parole."

John Levi paused to let what he said sink in. "Is Paloma worth all that to you, Angel?"

"What I want to know, Preacher, is why Paloma is worth all this to you."

"You can leave here and never get within four hundred yards of this apartment or any other place where Paloma might be, and I will hold on to the video. Your father has to stay away from her too."

"The bitch called me here."

"You call her 'bitch' again, and I'm going straight to the police."

"Look, man, move your truck. Let me out and she will never see me or my daddy again. But you need to tell her to stay away from us."

John Levi backed his truck out of the way. Angel sped out in his Camaro. John Levi waited in the parking lot, listening for the sound of a police siren. No siren and no police car.

He called Paloma's cell phone. Cynthia answered. "He's gone, hopefully for good. May I come up?" he asked her.

Paloma answered the door. She looked terrible. Her hair was dirty, her mascara was smeared around her eyes, and her eyes were red. She was dressed in stained shorts and a torn T-shirt under an open robe. Without saying anything to him, she sat on the couch where they had spent so many evenings together and pulled a blanket around her. She closed her eyes.

"Did you call Angel to bring you drugs?"

She said nothing. Cynthia stood next to the TV, a frantic look on her face.

"Paloma, did you call Angel to bring you drugs?"

"That's none of your worry," she finally answered.

"But I am worried about it. You have come so far."

"How far is that? I'm still me. I still have the same past. I still have the same dead-end future. You blame me for wanting a little escape from me? Actually, I don't care if you blame me. It's none of your business."

"Momma, Momma." Cynthia started to sob.

"Paloma, I have some bad information on Angel Bodine. He's on parole. I told him that if he or his father ever got within four hundred yards of here or wherever you are, I will turn him in . . . We've got him, Paloma. You are free of him."

"Really? Who says? You? Tell me this. Am I free of me?"

"What do you mean?"

"Maybe I want a hit of meth occasionally. Maybe little ole me needs it. Are you my daddy? Actually, my daddy doesn't give a shit."

"Cynthia," said John Levi, "can you step into your bedroom?"

"No. No, I won't. You will be out of our lives, but I will be still with her. Momma, what about me? What about what I want? What about what I need?"

"Cynthia, your mother is who she is. I can't outrun my past. I can't be someone else." She shifted her gaze to John Levi. "Cynthia is the one you love. Not me. Will you take Cynthia in? Can she live with you?"

"*Momma, don't say that! Don't even think it!*" Cynthia ran to her mother and climbed onto her lap. "We can do this, Momma," she sobbed. "We can do this by ourselves. I'll drop out of school and find a job. We can make it on our own."

"No, you don't have to do that, Cynthia," said John Levi. "I'll continue to support you two. If you will have it. I never intended to stop. I never want to stop."

Cynthia said, "But how long can we count on you? We can do this alone."

Paloma stood up. "I am exhausted. I need to go to bed." She staggered off to her bedroom.

Cynthia said to John Levi, "You need to go."

"Do you want to talk about the way things are?" he asked Cynthia.

"I can see the way things are. You need to go."

"Cynthia, I am always here for you and your mother. As a pastor and a friend. You can trust that."

"You broke my mother's heart. You broke mine. You need to go."

"Promise me you will call me if you need anything. I will keep paying the rent. The car is your mother's. I'll sign it over to her. You don't have to worry about that. Please, please, please don't drop out of school. There is no need."

"You are forgetting that this is for Momma and me to decide now."

"Will you at least promise to tell me if she is threatening to go back to drugs?"

"Why? What could you do? Pray? Like that's going to help her. Leave now, please. "

John Levi was despondent as he drove away. "*I did this. I did this to all of us.*" He had learned in his ministry classes in seminary that he could not look for love for himself within his own ministry. He was called to love others in his ministries. He had to look for love for himself elsewhere than his church. But the ministry books never reckoned on Paloma and Cynthia. He wasn't only worried that Paloma would go back to meth. He was worried that Cynthia would start cutting herself again and using drugs to treat her own depression.

He pulled to the side of the road to call Father Gutierrez. Thankfully, the father was free. He told Gutierrez the entire story of the last few days. "What can I do, Father, to make this right?"

"It's going to be hard for you to hear this. But there's nothing you can do, John Levi. You can't fix this yourself right now. You can't trust your own feeling of guilt to guide you to the right place now. If you tell them you want to be back in their lives like you were, they won't trust you. Even you need to admit that this is one time you can't do God's job."

"But God isn't doing it."

"You don't know that. You really need to learn something important from this if you are going to stay in ministry. Remember 'meekness' and 'poverty of spirit'? You need to learn the value of those. What you have seen in that impoverished neighborhood has awakened in you a strong spirit of love. But you need *poverty* of that spirit. You need to put some limits on the *way* you love. Most of the world hungers and thirsts for justice. The difference between the world and us is the *way* that we seek to satisfy our hunger and thirst. We must have the meekness and poverty of spirit to be faithful to God's way until God eventually satisfies our hunger and thirst for justice and mercy."

"I wish that God would hurry. Not what I wanted to hear, Father. God's way seems so ineffective."

"I want to leave you with one other thing. I haven't met this woman, so I don't know her at all. But from what you have told me about her and her terrible past, by being around her so much, you may have just delayed what is happening now."

"What is happening now?" John Levi asked.

"She is despairing of herself. She is losing hope. You gave her hope by being there so much. You affirmed her worth. Now she has to find another, better source of hope besides just you. Unless this is real love on your part, unless you are able to commit to her truly, you were going to have to stop giving so much attention to her and her daughter sometime. And whenever you did, this crisis was probably going to occur."

"But I am blaming myself now for leading her on by giving her that much attention in the first place."

"If you hadn't, she might have gone back to drugs right away. By being with her so much, you gave her and her daughter a glimpse of hope. You showed her that she can do it. Don't beat yourself up too much."

Chapter Sixteen

"Momma's gone."

— Sunday September 8, 2019 —

John Levi had not seen or spoken with Paloma or Cynthia for almost two weeks. He had telephoned and left messages but they did not respond. He confirmed that Paloma had gone back to work. He had been tempted to drop by to see her there. He had parked close to their apartment and had almost knocked on their door. But he respected that they had told him to stay away.

John Levi stepped sadly into his Peace pulpit for his evening worship sermon. He had scanned the congregation during morning worship, hoping to see Paloma's and Cynthia's faces. But of course he did not. Cynthia did not even come to the teenagers' morning Sunday school class. He told himself to rejoice because of the people who were present, but all he could think of was Paloma and Cynthia and his guilt for their pain.

He preached from Luke 18, verses 1 through 8, a parable that Jesus told "about the need to pray always and not to lose heart." The parable is about a powerless widow who had been treated unjustly by an oppressor. When she went to a judge for protection, the judge refused to grant her justice. Rather than giving up, the widow kept coming and coming to the judge until finally he gave in and granted the widow the justice she demanded.

"I am asking each of us," John Levi preached, "to consider why Jesus would compare this unjust judge to God. In this parable, this judge has the power to grant justice to the victim of injustice. And at the end of the parable, Jesus says that God also has the power to grant justice to the victims. So the judge and God have this power in common."

"What else do they have in common? They have both delayed in granting the justice they have the power to grant. Why did the judge delay? Jesus said it was because the judge did not love God or his neighbor. But why does *God* delay in bringing justice to an unjust world? To me, the line in the parable that God will 'quickly' bring justice is a hollow one. Why do I say that? Because I see so much of the *injustice* of poverty, the *injustice* of the powerful taking advantage of the poor, the *injustice* of the indifference of so-called Christians to the poverty of poor children. God, like the judge, *has* delayed bringing justice. Why the delay?

"Jesus says in this parable that God delays in bringing justice to the human community because *we* have not been persistent enough in asking for an end to injustice. It's on us, not God, says Jesus here. God is ready, willing, and able to put this out-of-whack world back into whack. God is just waiting for us to ask for it long and hard enough, as this widow did of her judge.

"Brothers and sisters, who am I to challenge Jesus? I am just a preacher. Do I believe that the reason for the persistent injustice I see in this neighborhood is because we have not asked God long and hard enough for the end of the injustice? No, I do not believe that. I do not believe that this world is broken because we have not asked God loudly and long enough for God to fix it. But I am just a preacher. So who am I to challenge Jesus?

"But I will say this. As the old-time preacher says, 'When you pray, move your feet.' One of Jesus' Beatitudes, which I have preached many times from this pulpit, is, 'Happy are those who hunger and thirst for justice, for they will be satisfied.' We can't 'hunger and thirst' for something without working for it too. If we aren't working for it, we aren't really hungering and thirsting.

"I have told you before about my friend who has had a hard and unjust life. As a child she prayed and prayed, persistently, for God to help her. She insists that God has not helped and that here prayers have gone unanswered, so she has given up praying and even given up believing in a powerful and loving God. Those of us who hunger and thirst for justice for her, for a fair life and an end to her exploitation by unjust men, must do more than ask God to help her. We must help her. We must move our feet for her and for every person among us who suffers from the random injustice of life and the malicious cruelties of men."

As John Levi sat down, he saw Cynthia standing alone in the back of the sanctuary. Her hair was matted and he could see that she had been crying. As the service was ending, John Levi walked to the back of the sanctuary by a side aisle. He took Cynthia by her arm, walked out the door, and took her to the side.

"What's wrong?"

"Momma's gone."

"Gone? Gone where?"

"I don't know. I'm scared."

"How long has she been gone?"

"Since sometime Wednesday night or early Thursday morning. She came home from work on Wednesday evening really upset. We ate together that night. She said she had quit her job. I asked her why but she wouldn't tell me. I went to bed about 10:00. When I got up, she was gone. I haven't seen or heard from her since."

"Is her car gone?"

"Yes."

"Has she called you?"

"No. She left her cell phone behind."

"Where do you think she went?"

"I thought she must have gone to the Bodines' club or house. I walked to their house. The old man denied that she was there. I refused to leave until he let me in to look. I got inside and looked through the entire house. She wasn't there. No one was there but the old man."

"Cynthia, you went into the Bodine' house on Lulu? Did the old man mistreat you?"

"No. He asked if I wanted some food and to spend the night. I got out of there as quickly as I could. The place had a terrible odor to it."

"Cynthia, that was a brave and a really foolish thing to do. I wish you had come to me first."

"I didn't think you would help. You turned your back on us. I'm only here now because I have nowhere else to turn."

"You said she took the car?"

"Yes."

"Give me a minute and we will drive the neighborhood together to look for it."

John Levi walked back into his office in the fellowship hall. He took off his worship stole and robe. He picked up his cell phone and called his former law partner's cell phone. He got only a message and he left a callback request.

"Jesus," he thought, *"she's been gone Wednesday, Thursday, Friday, and Saturday nights."* He counted the nights off on his fingers. *"It's Sunday night. She abandoned Cynthia for four-plus nights with no communication, just like in the old days. She's either hurt or in the hospital. Or she's dead. Or she's with someone and can't get away. Or she's using. Yeah, she's probably using again. Or . . . she's in jail. Let's hope she's in jail."*

John Levi checked online the inmate populations in the Tarrant County jail, Fort Worth jail, and Arlington and Mansfield jails. No hits. He checked the criminal district court clerk website. No new charges for Paloma Ibarra.

He thought, *"The next step is to drive the neighborhood looking for her car. If that doesn't pay off, we have to start calling hospitals."*

He walked back down to Cynthia. "Sorry I took so long, sweetheart. Do you know of any friends or relatives at all where she might have gone?"

"No. None."

"Do you know if she was getting phone calls from someone Wednesday night?"

"I checked the phone she left behind. No incoming or outgoing calls."

"Has she ever left her cell phone behind before?"

"She forgot it once. But she came right back to get it when she did."

"What do you make of her leaving her cell phone?"

"That she has given up. John Levi, I'm scared." She started to cry.

John Levi's phone rang. It was his old law partner, Charles Needham, responding to his call.

Needham said, "I'm calling you back. Is this about Paloma?"

"Yes it is. Did she get fired?"

"No, she didn't get fired. She quit after a big blowup. Is she okay?"

"No, she's not okay. She's been missing for four nights."

"Oh damn. What do you mean, 'missing'?"

"She left her daughter Wednesday night and hasn't been back. We don't know where she is. What happened at work?"

"I feel responsible. Shit, shit, shit. You know Doug Price? Young lawyer who joined the firm just after you left? He's a pain in the ass but he works hard and can take a good deposition, so we keep him around. He's too hard on our employees generally. When he's under stress, he takes it out on innocent people. Reminds me of the way you were early on."

"I'm going to let that pass."

"Paloma had a bad week. She was obviously in a bad way about something. She has always kept to herself, but last week she wouldn't respond to people even when they said hello. She just buried herself in the file room. I almost called you and am really sorry now that I didn't. So anyway, Doug couldn't find something in one of his files. So he loses it and goes into the file room and starts yelling at Paloma. 'Recite the alphabet to me!' he's yelling at her. 'Recite the alphabet to me!' We can hear him all over the office. I run down there. Paloma has ducked into the ladies' room to get away from him."

"Was she crying?"

"Not Paloma. She was cussing him."

"So she quit?"

"Not right then. She was still in the restroom. Darla Henderson went in there to try to calm her down but Paloma wouldn't talk to her. I read Doug the riot act."

"He mouthed back that Paloma was unfriendly and that his secretary was always complaining about her and her attitude. 'Why is she even here?' he demandd to know. 'There's not even a resume on file for her. She doesn't fit in.' That was when I made the big mistake."

"Oh God, what did you do?"

"It was innocent, John Levi. But I am sorry. I thought that if Doug knew what a hard life Paloma had been through, and what you were trying to do for her, he would let up. So I told him some of what you have told me."

"Like what?"

"Her parents' addiction. Her mom's death. Her poverty growing up. That she was forced into prostitution and addiction to support her siblings."

"Oh God, Charles. Did that asshole tell someone else?"

"Yes."

"Who?"

"His secretary."

"The one who was telling him that Paloma didn't fit in? Is this the one who is so outspoken about her Christian faith?"

"The same one."

"So why did Paloma quit?"

"John Levi, I didn't see or hear this firsthand. But I am told that Doug's secretary was holding court in the breakroom, telling her buddies that Paloma was a prostitute and an addict, when Paloma walked in and heard it. Some of the secretaries were giving her the stink eye. Paloma grabbed her purse, walked down to my office, said 'I quit,' and left."

"Why didn't you call me?"

"Honestly?"

"For Christ's sake, Charles. Of course, 'honestly.'"

"I was afraid of you. I was afraid of what you'd say."

"Oh, you were not!"

"Yeah, I was. Doug begged me not to tell you. I figured Paloma would tell you."

"Charles, she's been missing since the night she quit. She told me nothing."

"You think she ran off just because of what happened at work?"

"No. Most of it is on me."

"Can we help you look for her?"

"Of course not. You'd have to know this neighborhood."

"When you find her, will you tell her that she still has a job here?"

"With your people? Hell no. She's not ever going back there. Unless you fire them all."

"John Levi, I have to ask this. Why don't you leave what you are doing and come back to practice law here? You can't win with the Palomas of this world. Your God is winning. You can't control anything in that neighborhood for people like that poor woman. The outcome is out of your hands. Aren't you ready to give up all that frustration? We don't have to let our clients get so much under our skins. I worry about you."

John Levi hung up without answering.

John Levi and Cynthia drove the neighborhood. They started at the Bodines' house, but the only vehicle there was the old man's. Paloma's old Lexus was not parked at The Hacienda.

"Cynthia, I am going to take you back to your apartment so you can wait for your mother's return there. Then I am coming back here to talk to some folks."

"I want to go in with you. I am sick of just waiting around."

"But if she comes back, it shouldn't be to an empty apartment. Should it?"

"I guess not. But call me on Momma's cell phone about what you are doing."

"If she shows up, do all you can to keep her there. And call me right away. Okay?"

"Okay, John Levi. Why *did* you stop coming around?"

"Your mother hasn't told you?"

"No, nothing. Every time I asked her about it, she would either get angry or cry."

"Are you angry with me?"

"Disappointed."

"Cynthia, I love you and your mother. I have missed you both very much. Let's just find her and then we can sort this out."

"Will you pray with me?" pleaded Cynthia.

John Levi hesitated. "Cynthia, the way I am going to pray is to try to find your mom and make this right."

He saw confusion in her eyes. So he took her hands in his and bowed his head. "Jesus, as much as we love Paloma, we know that you love her more. Help me to find her and bring her home to Cynthia. And restore our hope. Amen."

After John Levi picked up some tacos for Cynthia and took her back to the apartment, he called Rafer Thompson. "Rafer," he said, "I need a favor."

"I'm here for you. What's going on?"

"Can you have a friend on the force run a check to see if a woman is locked up anywhere around here? I have checked the Fort Worth, Arlington, and Mansfield jails, but I can't check the other jails in Tarrant County."

"Sure. What's the name?"

"Paloma Ibarra."

Silence on the other end of the line.

"Don't say 'I told you so,' Detective."

"I was only thinking it. I'll call you back."

John Levi started driving the grid of streets in the neighborhood, looking for the Lexus.

Thompson called him back. "No hits on any jails in Tarrant," he reported. "Have you tried the places she used to use?"

"Her daughter tried the main one. The owner even let her in the house to look around. Wasn't there."

"Wait, her teenaged daughter went into Luther Bodine's house on Lulu?"

"Yeah, I told her that it was a foolish thing to do."

"If the mother is using again, which she probably is, she is likely some place where she thinks she won't be found. If you will let me come along to protect you, I can get you a list of meth houses in the neighborhood and we can look them over."

"A list? Enough to make a list?"

"It's a plague. Life is just too much for some folks. Meth is like a ticket out of hell to some of them. Then they come back to an even worse hell. "

"How much time do you need to get the list?"

"I'll meet you at the church in an hour."

John Levi kept driving the streets on his own, recognizing that Paloma had probably parked the car where it couldn't be seen. Then he met the detective at Peace.

Rafer opened his truck's passenger's-side door and sat down. "Evening, John Levi. I can't give you a list."

"Why not?"

"My wife won't let me. She says you are about to get yourself in trouble, and I am going to get myself in trouble if I help you. If I give you this list without coming with you, I'll just be getting you in trouble without being there to get you out. She put her foot down when she saw me putting on my holster and handgun."

"It's good she's worried about you."

"You know who's worried about you, Reverend? Me. My wife. Most of your church. A lot of people in this neighborhood. You know who's not worried about you? Two people, and so far as I can tell, two people only.

You aren't worried about you. And Paloma Ibarra isn't worried about you. In fact, I'm wondering if she hasn't run off so you will come looking for her."

"I don't think that's the entire reason she ran off," said John Levi. "Although I wish that were all there is to it. I am afraid Paloma has given up. And I am betting that she is feeling a lot of self-loathing because she has betrayed her daughter again. Her daughter is really worried about her. And so am I. Hopefully so is God."

"So how's God doing on this, Reverend? God's worried, and you and her daughter are worried. But if God can't keep her from going back to methamphetamine, how can you or her daughter? If God could prevent it, don't you think he would have just for her daughter's sake? By taking away the mother's craving for meth? Or making her love for her daughter more powerful than her hunger for meth? Not even God can keep a meth addict from her meth."

"Rafer, I feel responsible for this. I have to find her and bring her back. At least I have to try."

"I hate to say this, but I say it out of affection for you. You are wasting your time and putting yourself and your ministry at risk over someone you probably won't be able to find and who probably won't be rescued if you do find her. I used to carry a badge and I still had a hard time finding someone who didn't want to be found. And if you do find her, what will you do then? What words are you going to say to her that you haven't already said and that she hasn't already heard? And if you find her and she doesn't want to be rescued, what are you prepared to do? Kidnap her? The more I talk, the more I realize that my wife is right about my not going with you. And that you shouldn't go looking for her either."

"Like you said, maybe she left so that I would come after her."

Detective Thompson suddenly took John Levi's keys out of the ignition.

"Rafer! Don't do that! Please give me my keys back."

"Now I am rescuing you from yourself. I am doing you a favor. There are a lot more bad things that can happen from your going after her than there are good things."

John Levi held his hand out to Thompson.

"It's my decision whether to go after her, Rafer. Give me my damn keys."

"Just like it was her decision to run away. Doesn't it occur to you that trying to find her tonight has more to do with you than it does with Paloma or her daughter? Or even God? You just aren't used to losing, are you?"

"I hope you're wrong. What if I am the only chance God has to rescue her? What if God is making me feel responsible for her running away so I will try to find her? Anyway, thanks for the worry . . . Now, give me my keys."

"You be careful out there. Don't get angry or impatient and do something dumb because you are so sure you are doing what God wants . . . Maybe God is speaking to you now through me. Ever thought of that? Ever wondered why one person can be so sure about what God wants and another person can be so sure God wants the opposite? Maybe it's because it's not about God. It's all about the people claiming that God wants them to do what they already want to do . . . I see I am not helping. I wish I could talk you out of this."

"Give me my keys. Give me my damn keys."

Detective Thompson gave John Levi back his truck keys and watched as he drove toward North Main Street. Then he called a police friend who was on patrol, filled him in on what was going on, and asked him to be on the lookout for his pastor in the orange pickup. The officer told Thompson he would try but had a large area to patrol.

"So your pastor got no sense, huh?" the friend said.

"He just thinks God chose him to be the one to fix the world," said Rafer. "Hasn't learned yet that he can't."

John Levi continued his search by driving to The Hacienda. There were about ten vehicles in the parking lot, but the lights were off on the building and the front door was dark and closed. Paloma's Lexus was not there. John Levi parked his truck at a coin-operated car wash across North Main.

John Levi had never been in The Hacienda building, but had been told by Paloma about the bar entered through the front door and the club through an inside door at the rear. *"Since this is Sunday, maybe the bar is closed but the club is open,"* he thought. He got out of his truck, walked across the street, and went to the front door. He rapped loudly on the heavy wood. There was a peep hole at eye height, and he saw a quick blink of light through the hole. But no one would answer his knocking. He walked around to the rear of the building. No windows were open. He thought he heard music but he couldn't be sure. The air conditioning system was running. He walked across the street and climbed back into his truck.

As he was sitting there, he saw Angel Bodine drive up in his gold Camaro, park, and walk to the front door of The Hacienda. Angel made a call on his cell phone and the door quickly opened. John Levi jumped out of his truck and yelled to Angel, but Angel did not hear or chose to ignore him. John Levi rapped again on the front door, yelling Angel's name. He began kicking the door. He took a plank of wood from a dumpster from the lot next door and began beating on the door with the wood. The door suddenly swung open. A huge man shoved John Levi onto his back. "Get the fuck away from here. We're closed."

John Levi scrambled to his feet and stepped back from the man. "If you are closed, why are all these cars parked here? And why did Angel Bodine just get in?"

"Reverend, you need to get away from here right now."

"How do you know I am a reverend?"

The man blinked. He opened his mouth but no words came out.

"Angel just told you who I am and to get rid of me, didn't he?"

"You just need to leave now, sir."

"What's your name? Wait a minute, Paloma told me the name of a bouncer who works here. What was it? Steve? Seth? Seth! That's it. Are you Seth? Paloma said she helped you and your family once. She said, 'Seth is a good man who hates the Bodines as much I do.' You are on parole for something and that's why you stick with this miserable job. You are Seth, aren't you?"

Seth stepped out and pulled the heavy door closed behind him. "You really need to go now. For your own safety."

"Seth, I'm just looking for Paloma. I'm trying to find her to take her back to her daughter. Paloma's been missing since Wednesday. You have children. Imagine how worried they would be if their mother was missing for four nights. Can you help me?"

Seth took John Levi by the arm and took him around the corner of the building away from the parking lot, where it was pitch dark.

"She hasn't been here when I been here. I been working every night since Wednesday, and I ain't seen her," said Seth.

"You telling me the truth?"

"Take it or leave it. I ain't seen her. That's all I'm saying."

"Any idea where she might be?"

"Get the fuck out of here." Seth grabbed John Levi by the arm again, pushed him off The Hacienda property and out into Main Street. "Stay the other side of this curb." Seth poked John Levi hard in the stomach with his forefinger, knocking the breath out of him.

John Levi took one of his cards out of his pocket—one with his name and church and cell phone number on it. He pushed it into Seth's hand. "I know you are better than this. If you hear anything, please call me on this number."

John Levi walked back across the street to his pickup. A marked police cruiser without lights or siren drove to the side of the truck.

"You Reverend Jones?" asked the uniformed officer alone in the cruiser. The name tag on his uniform shirt read "Guillermo Martinez."

"Yes, Officer. Is there a problem?"

"Rafer Thompson called me about you. You need to go home now."

"Is that an order, Officer?"

"It's a strong suggestion."

"Thank you for your concern. I'm almost finished here."

"I understand you are looking for Paloma Ibarra."

"That's right. Can you help me?"

"Has she broken the law?"

"Not that I know of. But I am afraid she is a victim."

"A victim of what?"

John Levi hesitated. *A victim of life,* he thought. *A victim of terrible parents and horrible luck and evil men and meth and bad decisions, none of which this cop cares anything about.* "You name it," he said to the officer.

"Then it's not my problem. But it's not your problem either. You need to get off the street now, sir."

John Levi got his back up. "Officer, I am not just the pastor of Peace United Methodist Church, which is about a mile from here. I am also a lawyer licensed to practice law in this state. So as a pastor I am carrying out my duties by looking in my parish for a member of my church who may be in trouble, and as a lawyer I know my rights as a citizen to be here now 'on the street,' as you put it."

The officer stared at John Levi. "Next time you see Rafer Thompson, tell him I tried. And, Preacher, take my word for it. I been knowing Paloma Ibarra for a long time. She is always in trouble, and she always will be. Trouble is where she lives. You are on your own, sir." He drove away.

"Yes, Officer, but do you see this woman?" he thought.

John Levi drove back to his church. He telephoned Cynthia to let her know his lack of progress. She had heard nothing from Paloma. John Levi persuaded her to stay in the apartment. Then he began telephoning hospitals to ask if Paloma was a patient. He got nowhere.

He called Cynthia back. "Cynthia, what is the name of the bar on North Main where your mom went to work after she quit the Bodines?"

"The Runway. No, The Landing Strip. Close to Meacham Field."

"Did she ever mention the name of someone who worked there? Someone who was a friend?"

"She mentioned a night watchman and cleanup guy named Lemon."

"Lemon? Like the fruit?"

"Yes."

John Levi drove farther north on North Main. He found The Landing Strip, another cube of cinder block painted white with no windows. It was after midnight now. The neon sign and the light over the door were unlit. There were no vehicles in the gravel parking lot. He knocked on the front door but there was no response. He looked the bar up on the internet and called the listed phone number. No answer. He walked around the back of the building. There was Paloma's Lexus parked in the alley. He still had a set of keys to the car. He unlocked the car and sat in the driver's seat. He leaned on the horn until the back door of the bar opened and an older man peered out. "What's the big idea?"

John Levi walked to the man with his hand outstretched. "I'm Reverend John Levi Jones. I'm pastor of Peace United Methodist Church about two miles from here. A member of my church has gone missing since Wednesday night. I'm trying to help her teenage daughter find her."

The man took John Levi's hand and shook it. "You talkin' about Paloma?"

"Yes, sir. That's her car right there. Is she inside?"

"No. Wish she were. Come on in." The man held the door open.

John Levi walked inside. The door opened into a storage room with kegs and cases of beer and boxes of liquor on shelves. The man invited John Levi into another cramped room where it appeared he lived. He offered John Levi a cane chair while he sat on his cot. The man was dressed in an old-fashioned night shirt. He was about five and a half feet tall and thin. He looked to be in his sixties. His skin was dark brown. He was bald with a white fringe of hair around his head. An earring stud was in one ear. A day-old white stubble was on his chin.

"Thank you for your hospitality, especially so late at night. Does your name happen to be Lemon?"

"Yes, Reverend, Lemon P. Wilson." They shook hands again.

"What does the 'P' stands for?"

"'Pee.' My momma said I peed and peed the color of lemon when I was first born. So she named me 'Lemon Pee.' How did you know my name?"

"Paloma's talked about a friend named Lemon who worked here."

"I am pleased to hear that Lomie considers me to be a friend. She can be one sweet young woman. Is she all right?"

"You don't know?"

"No. What happened? You said she's missing? I last saw her here on Wednesday night. I was wondering why she don't come back for her car."

"We didn't know her car was here until I spotted it a few minutes ago. So it's been parked in the alley since Wednesday?"

"Yes, sir, it has."

"Mr. Wilson, what happened here on Wednesday evening?"

"I just clean up here, stock the bar, and act as night watchman. I go into the bar three or four times a night when its open to mop and make sure there is enough beer and booze. Middle of the night or so, I see Lomie sitting at the bar drinking tequila. Lomie, she battles the blues. She looked as down as I ever seen her. I'm not supposed to talk to the customers. But Lomie worked here and she looks bad. She was always looking after me, bringing me food and stuff, so I thought I'd return the favor and see how she was doing. She hugs me, which upset the bartender. She's crying. I asked what's wrong. All she says is to ask me the best way someone can kill themselves. She's drunk but it still really scared me. I tell her she is way too young and beautiful to talk like that, she has a long life ahead of her, she has her daughter to live for, and that it's just the booze talking. Can I call her a cab? No, she has her car here. Then this young man comes into the bar. Slicked-back, black hair. Black goatee. Chains around his neck. Looks to be about Lomie's age. I don't know him. He is standing at the door like he is looking around for someone. He sees Lomie, and sits right down on the barstool next to her. He is talking to her really low. I go back and stand in the hallway. I can't hear them, but I can see that she is angry with him. I did hear her tell him to go fuck himself.”

“Could you hear what she called him? What name, I mean?”

“No, but the bartender knows him. She calls him Angel. So Angel keeps buying Lomie more tequila shots. Then I see him open a narrow little bottle and take out something, maybe a pill, and drop it into her shot glass of tequila. She drinks it down. God knows Lomie can hold her liquor, but suddenly she just starts gibbering and weaving on the stool and falling asleep. Reverend, I just know he put something in her drink.”

“Did you report it to someone?”

“The bartender. She told me to shut up and mind my business. She never liked Lomie when she worked here. Lomie was too popular with the men who came to drink here.”

“Then what happened?”

“Lomie throws up. My job is to clean it up. I go get my mop and bucket. When I come back, this guy is carrying Lomie out like she is a baby, you know, cradling her in his arms. I finish my mopping and step out the back. This Angel guy is parking Lomie's car in the alley where you just saw it. He gets out, closes and locks it, and walks around to the front of the building. I followed him around. He gets in a Camaro and drives off. Lomie is in the passenger seat, passed out.”

“Which way did he drive?”

“Turned right out of our driveway on Main, headed back south.”

“And you haven't seen or heard of her since then?”

“No, sir.”

“And the guy?”

“Him neither.”

“Did you get the license plate of the Camaro?”

"Didn't think to."

"Lemon, here's my card. That's my cell phone number. If you see or hear anything or if someone tries to move that car, call me, okay?"

"Sure will. I sure do hope that Lomie is okay. Never met anyone like her. She could be mean and funny and sweet and nasty all at once."

"That's Paloma."

John Levi got back in his pickup and drove back south on Main. Now he knew that Paloma was where her car was not. As he was turning east on Northeast 28th Street to head toward Lulu and the Bodines' house, his cell phone rang.

"Reverend Jones, this is Seth. At The Hacienda."

"What's up?"

"What I am about to tell you, you can't tell anybody this came from me. Swear to God?"

"I swear to God."

"I heard Mr. Luther and Angel talking as they left the club tonight. Paloma is at their house. Been there for days. Angel gave her enough meth to knock her out. They got her in their back bedroom. You got to get her out of there, Reverend Jones."

"How long ago did you hear them say that?"

"About five minutes after you left here."

"If I call the police, Seth, and give them your number, will you repeat to them what you just told me?"

"Why?"

"So the police can force their way into the Bodines' house and get her out."

"Can't you just tell them what someone told you?"

"The police are not big admirers of mine, Seth. And they need to hear from the person who actually heard the Bodines talking."

Long hesitation. "I can't."

"Why not?"

"I'm in violation of my parole. I have to stay away from the police. I can't go back to prison. That's the main reason the Bodines trust me. I got a family to support. Reverend, you already swore you wouldn't tell anyone what I said. You swore to God. That's the only reason why I told you what they said. You going back on your word to God?"

"No, Seth, I am not. I will not. "

John Levi felt all alone as he headed toward the hell the Bodines had created on Lulu. "God be with me and Paloma," he prayed aloud. "God be with us. It's about time You were."

Happy Are Those Who Are Meek

"Reverend, you are in some deep shit."

— Monday, September 9, 2019, 4:00 a.m. —

Detective Alphonzo Washington of the Fort Worth Police Department Homicide Division was close to the end of his shift when the call came in for a double homicide on Lulu Street in the North Hill neighborhood. Washington's usual partner, Detective Eugene Castillo, was ill. Washington was not fluent in Spanish, so he asked the homicide dispatcher to arrange for a Spanish-speaking patrol officer on the scene who could help him in the neighborhood.

Washington arrived at the location. Crime Scene Search personnel were already there and had placed yellow tape around the house. A heavy gate in the front appeared to have been rammed and broken open by something heavy, probably a truck. A rusted yard chair was on its side on the narrow front porch. Inside there were three dead—an older and a younger man and a Rottweiler. The older man had been once shot in the chest and lay on his side in a pool of blood. He wore only an undershirt, shorts, and slippers. The body of the younger man was nude. He had been hit in the head at least twice, probably with the metal bat next to his body. One of the blows had split his skull and left a deep indentation. He also lay in a pool of drying blood. A nine-millimeter semiautomatic Glock lay close to his hand. There were four spent and ejected shell casings close to the younger man's body. The dog had been shot in the spine. A trail of blood was on the wooden floor from the front porch to the young man's body.

Washington asked the sergeant in charge of processing the crime scene, "What do you make of this mess? Any chance the old man hit the young man with the bat as the young man was shooting him?"

"I suppose it could be possible that the blow that crushed the young man's head could have been delivered at the same instant he shot the older man. But we found IDs for both of them in the back bedrooms, so both of them lived here. Someone rammed open that front gate with a vehicle. Why would someone who lived here need to do that? And if one or the other of them rammed open the gate, why are they dressed that way?"

"Has anyone run a criminal check on the dead?"

"Bad dudes. Younger one on parole for sexual abuse of a minor. Lifetime registered sex offender. Both have drug convictions. A uniformed officer who works this neighborhood tells me that these two are suspected of manufacturing meth in this house. The older one owns a bar and club up on North Main called The Hacienda."

"Wait, is that Luther Bodine?

"In the flesh—dead flesh, that is. And that's his son, Angel."

"Find any makings?

"The whole deal in a back room. Cookers. Meth components. Crystal meth itself. Pipes. Lots of coke and weed. The windows are sealed so no smell or sound gets out. They weren't just making the shit here. They were selling drugs and sex here. There's two bedrooms with handcuffs, sex toys, video equipment, the works."

"Any cash lying around?"

"Wads of cash in the pants of these two in their bedrooms. And there's a safe in an office. We need a warrant to bust that open."

"So this is likely a drug killing?

"Maybe."

"Any sign of anyone else?"

"There are women's clothes in the back bedroom. Young woman's, by the look of them. Lying around on the floor like they had been taken off quickly. Blouse, skirt, stockings, shoes, bra, panties. Only one earring, a big hoop. And a purse. ID inside of a Paloma Ibarra, aged thirty-two. Hot-looking Latina with a deep scar on her chin. I am guessing that she had been in bed with the nude man here. Maybe she split the man's head with the bat and then took off so quickly she left her clothes. That doesn't explain the shooting though."

"But she didn't take the money out of his pants."

"No. Maybe just too scared. Brained him and cleared out."

"Lots of loose ends. Your team taking samples of the blood on the floor?"

"Of course."

"Really interested if we have blood from someone else besides these two and the dog."

"There's some blood trailed out on the porch into the yard. Or the other way around."

"Anyone spoken to the neighbors?"

"Uniforms doing that now."

"Anyone own up to seeing anything yet?"

"We'll see."

Washington went to his cruiser and transmitted a lookout for a person of interest named Paloma Ibarra, age thirty-two. Her ID in his hand listed a house on Irion, not far from the murder scene. He walked back into the front yard. A crime scene tech was processing the front gate. "Detective," the tech called out to him, "here's something interesting." He shined his flashlight on an inside flange of the broken gate. There was a scraping of dark orange paint on the flange.

"What the hell color is that?"

"You know what it looks like to me? University of Texas colors."

Washington went back to his radio and called in a lookout for an orange vehicle, probably a truck, with heavy damage to the front grill and front quarter panels forward of the front wheels.

"Detective, can I talk to you?" Uniformed officer Guillermo Martinez stood in the street a respectable distance away.

"Yes, Officer, what can you tell me?"

"I've been going door to door in the neighborhood. Most of the neighbors denied even hearing shots. One admitted to hearing them and finally told me that this father and son ran a drug and prostitution operation here. The old man paid off the neighbors to keep them quiet. This neighbor said that she has seen young girls being taken in and out of this place and a bunch of older men coming and going late at night. But this person denied seeing or hearing anything this morning. People are scared."

"You get names and addresses of the people you've talked to?"

"Some. Some won't give me their names."

"Then we will have to take them downtown for questioning."

"There is one more thing."

"Tell me."

"An old lady who lives across the street said she looked out her window after she heard the gunshots and saw an old pickup, red or maybe orange, parked in the front yard through the open gate."

"How old?"

"Old. Sounds like vintage."

"Anything else?"

"Yes. Do you know Rafer Thompson?"

"Detective Rafer Thompson? 'Rafer the legend'? I met him once or twice before he retired. What about him?"

"He's an old friend. He called me earlier tonight, maybe at 10:30 p.m. He asked me to look out for his pastor. Reverend John Levi Jones is his name. Said he was driving around the area trying to find some female junkie who had been missing for a few days, a woman he had been trying to save from drugs."

"Keep going."

"Before midnight, I spotted Jones on North Main parked across from a place named The Hacienda. I told him to go home. He said he wasn't going until he found this woman and that I couldn't make him. He's a lawyer and a minster. Laid a real attitude on me. I told him that I had known the addict he was looking for a long time and that he was wasting his time trying to save her. He blew me off."

"The Hacienda is owned by Luther Bodine, isn't it?"

"That's what I understand."

"Bodine's dead body is lying in that house, shot once in the chest."

"Really? Good riddance. Justice done, as far as I am concerned."

"Describe this Jones to me." Martinez provided the description as Washington made notes.

"What was he driving?"

"Old, classic pickup. Burnt orange."

"The name of the junkie this John Levi Jones was looking for?

"Paloma Ibarra."

Washington got back on his radio and put out another lookout for John Levi Jones as a person of interest in a double homicide.

Washington turned back to Officer Martinez. "You got Rafer Thompson's cell phone number on you?"

After getting off the phone with Detective Washington, Rafer Thompson called John Levi and left a message on his cell phone. "Reverend, you are in some deep shit. You can't preach your way out of this one. The police have placed you and that woman you were looking for at the scene of some murders. I am not going to say 'I told you so.' I *am* going to tell you that you need to call a lawyer right now and have the lawyer arrange for you to turn yourself in. I mean right now. Listen to me, for once. Do not waste time turning yourself in." Thompson left Detective Washington's telephone number for John Levi's lawyer to call.

CHAPTER FOUR

"Cynthia needs to be free of me."

— Monday September 9, 2019, 6:00 a.m. —

John Levi Jones was in panic overload. Thoughts and feelings tumbled chaotically through him. He couldn't get control over their flow. He had almost been killed and he had killed a man. Nothing he had ever done had prepared him for this. How stupid and naive had he been to break into that home without realizing what violence and evil he was unleashing! And his leg hurt like fire from where the Rottweiler had bitten him. Dried blood stuck his trouser leg to the bites. He could not concentrate to drive. His hands and arms shook. He could not see clearly. He wanted to turn back the clock but of course he couldn't.

He knew from Rafer Thompson's phone message that the police were after him and Paloma. They had both been placed at the scene. He needed to find Paloma to urge her to tell the truth about what he had done and about her own innocence. He needed to make sure than the truth came out to exonerate her, whatever the cost to him. If he didn't tell the truth about himself, they would never believe his truth about her. It would be so convenient for the police to lump her in with his guilt. The thought claimed his mind that he had to reassure her that he would, finally, protect her and that, finally, she could trust him.

When his thoughts and emotions coalesced in this one righteous purpose of protecting Paloma and Cynthia from what he had done, calmness came over him. *"Greater love hath no man than to lay down his life for his sister,"* he thought, paraphrasing John's Gospel. He discovered that he had driven for more than an hour north of Fort Worth on I-35, had passed

Denton, and was nearing Gainesville. *"What? Was I unconsciously fleeing?"* he thought. *"Am I a coward deep in my bones?"* He knew that he was. He turned his battered pickup truck around and headed back to Fort Worth, now fighting rush-hour traffic.

His conduct in that house proved to himself that he was a phony, just as Paloma had once said. He had made such a self-righteous show of following Jesus, but he had killed a defenseless man with a bat. He had brought shame to his faith and his church. Giving himself up for Paloma was the only way to get back on the way and bring something redemptive out of this evil.

He listened again to the phone message from Rafer Thompson. *"I'll call a lawyer like Rafer says, but only after I find Paloma . . . Or I'll act as my own lawyer! That's it. That's better. I'll represent myself. Another lawyer would just try to talk me out of telling the truth. The truth is all I have left to protect her. And to be true to my faith."*

Paloma had fled the Bodine house on Lulu in a frantic fury. Because she was still in the throes of a meth high, she was unsure that what she thought she had heard and then seen in the front room of the house was entirely real. She had in the past suffered dreams that led to hallucinations while on meth. Was that sound really gunfire she had heard as she lay in bed? Was that really the smell of gunpowder instead of the meth smoke? Had she really seen Luther down and dying in the front room floor, blood gurgling and air spewing out of a hole in his chest, and his hound lying bleeding and crying next to him? And was that really John Levi standing over Angel and then hitting Angel over the head with a bat like he was a snake to be killed? Was it a dream and then a hallucination, or had John Levi really hit him?

But she knew she had really fled limping from the house in the blanket with the sense to snatch Angel's car keys. As the cooler air of the outdoors struck her senses, she was sure that she had actually seen John Levi's pickup standing inside the broken gate of the yard. *"No,"* she thought, *"there was something real to what I heard and saw."*

She drove slowly in the Camaro, trying to avoid attention and to remember the way to her apartment. *"That had to have been John Levi. He had to have broken in there to get me out. Why can't he leave me the hell alone? I'd have gone home eventually. Oh my God! He must really have killed Luther and Angel and that goddamn dog. What did I get him into?"*

Depression struck her like a bat, made worse by the horror of what she had just seen. The withdrawal from meth and the weight of her depression made it hard for her to keep her head upright and use her arms to drive. The world seemed tilted on its side. She took her foot off the gas and let the car roll to a stop on its own. She could barely see to keep the car in her lane. *"I can't do this,"* she thought again. *"I can't get myself free of this. John Levi and Cynthia helped me so much and I went back to the meth anyway. That fucking Angel put something in my drink, but I still didn't have to use meth so many days. I had the chance to get free but I wanted more meth. Cynthia gives me every reason to stay away from meth but I can't. I'm too fucking weak. I'm too fucking broken. Cynthia needs to be free of me."*

She sat in the car in the middle of her lane on a two-lane street, as traffic increased. Cars and pickups had to pull around her, some honking. A pickup stopped on her left next to her side window. A young man asked her through his window, "Ma'am, are you all right? You need to pull over and get out of the road. The police are going to get you." She woke up from her dream, and sped off in front of him. She found her apartment building and parked in the lot. She tried to think as she fought off her headache and through her nausea and weakness. She lost track of time, falling in and out of sleep. She reached a resolution. *"The only way out is for me to kill myself. John Levi will take care of Cynthia. Everyone will be better off. You win, Life. I give up."* It didn't occur to her that if what she had seen at the Bodine house was real, then John Levi was facing prison time. *"I'll crash this car and kill myself. I won't wear a seat belt. No one will know I did it on purpose."* She needed to pee and say goodbye to Cynthia. So she got out of the car with the blanket still bundled about her, climbed the stairs, and knocked on the apartment door.

Cynthia opened the door. "Oh, Momma! Momma, Momma, Momma! I'm so glad you are okay!" Cynthia grabbed Paloma and hugged her hard. "Are you all right?"

"I'm okay. I just need to make it to the bathroom right now." Paloma struggled out of her daughter's hug and reeled into the bathroom. She threw down the blanket, looked at her own naked body with disgust, and sat down on the toilet to urinate. She looked at her face in the mirror over the sink. *"You look fifty-two, not thirty-two."* She felt firmer in her decision to end her life.

She went into the bedroom. She pulled on some jeans and a sweatshirt, forgetting underwear. She put on sandals and stepped into the living room. Cynthia was opening the front door. It was John Levi. What looked like blood was caked on one leg of his pants.

"Paloma, I'm so glad I found you," he said. "Are you okay? Are you hurt?" He walked toward her.

Paloma retreated into the bedroom, slammed the door, and locked it.

"Paloma, please come out and talk to me. Don't be afraid of me."

"Afraid of you? Get away from here. Take Cynthia and get as far away from me as you can."

"Paloma, I love you. I love Cynthia. This is my fault."

Paloma flung open the bedroom door. "Hell yes, it's your fault. It's your fault for giving me stupid dreams." Paloma waked past John Levi, shoving him away from her as he tried to hug her. She walked into the kitchen. She retched on the floor. "I can't live out your dreams for me."

Cynthia spoke up. "But Momma, you were doing so well."

"Which just makes it worse," Paloma responded. "I need to get out of here." She made for the door.

"Where are you going?" John Levi and Cynthia said at once.

"Somewhere else."

John Levi stepped in front of the door, barring Paloma's way. "Cynthia," said John Levi, "I need you to trust me. I need you to go into your bedroom and close the door so your mother and I can talk."

"No way. I'm staying right here. Talk in front of me."

"*Get out of my way!*" screamed Paloma.

"Paloma, listen to me. The police are after both of us. Me *and* you. They know we were there."

"Where is 'there'?" demanded Cynthia. "What happened?"

"How do they know I was there?'

"I don't know. Didn't you leave your purse there?"

"Shit. That proves nothing . . . Get the fuck out of my way! Take your hands off me! I am sick of having men putting their hands on me. From now on I am deciding what I will do. I want to leave. Get out of my way!"

"Paloma, you did nothing wrong."

"I've done everything wrong. From the moment I was born and every moment until now. You want to do something for me? Something that I want, for a change?"

"Yes. You know I do."

"Then take care of Cynthia. And let me go!"

"I will tell the police that I was the one who killed Angel. I hit him with the bat when he was down. You were just there. You did nothing. You told me to go away but I broke in anyway. I will get you out of this."

"Get me out of it? You can't get me out of my life. Can you? *Can you!?* God Almighty can't get me out of this life. You say you love me. You don't love *me*. Why can't you love me for who I actually am? Not your fucking project. *Get out of my way!*"

"Paloma, now you are talking like Luther."

"Well, Luther isn't talking any more. Because of you and me."

John Levi said, "Paloma! *Not* because of you."

Cynthia had turned full-faced and wide-eyed to John Levi. "Is Luther dead too?"

John Levi nodded his head.

"You killed Angel? You killed him? Did you kill Luther too?" Cynthia began to cry. "How will you take care of me?" John Levi went to her to reassure her.

Paloma took the chance to run out the front door, limping as she usually did when she tried to run. John Levi went after her but was too slow because of her head start and the bite wound on his leg. Paloma jumped into the Camaro and roared off. John Levi got to his pickup and tried to follow.

Paloma drove east on Long Avenue to I-35 and headed north. John Levi was unable to keep her car in sight after she reached the interstate. He kept driving north on 35, trying to see if she had taken an exit, but he could not spot the Camaro. On a hunch he headed east on Loop 820 off of 35. He had driven about a mile when he saw traffic backed up and stopped approaching an overpass. He drove on the right-hand shoulder past the traffic until he saw Angel's gold Camaro piled into a column supporting the overpass. The front of the car was mashed in nearly all the way up to the passenger compartment. John Levi ran up to the Camaro. Paloma was bleeding from the forehead where she had been thrown forward on collision against the windshield. She was holding her chest where she had hit the steering wheel and gasping for breath. John Levi was unable to yank her door open because of the damage. John Levi stood beside her as cars leaked by single file, the drivers staring. He tried to comfort her and keep her conscious. All she would do was sob and repeat, "I can't even kill myself. I can't even kill myself."

A North Richland Hills police cruiser arrived. An ambulance and a fire truck came right behind the cruiser. The firemen were able to pry the driver's-side door open and free Paloma. They were also spraying the crushed engine with foam to prevent fire. Paloma kept asking them to let her die. The EMTs were able to stop the bleeding from her forehead with pressure but were concerned she had bleeding in her brain and bleeding in her chest or a collapsed lung. John Levi warned them that she probably had meth in her system. He didn't know if that might make a difference in the drugs they might give her, but he didn't want to take a chance. The ambulance left with Paloma, its lights flashing and siren screaming. John Levi was not allowed to ride in the ambulance with her.

The police office asked John Levi for Paloma's name and the owner of the Camaro. John Levi's mention of meth had heightened the interest of the cop. He asked John Levi for his driver's license. John Levi handed it to him and said, "If you put this information into your system, I think you will find that I am wanted by Fort Worth police." Another office had arrived by then, and the first officer told him to watch John Levi as he got on his police radio. The officer came back, cuffed John Levi, and put him in the back seat of one of the cruisers. John Levi asked if he was under arrest, but the officer didn't respond. After about twenty minutes, an unmarked Fort Worth police car arrived. Two police detectives exited the car and spoke to the officers. Then they got John Levi out of the cruiser.

"Reverend John Levi Jones?" asked one detective.

"Yes, Detective."

"I'm Fort Worth Homicide Detective Alphonzo Washington." He held up his badge for John Levi to see. "This is my partner, Joseph Crump. We are investigating two homicides that occurred in Fort Worth early this morning at a house on Lulu Avenue. Rafer Thompson has told me all about you. Let's take a ride, shall we?

"Detective, can you tell me if Paloma is all right?"

"I cannot. We'll get it all sorted out."

"Detective Washington, as Rafer probably told you, I am a lawyer. And I want you to note that at the very beginning of our interaction, before there were any discussions, I told you that Paloma Ibarra was not in any way responsible for the deaths of Luther Bodine or Angel Bodine."

Washington looked at John Levi, squinting at him with his mouth wide open. "Noted."

"Detective, I want you to write down in your notebook what I just said about Paloma."

Washington took a small spiral notebook out of his pocket, opened it, made a note, and showed the note to John Levi. "That cover it for now?"

"Yes, Detective. Thank you. Is there any way you can take me first to the hospital where Paloma was taken? Just as soon as you can? I really need to know if she is all right. I need to let her daughter know too."

Washington sensed that John Levi might be willing to talk to him about what happened on Lulu. Two of the persons who witnessed what happened were dead. John Levi and maybe Paloma were the only other persons who could possibly say who shot and hit whom and why and in what sequence. It promised to be hard to prove a crime if John Levi and Paloma claimed their right to refuse to answer his questions. So Washington had a greater-than-usual interest in getting John Levi's account. Washington would honor John Levi's request to follow Paloma to the hospital to stay on John Levi's good side and to help avoid a claim of coercion if he gave a statement. "We can do that," he replied. "Let's get those cuffs off you."

"May I drive my truck there?"

The detective frowned. "Reverend, please understand, I want to accommodate you. You've been through a lot. But I really ought to be taking you downtown now. I'm going to be second-guessed by letting you go to the hospital. Your truck is evidence in a potential homicide case. I just must have it impounded."

"Can I get my things out of there?"

"Sorry, no."

"It's evidence because of the marks on the grill and sides?"

"Yes. And the orange paint left on the gate at the scene."

"What if I told you right now that I rammed open that gate with that truck?"

"Did you?"

"Detective, I have resolved to tell the truth about what happened. Whatever the consequences to me, I want to make it clear that Paloma Ibarra had nothing to do with the deaths of Luther and Angel Bodine. So, yes, I drove that truck into the gate to break it open so I could get into that house to get Paloma out."

"Tell you what, would you mind if I drove your truck with you in the passenger's seat while we go to the hospital?"

"Not at all."

"And we'll be followed by my car and a cruiser?"

"Good for me."

John Levi handed the detective his keys. Washington spoke to his partner and the patrol officer. The partner got on his radio and confirmed where Paloma had been taken. Then he and John Levi got into the pickup. Washington gave the keys back to John Levi. "Actually, it's your truck. You drive," he said.

As he pulled out into the highway, John Levi asked the detective, "You have a camera that makes videos with sound on your cell phone?"

"Yes."

"Then turn it on."

The detective fumbled nervously in his coat pocket and pulled out his phone. He checked to make sure there was plenty of power reserve. He activated the video and held it up about four feet away from the face of John Levi.

As John Levi was driving, he began to talk. "This is John Levi Jones. I am driving my 1956 Chevrolet pickup, color burnt orange. Sitting next to me in the passenger seat is Detective Washington of the Fort Worth Police . . . I forgot your first name, Detective."

"Alphonzo. And I am with the Homicide Division of the Fort Worth Police Department."

"Thank you, Detective . . . What day and time is it?"

The detective stated the date and time.

"Thank you again. My name is John Levi Jones. I am an ordained minister of the Central Texas Conference of the United Methodist Church, although I don't really expect to remain one for much longer, and a licensed attorney in the state of Texas, and I'm not sure about that either. I am fully aware that I am a suspect in a homicide case being investigated by Detective Washington here, that I have a right to remain silent and to consult with an attorney, and that anything I say now can and will be used against me in a grand jury or court of law. While I do not consider myself to be under arrest at this moment, I do not think I am free to go. Detective Washington has kindly allowed me to follow Paloma Ibarra to the hospital to see if she is all right. What I am about to say is completely voluntary and uncoerced. As I already told the detective, my only desire now is to tell the complete truth in order to exonerate Paloma Ibarra."

John Levi decided to pull the pickup off the highway and into a parking lot of a mall. The other officers driving their cars followed his lead. John Levi put the pickup in park and put his head into his hands on the steering wheel.

"Are you okay?" asked Washington.

"I think so. I was just starting to hyperventilate, thinking about what happened." He sat quietly for a moment. "Video still going?"

"Yes. Take your time."

"There is too much to recount here and now. Let me get to the basics. I had been trying to help Paloma Ibarra and her daughter Cynthia for about a year before today. Paloma has led a tragic life. Her mother was an addict and died of stomach cancer when Paloma was about thirteen. Her father is still alive but is totally disabled by alcoholism. She grew up in terrible poverty. She had been pulled into prostitution at the age of fourteen to provide for her siblings, and that led to her drug use as a teenager and afterwards. She worked in Luther Bodine's club and in his house. He was the one who brought her into prostitution and drug use as a teen. His son, Angel, became part of the operation. Both of them used Paloma in more ways than I can recount now."

John Levi's voice caught, and he paused to calm himself and to clear his throat.

"As I say, in their house she was used to lure men there to have sex with her and to buy and use drugs. Her daughter and Paloma came to me about a year ago, to help her stay free of the Bodines. I was able to help her get work and a place for her and her daughter to live. She was doing well. Then . . . When was it? Just last night? My God, it was just last night, Sunday night.

Cynthia came to evening worship at my church and said that her mother had been missing since Wednesday night. Paloma had a setback at her work and in her personal life and had evidently relapsed. She was always likely to fall into self-doubt and self-hatred. After what she had been through, why wouldn't she?"

John Levi took a long swig out of a water bottle on the seat.

"I went looking for her Sunday night into Monday morning. I traced her to the Bodines' on Lulu. Someone told me that he heard the Bodines say she was there. I stood outside and called for her. I couldn't get into the yard or next to or behind that house. I made a terrible racket. Luther came out and told me to get away. He said that he ought to let me in so Angel could kick my ass. I kept yelling, asking Paloma to confirm that she was in there. She yelled out to me. Told me to go away."

John Levi was starting to hyperventilate again. He labored on, gasping between phrases.

"I couldn't let her stay there with those men. Not after what they had done to her and taken from her. I was afraid for her. I begged her to come out. It gets blurry after that. I rammed the gate with my truck and knocked it open. I went into the front yard, heading toward the front door, yelling for Paloma to come to me. Luther was standing in the doorway with a metal bat. He opened the door and a black-and-tan hound of some kind came out of the door after me. I threw something at him—the dog, I mean. I ran to the front door. Only way to get away. I thought I could get the door closed with the dog outside. Another great idea. The dog clamped down on my leg. That's where this came from." He points to his blood-stained trouser leg.

"Luther tried to hit me with the bat while the dog had me. I pulled the bat away from him. I'm now in this tiny front room. It's really dark in there. I must have been swinging at the dog with the bat. Then Angel suddenly comes out of the back into that room, screaming. I don't remember him having any clothes on. He has a pistol of some kind. The dog leaves me and attacks Angel. His father tries to pull the dog off him. Angel shoots his dog in the back, twice, I think. The explosions give off so much sound and light. He curses at me. He tries to shoot me. I hit his arm with the bat as he shoots. That's how close we all were. The bullet intended for me hits his father. Luther goes down. There is this half-second of weird stillness while this is sinking in with all of us. Then Angel screams at me for making him shoot his father. He is pointing the pistol back at me. I am maybe three feet from him. Just as he fires again, I dodge and hit him in the head with the bat. He goes down. I stand over him and hit him once more in the head with the bat."

John Levi takes a deep breath. "Only then did Paloma come into that room. Only after all the hitting and the biting and the shooting and the hitting had happened. She wasn't in that room—I'm sure of that—when all that was happening. She did not hit anyone, shoot anyone, bite anyone, threaten anyone, nothing. She did not ask me to do any of this. She never asked me to hurt the Bodines. Ever. This is all on me. In fact, she told me to go away before I busted in. She came out, saw what happened, and started yelling at me. Then she ran out the door, got in Angel's Camaro, and drove away . . . After a while, I followed her in my pickup. I think maybe I threw up in that room. I found her at her apartment. Then she got away from me. I followed her and found her in the wrecked Camaro on 820 . . . That's it. That's it. Can I go to the hospital now? I have to let Cynthia know if her mother is okay. God, I hope she is okay . . . Who is going to take care of Cynthia if Paloma is hurt bad? If I hadn't done this, she'd still be in the Bodines, but she'd be alive."

John Levi started to cry. He opened the door of his pickup. Washington reacted as if John Levi were trying to run. But John Levi only leaned out the door and vomited on the parking lot.

Chapter Five

"Your Honor, I am going to stay here and be accountable for what I have done."

— September 9 to September 16, 2019 —

Paloma was diagnosed with a concussion from her head hitting the windshield, and a hairline fracture of her sternum and contusions of her lungs from her impact with the steering wheel. Thankfully, there was no leakage of air from her lungs into her chest cavity. She was kept in the hospital for observation of her injuries for three days under custody of the police. She was then transported to the court for arraignment for the theft of Angel's car. She was bonded out to home confinement. She was on supplemental oxygen until the fluid in her lungs cleared and she could breathe normally.

Darla Henderson took care of Cynthia until Paloma returned to their apartment. Upon Paloma's return, Cynthia stayed home from school to care for Paloma. Cynthia was crushed that Paloma had returned to meth, had failed to contact Cynthia while she was gone, and had tried to kill herself. At first Paloma refused to talk and denied she intended suicide in the car crash. After Paloma had recovered from her difficulty breathing, Cynthia started urging her mother to talk things out about why she had given up. Paloma tried to use the excuse that Angel had laced her drink with some kind of date rape drug at The Landing Strip on Wednesday night. This didn't satisfy Cynthia because Paloma had chosen to stay at the Bodines' house to use meth for four more nights.

"Why was being with me not enough to make you want to live?" Cynthia asked her mother. Paloma responded that she was depressed and tired and had lost all hope. "I wasn't thinking right, honey. I was running away and then I was on meth."

"What about John Levi?"

"We never had a real relationship. I was fooling myself about that. He never cared about me. He just cares about you."

"Momma, John Levi killed a man for you. He put Angel out of your life forever. He put his life in danger to get you out of that house. Now he is facing prison for life. What more proof do you need that he loves you?"

"I am afraid that all he loves is who he hopes I will become. But I do know that if I hadn't run away that Wednesday night, John Levi wouldn't be in so much trouble. I think that maybe I wanted to kill myself in that Camaro partly to get away from that guilt. I was really angry with him for breaking into the house, but if I hadn't been there, Luther and Angel wouldn't have died and John Levi wouldn't be facing prison. I am scared that it is too late for any good to come out of any of this and that I started it all. I had going this normal, boring, *good* life and I didn't trust it. I didn't think I deserved it."

"You deserve it, Mamma. And I deserve it. Live it for me, if not for yourself. It's not too late. Something good will come out of this. I just know it," said Cynthia.

"It may be too late for John Levi," said Paloma.

Paloma was initially charged with felony theft of Angel's Camaro. The grand jury was considering other charges against her as the investigation progressed. Paloma was appointed a criminal defense attorney to be paid by the county. Someone posted the necessary 10 percent of her ten-thousand-dollar cash bond to obtain her release from jail pending trial. She was confined to her home. Of course, she was out of a job. Darla paid Paloma and Cynthia's rent and gave Paloma money for food and expenses, all from an anonymous source. The source was of course John Levi, funneled through his former law partner, Charles Needham. Needham had paid the 10-percent bondman's fee for Paloma's pretrial release with John Levi's money.

After staying for two hours at the hospital to satisfy himself that Paloma would recover, John Levi was transported by Detective Washington to the homicide office. There John Levi said he was too exhausted to add to his previous recorded statement. He was formally arrested, processed, and jailed without bond. John Levi's initial charges were criminal mischief for his destruction of the Bodine gate, burglary of the Bodine habitation, and murder committed in the course of that burglary. He was held in jail three days and two nights pending arraignment.

At the arraignment, the recording of John Levi's confession to Detective Washington in the pickup was admitted into evidence and played by the judge in his office. Assistant District Attorney Alison Wells informed the judge that her office would ask the grand jury to indict John Levi for the crimes he was already charged with by complaint, plus the crime of capital murder if the grand jury concluded that John Levi intended to kill Angel Bodine when he struck him the second time with the bat. Assistant D.A. Wells argued that John Levi should be denied any bail pending trial because his guilt was established conclusively by the recording, his conviction of the crimes was therefore certain, he faced life imprisonment, and he had the financial means to flee.

The trial judge was Walter Altshuler, the dean of all Tarrant County Criminal District Court judges, a former criminal prosecutor who had sat on the felony bench for more than twenty years and had presided over scores of murder trials. Altshuler was seventy-one years old, a great, white lump of a man with thick silver hair parted in the middle of his head and curling over his ears, bushy white eyebrows, reading glasses he peered over, and a surprisingly squeaky voice for a man of his size and gravity. He was not seeking re-election, so he had no inhibitions whatever about pushing for what he thought to be the right and fair result in his court.

When Judge Altshuler suggested to John Levi that he request more time to retain counsel, John Levi insisted to the judge that he was representing himself and refused to request a continuance. Altshuler admonished John Levi about the mistake he was committing. "It is well known and well repeated," said the judge, "that a lawyer who represents himself has a fool for a client. Mr. Jones, you are clearly in emotional turmoil over all this. I can see that as you are standing here. You even gave that recorded statement to the police when you knew better as a lawyer, and the substance and sound of your voice during the statement leave me no doubt about your emotional stress. You need the cool head of an experienced defense attorney to counsel you. The court advises you as strongly as it can to retain one." John Levi refused to retain a lawyer but also refused to give the judge a reason for his refusal. "Then the court on its own motion resets arraignment and receipt of your plea of guilty or not guilty. Mr. Jones, are you going to flee?"

"Your Honor, I am going to stay here and be accountable for what I have done."

"Tell me that you do not want to remain in jail pending indictment and trial."

John Levi actually hesitated. "No, Your Honor, I do not."

"Then I am ordering a one-million-dollar cash bond, with 10 percent of that one million to be posted in cash before you can be released. Also before release, your passport will be turned over to your pretrial release officer. During release, you are to remain in your home, except only when you are traveling directly to or from this court or unless you receive specific permission to go elsewhere from your pretrial officer. You will be fitted with an ankle monitor that will constantly report your location electronically. You will wear this monitor at all times, even while sleeping. If you leave your home, except for court or as permitted, you will be arrested and returned to jail, where you will remain at least until this prosecution ends. And you are to have no communication, direct or indirect, with . . . What's her name?" the judge asked D.A. Wells.

"Paloma Ibarra, Your Honor."

"No communications with Ms. Paloma Ibarra," replied the judge.

"And her daughter, Cynthia Ibarra, Your Honor?" asked the Assistant D.A.

"And with her daughter. None. Do you understand and agree, Mr. Jones?"

"Yes, Your Honor."

"In addition, I am ordering both sides of this case to have no additional communications, directly or indirectly, with the media. This case has already been the subject of a great deal of publicity. We are not going to try this case any further in the media."

"Your Honor, I would just like the record to be clear that the Tarrant County District Attorney's Office objects to Mr. Jones' pretrial release and the granting of *any* bond. Mr. Jones has no defense whatsoever to any of these charges."

The judge turned to John Levi. "Did you hear what Assistant D.A. Wells just said?"

"Yes, I did, Your Honor."

"You have no background or experience practicing criminal law. Am I correctly informed about that?"

"Yes, Your Honor," replied John Levi.

"Do you believe that you have no defenses whatsoever to any of these charges, as Ms. Wells just put it?"

"I . . . I . . . do not know, Your Honor."

"Then you need to retain competent counsel, don't you?"

John Levi said nothing.

"Ms. Wells, you just said that Mr. Jones has 'no defense whatsoever' to these charges. Since you are the only lawyer presently before this court with knowledge of Texas criminal law, please tell Mr. Jones about Texas Penal Code section 9.33."

"9.33, Your Honor?"

"Yes, 9.33."

"Excuse me, Your Honor." Wells' assistant, sitting next to her at counsel table, found and handed Wells a copy of the Texas Penal Code opened to section 9.33. "You mean the 'Defense of Third Person' section?" asked D.A. Wells.

"The very one, Ms. Wells."

Wells read silently. "I just don't believe that section applies here."

"Mr. Jones, I want you to note the existence of section 9.33. And I want you to think about the difference between your subjective conviction of your moral guilt and a legal conviction for murder under the Texas criminal law. I am not saying that both will not be present in this case. I am just saying that you ought to retain an experienced criminal attorney, one who is familiar with section 9.33, so you can make informed decisions about your defense. And I am also saying that if you do not retain counsel before the next hearing, this court will consider ordering you to undergo a mental competency evaluation to make sure you know what you are doing and have control over your remorse."

CHAPTER SIX

"Why don't you just hit yourself in the head with the same bat?

— September 2019 —

The "great deal of publicity" that Judge Altshuler referred to at the court hearing was a long article that had appeared in the local city newspaper the morning of the hearing. The writer cited anonymous sources for the story. John Levi could guess the identities of the sources from what was reported. One was surely Darla Henderson. Others were surely Rafer Thompson and Charles Needham. The other sources were probably neighbors of the Bodine house on Lulu, Seth, the bouncer at the now-closed Hacienda bar and club, and Elvira of Bonitas Chiquitas. The deaths of Luther and Angel Bodine eliminated the fearful silence of the neighbors, Seth, and Elvira.

The author of the article published a generally accurate account of John Levi's privileged upbringing and education, his success as a trial lawyer, and the ministries he started at Peace. The author exposed the Bodines' criminal records, their operation of their club on North Main with illegal gambling, drug use, and employment of underage girls, and their manufacture and sale of meth and seduction of teenage girls into prostitution and addiction in their home base on Lulu. And the author recounted the tragic history of Paloma Ibarra and her daughter and John Levi's efforts to save them from the Bodines. John Levi was painted as a selfless man who truly sought to walk the Christian talk but who was now facing indictment for his murder of evil men. And Paloma was painted as a weak woman who had failed to save herself and her daughter from her life of prostitution and addiction.

But the burden of the article was a scathing criticism of the Fort Worth Police Department for not stopping the Bodines long before John Levi had to stop them. The Bodines' criminal activities had gone on for years and years. Why had the police never stopped them? Why had The Hacienda and the house never been raided? Why had the Bodines never been charged? Why did a Methodist minister have to save this mother and her daughter? Had the Bodines bribed officers within the department?

John Levi read the article when he arrived home after his release from jail. He was sickened by the way it characterized Paloma. How mortifying it must be to her. And she had lost her anonymity. How could she ever escape these labels as a weak, addicted prostitute? And he was being made out to be a hero when he was the opposite. He had not killed in defense of himself or Paloma. He had just killed. He had no knowledge of any misconduct of the police. Paloma had insisted that he not complain to police because she was afraid she would be arrested. The writer implied that what John Levi had done was justified because the Bodines needed killing. What Christian could determine such a need or take such an action?

John Levi wished he could contact the article's author and correct the distortions about himself and Paloma. But Judge Altshuler had forbidden this contact. So the article strengthened John Levi's resolve to tell the complete truth to the grand jury and the trial court to save Paloma from prison and keep her with Cynthia. He would leave the consequences of his truthfulness to God.

He was still sickened at what he had done. He was shocked at his capacity to strike Angel with the bat as he lay defenseless at his feet. He had caused all this by taking it upon himself to break in. He had wanted to play hero. Now two men were dead, John Levi's own life was ruined, Paloma was facing prison, and Cynthia was threatened with a foster home, all because he had arrogated to himself the role of God.

But there was a deluge of support for John Levi in letters to the editor in the newspaper and in calls to local right-wing radio talk shows. One radio host lamented only that John Levi had not administered justice with his own gun that night. This talk show host speculated that John Levi had not called the police because he knew they had been bribed by the Bodines. Only rare objections to John Levi's actions as a Christian minister were written or voiced. Peace was deluged with donations of money, food, clothes, and furniture. New worshipers appeared the next Sunday at Peace to hear John Levi preach, only to learn that he had been suspended from ministry by his bishop. There was an outpouring of support for his actions from the people of the church neighborhood. A GoFundMe page was created by a neighborhood family to pay for his legal defense. Offers of testimony in support of John Levi were mailed to the Tarrant County D.A.'s office, some about the value of the ministries he had started at Peace and some about the criminal conduct of the Bodines.

The newspaper reported when the Texas State Bar suspended John Levi's law license because of his pending charges. Letters also poured into the bar offices in Austin in John Levi's support.

The newly elected Tarrant County District Attorney was Charlise Remington, a veteran criminal prosecutor who had become a private criminal defense attorney and vocal critic of the local police before riding into office on a reform platform. The Jones case was the first prosecution during her tenure that was being closely reported by the media. Remington was well aware of the public support for John Levi and the pressure on her not to put the case before a grand jury. But she was concerned that a unilateral decision on her part not to prosecute John Levi would be perceived by some as favoritism for an Anglo lawyer from a privileged home. So Remington would leave the decision to prosecute up to a grand jury. If a grand jury found probable cause that John Levi had committed all the necessary elements to be indicted, Remington wanted him prosecuted. Matters of his character and contribution to the church neighborhood and his motive in entering the Bodine house could be considered during plea bargaining or at sentencing after conviction. But she also directed Assistant District Attorney Alison Wells to inform the grand jury of any potential defenses that might be available to John Levi and to call to testify any potential defense witness.

John Levi persisted in representing himself despite Judge Altshuler's urging him to retain experienced counsel. John Levi sent a letter requesting to waive his Fifth Amendment right against self-incrimination in order to testify before the grand jury that was considering indicting Paloma as an accomplice to John Levi's alleged crimes. He received a letter in response from Assistant D.A. Wells informing him that the same grand jury considering his potential indictment was considering Paloma's as well. If he testified, it would of course be under a waiver of the Fifth Amendment right in both matters. The letter enclosed a transcript of his recorded statement to Detective Washington. The date of his appearance before the grand jury was set. He was urged by Wells to retain counsel well in advance of that appearance so the proceedings would not be delayed.

Charles Needham called John Levi to say that he was worried about him and wanted to see him. Needham appeared at the condo the next morning. He was not alone. He brought Doug Price with him, the younger lawyer in Jones' old firm who had so upset Paloma.

"What's he doing here?" John Levi demanded before letting them both in.

"Doug wants to apologize for the way he and his secretary treated Paloma."

"Won't do any good now. But come in."

They sat at John Levi's kitchen table. They all took a cup of coffee.

"Mr. Jones, I really regret how I spoke to Ms. Ibarra. And my secretary has left the firm. I seem to have started a domino of bad events. I am so sorry."

John Levi looked at him. "There a lot of pressure in litigation. It's easy to let off some of that steam against innocent bystanders. Charles will tell you that I have been guilty of the same conduct toward employees. I appreciate your apology. Maybe someday you can offer it to Paloma."

"How is Paloma?" asked Price.

"I do not know. I am not allowed to have any communication with her. That is one really hard part of this. I can't even talk to her daughter. I am sure they are both worried sick about Paloma being indicted as an accessory for what I did."

"Before we go any further, why don't we all agree that Doug and I are acting as your counsel during this conversation? That way we can never be asked what you say to us."

"Why would anyone question you?"

"You never can be sure. The assistant D.A. presenting your case to the grand jury is Alison Wells. She is *all* about winning. She could pull anything."

"How do you know that?" asked John Levi.

Gerard interceded. "We hired Doug out of the D.A.'s office. He prosecuted violent crime there. He also worked in the grand jury section. He still has friends in the office."

John Levi said, "So you brought him here for another reason than to apologize. I don't appreciate that, Charles. We have fought too many wars in the same foxhole for you to deceive me."

Charles asked Price to step into another room.

"John Levi, you are my friend. People in the D.A.'s office have told Doug that if you hadn't given the recorded statement to the detective, the D.A.'s office would be having a really hard time making *any* case against you. And now you intend to go before the grand jury? Do you have a death wish?"

"I am not going to talk to you about this. I am going to do this as a Christian, not as a lawyer."

Charles pulled his chair closer to John Levi's, so they were almost nose to nose. "Do you know how dumb that is? Do you *want* to go to jail for the rest for your life?"

"What I want is to make the right decision. I realize that I am applying different standards than a lawyer's to this. I need to testify to protect Paloma."

"But you already protected Paloma in your statement."

"I need to be sure the grand jury believes me. They will be more likely to believe me about Paloma if I also tell them the truth about myself."

"You don't want a lawyer, because you know a lawyer would tell you what I just did."

"You will never understand."

"How do you know that?"

"Charles, this world sucks. It's broken for most people. People like Paloma are born screwed and people like me are born protected from everything and everyone screwing people like Paloma. It's totally random and unjust. And you know the reason why the world is so broken?"

"I have a feeling you are about to tell me."

"Because we don't follow what God teaches. A priest in Austin told me once that most of the world hungers for the world to be put right. But for those of us who choose to be Christians, there are limits to the way we can pursue this. I ran right over those limits because I was angry that all my work for Paloma and her daughter had been undone by the Bodines. They had defeated me and God. I wanted to get that poor woman out of the clutches of those evil, miserable men forever. All that mattered at that moment was my hunger to do that. So I made the world worse. Now I am going to go back to following God's teachings. And one of those is to tell the truth."

Doug Price abruptly stormed in. "Why don't you just hit yourself in the head with the same bat? That's what you will be doing if you go into the grand jury and stick with your story that you brained that man out of nothing but anger and a hunger for justice. You can be sure you will be asked about that. What if there are grand jurors who are sympathetic to what you did and who are looking for an excuse not to indict you? This is still Texas. Can't you say that you were scared and disoriented by the gunfire and the smoke, that you'd never been in such a situation in your life, that you broke in to save Paloma's life, and that you hit that scumbag with the bat a second time because he was making a move to shoot you? Without calling him a 'scumbag,' that is?"

"So lie."

"For God's sake, Mr. Jones. You don't have to confess *in court*. Confess to that priest later. Repent privately. What's one more lie when you killed a man?"

"For God's sake, and for Paloma's, I need to tell the truth to the grand jury. You two need to leave now."

"John Levi, Doug knows how grand jury proceedings go. Please forgive him . . . for giving you very good advice, by the way. Can you at least listen while he fills you in on what will happen? Can you live in the world the way it is until after this prosecution is over?"

John Levi poured more coffee. He sat down opposite them at the table. "Let's hear it," he said. "What's likely to happen when I testify? Who's going to be asking me questions? Will I be allowed to say whatever I want? "

Three days before John Levi was scheduled to go before the grand jury, he telephoned his parents' number for the third time since the incident on Lulu Street. They had not returned his previous two calls. This time he left a longer message than before. "Mother and Father, I understand why you are not calling me back. If you had called back, I would have apologized for all that I am putting you through. That's it."

Two days before his appearance before the grand jury, John Levi received a letter from Father Gutierrez inviting a telephone call. He decided not to respond until his appearance before the grand jury was over. He was afraid Gutierrez would also try to talk him out of appearing.

Then the day before the grand jury appearance, Gerard Jones came to John Levi's door.

"Father!" John Levi stammered when he opened his door. "I am so surprised to see you. And pleased. Can you come in?"

"Just for a moment."

Father and son stepped inside John Levi's den. They stood awkwardly facing one another. Gerard Jones spoke first.

"I have come to apologize to you."

"*You* have come to apologize to *me*? I am the one to apologize to you . . . for being so self-centered and judgmental. I have not been a loving son to you and mother. I owe you everything . . . regardless of our disagreements."

"No, you don't owe us *everything*. You have accomplished so much without our support. We should have supported what you are doing up there in your church. We are sorry . . . May I sit down?"

Gerard Jones walked shakily to a couch. John Levi got him a glass of water and sat on the couch with him.

"This is hard for me, Son. And for your mother. At first when you were arrested, we were mortified. We couldn't face our friends. People would whisper about us at the club. My customers wouldn't talk to me. We hid in our house. But then we read that article in the newspaper about your ministries. Son, we had no idea. We should have. We should have come to your church to see for ourselves. You are helping so many people in trouble. And that poor Paloma woman! What a life she has led! It's just so admirable what you have tried to do for her and her poor daughter."

Mr. Jones took a long drink from the glass and wiped his forehead.

"You know who turned us around about this?" asked Mr. Jones. "Eugenia."

"Eugenia, your housekeeper?"

"Yes. Eugenia. She told us that her entire church was praying for you and that poor woman and her daughter. We were just blown away by that. She told us she didn't care if we fired her but she was going to say to us what we needed to hear. She said we ought to be proud that we raised a son with such a heart. She asked us how many parents could say they have a son who would risk his own life to get a poor woman out of a place like that. It really brought us up short."

"Father, I don't know what to say. I'm not proud of myself because of what I am putting people through. I need to apologize to you. But it means so much to me that you have come here."

"Can we help you in any way?"

"You just have, Father."

"Surely you won't be indicted."

"I am afraid I will be. But please don't worry about that now. We'll get through whatever is to come. Love will get us through. Would you pray for Paloma and her daughter?"

"Of course. And you."

"Father, you say that Eugenia told you what you needed to hear about me. You know who told me what I needed to hear about being grateful to you and Mother? It was Paloma."

"How remarkable. Maybe we can meet her someday."

"I will call Mother in a bit. To tell her I love her."

Mr. Jones couldn't bring himself to hug his son. But they parted with a tearful handshake.

Chapter Seven

"I played God."

— Monday, October 14, 2019 —

Assistant District Attorney Alison Wells met John Levi Jones in the waiting area for the grand jury. John Levi appeared in a black suit, white shirt, and black tie, his funeral attire. Hidden under his shirt and suit coat was a cross on a chain, which he almost never wore. Before he left his condo that morning, he had prayed over and over the centuries-old Jesus prayer: "Lord Jesus Christ, Son of God, have mercy on me, a sinner." Charles Needham had driven him to the criminal court building and let him out at the side entrance on the basement level, where no media were on watch.

"Are you still representing yourself?" Assistant D.A. Wells asked.

"Yes, ma'am." he replied.

"Are you still intending to waive your right against self-incrimination?"

"Yes."

"Are there any questions you intend not to answer?"

"No, I intend to answer all that are put to me."

"Did you bring your signed waiver of rights form?"

"Here it is."

"While we are speaking, are there any witnesses you request I put before this grand jury before it reaches a decision in your case?"

"Not at this point."

"Any questions of me now?

"No."

"Please wait until I call you in. One juror is running a few minutes late."

John Levi sat silently in the only chair in the tiny waiting area, praying quietly, "Lord Jesus, may my truthfulness be worthy of you, may my truthfulness be worthy of you." He thought to himself, *"I wonder if this is how a man about to be executed feels?"*

Within minutes he was ushered down a hall and into a windowless room about thirty by thirty feet with soundproof paneling. Just inside the door was a small square table with a chair on either side. He was directed to sit in one of these chairs facing the room. In the chair to the opposite side of the table sat a court reporter with her stenographic machine. A tape recorder and a Bible sat on the table. In front of him at a desk sat Assistant D.A. Wells. Twelve chairs were arrayed along the three remaining walls of the room, four to each wall. These were filled with twelve people, whom he inferred were the grand jurors. He looked closely from face to face to make sure he did not recognize any. As he did so, every juror stared intently at him. A few smiled and nodded but most withheld any sign of emotion. All seemed curious and concentrated.

Wells ran through his constitutional rights. She asked him if the waiver of rights form he had just delivered to her was indeed his. This was marked as an exhibit. She confirmed that he had requested the opportunity to appear before this grand jury and was not under subpoena. He affirmed that he was a licensed attorney, that he understood the rights Wells read aloud, that he waived his rights, and that he was not requesting more time to consult with an attorney. She also established that he was not under any undue emotional of psychological duress and felt mentally competent to appear. Last she established that he understood what potential criminal charges were being considered by the grand jury as well as the potential defenses. She read the elements of the crimes and defenses into the record.

"Mr. Jones, having heard all this, is it still your request to testify today before this grand jury?"

"Very much so, Ms. Wells."

"Why?" A voice came from the grand juror chairs.

"I'm sorry?" replied John Levi, searching for the person who asked.

A red-haired woman who appeared to be in her twenties sat in a chair directly ahead of him and behind Wells. "Why do you want to testify?"

In all his days before trial juries, no juror had been allowed to ask a party or a witness a question. John Levi looked at Wells for direction. Wells nodded her approval.

"Let the truth telling begin," he thought.

"My motivation is to help you conclude that Paloma Ibarra is innocent of any crime. My motivation is to tell you the truth of what happened. Those two motivations are the same."

"So you are here to exonerate yourself too."

"No." He paused. "After what I did . . . I find it hard to explain. I failed my faith. I failed the ethical standards that applied to me as a minister. I have been so self-righteous at times. That night I showed myself to be a phony. I can't undo what happened. All that is left for me is to be truthful about Paloma's lack of responsibility for what I did. I can't ask you to believe what I say about what Paloma did *not* do if I am not truthful with you about what I did."

Ms. Wells interceded. "I suggest that we start by considering the recorded statement which Mr. Jones gave to Detective Washington on the day in question. Mr. Jones, I inform you that these grand jurors have already heard the recording many times. The jurors have directed that this recording be played again now in your hearing so you will have the chance under oath to contradict, explain, or amplify your statement and to answer any questions they might have about it. Transcripts have been prepared of the statement. I am passing those out to every juror and to you. Any questions so far?"

"No, ma'am."

"Have you listened to this statement or seen a transcript of it since you made it?"

"No."

The recoding was played. John Levi was unsettled to hear the sound of his voice. It brought back much of the emotion he was feeling when he made it. Tears began to well up in his eyes. The court reporter handed him a tissue.

When the recording had finished playing, John Levi asked for a few more minutes to review the transcript. When he looked up from the document, Ms. Wells asked him if he had any corrections to the transcript.

"No, ma'am."

"Questions from the grand jurors?" asked Wells.

Seven hands shot up.

A man who appeared to be in his fifties and who sat to John Levi's right was evidently the elected foreman. He pointed to different jurors to ask her or his questions, careful not to use their names.

An older female juror went first. "Mr. Jones, in your statement, you said that Ms. Ibarra [reading] 'had a setback at her work and in her personal life and had evidently relapsed.' Do you see that on the transcript?"

"Yes, ma'am."

"What was the setback at her work?"

John Levi recounted what had happened among Paloma, Doug Price and his secretary. "So . . . Paloma quit."

"When did you find out about this?"

"When her daughter came to me on a Sunday night to say that her mom had been missing since Wednesday. The daughter told me that Paloma had quit her job. I called the senior partner to get the whole story."

"And the setback in her personal life?" asked the same woman.

"It was about me. I'm afraid I was the setback."

John Levi saw some jurors nod knowingly at one another.

"I was spending a lot of time at Paloma's and Cynthia's apartment. Got to where it was every night. Got to where it was until 11:00 p.m. almost every night."

"Why? Did you do that with anyone else in your church?"

"No."

"Why for them?"

"Because I wanted to keep Paloma from feeling the need to go back to meth. Because I loved being with them."

"We have been told that you were supporting this woman and her daughter financially. Were you spending your money on anyone else in the neighborhood?"

"Yes, but not directly. I was funding the microloan program myself. And giving money to the church for the church to give financial help to some families for rent and utilities and car repairs and stuff. But this was the only family I was giving money to directly."

"Again, why only to Paloma and Cynthia?"

"Because I couldn't let Paloma get back into the clutches of those men. I couldn't stand by doing nothing while Cynthia's heart was broken again. I didn't know anyone with stories like theirs."

"Why didn't you give them money through the church? You didn't want the church to know?"

"I guess I didn't."

"Why not?"

"Because it was a lot of money. Because of Paloma's past and the way she looks. I didn't want people to misunderstand."

"That this was romantic?"

"That this was romantic and sexual."

"Was it?"

"It wasn't sexual."

"Was it romantic?"

"I am afraid it was for her. For me . . . I'm still not sure."

"You're still not sure if you have romantic feelings for her?"

"You'd have to see Paloma. You'd have to be around her."

"We have."

"What? Did you say you have?"

Ms. Wells interceded. "We are not supposed to disclose who has appeared before the grand jury."

John Levi thought, *"Paloma has testified here. I hope she did not get herself in trouble. Why would she do that?"*

"What about how Paloma looks?"

"She is like no other woman I have ever known. Her story. Her courage. Her presence. Her face."

"Her body?"

"Everything about her. Her passion. I liked being around her. And Cynthia. I felt that I was helping. I liked the feeling of making a difference. I hungered for it. They were the first people I was able to actually help in that neighborhood."

"Did you ever have sexual relationship with Paloma Ibarra?"

"No, never."

"Did you want to?"

"Part of me wondered about it and wanted it. But it wasn't possible."

"Why not?"

"Because she needed to learn that a man could care for her without it being motivated by sex. Because I couldn't take advantage of my being so financially supportive. Because it is forbidden to a Methodist minister to have such a relationship with a church member."

"So you still haven't told us the personal setback she suffered."

"A short time before she ran off, I told her I wouldn't be spending so much time at her place."

"Why not?"

"I was told by a member of my church that my truck had been spotted at the apartment every night. Members of the church who were opposed to the ministries we had started and to the new people who were coming into the church were going to try to use that to get me reassigned. They were going to claim to my bishop that I was in an immoral relationship with Paloma."

"How did she react?"

"She was angry and disappointed with me. She said I was a phony Christian. She said no one would have complained except for her background."

"You used the word 'phony' when you were describing yourself to us a minute ago. Is Paloma where you got that?"

"Yes. And she was right."

Another young woman requested the opportunity to ask questions.

"Are you in love with Paloma?"

Long pause.

"I don't mean to mince words. I love Paloma and Cynthia. I would do anything for them. I guess I have proven that. But I am not sure that I am *in* love with Paloma. I am almost forty, but I have never been *in love* with any woman. I've had relationships, but not that. So I have no frame of reference. She may have thought I was heading that way. I may have led her on by being there so much. No, I did lead her on. I should have observed that boundary sooner—the boundary between a pastor and a church member. When I put the boundary up late, she was hurt. I am afraid that she had imagined her future with me in it. *I* imagined a future with her sometimes. When I told her that I was going to stop being there so much . . . I think that added to why she ran away and went back to meth."

"So have you ever been married?"

"No."

"Never lived with a woman?"

"No."

"Why not?"

"Never met anyone I couldn't do without, I guess."

"Can you do without Paloma?"

"Yes. I'll have to. Can I ask a question? What does that have to do with this case?"

Assistant D.A. Wells started to speak but the juror responded first. "You said that you love Paloma and Cynthia so much that you would do anything for them. Does that include lying to keep Paloma from being indicted?"

"I understand why you would consider that. That is why I am trying to be so honest about myself. If you believe I am being totally truthful about me, I ask that you believe that I am being totally truthful about Paloma."

The juror continued. "We also ask you about your feelings about Paloma and Cynthia because we have to decide whether you went in that house intending to do whatever you had to do to get her out of there, including kill someone. Did you?"

"I didn't go into that house intending to kill anyone. I went in to get Paloma out and back to her daughter. I was so . . . I don't know . . . *possessed* by that desire that I really didn't count the cost. That was a big mistake. That was another boundary I crossed."

"When you were standing outside that house on Lulu, did you feel partly responsible for Paloma being in there?"

"Yes."

"So that added to your motive to get her out that and free from those men?"

"Yes."

A middle-aged male in a suit spoke up.

"Do you intend to stay in ministry?"

"That doesn't seem possible to me right now. As I said, I think Paloma was right when she said I am a phony."

"How?"

"I killed a man. I broke into a house and killed a man. Another man is dead who wouldn't be if I hadn't broken in. Not exactly, 'Happy are those who are peacemakers, for they will be called children of God,' is it?"

"Do you intend to keep your law license?"

"I think whether that is an option for me depends upon the outcome of this case. My license is suspended now."

"If you can get your license back, do you intend to keep doing *pro bono* work for the poor?"

"Absolutely. More than ever."

"In that neighborhood?"

"I love those people, so . . . if I can."

An older male juror asked, "What in the Holy Bible allows these so-called ministries in your church?"

"'So-called ministries'?"

"You know what I am talking about. Don't play dumb. The food and the clothing and the money loans and the legal help."

John Levi leveled a cold eye on the man, but then remembered why he was there and who was observing his every look and move. "I would refer you to Matthew 25, verses 31 through 46."

"So you think you are the equal of Jesus?"

"Obviously, I do not. What a question. Jesus never broke into a home and killed a man. But Paul wrote in Galatians, 'It is no longer I who live, but Christ who lives in me.' And in Philippians, 'Put on the mind of Christ.' So I believe that every Christian is called to continue the ministry of Jesus to the poor. Not to be his 'equal,' as you put it, but his follower. You know? In order to love our neighbors as ourselves? Don't you, sir?"

The foreman quickly called upon another juror.

A slim young woman juror in a stylish silver blouse and blue slacks asked, "Reverend Jones, what were your feelings toward Luther and Angel Bodine when you went into that house? Did you hate them?"

"I have thought about this a lot. I promised to be truthful to you, and I will be as best I can. And I am trying to be truthful to myself about this. The worst lies we tell are to ourselves. Yes, I hated them." Assistant D.A. Wells started writing furiously. "I hated them for what they had done to Paloma and to so many teenage girls. I'd like to be glib and say I hated what they had done but not them. You know, 'hate the sin but not the sinner.' But I hated them because they were taking Paloma away from Cynthia, again, and from her best self and her best future. But I also pitied them . . . for what they had done to their own souls. And I couldn't imagine what paths they had been down to lead them to where they were. I once asked Luther how he could sleep at night knowing what he was doing to so many young girls."

"What did he say?"

"He said that I had no idea what life he had led that had brought him to that point."

"How many times had you encountered them before that night?"

"Luther in the landlord-tenant court and outside in the parking lot. Angel outside the landlord-tenant court and outside Paloma's apartment a few days before she ran away this last time. And then at the house when I broke in."

"Why didn't you call the police that night?

"I didn't think I had time. And I was afraid if the police came and went in the house, Paloma would be arrested too."

"You broke in to save Paloma?"

"Yes."

"You thought she was in imminent danger of being hurt?"

"That gets blurry. Imminent? I just wanted to get her out and get her home."

"You had seen the scar on her chin and the missing ear lobe?"

"Yes."

"She had told you that Angel had done that to her."

"What? No, she never told me that."

"Reverend Jones, isn't it possible that before the night you broke in Paloma Ibarra had told you that Angel had cut her chin and cut her ear lobe?"

"I think I would remember that."

"Reverend Jones, say that it is possible she told you that. You had many late-night conversations with her. You can't remember them all. Say, 'It is possible.'"

"It is possible," he repeated half-heartedly.

The young woman continued. "Just before you broke in that night, you were having a conversation with Paloma Ibarra and Angel Bodine."

"Conversation? We were yelling back and forth."

"Just before you broke in, you heard Paloma say to you, 'Go away before you get me and you both hurt' from inside the house?"

"Something like that."

"And then, right after that, you heard Angel Bodine say to Paloma inside the house, 'I told you to keep quiet, bitch. Say another word and see what happens to you.'"

John Levi paused. "This sounds very precise."

The young woman turned to Assistant D.A. Wells. "May we please play the recording for him?"

"Let's recess for one minute. Everyone remain silent and in place, please. Is that all right with you, Mr. Foreman?" The foreman nodded.

Ms. Wells returned to the grand jury room with a laptop. "Mr. Jones, I want you to assume that there was a security camera on a porch two houses down from the house you broke into that night. Assume that there was an audio component to that camera. Assume that the police acoustics lab enhanced the audio. Assume the following is a portion of the enhanced audio recording.

She pressed play.

John Levi was startled to hear his own voice first: "Paloma! Just let me know for sure that you are in there! Just give me a word! Then I'll get the police to get you out."

Then he heard the recording of Paloma's voice, slurred and rasping: "John Levi, leave me the hell alone. Go away! I don't want to be saved. I don't want you. I want you to leave me alone! Go away before you get me and you both hurt."

And then he heard Angel's voice saying to Paloma from inside the house, "I told you to keep quiet, bitch. Say another word and see what happens to you."

The young grand juror continued, "That was the interchange just before you drove your truck through the gate, wasn't it?"

"Yes, it was." John Levi remembered the advice Judge Altshuler had given him. "'A lawyer who represents himself has a fool for a client.' If I knew what I was doing," he thought, "I would have made a request for any recordings. Thank God for this grand juror. She's a more effective lawyer for me than I am."

"You decided you couldn't wait for the police to arrive to protect Paloma."

"Right." John Levi was reliving the moment he decided to get in his truck and ram the gate. "That's right."

"Because of the threat that Angel made to Paloma."

"Okay."

"Right?"

"Right."

"So you went in there not because of any hatred of Luther or Angel, but to get Paloma Ibarra out before Angel hurt her again?"

"Right."

"You knew what he was capable of doing to her . . . and to other young women."

"Yes, I guess I did."

"You knew."

"I knew. Yes, ma'am."

The young woman folded her notes and nodded to the foreman, who took over the questioning.

"Reverend Jones, had you ever been in that house before then?"

No."

"When you went in, you were being badly bitten by a Rottweiler, and you were hurting and losing blood."

"Yes."

"Do you mind pulling up your pant leg so we can see where the dog bit you?"

John Levi complied. There were two rough scars on his leg from the bites and the stitches. Many of the jurors stood up in their seats to get a better view.

"Were you scared?"

"Honestly, I was just thinking of Paloma. I know my heart was pounding in my chest, and I was breathing hard . . . Yes, I guess I was scared."

"When the dog came after you, why didn't you run back into your truck?"

"Because I needed to get Paloma out of the house. And I tried to get free of the dog by running into the house."

"That's all you were focused on?"

"Yes." John Levi had started to sweat. Beads of sweat were appearing on his forehead and trickles were running down the side of his face.

"Do you need some water?" asked D.A. Wells.

"That would be kind of you." Wells poured water into a Styrofoam cup and handed it to him. "Thank you."

The foreman continued. "You are reliving this right now?"

"I am."

"Are you familiar with PTSD?"

"I have read about it."

"Are you able to continue, or do you want a break?"

"Let's keep going, please."

"Did Luther Bodine try to hit you with that bat?"

"Yes."

"Did it seem to you that he was swinging at you with intent to put you down?"

"Yes, sir."

"And if he had succeeded in hitting you and knocking you down, do you think the dog would have mauled you worse?"

John Levi thought, *"My God, of course it would have."* "Yes, it would have."

"That dog could have killed you, or Luther Bodine could have killed you with the bat."

"I suppose. Yes."

"Angel came out of the back of the house yelling?"

"Yes."

"He fired his handgun repeatedly?"

"Yes, eventually."

"Had you ever been shot at before?"

"No, sir."

"Had you ever before been that close to a firearm that was firing?"

"I'd never been in the same place that a firearm was being fired."

"So you are not a hunter and have never been in the military?"

"No."

"Angel was how far away from you when he was firing?"

"Close enough for me to hit him with the bat."

"So, four feet?"

"Tops."

"There was a flash of light with each shot?"

"Yes."

"How loud was each shot?"

"Deafening. After the first one my ears were ringing."

"So you couldn't see or hear well?"

"Right."

"Angel wanted to shoot you? He tried to kill you?"

"Yes."

"He missed you by inches and killed his father instead?"

"Yes."

"Why didn't Angel succeed in shooting you?"

"I was dodging. And I hit him with the bat."

"The shot that hit his father was undoubtedly intended for you?"

"Yes."

"Okay, Reverend Jones. Please take a deep breath. Listen carefully to these questions. You already testified that you were deafened and blinded and upset and scared. Never been in a situation like this. Never even heard a gun fired before this. Angel is on the ground next to you after you hit him in the head the first time. Are you with me?"

"I am following."

"Angel makes a move with the handgun still in his hand to shoot you and you hit him in the head again in self-defense."

"What? No, sir. That's not how it happened."

The older male juror who had asked John Levi for his biblical justification for Peace's ministries butted in.

"Isn't it true that you hit and killed a defenseless man with your bat as he lay on the ground at your feet? A man who no longer posed any threat to anyone?"

This was the question John Levi expected and had resolved to answer truthfully, regardless of the consequences. "Yes, sir. I did that," replied John Levi.

"And you did it because you were angry that he had tried to shoot you. And he tried to shoot you because you had invaded his home and he was defending it."

"I was angry, but mostly at what he had done to Paloma and other young women."

The foreman objected. "I am still conducting this questioning now. You'll get your chance," speaking to the older male juror.

"Reverend Jones, tell us why you hit him while he was on the ground? What can you remember about that, given the shock of so much that had happened?"

"You can understand that I have thought through this a lot. There's no doubt in my mind that I hit Angel when he was on the floor as hard as I could. But piecing together *why* I hit him is harder for me. What was going through my mind . . . the image of Paloma the first time I saw her, how emaciated and angry and desperate she was, what the Bodines had done to her, the way they had exploited so many teenage girls, using their bodies, addicting them to meth. The way Cynthia had suffered. Angel's arrogance, his lack of conscience. These thoughts didn't last but an instant, but my mind was racing. I have resolved to be truthful. At that instant I hated him and the evil he had done. I wanted to stop him from ever doing those things to any woman again, particularly to Paloma. Next thing I knew, my arm went up and I hit him. I played God. I took God's role for myself. I had prayed for God to stop Luther and Angel one way or another. God hadn't done that. So I did."

"You say you 'played God'?"

"Yes."

"Earlier you said you 'failed your faith and your standards.' Is this what you were talking about?"

"Yes."

Grand jurors all shuffled in their chairs.

The older male juror who had interrupted the foreman interrupted again.

"So you intended to hit him?"

"Yes."

"So unequivocally 'yes'?"

"Yes."

"Are you happy he is dead?"

"Truthfully, no. Now I am sad I did it. I am sad about what Angel's life came to before that night. I am sad he no longer has the opportunity to repent."

The foreman spoke up. "Seriously? Do you think this man would ever have repented?"

"I don't know. But I eliminated whatever chance there was."

The slim young female juror who had questioned John Levi before asked permission to question again.

"You saw him raise his hand to shoot you?"

"No."

"But it was dark. You were unnerved, deafened, blinded. You were hurting from a bad dog bite. You'd lost blood. You still hadn't gotten Paloma out of there. Your heart was pounding and your mind was swimming?"

"I didn't see that."

"So it could have been happening just before you hit him again?"

"That he was trying again to shoot me? All I can tell you is that I didn't see that."

"No, all you can tell us is that you don't remember seeing that now."

"Well, I *don't* remember that now."

"But you have never before done anything remotely like hitting a man with a bat who was no threat to you at that moment?"

"I'd never hit anyone or anything with a bat. Or with anything else."

"And one reasonable explanation that you acted so out of character was that you saw him making a move with his hand toward you with that gun and you defended yourself. And Paloma."

"I didn't see that."

"But that would be reasonable."

Silence from John Levi.

"Say, 'That would have been reasonable.'"

"That would have been reasonable."

"You knew he would shoot you if he could."

"Yes, ma'am. I knew that."

"And if he shot you, and got you out of the way, you knew he was capable of hurting Paloma badly."

"Yes."

"Reverend Jones, the first you were *aware* that Paloma was in the door of that room was when she started screaming at you?"

"That's right."

"So you cannot deny that she was standing in the doorway when you hit Angel in the head with the bat as he was on the floor."

"I guess that's right."

"Or that she was there before you hit him with the bat?"

"I guess that's right too."

"So you would not contradict Paloma Ibarra, or call her a liar, if she were to testify that Angel was raising the gun to shoot you just before you hit him with the bat when he was on the floor."

"I didn't see that."

"But she may have. You just don't remember that now."

"I can't deny what she says she saw."

"And you would not contradict Ms. Ibarra if she also testified that she yelled out to you just before you hit Angel Bodine that he was about to shoot?"

John Levi looked around the room. Most of the grand jurors were nodding their heads at him, encouraging him. *"What has Paloma said to them?"* he wondered. "I can't deny what she says she saw or said."

Alison Wells asked him, "What did you come here to say about Paloma?"

"You're on," he thought. *"Don't mess this up."*

"That she is in no way responsible for *any* of my actions that night, or for any of the injuries or violations of criminal law. She did not ask me to come there or break in. In fact, as you heard, she told me to leave. She never touched the bat or the handgun and did not help me do so. I broke in, not her. Angel shot Luther, not her. I hit Angel, not her."

"What about her theft of Angel's Camaro?"

"Excuse me?" *"How stupid were you not to anticipate this question and have a response prepared?"* he thought.

"What about her theft of Angel's Camaro?"

John Levi blurted out the first excuse that came into his head. "She borrowed the car. She didn't steal it. She had driven that Camaro many times before with Angel's permission. Angel had given her permission to drive that any time she needed it. Plus, he was dead. He didn't care whether she drove it again. That was not a theft."

John Levi saw that many of the grand jurors nodded and made notes of his answer.

"Surely a lie to protect someone else is not the same as a lie to protect myself," he thought. *"God forgive me for this."*

"Lomie, it's time for you to take the wheel."

— Friday, October 18, 2021 —

Paloma testified before grand jury against the advice of her court-appointed defense attorney. When the attorney refused to notify Assistant D.A. Wells that Paloma wanted to testify before the grand jury, Paloma fired the attorney. Her fired attorney had warned that she would be asked about her drug use and prostitution at the Bodine house and about her theft and destruction of Angel's Camaro. So she went into the grand jury intending only to testify that she had seen Angel start to raise the handgun to shoot John Levi when he lay on the floor and to invoke her right to remain silent about every other matter. Paloma refused to sign the blanket waiver of her Fifth Amendment rights presented her by Wells before the session. Because of this refusal, Wells wanted to deny her the opportunity to testify. But the grand jury voted to hear Paloma.

Her grand jury session began with the playing of the recording of John Levi's confession to Detective Washington. The grand jury foreman asked her if she disagreed with anything that John Levi had said. She replied that the statement left out that John Levi hit Angel as he lay on the floor because Angel was raising the handgun to shoot John Levi. Most of the grand jurors seemed ready to accept this account. But an older male juror challenged Paloma to explain why John Levi would have left such a critical fact out of his statement if it were true. Either she was lying to protect her lover, he said, or John Levi did not see Angel's threat and was not acting in self-defense.

In response to this juror's aggressiveness, Paloma added that she yelled out, "John Levi, he is going to shoot" just before John Levi hit him. "So he had to have known what Angel was about to do," she said. By their expressions and body language, none of the grand jurors seemed receptive to that testimony.

"And John Levi and I weren't lovers," she insisted.

"Why not?" the older juror asked.

"I don't know. I guess he didn't find me that attractive. But we weren't lovers."

"But *you* love *him* enough to lie for him," he replied.

"Yes, I do. But I am not lying, sir."

Palma panicked. The jurors didn't believe her. She may have gotten John Levi into more trouble by her lies. So she decided on the spot to be so forthcoming about everything else that the jurors asked that they would understand the evil of the Bodines and that justice had been done in that house that night. She abandoned the Fifth Amendment's protections. She took the blanket waiver document from D.A. Wells' desk and signed it. "What do you want to know?" she asked the panel. "I'll tell you everything."

A young female juror asked Paloma to testify to the things which the Bodines had done to her and to other young woman. Paloma gave a long, emotional answer. She included that she had engaged in prostitution and drug use because of the Bodines for many years. She explained how it started and why it continued. She admitted that she was high from five nights of meth use when John Levi broke into the Bodine house to save her and that she stole Angel's Camaro in a panic to get away from the house. She gave the best answer she could to how methamphetamine is addictive and what had driven her to meth for many years. She described to extremely interested women jurors her relationship with John Levi and her love and her gratitude to him. When a woman juror asked her what she felt the most guilty about, Paloma said it was what she had done to her daughter during her daughter's entire life and what she had done to cause John Levi to be in such trouble. When a juror asked her to tell them about Cynthia, Paloma began to weep and could not compose herself. After discussion, the grand jury voted to excuse Paloma from further testimony.

Paloma had expected the grand jury session to be hard. Darla Henderson had become a good friend. Paloma asked Darla if she and Cynthia could spend the night before and after her testimony at Darla's apartment in southwest Fort Worth. Of course Darla agreed. Darla picked Paloma up at the criminal court building after the session was finished.

"Oh Darla," she cried, "I only made things worse. I am going to prison and so is John Levi. Will you take care of Cynthia while I am gone?"

"Of course I will. But don't give up. God will bring something good out of this."

"Do you really believe that?"

"Who else can we turn to in times like this except God, Paloma?"

"What has God ever done for me?"

"He brought John Levi into Cynthia's and your life. I like to think God brought me into your lives."

"Before this I didn't know people like you and John Levi existed. I didn't think God existed."

"Only God is good, Paloma, It says that in a Gospel somewhere, but I'm a Methodist so I can't tell you where. Let's see if we can put on a happier face before we get home. No point in worrying Cynthia more than she already is."

All that evening Darla talked incessantly and gaily. Paloma avoided telling Cynthia how matters had gone in the grand jury by invoking the grand jury secrecy rules. Paloma agreed to drink a glass of beer to relax. She had not slept in three nights so the beer knocked her out. She went to bed as soon as dinner was over and fell asleep immediately. Cynthia and Darla stayed up late watching old episodes of *Gilmore Girls* on Netflix.

Paloma experienced two new dreams that night.

In the first dream she was back in Angel's car, careening down the highway, wanting to die. But her mother was the one driving. Paloma was in the front passenger seat. Her mother was smoking a meth pipe and shrieking like a madwoman. Cynthia and John Levi were tied up in the backseat. The car was weaving around and through traffic and about to crash into a concrete column. Suddenly, Paloma didn't want to die anymore. And she didn't want Cynthia and John Levi to die. "*Mother, stop!*" she yelled. "*Mother, please stop!*" Her mother turned to her and said, "Lomie, it's time for you to take the wheel." Then her mother opened her door and jumped out, leaving no one in the driver's seat. Paloma strained and wrestled to slide behind the wheel to stop the car. But she couldn't move. The dream ended.

Then she had another dream. She was back in the front room of the Bodines' house on Lulu. She had a bat in her hands. Luther and Angel were there. So were Cynthia and John Levi. And so were Paloma's mother and father. She searched frantically for them when she lost sight of them in meth smoke and darkness. Then she found them again. She tried to hit Angel, Luther, and her mother and father with the bat. But she missed and hit Cynthia and John Levi instead. Cynthia and John Levi were down and bleeding. Angel, Luther and her mother and father were laughing at what Paloma has done. Paloma saw Angel's handgun lying on the floor. She picked it up and tried to shoot herself in the chest. She pulled the trigger but the gun didn't fire. She put the muzzle of the gun to her temple to try again. A hand grabbed the gun from her. She turned and saw that it was the Jesus depicted in the stain glass window behind the choir loft in Peace Church, a Jesus knocking at a closed door. "Knock and it shall be opened," Jesus said to her. "You have so much to live for." Cynthia and John Levi rose from the floor and hugged her.

Paloma awoke to find Cynthia sleeping peacefully next to her in the bed.

Chapter Nine

"Now we have to live the rest of our lives."

— Monday, October 21, 2019 —

A week after John Levi appeared before the grand jury, his front doorbell rang. He answered the door and there stood his pretrial release officer, Moses Murray. John Levi was accustomed to Murray dropping by unannounced to inspect his home and administer a routine drug test, so he welcomed Murray inside without asking any questions.

"You are a tea drinker, right, Mr. Murray? Can I make you a glass of iced tea?"

"That's all right, Reverend Jones. I only came by to remove your ankle monitor."

Just then John Levi's cell phone rang. It was Charles Needham. "Turn on Channel 5 now."

"Why?"

"Just turn on Channel 5 now. Do it!"

"Excuse me, Mr. Murray." John Levi walked into the den and turned on his TV. There was a live shot of a speaker's podium with no one behind it and with the American flag and the flag of Texas on either side. He was aware that Murray had followed him into the den.

District Attorney Charlise Remington stepped to the podium. With no preliminaries, she began to speak.

"The grand jury investigation into the deaths of Luther and Angel Bodine and the surrounding circumstances has concluded. As you know, the persons of interest through this have been John Levi Jones and Paloma

Ibarra. While grand jury proceedings are secret, given the intense media attention and public interest in this case, I feel required to make a limited statement. The grand jury received every piece of evidence and information it requested before reaching its determination. My office did not limit what evidence the grand jury heard. We insured that the jury heard all the evidence that we had and all that they requested. The grand jury itself was a fair cross section of Tarrant County. This was a very even-handed and thorough investigation. The grand jury worked very hard. There were more than ten sessions dedicated to this case alone. More than thirty witnesses testified live before the grand jury."

"Thirty witnesses!" John Levi exclaimed.

"The identities of the individual grand jurors are secret, and they may not divulge what was heard in the sessions. I ask the media and the public to respect that secrecy."

Remington turned to two documents. "Let me read to you now two documents which are being filed momentarily in the criminal cases pending against Mr. Jones and Ms. Ibarra. That will conclude my statement."

"The document as to Ms. Ibarra reads, 'The grand jury returns no bill of indictment against Paloma Ibarra.' The document as to Mr. Jones reads, 'The grand jury returns no bill of indictment against John Levi Jones.'"

"Thank you." District Attorney Remington turned to walk away from the podium.

A reporter for the Dallas newspaper yelled, "Will you tell us the vote in the grand jury?"

Remington paused and had a whispered conference with an assistant. She turned back to the reporter. "I will tell you this. A grand jury is comprised of twelve jurors. At least nine 'yes' votes are required to bring an indictment against anyone." She paused. "In this particular case, the number of votes in favor of indictment of either Ms. Ibarra or Mr. Jones was far less than nine."

Remington walked away from the cameras. John Levi turned off his television. He was thunderstruck. *"Now we have to live the rest of our lives. What's to become of Cynthia and Paloma? And me?"*

"Congratulations, Reverend Jones. Now you know why I am here to remove your ankle monitor."

"Mr. Murray, can you tell me if all the pretrial release restrictions on me are gone as of now? Or do I have to go back to court to get those lifted?"

"You mean the restrictions on contact with Ms. Ibarra and her daughter? As soon as those 'no bills' are filed in the court case, those pretrial restrictions are as dead as Luther and Angel Bodine."

John Levi winced. Murray saw it and said, "I'm sorry, Reverend. It's just that the court has received so many letters from people in the neighborhood about the Bodines, about how terrible Angel and his father were. As the person who might have been tasked with preparing a presentence report if you were convicted, I had access to those letters. Those men had hurt a lot of young girls for a long time. I don't mean to be insensitive, or flip. But I personally believe that justice was done all around in this case. It just took a while."

"Depends on whose justice," John Levi responded.

John Levi pulled up Paloma's and his cases on the district clerk's website. The 'no bills' had already been filed. The threat of prosecution was gone. The legal cases were over. Only God's trials remained.

"I need to go see how Paloma and Cynthia are," he thought.

John Levi peered through the narrow window next to the front door of his condo. Three television cameras were setting up outside. Reporters and crew were gathering. He walked outside. There was a buzz and a fury of activity when they saw him. Cameramen scrambled to start their cameras. The reporters ran toward him, two with their notepads open and their pens poised, three with microphones thrusting into his face.

They started yelling questions at him all at once.

"Do you feel exonerated?"

"Was justice done?"

"Are you going to sue the police for arresting you?"

"Do you consider yourself to be a vigilante?"

"Were you the one who shot Luther Bodine and his dog?"

"Did Luther and Angel Bodine deserve to die?"

"Do you believe that Luther Bodine bribed the police?"

"Have you considered running for mayor?"

"Are you and Paloma Bodine going to have a baby?"

John Levi stood in front of the throng with his hands upraised to ask for silence. He ignored all the questions.

"I respect your role as the press and the media. I know you are doing your jobs. But I have to try to put back together my life. I can't speak for Paloma and her daughter, but I am sure they want to do the same. We are not going to do this in front of a camera or in the newspapers. So I won't have any more to say to you about any of this."

The Fort Worth newspaper reporter asked, "Reverend, do you intend to return to pastoring your church?"

"I honestly do not know. It's not entirely up to me."

"Who is it up to?"

"My bishop, the other ministers of my conference, and the church and me, I guess."

"Do you intend to keep practicing law? The people in the church neighborhood still need your help."

"Again, I honestly do not know. It's not entirely up to me. The State Bar would have to lift my suspension."

"If you can't stay in ministry or in law, what will you do?"

"Something that's hopefully not in the news. Right now I want to make sure that Paloma and her daughter are okay. And that the Peace ministries to the neighborhood are continuing. That's all I have or hope to ever have for you, gentlemen and ladies. I hope you understand."

He walked away from the continuing questioning and into his condo. *"I wonder if the press is camped outside Paloma's apartment."*

John Levi was numb. It had been only minutes since he had learned he would not be prosecuted. He had received his life back as a gift, although a gift that would always be under the shadow of that early morning on Lulu Street. He sat immobile in his den while his cell phone rang and rang, and the voices of friends and strangers sounded faintly in another room.

Then he heard Father Gutierrez's voice. He jumped up and grabbed his cell.

"Hello, hello. Father?"

"I just heard the news, John Levi. I am so relieved. You must be so relieved."

"I am, Father. Although right now I am in shock. I had been reading about prison life, trying to prepare myself. Then this happens."

"So you didn't expect this?"

"Not at all."

"Your lawyer didn't predict this?"

"I was my own lawyer."

"Were you? Why was that?"

"Father, I went into the grand jury and confessed. I confessed to the police right after they found me. I didn't want to be lawyered up. I wanted to tell the truth of what happened to protect Paloma and to be held accountable. I had made such a show of my righteousness. Then I killed a man with a bat. I felt that all I could do was to tell the truth about it."

"And did you?"

"Yes."

"You admitted killing a man with a bat in the grand jury?"

"Yes."

"In self-defense?"

"No, because he needed to die. Because God hadn't stopped him from hurting young girls. So I did."

"You said this in the grand jury?"

"Yes, in so many words."

"And they returned a 'no bill'!"

"Yes."

"Extraordinary . . . John Levi. Are you regretting that the grand jury didn't indict you? Did you want to be held criminally responsible?"

"I didn't want to go to jail. But it seems wrong that no one seems to value the life of the man I killed."

"Was the 'no bill' unjust?"

"I think it probably was. No, it was. I am shocked that I am not being held criminally responsible for it."

"Well, this is still Texas."

"That's what people keep telling me. It's certainly not the kingdom of God."

"You think you'd be forgiven in the kingdom of God?"

"I am worried about the forgiveness that the man I killed would have received in the kingdom of God."

"If that man had been forgiven, he would have gone right back to exploiting innocent girls. John Levi, I want you to pick up your bed and walk. You know that story from John's Gospel? Of course you do. Don't let yourself be stuck in your bed of guilt. You still have a lot to offer people. What you do now is the question. I have been following your case in the newspapers. I have some understanding why you did what you did. The whole thing was incredibly brave and incredibly foolhardy. The justice system of your community has absolved you from criminal responsibility. Accept it. Don't confuse that with absolution by God. But don't *ask* God to punish you through the human criminal justice system. God's justice now is for you to accept this mercy so you can continue to be merciful to people in need. 'Happy are those who are merciful, for they shall receive mercy.' Maybe we can reverse that. 'Happy are those who receive mercy, for they can be merciful' . . . Does any of that feel right?"

"I am too numb now to feel that anything is right."

"What is that young woman going to do now? Paloma?"

"I don't know. That worries me."

"Now you are free again to help her and her daughter. And a lot of other people. What are *you* going to do now?"

"I don't entirely know what my options are."

"Take your time. If you'd like, I'd love for you to spend time with me here in San Antonio so you can hash this out. I'm sorry you didn't return my calls when you were in the grand jury process."

"I was afraid you'd talk me out of going before the grand jury."

"Maybe I would have tried. But that decision is behind you now. And it seems to have worked out for you."

"Father, I would really cherish having some time with you. But I don't know what my schedule will be yet. May I call you when I know?"

"Of course. I'll await your call. I'm always here for you. Peace, John Levi. Peace."

"Thank you, Father. If only I can find some peace. I'll call you as soon as I know."

John Levi hung up. He checked his many voice messages. There were two from Cynthia and one from Paloma. Paloma was crying when she left hers.

He called Paloma's cell number. Cynthia answered.

"Cynthia, it's John Levi. How are you and your mom?"

"Oh, John Levi! It's so good to hear your voice! We have been so worried about you! Have you heard the news?"

"Yes, of course."

"Isn't it great? Did you expect that?"

"I did for your mom. Not so much for me. Can I talk to her?"

"Momma, it's John Levi on the phone."

Paloma came on the phone. "Can you come over?"

John Levi felt a shiver from just hearing her voice. "Are there press people outside your apartment?"

"No."

"Do you think this is wise?"

"I just need to see you. I need to apologize. I need to thank you. Please, we *both* need to see you."

"I'm on my way."

John Levi took an Uber to the apartment. His truck had not been returned to him from police impoundment, and Paloma still had his Lexus. He knocked on their door. Cynthia and Paloma answered the door together. They both looked like they had been crying for hours. Before he could get the door closed behind him, they enveloped him in a hug. They started crying all over again.

"I am so sorry. I am so sorry. I am so sorry," sobbed Paloma. "I can't believe I put you and Cynthia through what I did."

"Thank you. Thank you. Thank you!" cried Cynthia.

John Levi tried to respond but the words choked in his throat.

Chapter Ten

"She saw that God had been there all along."

— late October to early November, 2019 —

Things weren't the same when John Levi visited Paloma and Cynthia, particularly when John Levi and Paloma were alone on the couch. There was no flirting and no veiled signs of physical attraction.

Paloma was much more open about herself. What he had gone through for her had been a reckoning for her. She had spent hours brooding about her responsibility for what he had suffered. She shared her repeated dream about her mother and her two latest dreams. She was sure these last dreams were a breakthrough by God into her consciousness. God was telling her to take control, to no longer let herself be a victim of her mother's neglect and of meth, and to live in hope in the future. She apologized about how hard she had made it for John Levi to talk about God with her. She now saw how hard God was working to help her through John Levi. Cynthia's new faith had helped convince her. Before John Levi came into her life, she wasn't ready to accept that God was present. But now she saw that God had been there all along in Cynthia's love, and she had been blind to it. Now she saw her decision not to abort Cynthia as a God thing. The bullet's near miss of John Levi and the death of Luther was God's doing. Angel's death was God's justice and protection of her and Cynthia through John Levi.

John Levi just listened. Paloma was now the one between them with faith in God's activity in the world. He held his tongue about his doubts. Angel's missed shot was due to John Levi's hitting Angel's arm as Angel was shooting and Luther being in a place where the bullet was randomly directed. It wasn't the actions of God. But John Levi was silent because the result of Paloma's newfound faith was a complete good. She wanted to show her gratitude to God and John Levi by helping people in trouble as she has been helped. She had only to figure out how to help them. He marveled that he had to kill and almost be killed for her faith in God to appear.

Paloma's eagerness to talk out her pain and anger at her past provided the opening John Levi needed to suggest again that she go into an inpatient rehab program. He found a ninety–to–one-hundred-twenty–day program outside of Dallas which he suggested to her.

Paloma had objections to entering the program. She didn't want to be belittled in group counseling sessions. She had watched the Sandra Bullock movie *28 Days* and didn't think she could endure such humiliation. She was scared at being so vulnerable to strangers. John Levi suggested that they go through an orientation at the facility. Then she could make her decision based upon facts, not a work of fiction. Paloma agreed.

But who would take care of Cynthia while Paloma was gone? Would she be unable to see her daughter for the entire program? Would Cynthia experience this as another abandonment by her mother? And where would Cynthia get the counseling she needed?

John Levi would take care of Cynthia while Paloma was gone. Cynthia could continue to live in Paloma's apartment. He would spend the nights there. He would drive Cynthia to every visitation day at Paloma's rehab facility and make sure she was available for every phone call from her. He would pay for counseling sessions for Cynthia with a young, female licensed professional counselor he trusted.

And what about the cost of her rehab and Cynthia's counseling? Paloma went online and found that the monthly cost for her would be just less than ten thousand dollars. John Levi said he would pay these costs more than willingly. Paloma felt guilty accepting this. She had felt guilty before about his financial support, but now John Levi had suffered so much for her. She was no longer able to claim the fiction that she would one day pay him back. And how could they ever be true friends when the relationship was so unequal? John Levi's response was, "Maybe God chose me to help you because I have so much money. Ever think of that? When you and I first met, you were angry with God because God hadn't helped you. Now are you going to say no to God's help? For God to work, you have to accept God's grace. It's kind of a partnership." Paloma was persuaded.

John Levi, Cynthia, and Paloma visited the inpatient facility. It was in a beautiful wooded and secluded setting. She was reassured about the counseling and fell in love with the place. It was so unlike the world she had always lived in. There was an opening in only three days.

So three days later, John Levi drove Paloma back to the facility. Cynthia decided not to come because she was afraid she would cry and cause her mother to back out. John Levi parked his truck and carried Paloma's bags to her room while she was registering. When it was time for him to go, Paloma asked him to pray with her. He was not sure what to pray. Given that Paloma's faith now seemed stronger than his, it seemed that she should be the one praying. But he faced her and took both of her hands in his and watched as she bowed her head. He did not bow his head, but instead bent his knees so he could watch her face. The words flowed out of his mouth, and he was surprised by them. "Lord Jesus, we thank you for bringing us together out of the valley of the shadow of death. We thank you for the strength and hope and honesty that has always dwelled deep within Paloma and that has brought her to this place after so many years of suffering and injustice. Help her to endure the honest conversations and hard soul-searching of this program. Help her to feel sure than Cynthia is safe and cared for and will always love her. Help her to be sure of my love. And help her to be sure of your love and her future in you. We pray all this in your holy name. Amen."

Paloma hugged him, turned, and walked eagerly toward the counselor waiting for her. She turned a corner without looking back to him. He stood there for a moment but she did not return.

As John Levi climbed into his truck for his lonely drive back to Fort Worth, he felt guardedly optimistic that Paloma would successfully complete her rehab and start a new life free from her past. But he also felt an unwelcome sense of regret that she would never again need him in the same way she once had.

Then he thought, "*Where did that prayer come from?*" Then, "*It came from her need for it, that's all.*"

Then, "*What will I do with myself now?*"

CHAPTER ELEVEN

"I don't think Jesus is changing the world quickly enough for you."

— Friday, November 15, 2019 —

John Levi telephoned the bishop's office, asking to schedule an appointment to discuss the lifting of his suspension from ministry. John Levi was uncertain how long he would continue in ministry, but Peace Church was floundering in his absence. Worship attendance had halved. John Levi felt he needed to return to the church and its pulpit at least for now.

The meeting with Bishop Morris Leary took place at the bishop's parsonage because the bishop wanted an entirely private and personal conversation. And he wanted to share a private meal with John Levi.

John Levi arrived at the episcopal parsonage thirty minutes early and waited in his new, used Jeep at the curb. He had sold his pickup because it was too conspicuous and bore too many bad memories. After all the publicity, he wanted some anonymity as he drove. As he sat reading the Jeep user manual about all the icons on his dashboard instrument panel, he was startled by the bishop tapping on his passenger's-side window. He had spotted John Levi sitting in his car and had walked out his front door to invite him to come in early.

As they were walking toward the door, Leary said, "You are limping. Is that from the dog bite?"

John Levi wondered how Bishop Leary knew about the Rottweiler bite and what he knew generally about what happened that night.

"Yes, it is. But I am much improved. Thanks for asking. How did you know that I was bitten by a dog?"

"I read it in the newspaper."

Bishop Morris Leary was bishop of the Methodist conference of which John Levi was a member. He had pastored churches in the Houston area for thirty years before being elected bishop and assigned to lead the conference. He was known to be an honest, urgent, and unspectacular preacher who was at his best in a one-on-one pastoral setting. His churches were known for their crisis and grief counseling ministries. Since becoming bishop, he had urged the churches in his conference to expand their counseling ministries as well.

They walked inside. Leary welcomed him into his den. They sat in leather chairs facing one another over a coffee table. "I have a pot pie warming in the oven. Chicken pot pie okay with you for lunch?"

"Sure."

"John Levi, I know you have been through a great deal. I know you have recounted the events of that night many times. I read all the newspaper articles I could and believe I have a fair understanding of what happened. I understand that you broke into that house to try to save a victimized woman, that there was gunfire, and that you killed a man with a bat after you had already knocked him down. But I need you to answer my questions to help me decide what is to be done about your ordination. And I am concerned about you personally. In fairness, I need to disclose that what you say may help me decide if I need to bring internal conference charges against you to revoke your ordination. Are you willing to answer my questions?"

"Yes, Bishop."

"Why do you think the grand jury didn't indict you?"

"I don't know. Maybe they thought justice was done that night."

"By you?"

"By me."

"What do you think?"

"No."

"No?"

"I don't think that justice was done that night by me."

"Did you hit that man on the ground because you wanted to do justice?"

"I hit him because I was angry at him and what he had done to Paloma. I hit him to keep him from ever hurting her or any woman again . . . I was wrong to do it. I gave in to a sinful impulse."

"Like the impulse of driving through the gate and going into the house?"

"Not the same. Going in after Paloma was one impulse. Killing a man when he was down was different."

"Does whether you did justice depend upon whose justice we are talking about?"

"It wasn't legal justice for me to hit him while he was down. And it wasn't God's justice either."

"Why not?"

"Because it was merciless."

"Where do you think God was in all this?"

"I am afraid that I thought I was God at the time."

"Amazing honesty. What about now? Now where do you think God was?"

"I am still working through that. Paloma thinks God sent me in there and that God struck the blow through me."

"Paloma is the name of the woman?"

"Yes."

"What do you think?"

"I don't think God wanted me to hit a man while he was down—if God was to be found anywhere that night. I'm not sure about that anymore."

"Are you angry at God? Or at the church? Where are you in your faith?"

"I was angry at God. Now I am not so sure how much power God has to fix this world. I am not even so sure about God's power to fix me."

"Tell me some more about that. What happened to you at Peace?"

"I have seen the face of injustice and evil. I have *been* the face of evil. For an instant evil took me over in the name of justice. I have seen some victims of a broken world. You asked me about the church. The church is hiding from evil and injustice, pretending evil and injustice don't even exist. But I broke into a house and hit evil in the head with a bat."

"How do you respond to those who say that it is up to God to decide when and how to fix this broken world?"

"How do I respond? I respond that anyone who says that has never seen the face of evil and injustice. You know what it was like when I was outside that house that night, Bishop? It was like I couldn't wait on God any longer to free that woman from those evil men and that evil drug. Paloma had given up praying because God had done nothing. I needed to go in that house to do what God was failing to do . . . I'm sorry, Bishop, but to me this is the truth."

"But you used means that God would not use and has taught us not to use."

"What means should I have used, Bishop?

"The means you were using before the moment you broke into that house. Just being there outside that house and pleading with that poor woman to come out was offering her a lifeline. Even confronting those men with their evil. All that was within God's way. You had been so merciful to that woman and her daughter. You had supported them and loved them. Just as you and Peace are being merciful to so many in your neighborhood. I think I understand why you broke in. It was courageous and motivated by concern for her. But God is spirit, and the word of love, and acts of mercy. God is not a bat."

"But what if the only way to get her out was with that truck and even that bat? What if God's means are totally ineffective in the face of real evil in a situation like that? What if that's why God seems ineffective and absent?"

Bishop Leary looked at John Levi blankly.

"Bishop, am I going to be allowed to stay in ministry?"

"Do you want to?"

"For now, anyway. I don't want the Peace ministries to die."

"You are a wealthy man, correct? You don't need any income?"

"Correct."

"Have you thought about going back to law practice full-time and opening some *pro bono* law firm in that neighborhood?"

"That is an alternative to staying as pastor at Peace. *The* alternative actually. If I can keep my law license."

"Can you?"

"I talked to the State Bar. The decision of the grand jury not to indict ends the option of disbarment as far as the Bar is concerned. They are probably going to ask me to undergo a psychological evaluation and counseling. I'll be on some kind of probation for a while. Depending on the circumstances, hitting a man in the head with a bat is not the same kind of violation of a lawyer's rules as it is a minister's. I mean, it's not like I stole some client's money. Now *that* could get me disbarred."

"What will make you decide between full-time law and ministry?"

"Whether I believe that the God revealed by the life of Jesus is truly God. And I have to find some peace with why that God lets so many Palomas suffer in this world, and lets so many Luther and Angel Bodines continue with their evils."

"It sounds as if you have grave doubt about the value of Jesus' teachings?"

"I believe in those teachings more than ever. I've seen what happens when they aren't followed. I just have some doubt about their power to combat evil and injustice. And whether God is behind them. And about my capability to live by them."

"Me too," said Bishop Leary. "About myself, I mean. John Levi, give me a minute, please."

Leary left the den and made a phone call. John Levi felt as if the jury had retired to deliberate his fate. John Levi could hear Leary making a few notes on a pad. Leary came back and resumed his seat.

"Here is what I am thinking. You have caused some embarrassment to the conference and to Methodism. But that is partly the conference's problem. We haven't been preaching to our churches as we should have. We haven't been as committed as we should have been to Jesus' teachings. Yours is an extraordinary story of commitment to the word. I am talking about the Peace ministries to the poor, not when you broke into that house and killed that man."

"You have a problem with your faith. And that relates to your problem with boundaries. Your hunger and thirst for justice come from the spirit of Jesus. I have no doubt of that. You hunger for justice so deeply that you leave no conviction unsaid and no action undone that you think are needed to fight injustice. But that's because of your doubt that God will bring about justice if we follow Jesus' way. You think *you* have to bring justice about, with your own way. You need to be humbler and more able to accept the limitations on ministers in your pursuit of social justice. You must be more willing to rely on God for the end of defeating injustice while you follow Jesus' means. If you can't develop the necessary faith in God for that reliance, you need to think seriously about returning to full-time law practice."

"Are you saying that a *pro bono* law practice seeking justice for the poor is not faithful to God's means?"

"No, I am saying that lawyers fighting for the poor don't have to believe that the advent of a just world is in God's hands rather than in their own. Lawyers fighting for the poor don't even have to believe in God. But ministers hungering for justice must accept God's means and limitations. Jesus didn't hit his opponents with a bat. He didn't lead a violent insurrection for the poor. He didn't return evil with evil. He was non-violent. He loved his enemies. And he is changing the world . . . I don't think Jesus is changing the world quickly enough for you."

"No. No, he is not."

"So here it is. You need time to think and pray and decide if you want to remain in ministry or if you want to go back to law full-time. You need to search your soul for a faith in God's ways and means. I mean, is Jesus your Lord or not? And the public needs to see that the conference has something to say to this Elijah, this Savonarola in our midst in North Hill. So you will attend thrice-weekly secular counseling for at least six months and probably longer. You will have to agree that I can receive reports from this counselor about your sessions. You will also meet separately at least twice a week with a spiritual counselor of my choice. I think it will be a former professor of

Christian ethics and spiritual formation at Perkins Seminary at SMU. I will need reports from her as well. You will be completely absent from Peace for at least one more month. After a month you may be able to come back to preach, depending upon what I decide about your progress and what you have decided about your faith and ordination. I will preach at Peace every Sunday during this month. I want you to stay out of the public eye. No statements or interviews for now. How does that sound?"

"I thank you for being willing to preach yourself. You will need a translator."

"John Levi, I have something else to say now to you. Life is long. God is not finished with you. Jesus is in your heart and mind, and you won't be able to get him out. But your demands of God are not going to come true. Scripture tells us that God hates injustice and sides with its victims. God suffers with the poor and intervenes for them. That's what Scripture tells us. But experience tells us that God comes slowly and gently. You know the story in 1 Kings of Elijah on Mount Horeb. God comes in God's word and in acts of mercy, not in the earthquake and the fire. And not in the bat or the grill of an old pickup. God comes persistently and eventually persuasively, but still sacrificially. God allows a lot of injustice and evil to continue. There can be no honest denial of that. But you keep demanding of God a house cleaning of the evil in creation *now*. I don't believe that we can count on that. And even if God is going to do that someday, we can't do that. We should do what you are doing in those ministries at Peace, including the legal clinic, but we can't be the earthquake and the fire. You need to decide if you can follow a God who is not going to make justice happen the way and when you want it to happen, a God whom I am afraid you believe is weak. We all must find our places somewhere between indifferent inaction and autonomous action."

"Spoken like a bishop."

"Thank you—I think."

Chapter Twelve

"We need a faith that transcends this belief in the almightiness of God."

— Sunday, January 6, 2020 —

On the eighth Sunday after his meeting with Bishop Leary, John Levi stood in the pulpit at Peace for the first time since his arrest. Word had gone out about his return. The sanctuary was packed. Newspaper and television reporters stood against the back wall. Bishop Leary was there in support and to hear what John Levi had to say after his forced sabbatical. As John Levi stood up, most in the congregation applauded. John Levi waited until they were done, without acknowledging their support.

John Levi started his return sermon with the Apostle's Creed. "I believe in God the Father Almighty . . ."

"Every time we repeat the Apostles' Creed, we affirm that God is 'Almighty.' So we claim to believe. 'Father,' we pray, 'you are almighty. Cure my cancer.' Or 'Father,' we pray, 'you are almighty. Save me from an unjust person or a random tragedy.' Or 'Father, Almighty One, end birth defects, or child hunger, or the suffering of the poor, or war.'"

"But hunger and birth defects and injustice and war most certainly continue. Greedy people continue to take unjust advantage of the poor. Some people are randomly born to parents who are drug addicts while others are just as randomly born into homes of privilege. If God is 'Almighty,' then God either causes or allows every event."

"We need a faith that transcends this belief in the almightiness of God. God *cannot* act contrary to God's character. God must be faithful to God's self.

"What is the character and nature of God revealed in Jesus? God is love. But not any love. God is sacrificial, self-emptying, and humble love. God is a patient love that does not insist on its own way. God is a love that bears all things and endures all things, as Paul wrote about love in his first letter to the church at Corinth. This is clearly a love that is *not* almighty.

"Why would we choose to worship such a God? A God who suffers our defeats with us but not one who rescues us from every defeat? Why worship such a 'weak-ass God,' as a friend of mine asked me about a year ago? Why not worship our capacity for coercive power as our God? If we do, we can achieve justice and mercy with a truck and a bat, with a clear conscience and a divine mandate.

"We choose such a God of selfless love because there is that within us that hungers and thirsts for love to be more powerful and transforming than coercion and violence. We choose to worship such a God of love because the justice and mercy which can be accomplished through coercion and violence *will be corrupted by that violence and coercion.*

"This god Love—Love with a capital L—is already present in our hearts and minds. The capacity for this Love includes a hunger and thirst for justice and mercy. Yet even if all we humans ever do is choose a part of ourselves to worship, we should make this humble, self-sacrificial capacity for Love within us our god. Not *al*mighty, but mighty in Love's ability to save and transform *if* more of us will truly follow and worship this Love.

"So no more complacency. *God is here as much as God will ever be here.* No more praying and waiting for God to intervene from up there to down here to rescue us. No more leaving it to God to bring justice and mercy in the end. No more depending upon God to die for us so we don't have to die for anyone.

"We need to admit that there are other gods in the world. And not only in the world, but also in our own minds and hearts. These other gods can and do defeat our god Love in the short term. Coercion and Violence. Fear and Lust to Dominate. Racism and Tribalism. Cruelty and Indifference. Disease and a random, amoral Creation. We are in a life-and-death contest between our god Love and these other gods. In that contest we must use only the tools granted us by Love, not the tools used by these other gods. We hope that our god Love will ultimately triumph. But even if Love does not triumph, we choose Love and Love's tools.

"Despite all the power of these other gods, we know that it is our god Love who holds human creation together every single day through millions of quiet, gentle, self-sacrificial acts of mercy by Love's disciples while these other gods try to tear us apart.

"Most of these competing gods defeat their opponents as fast as they can and move on. They are heedless of the damage they cause, particularly the gods Violence and Coercion. Love remains and endures after Violence and Coercion leave. Love knows no time line and holds past, present, and future in its embrace. Violence and Coercion thrive only in victory or its unscrupulous pursuit. Love is present in victory *and* in defeat. We can lose with any gods, even with Violence and Coercion. We choose to win or lose with Love and its tools.

"1 John 4:16 reads, 'God is love and those who abide in love abide in God, and God abides in them.'

"And I say now: 'Happy are those who choose this gentle, self-sacrificing, self-emptying Love as their god.' Amen."

After the service had concluded, Bishop Leary asked John Levi, "What about your *pro bono* legal clinic? Is that not a tool of Love? I hope you are not going to give that up."

John Levi smiled. "Surely Love calls us to use the peaceful tools our society provides for protection of the weak. Surely Love wants us to keep this ministry open."

"I am sure Love does," the bishop replied.

CHAPTER THIRTEEN

"I have big news."

— March 2020 —

Paloma was within one week of finishing her rehab. John Levi and Cynthia were to drive there to see her and to discuss her future. John Levi had been back as pastor at Peace for two months, and the church and its neighborhood ministries were recovering. Worship attendance was actually increasing from what it was just before the incident on Lulu.

Cynthia had started staying overnight at John Levi's condo rather than the apartment close to her school. His condo included two bedrooms and two full baths, so there was plenty of room. Cynthia's overnights there started on weekends but increased to more weeknights. On school mornings she and John Levi would rise early, eat breakfast together, and drive to her school. Cynthia moved more of her belongings to his place. When John Levi asked why she was doing this, Cynthia said only that her momma was coming home soon. John Levi understood without asking that the home Cynthia was speaking about was his condo.

John Levi was surprised how much he continued to miss Paloma. Months had passed since he had spent any time alone with Paloma. He caught himself picturing her here and there as he went about his day. Seeing Cynthia every day reminded him of what he loved in Paloma. Cynthia had the same shape face and the same expressions and mannerisms as Paloma without the profanity and sarcasm. Slowly, only partly because Cynthia wanted it, John Levi began indulging the idea that he, Paloma, and Cynthia would become a family. He frankly didn't care anymore what his church would think about it. He wondered if he could live without Paloma. And he wondered if he could live with her. There would be so many rough edges on both of them to be ground down within their relationship. And, although he hated admitting this to himself, he worried if he could ever satisfy Paloma sexually, or if lovemaking would be torture for her because of the way she had been treated by men in her past.

John Levi and Cynthia drove to the rehab facility. Paloma was already waiting for them under the pavilion at the front entrance. Cynthia jumped out of John Levi's Jeep and ran to her mother. John Levi followed slowly. Mother and daughter were laughing and looking one another over. Paloma was in full flower. She looked rested, happy, healthy, and absolutely beautiful.

The three of them walked into the dining hall for lunch. They went through a cafeteria line side by side, pushing their trays along. John Levi remembered the day of Paloma's eviction trial when they went through a cafeteria line at a barbeque place and she leaned her exhausted head on his back, the first time he felt attracted to her physically. This day, Paloma was asking Cynthia about her school and laughing at her stories about her recent band adventure. As they arrived at the cashier and John Levi was paying for their lunches, a woman about Paloma's age walked up to her, nodded at John Levi, and asked, "Is this him?" Paloma nodded yes. The woman responded, "What a hunk." Paloma laughed and pushed her away.

They sat down and talked so much they lost track of time and their food. Paloma wanted to know all about the church and Cynthia's counseling sessions and her school. John Levi and Cynthia wanted to know about the group counseling sessions and whether Paloma had made any friends. Eventually, they were the only people left in the dining hall.

"Well, I have big news," announced Paloma.

"How big?" John Levi smiled. "*I have some big news myself. We are all going to live together in my condo.*"

"The biggest. I have been offered a job here. I will be a counselor and mentor to women going through the program. They have been impressed by my story and the progress I have made and how I have related to the other people in my group. They want me to stay on as a member of the staff."

Cynthia was suddenly silent. John Levi said, "Paloma, that's great. You have really profited from your stay here. It's great that they see what we have seen in you all along," nodding to Cynthia.

"This program has opened my eyes. I have made so many mistakes in my life. But I can't live in them any longer. I can't be defined by them. I have to forgive myself and move on. I have to stop being angry at myself and at God. And I have to ask forgiveness from Cynthia by making us a new life."

Cynthia spoke up. "Will you commute from Fort Worth every day? How can you handle that?"

"That's one of the neat things about this. They have duplexes on this campus for their staff who are former patients. And for our kids. You and I have our own little place. Bigger than the apartment we have now. Really cute. Already furnished but we can bring in our own. You will have plenty of teenagers around. And they have group counseling sessions for what kids like you have gone through."

Paloma was really smiling, talking faster and faster. It was infectious. Cynthia started smiling a little.

"I will be paid more than I have ever made before at a legitimate job. And we will get the duplex and utilities free. They will help me eventually start community college. I am so excited about studying psychology. I want to become an addiction counselor. This whole program is a godsend. Oh please, Cynthia, be excited for me! For us!"

John Levi had never, ever seen Paloma so positive about anything. She was another person, born anew.

"Where will I go to school?" asked Cynthia.

"The middle school and high school are within a mile of here. What's wrong, honey?"

"What about me? What about my friends? And my band? And what about John Levi?"

"Cynthia, I know this is a big change. But we *both* need a change. And this is a good one. This is a chance for me to make something good come out of all the bad that has happened. This is a chance for me to help people, not just to be helped. What will I do if I go back to Fort Worth and that neighborhood? Where will I work? How will I be able to support you in Fort Worth? If I worked as a waitress there, I'd have to be gone at night and on weekends. You'd be alone again. Here I'll work days just a short walk from our home. If I go back there, I will never get free of my past. That place is a dead end to me. It's a coffin."

"I thought we three could be together."

"You mean, *we* three?" Paloma drew a circle with her finger pointed in turn toward each of them.

"Yes. Don't you love him? He loves you."

"Perhaps I should leave?" John Levi said.

"No, please stay. Cynthia," said Paloma, reaching out to take Cynthia's hands as Cynthia drew back, "there are all kinds of love. John Levi has never loved me like that. And I don't love him like that. I thought I did. You and I talked about that. But I have realized while I have been here that I don't. I love him, and I love how God loved me through him, and I love how he helped us. I will always be so grateful to him. But he is not my life's match. I can't be in a relationship when I am the only one receiving anything in it.

I need to learn who I am. They have taught me here that the way you learn *who* you are is by *giving* yourself to others in trouble. As you get older you will understand. We can't ask John Levi to support us forever. So I am asking you to support me in this. I know I haven't earned your trust. But I will. So please start trusting me now. Do you want to see our place?"

"It's ready?"

"I'm already in it. I had to jump on it when it became available. I can still give it up if you say no. Please don't say no."

Cynthia looked over her new residence. She met other staff and a few of their teenage children. She didn't say no to the move. She couldn't do that to her mother. She was too loving a person.

John Levi never mentioned to Paloma the option of her returning to Fort Worth to live with him and Cynthia in his condo. He had thought that if Paloma decided to live with him, he would take it as a signal that he should resign his ordination and go back to full-time law practice. Now that she had decided on another future for herself and Cynthia, John Levi had to decide on the rest of his life alone.

Chapter Fourteen

"Who washes away the sins of the world with the tears of children."

— March 2020 —

John Levi drove Cynthia back to Fort Worth. As they drove, John Levi said to her, "Cynthia, your love for your mother and her love for you have gotten both of you to the brink of this new life. Please always hold on to that."

"And I think it was God too," said Cynthia.

"Yes," responded John Levi. "I don't think there is any difference between God's and your mother's and your love for one another."

He helped pack Cynthia's clothes and check out of her school. He drove her back to the rehab place the next day. Later he rented a truck and moved their clothes and some of their furniture to the facility duplex. They all said a tearful goodbye and promised one another to telephone, text, and visit often. But John Levi realized that Paloma needed to move on from him. The communications and the visits were sure to become rare.

Whether to remain in ordained ministry became an hour-by-hour decision. He could always go back to law practice. The State Bar of Texas was not threatening to take his license if he completed his counseling. He buried himself in Peace Church's neighborhood ministries. He started studying Spanish.

Every morning he awoke and had to make a new decision to go to the church and the neighborhood. He was still wrestling with what he believed about the way of Jesus. Poverty and injustice were still thriving all around that neighborhood. Why shouldn't he just fight against this poverty and injustice with all the legal tools at his disposal, using the legal system as a bat, demonizing his opponents, taking no prisoners? Why not just leave Jesus out of it?

One morning he received a telephone call from the principal of the elementary school across the street from Peace. A third-grader named Melissa had head lice again. The school policy was that a child with head lice had to leave school immediately. The lice would have to be killed by use of a special shampoo and the nits would have to be combed out before the child could return to class. Melissa's parents were both in prison and the uncle who had custody of her was away at work. Melissa had been infested with head lice so often that the uncle had given John Levi written permission to treat the lice at the church. Peace had a supply of the necessary shampoo in stock. John Levi told the principal to send Melissa over in a few minutes. He would be waiting for her.

The church had a policy that a woman had to be present with John Levi at Peace whenever he shampooed a child's hair and combed out the nits. John Levi telephoned a number of women in the neighborhood to ask them to come, but none answered. No female teacher was available to help. John Levi arrived at the church. There was a woman there. It was Jewel McKenzie. She was the Communion steward and was resupplying the bread and grape juice for the coming Sunday's service.

Jewell had become less vocal in her opposition to John Levi since he had been arrested. She even told Rafer Thompson that she admired John Levi for having the guts to break in to the Bodine's house to get that woman out. "At least he didn't just stay outside that house and pray," she said.

He considered calling the principal to tell them he couldn't help with lice this time. But John Levi knew that Melissa was really embarrassed. She had become the butt of ridicule by her classmates, who called her "Me-lice-a." John Levi didn't want Melissa to have to go home alone to wait for an uncle who wouldn't do anything to help her. What John Levi wanted was to treat and eliminate the lice so Melissa could go right back to school in time for her free lunch. He decided to ask Jewel to stay in the building.

"Jewel, I need your help, please. Or should I say a sweet third-grade girl named Melissa needs our help."

"What now?"

John Levi explained the problem. He just needed her to remain in the kitchen while he carried out the treatment.

"What if I get head lice?"

"You don't have to be close enough to her to get them."

"What about you? What about the building?"

"Jewel, I have already done this for her three times. I haven't gotten head lice and neither has the building."

"Three times before? Hasn't she learned anything? Where are her parents?"

"They're in prison. Her uncle won't clean her sheets and pillow case, so she keeps getting lice. That's not Melissa's fault."

Melissa knocked on the outside door. John Levi hustled over and let her in. She had been escorted by her teacher, who had to leave.

As soon as Melissa stepped inside, she started bawling. She gasped for breath between sobs. Snot ran out of her little nose and she tried to wipe it off with her hands. Her face was a mess of snot and tears. John Levi comforted her, telling her they could get rid of these little pests in an hour and she could go right back to school in time for her lunch.

Jewel watched Melissa as she was crying. Jewel's face softened. A look of pity came over her. Her eyes teared up.

As John Levi took Melissa into the kitchen to shampoo her hair over the sink, Jewel followed them. He sat Melissa on a high stool, draped a towel around her, and leaned her backwards under the faucet. Melissa continued to cry while he shampooed. So did Jewel. When Melissa fidgeted, jerked her head up, and almost hit the faucet, Jewel jumped forward and kept her from being hurt. As John Levi shampooed, Jewel held Melissa steady, wiping her own eyes as often as Melissa was wiping hers.

John Levi was amazed at the Jewel McKenzie he was experiencing for the first time. *"John Levi,"* he asked himself, *"do you see this woman? You didn't give her enough of a chance."*

"What could a lawsuit do for Melissa or Jewel? Or a bat? What could Love?" he thought.

Then John Levi had a vision that the sink was a baptismal font, and Melissa's and Jewel's tears blessed and mingled with the tap water and became the water of baptism, and John Levi was baptizing Melissa and Jewel and Paloma and Cynthia and himself and the entire world with the tears, as he was chanting over and over, *"Lord Jesus Christ, Son of God, who washes away the sins of the world with the tears of children, have mercy upon us and grant us peace."*

On March 13, 2020, the President of the United States declared the COVID pandemic a national emergency.

What could lawsuits do? Or a bat? What could Love?